HOMEROOM

HOMEROOM

A Shelter from the Storm

A Novel

Bob Nelson

iUniverse, Inc.
New York Lincoln Shanghai

Homeroom
A Shelter from the Storm

iUniverse books may be ordered through booksellers or by contacting:

iUniverse
2021 Pine Lake Road, Suite 100
Lincoln, NE 68512
www.iuniverse.com
1-800-Authors (1-800-288-4677)

This is a work of fiction. All of the characters, names, incidents, organizations and dialogue in this novel are either the products of the author's imagination or are used fictitiously.

The quote from Lord Buckley on page 212 is used by permission from Laurie Buckley. (TXu 1-202-666)

ISBN-13: 978-0-595-40830-6 (pbk)
ISBN-13: 978-0-595-85192-8 (ebk)
ISBN-10: 0-595-40830-3 (pbk)
ISBN-10: 0-595-85192-4 (ebk)

Printed in the United States of America

This is not a memoir.
It is a novel.
Truth is sometimes
best revealed through fiction.

Dedicated to all my students who have enriched my life.
They have taught me more than I could ever "learn" them.
Especially Nancy Vallera-Zuppa and Ronna Dillinger.
They weren't the model for any character in the story,
but they validated the author numerous times.

A Tuesday morning, in early May

At 7:50, ten minutes before the start of the school day, at West High School, on the second floor in A Hall, he knew exactly what he would find. As usual, as he meandered down the hallway there were twelve students randomly interspersed, standing by their lockers, although four or five students were sitting finishing some homework assignment, copying someone else's work. Most of them were girls and mostly they were talking about boys, who was hot and who was not, who did what with whom, and who wouldn't be caught dead with whom. He was invisible like any other day. He was always invisible. He counted on his invisibility.

At the end of the70 paces of hallway was the Hub. All the upstairs hallways branched off form this one intersection like spokes from the middle of an impor-tant wheel. B Hall went slightly to the left, with approximately 25 square feet of empty space, C Hall slightly to the right, equally spaced. Between them was the main staircase, double in width in order to accommodate most of the student body. D Hall was a perfect right angle from A Hall, but it didn't really begin for another 45 feet. The end of D Hall served as a balcony looking over the cafeteria. The junction of all the hallways formed a huge meeting ground for the students, the chosen students; the Hub was an open arena for upperclassmen. Underclass-men still were expected to stay downstairs, in the abyss of rejection known as the cafeteria. The library and the parking lot provided the other ghettoes for high school society. In high school even where you spent your last few minutes before class separated you, labeled you. He knew this, and he knew what he would find at the end of A Hall. He counted on it.

He reached the end of the hallway and leaned his back against the corner of the wall. He could see the entire Hub from this perspective. There were approximately 100 to 200 students in various groups standing around talking and laughing, but none of them were saying anything, anything of sustance. To his left were several groups of juniors and a few scattered seniors. Everyone was distributed in what looked like a random fashion, but he knew that there was a subtle pecking order radiating out from the group directly across A Hall from him, the closest group to him in proximity and furthest in reality, THE SENIORS WHO MATTERED. In the middle with his back to him was one of the star football players with letter jacket hanging over one shoulder and a cheerleader draped over the other. He was surrounded by a group of fans, guys and girls, all laughing and smiling and gig-gling over every mindless thing that was said.

"You are a Moron!" He shouted. And the football star turned slowly around still smiling, barely aware certainly not stunned, never entertaining the thought that the remark could possibly have been directed toward him. The first bullet entered the football star's mouth and he maintained his look of blasé astonishment *even as the exit wound removed the back part of his head. The blood and pieces of brain splattered over the group, but recognition wasn't immediate. There was a split second before anyone could grasp what was happening; a flash before everyone's face registered disbelief and shock. It was as if time stood still, but he knew better than to relish the moment too long. The sounds—explosions, ripping and tearing sounds, splashing sounds, and even the screams—all seemed to precede recognition on the faces. He moved the Uzi a scant six inches in either direction and began spaying bullets back and forth. First he made sure all of the ones standing across from him with the football star went down, and then he pivoted to his left, spraying bullets the entire time, spreading the Hub with pellets of venom. Before he had finished the semicircle, the clip ran out. He reached inside his jacket, pulled out a new clip, reloaded, and in less than a second, was continuing the carnage. He made one complete swipe to the left before he turned 180 degrees and took care of those in A Hall. He knew they would have further to go to escape, and he actually had to aim to get some of them, but he still got them all. He whipped around to see if anyone in the Hub was still standing or trying to make it to the stairway. No one was really moving although there were still some cries and some feeble attempts to crawl or hide. He sauntered down D Hall toward the cafeteria, shooting anyone else that was still moving or crying. He emptied and changed two more clips, and was quite satisfied with the results of his butchery. When he reached the end of the hallway he turned, and shot some more bullets in the dead bodies.*

"Who matters now!" He said in a way that was more like spitting than talking. He was not sure what waited for him downstairs, and he didn't care.

CHAPTER 1

TWO-FIFTHS OF A TEACHER

In A Hall, close to the stairwell and about as far from the Hub as possible, Mr. Harmon resided in the classroom sanctuary known as A 216. For the students, it indeed was a safety zone and a bit of alternate universe. In A 216, he taught psychology by fact and reputation. However, entry into the refuge of A 216 by a newcomer would provide no clue as to the purpose of the room or the contents therein. At the front of the room, running parallel with the door was the blackboard, usually blank but with the telltale eraser marks to indicate recent heavy use. All of the 30 student desks, in six equal rows, faced this blackboard. To the right of the blackboard was the mural that took up the entire length of the wall. The mural was composed of surrealistic and stock psychological images—Dali's melting clocks, the ambiguous old woman-young woman portrait from Gestalt lectures, the figure/ground example of vases and faces, and right in the middle, a great big ostrich whose head was a hand. The back wall was a second blackboard covered with butcher paper to provide a graffiti board for students. Harmon wanted the graffiti board to be a forum for independent thought and free expression, an opportunity for philosophical discourse, but originality seldom appeared. Clichés and rock lyrics were the closest things to deep philosophical thought, but mostly little personal notes were written, and love notes—MR + NA 4 ever XXOO!! On the left side of the room were Harmon's desk, some file cabinets, and a cluttered table. The desk was pushed back into the corner facing the wall. Harmon would never let the desk come between him and the students. This indeed was the organic part of the room because Harmon never knew what treasure he would find in this part of the room. It was not surprising to find poems lying around, but he also found toy figures, a stuffed tiger, a plastic penguin, and space alien. One Monday he came to class and found the feather and two inch shaft of the top part of an arrow. He liked that his classroom was full of surprises.

If A 216 was a safety zone for students, it was something even more profound for Harmon. He saw A 216 as the place in the world where he was supposed to be. It was home. His insecurities might still surface, but now at least he had a place to subdue them. He might have had an insecure youth, and an early adulthood full of self doubt, but now he had a corner of the universe where he felt competent.

For example, after twelve years of teaching, notes from the principal no longer intimidated Mr. Harmon; they no longer seemed like ominous threats. At West Side High School, an affluent school in an affluent suburb, a request to meet with the principal seldom elicited more than a perfunctory reply. Usually such a request centered on checking the Social Security number for a government form or some such formality. Although he had received the note during the first period, Harmon waited until his second-period conference period to head toward the office. The chances were slim that he would actually see Dr. Randich, the building principal. Besides, meetings with principals tended to be very short. Harmon couldn't remember ever being in the office for more than five minutes. The exception, of course, was the meeting with the Swensons, which lasted an inordinately long time. In reality, the meeting lasted less than fifteen minutes. Yet in ways that Harmon acknowledged only to himself, the meeting was still reverberating in his head some seven years later.

As he made his way to the principal's office, Harmon encountered Clark. "What are you doing here? Don't you ever go to class? It seems like I see you in the hallway every time I leave my classroom." The last statement was delivered while his arm was around Clark's shoulder and they walked together down the hall.

"I'll do anything to get out of class."

"Why are you out of class? You're a senior; you can't afford to goof around."

"Old habits are hard to change."

"What does that mean?"

"Mr. Harmon, I might ask you the same thing."

Harmon turned to notice Allison, the Counselor. She was accompanied by a man and a woman, who Harmon immediately guessed were parents touring the building. This kind of tour was not uncommon and Harmon guessed their purpose, but first he had to finish with Clark. "You'll have to explain that old habits remark in Homeroom."

"How's the best psychology teacher in school?" Allison asked with a cheerful tone, and Harmon took the question as the first cue to how she wanted him to respond.

"I hate to be the one to break this to you, Allison, but I am the only psychology teacher in school."

"Well, I guess that makes me right, then. Mr. Harmon, I want you to meet Mr. and Mrs. Martin. They are thinking of enrolling their son, Peter, in West Side next year."

"Hello, it's nice to meet you. Are you moving into the district?"

"We are considering it," Mr. Martin said.

"We want a good school for our son," Mrs. Martin continued, "but one that is not too strict or unrealistic in the academic demands."

Allison stepped in. "Peter is very bright, but he hasn't always been challenged at school. His grades are much lower than his PSAT scores would indicate."

Harmon knew that Allison meant much more than she was actually saying. He could guess what she wanted from him and why she had stopped him in the hallway. They had established an unspoken language based on mutual respect and a parallel interest in the needs of students. With just those few clues, notes if you will, Harmon knew the melody that Allison wanted him to play; their communication had become like music, more tone and rhythm than anything else, more nuance than content. There was nothing mysterious or magical about their communication. They were just in tune with each other's views and philosophies.

"What are you doing out of your classroom anyway? Are teachers allowed out of their ivory tower these days?" With her questions, Allison established Harmon's identity as an intellectual for the audience. With her tone, Allison gave Harmon the entire hint he needed to understand the melody she wanted. He knew his part. The ivory tower reference and the mention of the SAT scores let him know that she wanted him to play the role of an achievement-oriented teacher, but her tone let him know that she wanted him to play an upbeat, casual rhythm.

"Second period is my conference period, Dr. Randich sent a note that he wanted to see me, and I figured I'd take care of the meeting while I could."

"Couldn't handle the tension, eh?" Allison was teasing him and a casual, witty reply for the Martins' benefit was called for. He was confident that he knew why she wanted him to play this variation of a familiar song. Harmon had a great deal of affection for Allison that sprang from his deep professional respect; for example, he liked that she insisted that everyone call her by her first name only. She was in her early fifties, perhaps ten or twelve years older than Harmon. Her hair was pure white and shoulder length. She wore mostly sweaters and layers of clothing that may have been intended to hide the fact that she was slightly overweight, but this also had the effect of enhancing her natural warmth. Her office was almost always filled with students and more often than not, laughter was the most prominent sound. The Top Ten Graduates annually selected her as one of the Most Influential Teachers, but the dropouts and potential dropouts loved her even more. More than a few students had graduated because of her efforts. Few realized how many suicides she had thwarted or how many drug rehabilitations she had started. She was trusted and loved by the students, and of course, unappreciated by most of the faculty. Harmon knew of her accomplishments and viewed her as an ally and confidant.

They had talked many times over the years. Allison was one of the few people with whom Harmon could be really open and vulnerable. She could accept his insecurities without judging him. His constant questioning tormented him. Allison accepted his questioning and still believed in him.

Harmon responded to her teasing. "No tension. Meetings with principals don't bother me. I've learned to cope. I just pretend that the principal is calling a meeting to give me some sort of award or recognition of my teaching excellence."

"When you won the Teacher Award…" She turned toward Mr. Martin. "Mr. Harmon got the Teacher Award, when? Two years ago?"

"More like five years."

"Really? That long. Time flies when you are having a good time. Well is that how you were told? Did he call you into his office?"

"No, not at all. The committee told me by phone."

She laughed out loud, something she did quite easily and often. "Have you ever heard of anyone being called into the office to get an award like that?"

"No, but I figure, if reality isn't a choice, what good is it? You choose your reality and I'll chose mine. I mean, who says delusions of grandeur have to be dysfunctional."

Allison turned toward Mrs. Martin. "Mr. Harmon is one of the most respected members of our faculty, at least that's what he tells me. But he has some unconventional methods. I hear you have been eating chalk."

"Who told you that?'

"One of your students said that you started eating chalk in the middle of a lecture. Is it true?"

"Of course not. That would be crazy."

"My point exactly," she said as she looked at the Martins.

"Let me tell you what happened. I was in the teacher's lounge with Mrs. Brooks. She had received a gift, a box of mints. The mints were long and cylindrical; they looked like chalk. In the next class I used a mint as a piece of chalk and in the middle of writing something on the blackboard; I took a bite of the mint."

"Was it good?"

"The look on the students' faces was priceless, but the mint was just a mint. I've never liked mints. They're like trying to fool your stomach into thinking you had dessert."

"You know the student who told me wants to drop your class."

"No he doesn't."

"Who said it was a he? But you're right. His parents want him to drop the class."

"I don't believe you. Did I ever tell you about the time I taught a whole class with my shoes on the wrong feet? You could see the glimmers of awareness slowly spread from one student's face to another until the whole room wasn't sure if they were seeing what they were seeing."

"Yes, you have told me many times with a growing glee that, frankly, worries me," Allison spoke in mock disgust.

"Hey. I was lecturing on perception." Harmon explained with an equal amount of mock exasperation. "It seemed like a good idea at the time."

"Mr. Martin." Allison turned toward him. "I hope you don't think the whole faculty is like Mr. Harmon," which was exactly what she wanted Mr. Martin to think.

Mr. Martin seemed to validate her intentions with his response. "We can only hope."

Harmon knew what Allison was trying to do by introducing him to the Martins and bringing up the chalk incident, which had happened three years ago. Their son probably did not get along well in school, and they wanted an environment more comfortable and safe for someone alienated; yet they still wanted a good education. He decided it was time to address the second part of their concerns more directly. "Don't get the wrong impression; I take my job very seriously. I still teach my subject, and I teach it well. I just feel that there is more than one way to skin a cat, so to speak. I prefer the way that is least painful for the cat. If there is one thing I believe, one mantra it is this: education shouldn't hurt. For example, if a class is acting up and I need to get them under control, I can get complete silence by telling my favorite joke. Allison, have I ever told you my favorite joke?"

"I don't think you have, but knowing your sense of humor, I believe you." Allison turned to the Martins. "Mr. Harmon is notorious for his sense of humor, or should I say, lack thereof. I can't tell you how many times students have come to me asking me to explain some joke you have made in class."

"Hey, I resemble that remark. But I have scientific proof; I mean I have field-tested this baby. If I have thirty students who are talking or acting up, I can tell this joke and twenty-eight will sit in stunned silence."

"What about the other two," Mrs. Martin asked, and Harmon and Allison knew they had captured the more resistant of the two Martins.

"The other two? Why, they will be convulsed in laughter with me, naturally."

"Okay." Allison knew her lines perfectly. "I know I'm going to regret this, but what is your favorite joke?"

"Do you know what Custer's last words were?"

"No."

"Have you **ever**…seen so many Indians?"

Allison tried not to laugh, and mostly she succeeded, but one look at the stunned face of Mrs. Martin, and she found herself smiling and eventually laughing out loud. "That is the most…the worst…. joke I've ever heard. It's not even funny."

"Exactly. But you have to admit, the joke captures the human experience in some terribly profound and universal way."

"You really enjoy teaching, don't you?" Mr. Martin asked. "I haven't met many teachers who show their joy as much as you."

"If I didn't teach, I'd have to work for a living."

"Tell them how your students do on the Advanced Placement exams."

"They do all right compared to the national norms."

"They consistently outscore the national norms even though his class is one semester and he competes against year-long classes. His students also do well on the SAT and many test out of freshmen psychology."

Harmon shrugged, "We put too much emphasis on tests. You know, I tell my students, nothing of any real value has ever been measured by a test."

The Martins twisted their collective heads and Mrs. Martin wrinkled her brow. So Harmon asked her directly. "Would you rather have you son make a perfect grade on the SAT or be a perfect father to your grandchildren?"

"I'm not sure they're exclusive," Mrs. Martin responded.

"Of course not. But only one can be measured by a test, and it is not the most important one of the two."

She nodded slowly.

"If my job were just to prepare people for a test, I'd get a different job."

"What is your job?" Mr. Martin wanted to know.

"I teach."

"What does that mean?"

Harmon smiled, slowly starting with a sly grin that spread across his whole face lighting up his eyes, before he spoke. "I could probably spend the rest of the week answering that question on a variety of levels—behavioral, emotional, intellectual, spiritual—but for now let me just give you the short answer: teaching is making people better."

"Better? In whose opinion? By what standard?"

"That is a very good question! And my answer tells you why I'm not an administrator, why I decided long ago that I never want to be a principal. They want to make better schools; I want to make better people. I want my students to be better people not in my opinion, but in their own opinion. When they finish my class, I want them to feel that they are better than they were before they took my class."

There was a silence, the type of dramatic silence that expressed closure. Harmon bid goodbye to the Martins and walked into the principal's office, confident that he had made a good impression on the Martins, or, more accurately, that he and Allison had made the desired impression. The Martins might not be aware of how studied and practiced the casual interplay was; Harmon knew, but he was also aware of how genuine it was. Nothing he had said to the Martins was false, neither in tone or content.

Harmon presented himself to the principal's secretary.

"Hello, Mr. Harmon," she said.

"Dr. Randich wants to see me."

"Yes. He's expecting you. He'll be right with you."

Harmon sat down and wondered if people who make him wait in outer offices were really that busy, or was making people wait some sort of mandatory gesture, a necessary ritual of power. He probably would have sat pondering the question indefinitely. He slowly realized that Mrs. K, the secretary, had failed to address him by his first name. Among the faculty, there was a saying that one was not really considered a faculty member until Mrs. K called you by your first name. Harmon couldn't recall her ever having done so.

Mrs. Kennison was the type of secretary one associated with a large corporation not the typical grandmotherly type typically found in a typical high school in a typical suburb. She was the essence of professionalism, efficient, cryptic and more polite than friendly. She had a checklist for everything, and she knew where the lists were and what was on them. For example, she knew the deadline for summer school teaching applications in September. In his twelve years of teaching at West Side, Harmon never asked her a question for which she did not immediately know the answer. The faculty believed that she had the final veto in the selection of a building principal. That rumor probably was false, but she had been the only secretary the school's 27-year history. Dr. Randich, on the other hand, was the fourth principal.

Mrs. K announced Harmon and he walked into the office. The office was very neat, with everything in place. The desk was very large, with dark, shiny wood. Behind the desk was a large window that looked out onto the front lawn of the school. On one side of the window were Randich's various diplomas, including a Ph.D. in education. On the other side were portraits of his wife and children. Scattered on the walls were various awards that had been given either to the school or to Dr. Randich personally. Most schools have autographed letters of congratulations and appreciation from different politicians and celebrities, but few schools have a collection as extensive and impressive as West Side. There were letters from Presidents Ford, Carter, Reagan, Bush and Clinton, the last five governors of the state, secretaries of education, and several other celebrities.

Most of the recognition had come from the academic area. Traditionally West Side won more National Merit Scholarships than the all other schools in the district added together. Over the years, an average of nearly 95 per cent of the graduates had been accepted into a college, and nearly 90 per cent go on to graduate from a four-year college. West Side was a school of academic excellence in the midst of a community of economic and intellectual success. The school's accomplishments were impressive, the standards were rigorous, the expectations were high, the pressure was relentless, and the cost had been quite high.

Five years ago, an eighteen-month period was marked by nine suicides. Nine completely different students with nine completely different profiles, with nothing in common except that they were enrolled in West Side High.

Randich became principal the next year and in the past three years, there had been no suicides, none, positively zero. There were many reasons behind the decrease in suicides, but any investigation into the reasons had to start with Allison the Counselor who was hired by Dr. Randich. He allowed her a tremendous amount of flexibility and freedom in restructuring the counseling department.

Dr. Randich himself had been recognized by the PTA for his excellence as principal, by the community for his public relations work, by the district for his professionalism, and by the state for the total achievement of the student body. He was declared Administrator of the Year by the State Board of Education last year, an accolade seldom given to a building principal instead of a superintendent. He handled all of these awards with the wisdom of humility. Randich knew that he did less to earn the awards than he reaped the benefit of other people's hard work. Harmon liked that Randich saw things that way. Randich let teachers teach. He did not over administrate, and that is why Harmon felt that Randich deserved every award he received. Yet Harmon always wondered how Randich would have handled the Swenson situation.

Dr. Randich represented the best of a new breed of school principals. There used to be an old saying that the only requirement for being a school principal was a losing record because almost all principals were former coaches. Randich was different because he had an academic background. He taught real classes for a few years before he became an administrator. Unlike past principals, his faculty meeting were not sprinkled with sports metaphors. Instead he used the current terms in educational literature—"empowerment", "accountability", "objective driven curriculum", "research based instruction"—these were all phrases likely to have been slipped into a conversation with Randich. In his office were copies of Educational Leadership, The Kappan and other educational journals, and they had all been read.

In the past, "the Good ol' boy", approach had been very ineffective, which was its most endearing quality as far as Harmon was concerned. If there had been a lot of silly rules, they weren't really enforced and Harmon could choose which rules to ignore. Harmon found that the old principals had a limited perspective. For example, Bruce Shakleford, the principal before Randich, seemed concerned only with a teacher dress code. He was obsessed with the idea that every male teacher should wear a tie, an obsession Harmon could never understand. On days that he didn't wear a tie, there did not seem to be an outbreak of ignorance. Dr. Randich found no research to correlate student achievement with teacher fashion; therefore, ties were a non-issue for him.

With Randich, student achievement was the main issue, the only issue, for his administration. Every program, every policy, and every decision were weighted from the perspective of how it would affect student achievement, a more professional approach from that of the past, and much harder to ignore. Randich certainly improved the instructional climate. Having lesson plans proved to be a good idea. Having to justify class activity in terms of instructional outcome was a good idea. Those teachers whose instructional methodology centered on movies judged on length rather than quality, or pop quizzes on football games, or word searches found Randich's policies to be intrusive. For those who had always been conscientious, who strove for improvement, and who spent a great deal of time thinking about teaching, Harmon being among those, Randich let them teach and refine their craft. Randich respected good teaching.

Still, Harmon felt vaguely at odds with Randich. There was a dissonance that was difficult to articulate. They seemed to be opposites in some sort of silent, fundamental way. To Harmon there was something depersonalized in Randich's efficiency. Harmon feared that Randich was part of the "Cult of Uniformity" that permeated education. The Cult revered standardized instruction to the point of eliminating individuality. The antithesis of the "do your own thing" mantra, the objective was for every teacher of a given subject to teach the same material the same way on the same day to every student. Although Harmon acknowledged some value in curriculum alignment and instructional consistency, he also perceived a threat to creativity, both for teachers and students. With the Cult's emphasis on objectives and standardization, education became very precise, almost scientific, but people are not precise. People are fuzzy, and to treat all of them the same was not only foolish and counterproductive, but ultimately, it seemed to Harmon, violated something sacred. True, the Cult of Uniformity provided excellent guidelines for teaching and testing, but it had little to offer people. The Cult elevated normalcy as if were a lofty objective. The Cult appealed to those teachers who taught subjects, but it was a vague threat to those teachers, like Harmon, who taught students.

However, Harmon was never quite sure how to classify Randich, obviously the darling of the Cult that tried to make everyone into everyone else. To Harmon, the Cult was evil, dictatorial, malicious, but he also knew it was just a metaphor. Harmon used the term because they helped express his viewpoint, but he knew they were just images, useful allegories, used in conversations mostly with Allison as a joke. There really was no Cult, but in Harmon's mind, educators acted as if there were. His reality was congruent with his fiction.

Even at that, Randich defied easy classification. He did not seem to agree with Harmon on most issues, but they seemed to share a mutual respect. Randich had always been very supportive, courteous, and professional to Harmon. Yet Harmon could not shake his uneasy feelings, his unconscious tension and insecurity. His doubts were galvanized on the Swenson issue. How Randich would have handled the Swenson case was a question that haunted Harmon.

Nancy Swenson was a brilliant student, valedictorian of the class two years before Randich came to West Side, right in the middle of the rash of suicides. Her SAT scores were near perfection. She had won many academic competitions and awards when she enrolled in Harmon's class the fall semester of her senior year. She could fit an elective into her schedule, and Harmon's class had a reputation as being more college preparatory than most electives.

The class was psychology, and Harmon made the subject both academic and relevant. Sprinkled between lectures on various psychological theories were "hands-on" activities geared to produce self-realization and awareness. The objective was to make psychology real and demonstrate how psychology pertained to the students' lives.

Nancy completed the first grading period with the highest grade in class. She seemed to enjoy class and often exhibited her peculiar laugh that was part chuckle and part giggle. However, there was a dark side to her high school career that soon became apparent. Her academic achievement hid her feelings of social incompetence and the more the subject of friends and emotions became the topic in class, the more uncomfortable and alienated she felt. She did have friends, but they had nothing in common except grades. Emotions were familiar only in a very abstract, depersonalized way. They could all dissect and analyze feelings but never really experience them.

On one particular day, Nancy's conflict became quite visible to Harmon. The objective for the lesson plan of the day was to illustrate the connection between self-concept, values and behavior. The first step was for the class to give five answers to the question "Who are you?" Then the class was asked to prioritize a list of values from most important to least important: friendship, money, romantic love, family, religion, and school. Then the class was asked to draw a map of where they spent their time in a week. All of this was followed by a discussion trying to show a connection between values and expenditure of energy, and self-concept. Hopefully, there would be congruence between values and where one spends one's time, and both of these would be reflected in the self-concept. Usually, Harmon found this activity would produce an energetic discussion, and without a great deal of self-disclosure in front of class-mates, the students would have a tool for assessing the way they spent their time. Typically, for example, a student might realize that family is very impor-tant but that little time was spent with the family. Nancy, however, was the only student Harmon ever had who just lowered her head and gently wept during the entire discussion. She sat in the first seat in her row so no one noticed except Harmon. When he tried to talk to her after class, she rushed off and wouldn't say anything.

The next day, he confronted her on the way into class. "Your reaction in class yesterday...I think you should talk to somebody about it."

"Who?" she asked.

"Your counselor."

She shook her head.

"Your parents?"

Again she shook her head.

"Your clergyman?"

"No. They couldn't help. None of them. They wouldn't understand. I'm okay. It's all right."

"Well, if you want to talk, you know, just to have someone to listen to you...I'm usually around after school, and I'm a pretty good listener."

She started showing up that Friday. Harmon listened. During the first meet-ing, Harmon developed a sense of how alienated from her classmate's Nancy felt. Mostly she felt like an immigrant from a different culture. She talked about, as she put it, "those ghastly Homecoming Mums and their insidious cow bells that seem to scream how popular everyone is and how unwanted I am."

"That's funny," Harmon said, "I always thought those Mums were just a cruel and unusual punishment for teachers. I wondered what karma conjured up their existence."

On the second Friday, they went beyond their mutual disdain for Home-coming Mums and other high school rituals. Nancy revealed that although her academic achievement insulated her from herself as well as her classmates, she was beginning to question the merit of her approach to life. "What good is it to be smart if there is no fun in it?"

Harmon asked, "What do you do for fun? What is your idea of a good time?"

She was silent for a long time before answering. "I like to go to the library and read out-of-print books. Pathetic, huh?" Then she cried.

On the third Friday the subject of suicide came up. She revealed that she had thought of suicide quite often in junior high school. When Harmon pressed for assurance that those thoughts were all past tense, she insisted that suicide was an issue from the past. When he asked if anyone else knew about her thoughts of self-destruction, if there was anyone she could talk to about these thoughts, especially her parents, she broke into tears and almost screamed. "**NO**! They must never know. Promise you won't tell them. Promise! Promise!"

Harmon maintained steady eye contact and spoke very softly, "I can't make that promise."

"Oh God! You must." By then she was crying hysterically and started to run out of the room. Harmon stopped her.

"I don't feel a need to tell your parents now. Your thoughts of suicide are all in the past, right?"

She nodded and Harmon touched her arm and stared into her eyes before he spoke, "I can't promise I won't tell them in the future if I think that I have to. What I can promise you is that I won't talk to them without asking you for permission first. I will never go behind your back. I will not betray you. You can trust me."

He had managed to comfort her with his assurances, and they talked for a long time that afternoon about a wide range of subjects, all revolving around her fears and "this awful life-sentence of loneliness that is my life", as she put it. She continued to weep during the conversation, but she wept more quietly. Finally when the hour was getting late and Harmon knew that Nancy needed to go home, he tried to elicit from her a promise that she would not kill herself, that she would talk to him first.

"You'd just try to talk me out of it," she said as the tears began to flow a little quicker.

Harmon nodded. "You're right. I don't want you to die."

Her eyes met his and she stared for several minutes before she partly whispered and partly sobbed, "Why?"

Harmon gently grabbed her hands, making sure there was eye contact; he spoke very slowly so that each word was heard fully. The effect was giving a nonverbal underline to what he was saying. "Because I value you. Because you deserve to live. Because I would miss you."

"You don't even know me," she said between clenched teeth holding back sobs.

"Because I want to get to know you better. Because I think you are worth knowing."

She sat in silence staring at him for what seemed like a very long time. Her head was tilted slightly sideways as if what she was hearing was so incredulous as to be totally unbelievable. "You know, you have never asked me about my GPA or SAT scores or my college plans."

"But I know you," Harmon said. "I know you at some other level, a deeper level. I know you are lonely. I know you hurt. I know you cry. I know you like to read old books. I know you hate Homecoming Mums. I know you laugh at my jokes. Really, what else is there?"

There was a long pause that in any other circumstance would have been unbearable, but here it was somehow comforting, somehow extending the developing realization of the truth of Harmon's words. It enabled Nancy to stop crying and finally, she broke the silence. "What else is there? The fact that I realize they are jokes, I would think."

Her response was like pulling down a window shade. Harmon marveled at her ability to almost instantly compose herself, but he was also a little unnerved by it.

They both laughed, experiencing the kind of laughter that lasts longer than the joke merits. When they stopped, they would start again. Finally the laughter provided a convenient stopping point and exit for Nancy. They said good-bye for the weekend, but not before she did promise that she would never kill herself without first talking to him.

When Harmon arrived at school the following Monday, Nancy was standing looking very calm and composed. Her posture was quite proper, and she was clutching her textbooks, sort of hugging them. She had a smile on her lips and as Harmon approached, a couple of students who had been asking her about homework walked off, thanking her for the help. When he opened the door, she briskly walked into the room, and her demeanor immediately changed. Her smile evaporated. She dropped her books onto the desk tip and slumped into the chair. She looked like a balloon that had been deflated. Tears came slowly but steadily as she talked. "I spent the entire week-end thinking about death. I kept daydreaming about my own funeral. Whenever I would close my eyes, I would fantasize blood flowing, sometimes gushing from me." Her tone became almost hysterical, "Oh Mr. Harmon, help me! I am so scared!"

She fell onto the desktop in convulsive waves of anguish.

Another student entered the classroom. He left at Harmon's wave, but he closed the door and stayed in the hallway to make sure no one else burst in.

Harmon turned toward Nancy. "Do not kill yourself!"

"Why? I need a reason."

"Because of my hurt. The pain….I wouldn't be able to…." Harmon couldn't complete his thought, but what he said was enough to get her head off of the desk even if the tears did not stop. "Nancy, listen to me. This has gone on long enough. We need to get you some help. Some professional help. You need more than I can give you."

She nodded, "I know. I can't go on like this. I can't take it anymore."

"You will get better. You will feel better. Trust me. I know you feel….hopeless. But don't give up. We.. you can get through this."

She looked at him for the first time. She saw the sincerity in his eyes and her tears temporarily halted. She nodded slowly as he continued to talk in a quiet but deliberate voice. "I want…..I have to have your promise that you won't do anything."

She nodded, and he felt that the emergency had passed but he didn't feel particularly comforted.

"We are going to have to tell your parents. Any help will have to come through them."

"I know. I know," she said. She began to look around the room. Her sobbing had stopped and her breathing was returning to regular pace. She had made one of those rapid transitions that Harmon found so confusing. One second she was crying hysterically, the next she was vary composed and articulate. "Mr. Harmon, you don't understand. Talking to my parents would be the goal of therapy. It cannot be a prerequisite."

Harmon understood exactly what she meant, and he recognized the logic of her words. He tried to compose a response, but he could think of nothing to say.

She continued to stare at him, waiting for the response that was not forthcoming. Finally she took a deep breath and mustered up some inner strength. She continued her visual inspection of the room. She stood up and walked around the room, touching desks as she talked. "You know, this room is the only place in the world where I feel safe, this room, A 216, and the sanctuary of my church. But somehow this room is the only place that seems real."

Harmon nodded and tried to think of the right words to comfort her. "Safety isn't a place out there; it's inside of you. This room is always here, and it will always be here, but the best part of this room goes with you wherever you go and whatever you do. The best part of anything, you make a part of yourself."

She stared. "I'll have to think about that." She stood and straightened her skirt to remove any wrinkles, took a deep breath to compose her self and looked around the room as if taking inventory. "I tried to talk to my mother at church last Sunday, no, the Sunday before last. The sermon was about suicides and the spiritual ramifications. Everyone in the congregation, well, really in the community, is quite concerned about suicide. It is a hot-button issue this year. The minister called alienation, the type of alienation that causes suicide a 'scab upon the soul for which the only known salve is spiritual salvation', appropriate metaphors if rather graphic. He is known for his fairly vivid imagery. On the ride home, I told my mother how much I enjoyed the sermon. 'Felt enriched' was the term I used. She didn't agree. She thought suicide was ridiculous. She said those kinds of thoughts, suicidal thoughts, were," Nancy hesitated and then spit the next words as if eliminating a bad taste from her mouth, "**inappropriate**."

She slowly shook her head repeating the word, "Inappropriate."

She walked over in front of Harmon. Perhaps two feet separated them, "I can't talk to her. I can't tell her those feelings. She'll think I'm inappropriate."

Her pronouncement was followed by silence. Again she looked to Harmon for answers that he could not provide. He maintained eye contact but said nothing. Finally she broke the silence, "Yes, Houston, we have a problem. I can't stay where I am at, and the only other move is intolerable."

"No wonder suicide seems like an attractive alternative," he finally said.

She nodded and returned to her measured patrol of the classroom.

"How about your father? Can you talk to him?"

"Father? If anything, he is worse. Father is a doctor, a surgeon by trade. During his internship, he and his professors realized that father related more to disease than people. He could never muster an acceptable bedside manner. Human suffering is not something with which he sympathizes. In short, one does not talk to my father; one listens to him dissect and eradicate."

Harmon was beginning to feel real fear. "Can we at least eliminate suicide as a choice?"

She sat on the closest desktop. She stared at the floor and her eyes filled with tears, but the tears stayed there. "I don't want to die, but I need a reason to live. I need hope."

"Let me talk to your mother for you."

She looked up.

"I can call her right now. I'll go to the office and call her right now."

"She won't be in her office until nine o'clock."

"Great. That's my conference period. I'll call her then."

"What will you say?"

"I'll tell her about your feelings, your loneliness, and I'll have to tell her about your thoughts of suicide. We'll decide…I'll make her commit to a plan to get you some professional help."

"Nothing will ever be the same after that phone call," she said with a quietness that Harmon wasn't sure was hopeful or disturbing.

"Do you want things to be the same?"

"No, I suppose not."

"Come and see me after third period, and I'll let you know how it went."

She nodded and took a deep breath. He asked her, "How do you feel now?"

"Relieved. Resigned."

"This is the first step toward making things better. Do you want to stay here first period? Would you prefer to stay in the counselor's office? Do you feel like going to class?"

"No, I'll go to class. We're having a quiz in calculus. I didn't get to be valedictorian by missing quizzes." She smiled. "That's a joke."

She looked around the room. "I'll go to class. There is a certain comfort in routine. It is an effective insulation from feelings."

Nancy's choices and speech pattern comforted Harmon. She didn't sound like someone in imminent danger. The bell rang and the first class filed into the room. Nancy did go to class and she did make the highest grade on the quiz.

When class ended, at 9 o'clock, Harmon went immediately to talk to Mrs. Dalworth, the school counselor at that time. He apprised her of Nancy's suicidal ideation, and told her that he was going to call Nancy's mother. Mrs. Dalworth said she would look at Nancy's transcript to see if she could drop a class or make an appropriate schedule change. To her, there was no problem that couldn't be solved by a good schedule change. He looked up the phone number of Mrs. Swenson's business office, went to the teacher's lounge, and sat down at the desk facing the phone.

He wondered what to say, where to begin, how to introduce the subject. He thought to himself, "How do you tell a parent that her daughter is at risk of committing suicide?" He sat staring at the phone for several minutes trying to compose his thoughts. Finally, he realized that he could wait no longer and that the phone call was absolutely necessary. He dialed.

Harmon always had difficulty remembering the conversation with Mrs. Swenson. He could remember the details but never anything specific about the tone. He told her about Nancy's meeting with him on Fridays and her suicidal thoughts. He expressed his belief that Nancy needed to see someone professional as soon as possible. She was shocked by his revelations, but she immediately agreed to make an appointment that afternoon, right after school, sooner if possible. She did not resist anything Harmon said, nor did she display any denial. She thanked him and the call ended. He was stunned at how little time the conversation had taken. A scant minute or two was all. Yet the call was productive. He had said everything that needed to be said. Nancy was going to get help. He decided that he felt rather hopeful and satisfied.

That he did not see Nancy after third period did not register in Harmon's mind. He was too busy teaching and she was in class. He went to lunch without giving the call to her mother another thought. He had some time before his next class. He went to his room to collect his thoughts and mentally prepare. The lights were off as he entered the room, which he found odd. He hadn't remembered turning them off. When he turned the lights on, he saw Nancy slumped on a desk with her head in her arms as if she were napping in a similar position as she had that morning. At first he was startled, but then he spoke, "I talked to your mother; I think everything is going to be fine. She seemed to take…." At that point, Nancy raised her head and Harmon noticed the blood. Her eyes were glazed over, unfocused, and a pool of blood on the desktop was slowly cascading onto the floor with a sickening, dripping sound. Her left wrist was the source of the blood and there was a smudge of blood on her forehead from where her head had been lying, covering the wound when he first looked at her. Some of the hair on the top of her head was matted together by the blood. Her lips moved as if she was trying to say something but her eyes just stared at Harmon. She slid out of the desk and collapsed on the floor.

Harmon was never clear about the details of the next few minutes. He remembered only brief, disjointed images strung together in some horrible mosaic. Time stood still while simultaneously speeding up. He picked her up. He squeezed her forearm as if trying to push the blood back into her wound. He remembered hearing noises coming from his own throat, but he could never remember exactly what he said. He carried her to the nurse's office. Blood seemed to be everywhere. On the steps. On the floor. On his shirt. He was babbling incoherently and crying uncontrollably. The nurse got the bleeding to stop or perhaps only got it to slow down. Nancy lapsed in and out of consciousness. The only clear memory Harmon ever had was Nancy's words,

"Mother…suicide…unacceptable…inappropriate…unacceptable."   The ambulance came and took her to the hospital.

Nancy stayed in the hospital the customary sixty days that insurance allowed. Harmon wrote to her, or called her, or visited her about twice a week. Some days were better than others. The first week was the roughest. Twice she was put on suicide watch and visiting privileges were suspended. By the last month, she had progressed sufficiently to meet with her parents in family therapy. She reported that things were going better between them. She had maintained her class work and by early spring, she was ready to return to school. The day before she was scheduled to return to school, Harmon was called into the office to meet with the principal, the counselor and Nancy's parents. Mr. Shakleford, the principal, presided over the meeting. He began, "Dr. and Mrs. Swenson have asked me to call this meeting to ensure Nancy's smooth transition back into school."

Mrs. Dalworth spoke next, "We've looked into her transcript and her schedule. She only needs one English credit to graduate. We can drop her from calculus and physics, both are honor classes and there is a lot of homework in each. We could enroll her in marine biology and single survival. That would relieve the stress here at school."

Mrs. Swenson spoke up, "No, those are all elective courses." She said this with an audible disdain. They were blow-off classes, and she knew it. "Those classes are not intellectually challenging. Nancy needs to return to the structure and discipline of a good class to keep her mind active. She has kept up with her studies while in the hospital. I want to keep her in all of the same classes, with the exception of psychology. I want her dropped from it." She looked at Harmon as she made her last statement, with a look of hostility that Harmon did not understand.

Suddenly the tone of the conversation changed. Harmon became the focus rather than Nancy. He was being accused, but he had no idea of what he was accused. He wondered why he was even in this conference if she was going to be dropped from his class. Harmon felt Dr. Swenson's eyes boring into him, and suddenly everything became quite surreal.

Mrs. Dalworth continued, "We have arranged for Nancy to eat lunch in my office every day."

"I don't understand." Harmon spoke out for the first time. "Why would you want to isolate her from her friends at lunch? And why drop psychology? I think she liked the class."

"Well," Mrs. Dalworth responded, although Harmon didn't believe she was really expressing her own ideas. "We don't want her under a lot of social pressure like she was before. You know, in her vulnerable state."

Mrs. Swenson sternly looked at Harmon and sharply retorted. "We don't want her in your class; we don't want her to talk to you after school; we don't want her to see you anymore. Period."

"What?" was all he could think to say.

"We don't think it is in her best interest to be exposed to you."

"Exposed?" Harmon looked around the room. "Everything you say is what you want. What about Nancy? What does Nancy want?"

"She is very concerned about her class rank, and she doesn't want to jeopardize it."

Harmon looked around the room in startled amazement. He searched everyone's eyes for some glimmer of support. He had, after all, saved Nancy's life. Had he stayed in the lunchroom the whole period, as he sometimes did, Nancy would have lost too much blood and died. If he expected anyone to realize this fact, he was certainly in the wrong room. His eyes finally fell on Dr. Swenson. Dr. Swenson had an air of efficiency about him. He looked like Nancy, only more aloof and even more intense, like a tightly-wound spring. Harmon thought perhaps the healer in Dr. Swenson would prevail and bring logic to the meeting. "What do you think?" he asked.

Dr. Swenson spoke in a very measured, even, controlled voice, well modulated, very firm and cold. No passion surfaced. Everything the mother had said had apparently originated from Dr. Swenson. She did the talking for the family but he did the thinking. If she was passionate and energetic, he was definitive and calculating. "I think," he began, "you are lucky that we are not going to pursue legal action against you."

"What?" Harmon was stunned.

"Who gave you permission to talk to our daughter after school? Who gave you permission to conduct therapy on her? Are you even a licensed therapist or counselor?"

"I am not, and I never claimed to be. I was not conducting therapy or counseling your daughter. I was just.." Harmon didn't know how to describe or label what he had been doing. He found himself becoming defensive, although he wasn't quite sure of what he was accused.

Dr. Swenson continued to speak in such a dispassionate voice that Harmon actually felt frightened. "It is our position, our legal position, that our daughter never expressed, acted on, or had any suicidal tendencies until she came in contact with you."

No one moved. No one said anything. The tension was palpable. Dr. Swenson's pronouncement had the effect of being a time bomb hurled into the middle of the room; everyone focused on the ticking, waiting for the explosion. Harmon looked around the room for some sort of support. None was forthcoming, none from Mrs. Dalworth, and none from Shakleford. He sensed that the next words spoken would be very important, but he couldn't think of anything to say.

"We want you to stay away from he." Mrs. Swenson did the talking but Dr. Swenson's glare, which never left Harmon, left little doubt about who was the power behind the words. "We would transfer schools except she is in her last semester and her class rank would be compromised. We would pursue legal action except we don't want to upset her any more near the end of school; she still feels some misguided loyalty. Rest assured those are the only reasons. And if we hear of you talking to her…" The thought didn't need to be completed.

After an uncomfortably long silence, Mr. Shakleford spoke up. "Well, we all want what is best for Nancy. That's really the important thing. Don't you agree Mr. Harmon?"

He nodded agreement. There was nothing else he could do. "I don't want to be a source of conflict for Nancy."

"Good." Shakleford continued. "We all agree. Nancy will return to class tomorrow. She will have the same schedule with the exception of psychology class." He turned directly at Harmon with a sternness in his eyes that could not be mistaken, "And Mr. Harmon will have no contact with her."

Harmon wanted to protest. He thought of pointing out the illogic of thinking that an elective teacher during the senior year could implant suicidal ideas in a student. He wanted to rave at the injustice of being attacked for doing nothing improper. But he recognized the awful truth: to fight for her right to talk to him would have added more stress and pressure to her life. He did not want to engage in a battle with Dr. Swenson, a battle that Nancy would lose no matter who won. The issue needed to be addressed by Nancy and her therapist. The therapist would address this issue, and Harmon would eventually be vindicated. This moment was about her not him, and intellectually he knew that it was not in Nancy's best interest to clash with the Swensons. Still, emotionally, he kept thinking of her words that morning. "You know, this room is the only place in the world where I feel safe, this room, A 216." That port, that shelter from the storm, had been ripped away from her, and Harmon felt guilty for allowing it to be taken from her.

He did manage to see her one more time. At graduation, before the processional she pulled him aside behind the curtains backstage.

"Hi," she said. "How have you been?"

"Fine. You?"

"Good, better. Look, I'm sorry about my parents. You know, not letting me talk to you and everything."

"That's okay. I thought you might think it was me."

"No. I knew it was their idea; they wouldn't let me talk to you. My therapist and I talked about it…it just seemed like…you know, you have to pick your battles."

Harmon was looking around nervously. He didn't know what else to say. "Thanks, I felt really bad. I was worried that you thought I…that I had let you down, that I didn't care any more…that I broke my promise"

"No. No. I understand. But before I left. I just wanted to…I had to…thank you." She was looking around too, as if they were both afraid of being caught. "This is hard, but I have to tell you. When things were the worst for me, when everything seemed so hopeless, and I wanted to die, you were there. You reached out to me. You cared. Thank you. It made a difference. I mean, I sort of owe you the rest of my life."

She turned abruptly and headed for the stage. On the stairs, she turned. "I have to make a speech, you know."

"Nancy, I want you to know, that no matter what happens, no matter where you go, or what you do, or even whether we ever see each other again, my room, A 216, that safety zone is always there."

Very quietly she said, "I know. I count on it." Halfway up the stairs, she stopped and turned toward him. "You were right, you know, about taking the best parts of anything with you. I thought about it a lot in the hospital. I even mention in my speech that the best parts of high school, we take with us as we leave, and your classroom was the best thing about high school for me; it was my safety net, my shelter from the storm, and it will be a big part of my life forever." She turned, bounded up the last two steps of the stairs, and left his life forever.

In the countless times that Harmon replayed the conference with the Swensons in his mind, he became more and more convinced that he had done the right thing. Long ago any lingering feelings of self-doubt or guilt had been replaced by another feeling, one of anger directed not at the Swensons but at

Shakleford. "He should have supported me," Harmon thought, "instead of abandoning me. Shakleford should have defended me. Instead he sacrificed me at the hint of a lawsuit. Even in the absence of professional respect, Shakleford should have exhibited some sort of faculty loyalty. Instead, loyalty and respect were quickly abandoned at the hint of parental disapproval."

This feeling of betrayal had stayed with Harmon for all of these years, and he projected his fears of professional abandonment onto all principals; they were certainly the source of his doubts about Dr. Randich. Harmon never met with Randich without wondering how he would have handled the situation with the Swensons if he had been principal at the time. Would Randich have given Harmon the support he deserved? Would he have validated Harmon's role in Nancy's life? Did he respect his faculty members enough to defend them against parental attack? Or would Randich have taken the Swensons' side? Harmon vacillated in his answer to those questions. Part of him liked to think that Randich was too professional not to support his staff. The intellectual superiority of Harmon's position would appeal to Randich. However, another part of Harmon recognized that Randich was not very fond of the affective domain, not very comfortable with emotions. This fact caused Harmon to question how Randich would have responded. Policies that impacted cognitive growth were his usual jurisdiction. He acknowledged emotions but tried to avoid dealing with them. Emotions were too abstract and too elusive to respond to in a logical way; they were too fuzzy. Randich's adherence to professional standards and behavior might not permit him to endorse the behavior of a teacher functioning without a firm curriculum based rationale. Harmon was navigating uncharted waters and Randich required a chart and compass.

Yet whenever Harmon felt sure that Randich was too committed to the Cult of Uniformity to have confronted the Swenson's, Randich would do something uncharacteristic that would shake Harmon's perception of him. For example, Harmon was always surprised at Randich's support of Homeroom. Homeroom did not seem like a program Randich would endorse or even permit.

Homeroom was a kind of support group that Harmon conducted. However, most support groups are based on common areas of concern and have an-agreed upon objective. For example, drug rehabilitation support groups, eating disorder support groups and suicide survivor support groups have become accepted programs in many schools. Often these programs have a set curriculum with lesson plans. Unlike these groups, Homeroom had no common denominator among the students enrolled. In fact, this diversity of population was a defining characteristic and was considered one of the most positive elements of the program to many of the participants. Homeroom also differed from other support groups by the absence of specific objectives or defined goals. For example, a support group for eating disorders concentrates on supporting members in dealing with their personal eating obsessions. In Homeroom there were no common problems; therefore, there were no common goals. Each member was free to develop his or her own objective either consciously or unconsciously. Because the program did not delineate any end-targets, each student was free to pursue personal goals. In other words, by not providing a direction, Homeroom empowered students to determine their own directions and growth. To the students this lack of direction was called "freedom" and was considered one of the most positive aspects of the program. To Randich, Harmon feared, this lack of direction would be called something else, intellectual laziness, lack of clarity, stupidity, or confusion. Harmon was apprehensive that Randich would not approve of Homeroom. It violated all of the principles of the Cult of Uniformity; it was the arch-enemy, and yet Randich allowed it.

Prior to Homeroom the closest thing to a support group at West Side was the Anti-Social Club. Two years before Homeroom, during Shakleford's administration, Harmon had created the Anti-Social Club as an extracurricular activity. Meetings were held on Wednesdays right after school in Harmon's room. The Anti-Social Club was an oxymoron created in a tongue-in-cheek manner to foster communication of a free-floating, uncensored nature. Shakleford granted approval as long as no mention of psychology was used in the name. The purpose was to reach out to those students who were the most alienated at the school. At the time, the term "Social" was used by students to describe the most conformist groups of students; no one identified with the term or used it to describe his or her own group. "Socials" were always other students. The term Anti-Social carried a certain status as well as a covert meaning. This self-deprecating and tongue-in-cheek nature of the Anti-Social Club was expanded in recruitment announcements and posters. Billed as the "Society for the Prevention of Mental Health" or the "Friends of Those Who have No Friends", the Anti-Social Club was sort of an in-joke that had a loyal following.

Several faculty members, all members of the Cult, took the name too seriously and complained about the Anti-Social Club. Mrs. K, for example, refused to ever type the name on any list of extracurricular activities. Other faculty members felt that Harmon was rewarding the worst part of the school population. Mostly the members of the Anti-Social Club just laughed. Laughter was the main activity at any meeting. Topics, even serious topics, were discussed, but eventually everyone would laugh at some aspect of the topic. Generalities were never made specific. If a student ventured into an area of self-disclosure, the topic was gently steered away from him. Harmon consciously decided upon this policy because the population at meetings was constantly changing. Although there was a core of loyal attendees, he never knew from week to week who would show-up.

Homeroom was an extension of the Anti-Social Club. That was how Harmon had convinced Randich to allow him to have meetings during class time of the regularly scheduled day. Randich approved for several reasons. First, Homeroom was something he could tell the community the school was doing as a reaction to the problems of suicide and drug use. Harmon concluded that Randich didn't endorse Homeroom as much as he used it to relieve some community pressure. Second, Homeroom did not cost anything because, initially, Harmon was using his own conference period. Later Homeroom became his duty period, and it was not until last year that Homeroom became an extra duty period. Third, Homeroom was a personal statement of faith in Harmon. Randich was saying yes to an experienced, respected teacher. He was rewarding Harmon for years of good teaching with high evaluation marks. He trusted Harmon to do a competent job. The message was not lost on the rest of the faculty.

Still, there was a nagging doubt inside of Harmon. He never felt that Randich completely supported the concept of Homeroom. In fact, he was not sure that Randich completely understood Homeroom. Randich never asked for a detailed explanation. He did insist that the name be changed from the Anti-Social Club. Harmon remembered that when he had been in high school, the school day had begun with a fifteen minute homeroom. The purpose of the homeroom was to help the student with any number of problems including registration, attendance, permission slips, etc. The sole purpose was to benefit the student. This seemed like an apt description of the Anti-Social Club, and Homeroom was much more palatable for most people's tastes.

Because Harmon did not believe that Randich really supported Homeroom, when Randich began the meeting by asking the status of Homeroom, Harmon gave his usual noncommittal "okay". In Harmon's experience, usually principals did not want details when they asked a question; they wanted reassurance. In the past, this type of answer had always satisfied Randich; however, this time, something was different. Randich looked at Harmon from across his desk, legs crossed and his right elbow supporting his chin. His posture made him look casual but attentive. By ignoring the stack of papers in front of him, Randich gave the impression he wanted more than a perfunctory response.

Harmon wasn't sure what Randich wanted, but he replied, "Currently there are five Homerooms, three second period, and two fifth period. Second period meets on Monday, Wednesday and Thursday and fifth period meets on Tuesday and Thursday. There are no Homerooms on Friday. There are a total of 48 students enrolled, but only 43 attend consistently. There is a 93% attendance rate for all Homeroom with fifth periods, slightly lower than second period, which makes sense, because most students get out early. If they attend fifth period, they are staying late. On the other hand, in second period, the students are actually missing a class."

Randich continued to stare at Harmon, who wasn't sure if he had said enough or if he just hadn't said what Randich had wanted to hear. So Harmon continued, "This is the tenth semester of Homeroom. It has grown from two periods a week to the five, currently. I use my duty period and you have given me an extra duty period for the last two years. Each Homeroom has had roughly eight to ten students." Harmon wasn't sure if he had given Randich everything he had wanted, so he waited for Randich to reply.

"Is it working?" he asked.

"I don't know how to answer that. I think it is working. The kids seem to like it. It seems to generate a lot of loyalty."

"Have you ever tried to evaluate Homeroom? Have you ever tried to demonstrate measurable outcomes?"

"No." Harmon began to feel defensive, but he continued. "Not really. I mean, how do you measure something like Homeroom? It mostly tries to prevent things, you know? There were no suicides last week, but I don't know how many Homeroom actually prevented. I can't say no one got drunk or did drugs, but I feel sure that it was less than there would have been without Homeroom. There was less loneliness, and that seems like a good thing, but I don't know how to measure that."

"Well," Randich spoke slowly, dropping his hands into his lap but maintaining eye contact with Harmon. "I am afraid I have some bad news for you. We received our student numbers for next year from central administration. Our enrollment is down for the third year in a row. We are going to lose some teacher allocations. The teachers that stay will have to increase their loads. We won't fire anyone, but we won't replace any teacher who retires or transfers to a different school. The bottom line is." He leaned across the desk to emphasize the next words. "I can't afford Homeroom. Two periods a day. That's two-fifths of a teacher, forty per cent of a teaching load. Less than fifty students divided by five periods. I just can't allocate that many teacher hours on that few students just because they like it. The absence of any quantitative data to support Homeroom is troublesome, but frankly, there just aren't enough numbers to continue Homeroom."

Harmon nodded, but he wasn't going to accept the demise of Homeroom without responding. "Dr. Randich, I hope we aren't becoming a profession that is run by numbers only."

"Do you have anything that's better?"

Harmon just shook his head. "It all seems rather…dehumanizing."

"You may be right. Doing things based on formulas may not always be the best way, but at least it is rational rather than emotional. I can hang my hat on decisions based on data. What do you, Mr. Harmon, base you conclusions on?"

Harmon looked at Randich and wanted to say something very dramatic. "Tell me about your numbers when the suicide rate starts increasing again." But he knew it would do no good and would only create hostility. Besides he really did not have a good answer. Harmon still respected decisions made with logic over emotion, especially from an administrative viewpoint.

"Dr. Randich, I respect your decisions, and I appreciate your telling me like this. Of course, I disagree with the decision in this case. Is there anything I can do? Do you mind if I appeal your decision?"

"No, I don't mind at all. I don't think it will do any good, but there is a Board of Education meeting tonight. The budget will be the primary agenda item. I can introduce you to the trustees and you can make your own personal plea. Please understand, Mr. Harmon, my decision is all based on a formula, guidelines sent from the superintendent. I really have very little leeway. Do not take it personally."

Harmon stood up, shook Randich's hand, and left the office. "A victory for the Cult of Uniformity," he thought to himself. "At least, maybe now I know how Randich would have handled the Swenson affair." He felt hurt. He felt slightly betrayed, but mostly, he felt like he needed to talk to Allison.

CHAPTER 2

DOING NOTHING VERY WELL

Randich's last words echoed in Harmon's head. "Don't take it personally." But he did, and that was probably the biggest difference between the two. Harmon had no choice. Homeroom was a personal experience. With a pace slow but deliberate, he headed toward Allison's office. Suddenly he heard, in hushed, almost reverent tones, *"Angels in the snow."* He was not sure if someone had actually spoken the words out loud or if he had only thought them. The effect was the same: he stopped in the middle of the hallway. He thought of Genevieve. Whenever he tried to evaluate Homeroom, Genevieve came to mind. She, more than anyone else, had summarized her Homeroom experience with words that captured the ambiguity, the magical enigma that was at the heart of Homeroom: *"Angels in the snow."* His own attempts to analyze and make sense out of Homeroom failed to do justice to the experience. Homeroom always seemed to be more than the sum of the parts. How could he explain Genevieve's words to Randich? How could he make the Board understand her poetry?

Like any other teacher in a large, urban, high school, with 150 students each semester, Harmon did not always notice an individual student unless there was a specific reason. An unfortunate side effect of a large school district is that anonymity is the rule; individual relationships are the exception. Often the first thing a teacher notices about a student is the student's grades, especially on tests. And so it was with Genevieve. The first reason Harmon noticed her was her grades. She didn't make the highest grades in class, but she was close. However, what really caught Harmon's attention were the editorial comments that she would make in the margins of the test:

"Good question."

"Tricky."

"You're trying to fool us here." Her remarks evolved into more original and amusing comments:

"This reminds me very little of question number 2."

"I hate questions like this. I think I told you before that I hate questions like this." "The last three questions remind me of the questions on my math test except Mrs. Kaplan uses numbers."

"Have you ever thought about getting a job writing for TV Guide?"

Genevieve was very quiet in class. She sat in the back of the room, talked to no one, which was understandable for a transfer student, took competent lecture notes, did well on tests, and, most impressively to Harmon, caught all his jokes. After school, he noticed that she walked home every day. One day when his car was in the shop, Harmon ended up walking in the same direction. He asked her how she liked her new school.

"It's a school," she said.

"Do you do as well in all your classes as you do in mine?"

"Pretty much."

"Made any new friends?"

"Not really."

"I know it's pretty rough moving into a school the second semester, especially a school like West Side."

She shrugged her shoulders. "My mom is thinking of starting a support group like we had at my old school."

"Really?"

"Yeah, she'll call it DAM."

"What kind of support group will it be?"

"Mothers Against Dyslexia."

Harmon laughed, Genevieve only smiled but Harmon was genuinely impressed by her ability to sucker him in completely. She got him, and not many people did. At that point, Harmon took a more comprehensive look at this very quiet, competent girl with the peculiar sense of humor.

Her hair was very short and she dressed in a fashion that at some later point would be called the grunge look. If she was ahead of her time, she wasn't the only one. However, Harmon was convinced that her clothes were not so much a fashion statement as they were a necessity. While some other students would wear the same styles of outfits for effect, Genevieve's wardrobe was not a fad. Her clothes were never quite clean and the recycle rate of each item too short and regular to be merely a choice. Her shoes, Converse high tops, were not only dirty but they also had holes in the sides and bottoms. The shoelaces were frayed and one was tied together where it had broken. She tended to wear T-shirts that were actually undershirts. Her jeans had holes in the knees and one right below the seat. Other students wore jeans like that, but her jeans also had permanent stains of what looked like grease on the thigh of one leg and below the knee on the other leg. She continued to wear the same jeans when the weather turned cold and the other, more fashionable students had switched to corduroy. The bottom line was Genevieve looked poor not by choice but because she was poor. Being poor was not exactly a sin at West Side, but it was a novelty and was certainly considered bad form. Other students didn't consciously condemn the poor, but they tended to avoid them as if poverty were contagious.

Harmon invited Genevieve to join Homeroom. He thought Homeroom would provide an excellent way for her to met new students, but as often was the case, he really just wanted to get to know her. She had a difficult schedule with all academic classes. He settled for a perfunctory "maybe next year".

In the meantime, Allison had discovered the history behind Genevieve's move to West Side. For the past two years, her father had been disabled and could not work. Unemployment payments had been exhausted, and the family had been trying to exist on the meager amount of money that her mother could make with no formal education or training. Genevieve's aunt called and offered her a position that seemed to be the answer to their prayers. She was a manager of a franchise restaurant and made a comfortable living. The position she offered the mother was assistant manager. Although the pay was not great, by sharing rent with the sister, the family could raise their standard of living and pay off some debts. They moved into a West Side neighborhood and were beginning to see light at the end of the tunnel when the father's health took a turn for the worse and medical bills started mounting. The house they rented was close enough to the restaurant to walk, which was fortunate because their car broke down and they could not afford the repairs. Genevieve had to walk nearly two miles to school each day and this was becoming a problem as the cold days of January were becoming the even colder days of February. The school bus policy was to serve only those students who lived outside a two-mile radius of the school. It was because of this school bus issue that Allison became involved with Genevieve. She went to work getting the Director of the Transportation Division to make an exception for Genevieve. This was not an easy battle. Many principals and teachers had come to the conclusion that the Director of Transportation was the real power in any school district. That school districts exist for the benefit of school busses seems to be an irresistible conclusion. That year was Allison's first year at West Side and she did not give-up easily. After many phone calls to the principal, the superintendent and the members of the board, Allison prevailed. Genevieve was finally put on a bus route. During the struggle for the bus, Allison got to know Genevieve, and the more Allison got to know her, the more worried Allison became.

Allison had heard of the Anti-Social Club from various students. She knew it had changed names to Homeroom and was available to students during the day. She wanted to enroll Genevieve in Homeroom so she contacted Harmon to pursue the issue. Allison wanted Harmon to put Genevieve in his Tuesday Homeroom. In order to do this, Genevieve would have to miss her honors English class. Harmon hesitated. "I don't think it will work. Mrs. Davis won't let her out of class. I mean, no one gets out of honors English."

Allison nodded, but assured him that Genevieve was a special case.

"Maybe she is, but I have never asked to get a student out of her class. I mean there are certain things you just know in this world. Mrs. Davis is all business. She doesn't play around. You know? She does a tremendous job. I have all the respect in the world for her, although I probably don't agree with her about anything. I wouldn't dream of asking to get someone out of her class. I mean, Allison, you are new to this faculty, but you are messing with an icon of the faculty, the guru of the honors curriculum, the…"

"It was Mrs. Davis's idea."

Harmon was stunned. Davis was not the kind of teacher who was friendly to a program like Homeroom. Frankly, he was stunned that she was even aware of Homeroom. Allison handed Harmon a paper. "Genevieve turned this in last week."

The paper was a very disturbing character study with undertones of suicidal ideation and hints of delusional thinking. It was surrealistic and very bleak.

Harmon read it over and looked up at Allison. "What do you make of it?"

"No one knows how to interpret it. Is it a well-written portrayal of a crumbling mind, or is it some sort of autobiographical sketch? Is it even original? There are not enough samples of her writing to tell."

"What was the assignment, Psychos I have known and loved?"

"That may be the most disturbing part," Allison said. "The assignment was about the symmetrical organization of Hawthorn's <u>Scarlet Letter</u>."

"Well, there you are. No one in her right mind could answer that."

Allison did not laugh. "I'm really worried about Genevieve. I don't think I've ever seen a student have more difficulty adjusting to a new school. She has no friends. She doesn't eat lunch. She used to walk around the halls during lunch looking, lost and pathetic, until she was caught and given a detention. Mr. Harmon, now she just sits at this one table all alone. And this paper. I mean, I worry whether she has a good grasp on reality. Her records from the past school are incomplete."

She looked away for a brief second. "She scares me. No, let me put that differently, I am afraid for her. When I look into her eyes, there is something different from what I see in other student's eyes. Do you know what I mean?"

"I have no idea." Harmon wanted to comfort Allison, but he knew anything he would say along those lines would be a lie. "How can I help? What can I do?"

"I'm hoping Homeroom can provide some sort of base of support while we find out what is going on. Give her a safe harbor, a port in the storm. Watch her. Let me know if you find out anything. I don't want you to break confidentiality, but let me know if you find anything we need to do to help her." She held up the paper and waved it as she spoke. "If this is all made up, she has a great deal of talent and we need to make sure it is nurtured. If this is not made up, she has symptoms of schizophrenia."

"Schizophrenia. That's heavy. I don't know if I can handle that. I mean what can Homeroom do?"

"I'm no diagnostician. This may all be an overreaction by everyone, by me. In the meantime, she does need to connect with someone, anyone. I don't know, but Homeroom can't hurt, can it?"

"I don't know. If we get into one of those reality-is-a-choice conversations, it might take on a special meaning for her."

"Try."

"I will. I like Genevieve. I'll be glad to work with her. She seems different and if the Anti-Social Club—I keep forgetting—Homeroom means anything, it is kind of a celebration of being different."

Genevieve joined the Tuesday Homeroom, Wendy's Homeroom. Although there was the usual number of students in this Homeroom, maybe eight or ten, Wendy was the defining member. She provided the identity for this particular

Homeroom. Wendy had been a loyal member of the Anti-Social Club when she elected to join Homeroom.

Genevieve and Wendy had nothing in common. In fact, if one were to create a continuum on any characteristic or trait, Wendy and Genevieve would be placed on opposite ends. Wendy was well dressed; she made excellent grades in all her classes; she was an officer in the student council; she was a Homecoming Queen nominee; she was wealthy, well mannered, clean-cut, out-going, and confident. In fact, she had all the qualities that would have caused her to be hated by three-fourths of the student body. Wendy was different. She was that rare individual who could cut across stereotypes and break down clichés. She was almost universally adored. Student who didn't like anyone else at school spoke of Wendy with tones of reverence, and she had an almost magical effect on other students. Although she was drug-free, clean-cut, and immensely socialized, many of her best friends were none of those things. She did not alienate those who made different lifestyle choices. She accepted them and respected them. In fact, she was attracted to the seedy elements of the school. Sometimes she felt it was her mission, as she put it, "to protect and serve, a friend of those who have no friends." For example, she was often the designated driver. She would often spend weekends picking up friends from parties she did not attend and make sure they got home safely. She would help clean up after a beer bust at an absent parent's house. And on more than one occasion, she went into an "unsavory environment to remove a friend who couldn't move."

"My lifestyle is not without risks," she said one time as an introduction to an incredible monologue that had the phrasing and timing of a well-rehearsed comic routine, an impression that was strengthened to Harmon whenever he heard the story. This was his third time. She told the story on the first meeting of Homeroom. "Actually I was much worse during junior high school. I think I learned my lesson on Halloween of my ninth grade year." And then she launched into her routine:

Wendy's Monologue

Greg had been trying to get me to go to this Halloween Party all week. It was at some crack house. You know, downtown. Skid row. Like I really wanted to go to this place. "There'll be wild costumes and great drugs" were his exact selling points.

"How will we get there?" I asked. You have to remember this was ninth grade and we were all still a year away from thinking about driving.

"That's the great thing. I've talked my parents into taking us! They think it is some sort of haunted house for charity. They won't think anything is wrong when they see all the weird people going to the party."

"And this is good because? How will we get home?"

"Well, I haven't worked out all the details. Something will come up."

I didn't like the sound of "something will come up." So I told Greg, thanks, but no thanks. "I hate to turn down the social event of the season, but count me out."

So I'm alone at home studying and answering the doorbell for the local trick-or-treaters when I get a call from Greg. He is stoned out of his mind. At the party, someone gave him some weed that was stronger than anything he had ever smoked. "I can't feel the roof of my mouth," he said. Everyone at the party is in as bad a shape as he is and he doesn't trust them to drive him home anyway. He tried to give some directions to one guy but when he pointed north the guy just stared at the ceiling. He needs someone to come and get him. He wants me to be that someone. The fact that I have never driven a car before and that I have very little idea of how to start the engine does not dissuade him. The fact that there is an unused car in my driveway with car keys hanging by the door is a much more persuasive argument, to his way of thinking. My folks were at the country club in Mom's Lexus. Greg figures I could take Dad's Buick, go get him, and be back before they would miss me. It was a plan. And, he convinced me that it had some merit, which should have been my first clue that I wasn't thinking rationally.

I get the key from the key rack, open the garage door and try to start the car. No one has ever told me that the key has to go in upside down before it will fit into the ignition. It takes me five minutes to get the key into the ignition. Now, I've watched my Dad enough times to know that I turn the key to start the engine, but I haven't watched him closely enough to realize that I should let go as soon as the engine starts. So I sit there for another five minutes trying to figure out why the car is making this horrible grinding sound. When I finally give up and let go, to get out of the car and abandon my mission, the noise stops but the car is still running. I see the PRNDL on the dashboard and figure that has something to do with the driving of the car. I try to force the indicator to R because I want to go in reverse, but it won't move. I don't know what is wrong. I can't get the stupid handle on the steering wheel to move. In desperation, I slammed my hand on the wheel and kicked the brakes. When I touched the brakes, the handle moved into R. The car lurches backward. At full speed. I slam on the brakes, but don't switch out of R. I sit there trying to figure out what to do next. I play with the handle with my foot on the brakes. L makes the car go forward. I keep going back and forth between R and L. A few feet forward, a few feet back. Each time I twist the steering wheel.

Eventually, after five or ten minutes, I'm in the alley pointed in the general direction of the street. I'm off to rescue Greg.

I'm going okay until I reach the end of the alley. By now I have mastered the concepts of a gas pedal and forward motion, but I'm still a little shaky on the steering wheel. I turn right at the end of the alley and it only takes me one trip onto the sidewalk and into the bushes to realize I have to do something to the steering wheel to stop the car from continuing to turn. By accident I let go of the wheel to put my hands in front of my face to scream, and what do you know, the car straightens itself out. Like magic. What a wonderful machine, I thought. Just take your hands of the wheel and it gets itself out of a jam. I now proceed to drive downtown with my hands mostly off of the wheel.

I keep the little arrow pointed at L because it is working and I don't feel that I need to get any fancier than success. The car seems more sluggish than it is for Dad, but I'm not into performance anyway. The whole trip downtown is a blur of starts and stops and lurching forward. At one point I stop at a red light, when a police car pulls up next to me. I figure my adventure is about to end if he sees me drive across the intersection in my lurching style, but he turns right and doesn't see me going down the road. Fortunately, there are very few turns on my way. I stay off any expressways and only make two turns from the main street. I finally make it to the party, sort of.

I mean, I get to the house where the party is, but there is no place to park. More accurately, all the parking places require parallel parking, a skill I hadn't mastered in my 45 minutes of driving experience. I'm not sure what to do. I decide to just stop the car in the middle of the street and run in and get Greg. How long can it take, I ask myself.

I go to the front door and ring the bell. I figure that's the polite thing to do. Then I knock. Then I wait. Ring the bell. Knock, wait. I repeat the ritual about four times. In the meantime, two or three couples push past me into the house. I get the drift. Apparently, on this side of town, one doesn't have to knock to enter a house. I walk into the most bizarre scene I've ever seen.

The house has maybe seven rooms, but no furniture. Every room does have a source of music. Everyone is in some sort of costume only there doesn't seem to be any theme. I mean, there are like monsters with realistic makeup and vampires and ghosts. One guy walks by with his head in his arms. I don't know how he did that. There are witches in various stages of undress, including one topless cowgirl, at least that's what I think she was supposed to be. I'm walking around looking for Greg, asking for Greg. In one room everyone is naked, I think. The lights weren't very bright. It was the orgy room. Every room I enter I develop a little ritual. First

I look around for Greg and I say his name three times, each time a little louder. The people in the room follow a two-step response. In each room someone offers me a different drug with a different method of ingestion. I never knew there were so many ways to take drugs: smoke, snort, shoot up. In one room I was offered a suppository. Also, in each room I get a compliment for my costume. I mean, I'm dressed like normal person, a skirt and a sweater. But everyone says I have a great costume: a preppie. I'm the only one dressed normally and they think I'm weird. I finally find Greg, in the kitchen I think. He is half-unconscious but I manage to pull him to his feet and get him to walk, stagger, with me to the car.

My relief at leaving the party is short lived. When we reach the street, a near riot is ensuing. There are three cars behind my car in a mini-traffic jam. They can't pull around me; the street is too narrow. The first car is filled with seven Mexicans yelling Spanish at the second car, which has five Asians screeching Asian. Behind both of them is a street gang in a pick-up truck that looks like they're on their way to a drive-by shooting. Everyone is screaming at each other and no one knows what anyone is saying. I push Greg into the passenger side of the car and I take off as quickly as my lurching manner allows. I would have peeled out had I known how to get out of L.

By the time I get home, it is rather late and my parents are back. Mother's car is in the garage, which is a good thing. I wasn't sure how I was going to get the Buick into the garage. I was thinking of parking it and pushing it in. Now I just pulled in behind her. But I know I am in big trouble. After I pull Greg from the car, I brace him against the fence and tell him he's on his own. He starts to protest, but falls asleep before he can whine very much. He lives only four houses down the alley so I figure he's safe enough. I got my own problems.

I sneak into the back door. I hear my Mother. She wants to call the police. My Dad is trying to calm her down. "She's a good girl. Where would she go? She doesn't even know how to drive." None of these things seem to comfort Mother. I notice my textbooks on the dinner table, and I get an idea. I tip toe past them while their backs are turned and get my books. Then I sneak back into the garage and enter the living room. Mother is really angry. Dad doesn't know whether to slap me or hug me. I am all apologetic. "I needed to go to the library to do some research for a paper. I didn't want to spoil your evening."

Dad is already saying, "I told you so."

"I'm so sorry. I know I shouldn't have done that but I so needed these books." Mother lectured me for a half-hour; I acted humbled and repentant. I think my Dad was secretly proud that I had so much gumption and academic determina-

tion. When I showed them an "A" paper next week, all was forgiven. To this day, they have no idea where I went or what I was doing.

Although Wendy was quite capable of being deceiving her parents, she was completely honest with her friends. She did want to go to a good college and join the right sorority. She did want to dress properly. She did care about her grades, her resume, and her appearance. If some of her friends did not share her values, she could accept their differences, and they had no choice but to accept her. She cared deeply for her friends, and she did not let her loyalty hinge on superficial similarities. She was highly socialized and ambitious, but she accepted that her friends were not, and she did not make demands or try to change them. She had those two sides and both sides were real and genuine. She had no problem living with her dual nature. "What you see is what you get," she told Homeroom one time. Another time she looked directly at Harmon and said, "I am everything I pretend to be." He never knew what she meant.

As it turned out, Genevieve's first day in Homeroom was the first day for Wendy's spring Homeroom. After Wendy's monologue, Harmon began by explaining the rules of Homeroom, which explained confidentiality and his limits on the subject: "Everything we say in Homeroom stays in Homeroom. This is very important. I will not breach your confidentiality and I expect the same from you. I don't mean that you can't tell your parents that you are in Homeroom. Obviously, you have to have a signature on a parental permission slip. But never reveal specific information, even if you think it is safe. To do so would violate trust and might lead others to realize stuff we don't want realized. In other words, your stories are yours to tell, not for anyone else to tell."

Harmon always maintained eye contact whenever he made his plea. He tried to see if anyone indicated that they might have problems in this area. If he felt that someone's behavior was a cause for concern, he would confront him or her and get a personal promise. If everyone seemed comfortable with confidentiality, he would continue. "There are of course exceptions to this rule. If anyone reveals a threat to self or others, I will be compelled to report the threat to the proper authorities." He purposely used a word choice that felt awkward and stiff to emphasize the seriousness of the subject. Then he would look around making sure everyone understood. "In other words, if you are planning to kill yourself or anyone else, I won't sit on that information."

To try to change the tone of the meeting, Harmon would follow with the last rule in Homeroom. "The last rule is the Guido Menitto Rule: no physical violence. This is not really an issue; we've never had a fight break out, but

Guido always wanted the rule mentioned just in case. There is another rule but I forget what it is."

"There are two times when Homeroom is structured: on the first day and on the last. Most of the time, I will just ask if anyone has anything on his or her mind. I want to start by sharing our names and expectations for Homeroom. Keep in mind that every Homeroom is different because the people enrolled define Homeroom. Some Homerooms are very serious and get really heavy. Others have been silly and goofy. Either way is okay. Homeroom is whatever we decide for it to be, whatever we make it. Do not base expectations on past experiences in Homeroom. Still, I want to know what you hope will happen, why you are here. And while we are at it, tell us your name so we can start to know each other."

The whole process took maybe five minutes. The students began, one at a time, to introduce themselves. Nothing particularly noteworthy was said until Genevieve spoke. She spoke very softly while she seemed to be staring at her desktop. "My name is Genevieve. I'm here because Mr. Harmon invited me, Allison thought it was a good idea, and my English teacher agreed. They all think I'm crazy." Then Genevieve looked up directly at Harmon. "Do you think I'm crazy?"

Harmon sensed the seriousness of her questioning and the direct confrontation to his motivation. He knew she wanted and needed an honest, complete answer, but before he could say anything, Wendy interrupted him. "You make that sound like a bad thing. We are all crazy here. This is my second or third Homeroom, and that's the best thing about Homeroom, this is a place where it's okay to be crazy."

Harmon could sense that Genevieve needed more of a response. "I don't want to be evasive, but I think that your own opinion is more important than mine on this issue. Do you think you're crazy?"

"Sometimes." She dropped her eyes back onto the desktop. "I don't know what to think. I know I think differently than other people. I am different from other people." She glanced toward Wendy. "From other people here."

There was something in her words and the glance that touched Wendy deeply like a surgical laser penetrating the layers to her heart. Wendy nodded as she maintained eye contact and spoke to Genevieve, "We are all different, and it scares us too."

Harmon interrupted. "What is crazy? I mean, what do you mean by crazy?"

Genevieve started to answer, but her words were hesitant. "I don't know...I think,...maybe,...being out of control?"

"Out of control? Who is in control? I mean does anyone feel in control?" Daphne another member of the group was talking. "No, I think the first step in not being crazy is realizing you don't have control. Crazy is being different from the majority, and I for one, am proud to be crazy. Who wants to be like everyone else?"

"I know what you are talking about." Katie responded to Daphne. "But non-conformity is not crazy. Crazy hurts."

"It is still defined by the majority, by society," Daphne responded in an impassioned way to continue her argument. "If you're different and the difference is approved of, you are "Too Cool". If you are different in way that society does not approve of...."

"Like being too tall in junior high school." Wendy added with a tone that startled everyone because it was so out of character for her.

"Being tall is not crazy."

"You were never the tallest kid in school. I was."

There was something in the way Wendy's voice cracked that alarmed the group. They all turned to her and gave her their complete attention, and for the first time, Wendy's cheery façade crumbled.

"All through junior high, no one would have anything to do with me because I was a full head above everyone else. Even the tallest guy. Don't get me wrong. I had plenty of friends. They would joke with me, tease me. But no one, no one, ever took me seriously. I was there for them, but they were not there for me. I could get them to count on me, depend on me, but no one...valued me. No one took the time to know me." Tears had formed in her eyes and were slowly beginning to flow down her cheeks as she continued to speak and everyone else sat dumbfounded. "Every relationship was because I tried so hard. No one reached out to me. Like the time I stole my parent's car and went to get Greg from the drug party. I've told that story a hundred times and everyone laughs cause I didn't know how to drive and the party was so weird and everything. But no one ever realizes how scared I was. I've never been so frightened in my life."

The tears were flowing freely now but her sobs were silent. Her voice, lower in both volume and tone, had the effect of a verbal underline. "Greg never even said thank you. And my parents? My parents never knew. I mean they still don't know. I could have ended up dead with my throat slashed from some bizarre junkie, or in a car accident, or something, and they would never have known where I was, or why, or anything."

Harmon nodded. "It's like they don't even know who you are."

By now she had surrendered any attempt to control her crying, and her shoulders were trembling. Everyone sat quietly while she got the strength to continue. "I have done so many things—foolish, dangerous things—and my parents? They do not have a clue. They think because I make good grades, I'm safe. Little Miss Prom Queen Honor Society. How can I do wrong? How can they do wrong?"

"It's like they don't even know you."

"They don't know me." She nodded and sat quietly, sobbing. "You'd think your own parents would take the time to get to know you. I mean, what's so bad about me that they don't even want to know who I am?"

She cried silently for a few minutes, and the group let her. Then she looked up and tried to regain her smile with tears in her eyes. "Being different isn't crazy, but I tell you, being different can sure drive you crazy."

Harmon spoke next. "How can we help? What can we do?"

"I'll be all right. I'm okay." She had managed to stop crying.

Harmon nodded. "I know you are. But is there anything we can do to help?"

"Sometimes I just get tired of being alone…. sometimes. I'll be all right. It helps when I can talk."

"It just doesn't seem like enough."

"I just want someone to care about me." She started to cry again, but before she could, she was interrupted by Genevieve. Because she was new to the school, because she was new to Wendy, because she was new to Homeroom, her interjection surprised everyone and she was immediately given extra credibility.

"I appreciate you. What you did for Greg took a special person. A very special person. And I am glad that I've met that person."

Wendy was stunned. She sat still and let the words sink in. Uncontrollably, her tears started to flow again but in a new different way, more of a cleansing way. Her smile returned to her face and eyes, even with the tears. She mouthed the word "thanks" and then she walked across the circle and hugged Genevieve. They stood there hugging and patting each other on the back for a few minutes. As Harmon looked around the circle, he saw tears in everyone's eyes.

Homerooms are unpredictable, Harmon thought. Sometimes they start intense, but do not maintain the intensity. Sometimes they develop intensity, and sometimes they manage to avoid any intensity. Harmon was never able to predict how a Homeroom would progress, but, of all the Homerooms over the years, none started with as much intensity as the one with Wendy and Genevieve.

After that first meeting, Wendy and Genevieve expanded their relationship beyond Homeroom. Wendy would meet Genevieve for lunch and eat with her in the cafeteria, a gesture that meant a great deal more to Genevieve than to Wendy. Lunch period is the single scariest time of the day for most high school students, especially transfer students. With Wendy, Genevieve felt safe, even in the cafeteria. The safety zone broadened beyond school. Wendy took Genevieve shopping with her to second-hand stores in the funky part of town. They went to a few alternative music concerts at Genevieve's instigation. They even went to an art museum together. Eventually the new wore off of the relationship and they saw each other less and less. They soon realized that they had little in common. They still had Homeroom, and that was enough to support a powerful, nurturing friendship. In some ways, their friendship was enhanced when they realized that their mutual respect and loyalty were more evident each week in Homeroom than in superficial activities like shopping. They did not need to do anything together. Their bond had reached a place of quiet certitude that was stable enough not to need constant reassurance. They were confident and secure in their relationship. Their trust in each other did not need outside confirmation. Their closeness and warmth soon became contagious to the other members of their Homeroom and created an environment supportive of introspection.

Katie, for example, began one Homeroom by talking about her junior high school days. "I was into black in junior high. Black. Drugs and sex. Not necessarily in that order. Actually, come to think of it, it probably was in that order. Sex was not…you know, I never really lost my virginity, but I was..how should I put it…I was very popular. I mean, I really had a bad reputation. I reached the point where I wouldn't be caught dead with anyone who would be seen with me."

She looked around the circle to make sure everyone got the joke and waited for the polite, if uncomfortable, laughter before she continued. "And drugs. I never really got into drugs, certainly to the level everyone thought I did. I mean, I did a little weed, a lot of beer, one try at coke…that's all. I was in the envious position of being called a druggie without actually doing drugs."

Her eyes darted around the room. Her flippancy was getting a kind of attention she was not used to. No one laughed but everyone listened. When she started talking again, she mostly stared at her hands. "Black, black was my thing. I wore only black. All through junior high school, every blouse, every pair of jeans, every jacket, every thing was black."

"Why?" Harmon asked.

"Because that's who I was. I was black."

"I don't understand. What do you mean? Black was your.....what? A symbol of your philosophy?"

"Oh, yeah, that's it. No, I don't know. I only felt comfortable in black."

"Because?"

"Black is like the absence of any color, the absence of everything. And that's how I felt, like I was missing something, everything. Black described my mood, my mind, my personality, my whole approach to life. I was black. My parents never even knew. There were all these warning signs. My grades were dropping. None of my old friends came around the house anymore. I mean, my teachers and counselors called my parents and talked to them, but they just shrugged. 'She is going through a phase,' they said. 'All the kids wear black. So she's flunked a few classes. Her achievement tests are still high enough for college. She'll get it together when she gets to high school and grades count.' And me? I would go home every night, sit in my room, playing the stereo with lights out, crying." She took a deep breath to regain composure.

"My parents would sit in the living room watching TV. Cheers, the Cosby Show. I would sit in my room crying and I'd wish they would come in and find me. They never did." She took three deep breaths and blinked several times before she continued.

"One night, I couldn't stand it anymore. I wanted to die. I took a whole bottle of Extra Strength Tylenol. It was the strongest thing I could find. I wasn't sure if it would kill me, but I figured, what the hell, it couldn't do me any good. I laid down and waited. But nothing happened. Except I got a really rank taste in my mouth. No parents breaking down the door to rescue me. No flood of light whisking me away. Nothing. I just lay there getting bored as well as depressed. I started to cry. I got up and ran into the living room hysterically. I tried to tell them what I had done, but, I don't know, I must have just blabbered. But, you know, I thought they should have seen me, should have known I was saying something important, even if I wasn't making sense. They should have recognized something. My Dad just hushed me and said, 'Can't you wait till the commercial?' When I finally screamed what I had done, he assured me he would take me to the hospital to have my stomach pumped as soon as the show was over, which would be fifteen minutes at the most."

Everyone laughed because they didn't know what else to do. Even Harmon smiled, but he added, "Really? Did he really say that?"

She looked at him and knew that she had exposed too much to maintain any semblance of dishonest exaggeration. They wanted the real story and suddenly she wanted to tell them the real story. "No. He didn't say that. I did take the Tylenol and I did rush into the living room, but I never said anything. They were watching TV and laughing. I felt like I wasn't even there, like I was on some other planet watching the whole scene. I was like watching myself watching them watching television. It was like a reality warp, and I couldn't tell what was real. It was weird. But suddenly I knew that I didn't want to die. I ran into the bathroom and made myself vomit. I had had some practice at that too."

"After I puked my insides out, my parents still had no idea what was going on. I went into my bedroom and threw myself on the bed. I had no idea what to do next. Something inside of me told me that I couldn't go on the way I had been. I needed to change, but I didn't know what to change or even how to change. I sat up. The first thing I did was turn the light on in my room. I decided to let the radio make my next decision. I spun the dial as hard as I could. Whatever song I heard on the radio would determine my fate. The first two spins I got a commercial for car wax, which I ruled out as a substitute for suicide, and then a Spanish-speaking station. On my third spin, I got a religious radio station, Christian music. I haven't changed channels since. I picked up my Bible and started reading. Now I never go anywhere without it. I bought a new wardrobe, all pastel, and I have only recently allowed black to seep back into my closet. I have accepted Jesus as my Lord and Savior."

There was something about the definitive nature of her statements that bothered Harmon. He feared that her convictions were as temporary as they were intense. She seemed to being saying things that sounded right rather than sincere. He wasn't sure if she expressed her real thoughts or just what she thought everyone wanted to hear, like being a druggie without using drugs.

Daphne, another student who benefited from Wendy's model, was unlike Genevieve, Katie, or Wendy. Daphne was not a good student; in fact she was enrolled in the vocational program. Her vocational teacher recommended Daphne to Homeroom because she was concerned about Daphne's drinking. However, Daphne never discussed drinking. Although she came to school several times looking very hung over, she never came to Homeroom that way, and Harmon never felt there was an appropriate time to bring up the subject without divulging her vocational teacher's concern and breaking professional confidentiality.

Unlike the others, Daphne looked tough and independent. She had worked as a waitress and paid most of her expenses for the past three years. She didn't seem to have any friends at school. Her social life centered on work and the people she met there. They were mostly older, mid to late twenties. Most of the time, Daphne acted as if she belonged with this older group. There was only one time when her façade crumbled and she revealed the seventeen-year-old underneath the surface. Wendy began, innocently enough. "I haven't seen you at lunch the past few days. Where've you been?"

Daphne seemed uneasy about the question. "I was sick."

"Sorry. Did you have that crud going around?"

"Leave me alone. I was sick, all right? Leave it at that."

Wendy was genuinely hurt by Daphne's reaction. Her eyes showed her hurt as she tried to comfort Daphne. "I'm sorry. I didn't mean to upset you."

"Look." Daphne was clenching and unclenching her jaw. "Do you really want to know?"

Wendy nodded, "I don't mean to pry, if you don't want to…"

"I had an abortion on Monday. There, you satisfied?"

There was a gasp. The group was stunned. Then there was silence. Harmon feared what might happen next. Daphne's revelation was certainly a challenge to Wendy's Catholic upbringing and Katie's born-again Christianity. The silence continued for a long time before Daphne spoke, "My mother took me to a clinic. She said it was the best thing. I was just…I checked in and went into this room and….it was over. I was amazed at how quick…I was still trying to sort it all out and then it was over."

The group listened with silent intensity as she continued her story. "I could have gone to school the next day, but I wasn't ready. I missed the rest of the week. The only reason I came today was because of y'all, you know, Homeroom. Wendy, I'm sorry I jumped at you. I guess I really did want to talk to somebody about it."

Then she began to sob and her shoulders shook as she blurted out, "I feel so *diseased*."

At first no one moved and the only sound was her gasping and sobbing. Daphne was not the type of person to cry and no one knew how to react; she was always so independent. Wendy walked across the circle and hugged her. Daphne trembled and continued to weep on Wendy's shoulder. Finally, between gasping for air and crying from pain, Daphne spoke, "I didn't want to be a mother. I didn't want to be pregnant. But I wish…I didn't want to kill…Mother says I did the right thing…I know I made the right choice for me, but…I mean I couldn't be a mother. I just wish I felt more sure, had more time to…"

No one else spoke. Wendy continued to hold Daphne's hand with one hand while patting her on the back with the other. Katie was crying quietly. Genevieve went to the desk and got tissues for everyone. Katie finally said, "Daphne, I am so sorry. Is there anything we can do?"

"Just don't hate me."

"I don't. We don't. I'm just so sorry that you hurt so badly. I want you to know I'm here for you."

"We are all here for you," Wendy added.

"What would help?" Genevieve asked. "Should we listen and let you talk? Should we change the subject and distract you? How can we show you that we care?"

"I think you just did," Daphne said with the beginning of a smile. The tears flowed for a few more minutes but the crying became less and less intense. Everyone took a turn hugging Daphne. She didn't attend class the rest of the day. Wendy skipped class and took her to lunch.

Wendy continued to be the cement for this particular Homeroom. Her willingness to be vulnerable and the empathetic nature of her responses to everyone else provided emotional cohesiveness for the group. Although she never dominated the conversation as she had on the first day, she never avoided being the subject of discussion. For example, one day she mentioned seeing her family counselor, and the group wanted to know more. With her usual flare for dramatics and flippancy, she revealed how her family came to be in counseling. "Last summer, my boyfriend, my beau, my squeeze, Bill by name, was getting ready to go away to college, and one afternoon, I went over to his house to watch a movie. No biggie. But to my mother, I had violated some great rule of decorum. You know, like the Twelfth Commandment: Thou shall not visit a boyfriend without a chaperone. A girl, a good girl, just doesn't go over to a guy's house when there are no parents there. It is just bad form. It doesn't look right. What will the neighbors think? Blah, blah, blah, blah. So a month ago she wants to fight about this one more time. Well, she kept it up, going over and over about how improper it was, blah, blah, blah. I kept saying, 'Hey, that was last summer. Give it a rest.' And the more I'm saying that, the angrier she is becoming. I think the whole thing is ridiculous. Finally I start laughing at her and she goes ballistic."

"She starts screaming at me, 'Did you lose your virginity?'"

"Now I really think that is funny so I say, 'Lose it? No I think it still around here somewhere.'"

"She shakes her finger at me, 'Wendy, you know what I mean?'"

"'No, I don't,' I say."

"'Did you surrender your virginity?' she says."

"'What?' Like have I ever surrendered anything?"

"At this point, my sense of humor is being tested and the veins on her forehead are nearly popping out."

"'Did you have sex with Bill?' She screams."

Now I could have said a lot of things, and several ideas flashed through me head, some quite funny actually. I took a deep breath and said, 'Yes.' I figure it was the only thing I could have said to get her to shut up, and it seemed to work because she was silent for a long time before she responded with an icy, 'I see.'"

"It was then that she decided we needed to go to family therapy. Hey, Bill was going away. He was the only boyfriend I'd ever had. I have needs too. I wanted to give him that before he left. But the truth of the matter is, I only wanted to have sex with Bill. We never actually did it. I lied to my mother. I'm not even sure why."

"So we are off to family counseling. Mother wants the counselor to whip me into shape. Dad wants mother to be happy. And I just want them to get to know who I am. You know, there are a lot of parents who wish their daughter was as nice as I am. You know, they could do a lot worse."

Genevieve was silent during this discourse by Wendy. In fact, Genevieve was mostly silent during Homeroom. She seldom spoke after that first meeting, and she never initiated a topic. Harmon was never quite sure how to interpret Genevieve's silence. "Maybe," he thought, "Homeroom didn't really work for her." On the other hand, Homeroom did introduce her to Wendy, who became an obvious asset for Genevieve, but she never talked about anything personal. She was perhaps the only one in the group who maintained a distance and never opened up. As the year went on, her English teacher, Allison, and Harmon all became less worried about her. She ceased exhibiting any of the near psychotic behaviors that they had first feared. Something seemed to be working.

Homeroom had a structured activity twice during each semester. The first structured activity was the first meeting and the introductions. The second was always on the last meeting. Homeroom veterans called the last meeting Warm Fuzzy Day. During Round One, each person was to pay a sincere compliment, a warm fuzzy, to someone, anyone, in the group. The only requirement for the compliment was that the individual had to mean the compliment. In Round Two, each person would pay two compliments, one to one person and one to another. Round Three involved three compliments. After the completion of Round Three, everyone had given six compliments, but by going in rounds, the compliments became more and more personal. People would get in touch with the positive feelings that they had for other members, and the structure gave them permission to share those feelings.

Harmon never recalled any of the specific compliments in that particular Homeroom except the ones Genevieve gave to Wendy and to him. "Wendy, I want to compliment you for knowing how to be a best friend." Genevieve looked directly at Wendy and never wavered from her eye contact. Her voice was clear and steady as she went on. "You managed to give me something when I most needed it. I know that we don't have the same opinion on too many things, and I know we have different values. I know we don't hang out together anymore, and I know that we will soon be going separate ways, and we may not even see each other again. But I also know that none of that matters. You know that wherever you go, whatever you do, there will always be at least one person you can depend on to…value you. And I know that wherever I go and whatever I do, I have the confidence to know that you care about me even if you never have an opportunity to show it again. I can't tell you what a great gift that is or how much I appreciate it. You gave me an emotional stability at a time that I needed it most. You gave it freely without asking for anything in return."

"And, Mr. Harmon, I want to compliment you…. this is going to sound so weird…I want to compliment you <u>not</u> for what you do, but for what you don't do." She had turned to face Harmon directly and gave him the same type of eye contact that she had given Wendy, only now tears were beginning to pool in her eyes. "My father is very important to me. I love him very much. In the parts of the world, and the parts of other people that I like the most, I see so much of him. I don't know if that makes sense to anyone else. Well, anyway, I think my Dad is a very wise person. He once told me that the true measure of a friendship is not what you say to each other, but the ability to be silent together. I'm not sure if this is making sense, but I want to compliment you for accepting my silence, for not probing or pushing me. You have never pressured me into being anyone else but me. Thank you for accepting my silence and me; your acceptance has been the most beautiful thing any teacher has ever given me. I cannot begin to tell you how much it has meant to me to have one place I could go and not feel pressured, not feel that I had to pretend. One safe place. It's not anything you do, it's that you do nothing so well."

The semester ended; that Homeroom ended. Wendy, Daphne and Katie all graduated. Wendy went away to a very proper, if not stuffy, college on the East Coast. Typically, Wendy joined a very proper, if not stuffy, sorority, and typical of Wendy, she had her sorority organize a service organization for AIDS victims on campus. Genevieve returned to finish her senior year. She enrolled in two more Homerooms, one each semester, but for a variety of reasons, she was not as regular in attendance as she had been that first year. In fact, by the end of the second semester, she stopped attending altogether. Harmon was not sure if her lack of loyalty meant that she had outgrown Homeroom. He saw her periodically and when he asked her how things were going, she always smiled and said that things were better than last year, but she never went into detail. Still Harmon was certain that Genevieve's life had improved in some very fundamental way. She had friends, her grades were good, and she had several poems published in the school literary magazine. Her appearance was not quite as ragged as it had been although she still radiated her own personal sense of fashion. She had dates to both Homecoming and the Prom, and she looked beautiful at both. In short, she seemed to have weathered whatever storm her junior year had been. Just before her graduation, Harmon received a letter from her.

Dear Mr. Harmon,

I want you to know that I have been thinking about you. It has been hard for me to talk to you because I don't want you to worry about me. I guess that's not really true. It has been hard for me to talk to you because it's hard for me to talk. I do so much better with pen and paper. I would say that I am going to miss you except I haven't seen you much this year; yet I have always felt your presence in my heart, wherever I go. And I will always take that with me.

That first Homeroom was so good for me; it saved my life, or at least my mind. I needed Homeroom so much. The other students, Katie, Daphne, and Wendy, needed a place to vent their troubles and talk about them. I needed something completely different. I needed a place where I didn't have to face my troubles but where I could still be me and feel useful, valued. At that point I felt confused, hurt, worthless. I was a zero.

You see, my father was dying of AIDS, still is. His health began to fail right before we moved here. I had just found out about the diagnosis when I enrolled at West Side. My father is a very intelligent and creative man. He has always made a comfortable living with a variety of jobs usually revolving around his artistic skills. But always there was his work as a part time musician. He was in several different bands playing all around the state. Nothing big time, but a good supplemental income. Looking back at his professional lifestyle, I should not have been surprised at his sexual orientation. Suddenly the parade of uncles I had while growing up took on a new meaning. To this day, I don't know how Ma feels about all this. I suspect she tolerated more than she liked, but she loves him and what choice does she have? I don't know. We never talk about it. The subject is forbidden at home. All I knew was that I was sixteen years old and was forced to deal with his health, his sexual preference, our newfound poverty, and a new environment. My relationship with everyone and everything became strained. I questioned my own sexuality, my relationship with Ma, my relationship with Dad, my relationship with the world. I mean, where do I fit in? What caused me the greatest pain was the new way I had to look at my Dad. Trying to make sense out of him was exhausting. I wanted to love him and be loyal, but I wasn't sure who he was. All my doubts filled me with self-disgust and guilt.

And then Homeroom started. On that first day, I saw this beautiful, bright, cheery, personable Wendy. Everything I wasn't. You know what Wendy is? She is perky. I've always hated perky. I felt intimidated and pulled back into my protective shell of judgementalness and condemnation. And Wendy shared her pain and vulnerability. With me! It was a miracle for me. Suddenly, I realized that other people hurt. Perfect people hurt. Now that may not seem to you like much of a stretch intellectually, but it was a great realization for me emotionally. Other people with other lives had other pains. I was not alone.

Then I reached out to her, I made a difference. She let me touch her, reach her. I counted. I was significant. All through that semester, that feeling became the new foundation upon which I built a new life, a new me. I want to say it became the core of my sanity. That sounds too melodramatic, but it is accurate enough to be scary. I would look around that group during Homeroom and watch the eyes of everyone, and I would see all this anxiety and fear, feelings we all shared, and I knew I was not alone. I was not crazy.

And you, Mr. Harmon, were always there, not just in attendance, but really there. You know what I mean? No matter who was talking or what they were talking about, you listened and communicated that you were there for them. My Dad used to say that the only thing you can ever really give someone is your presence. And man, did you ever give that. I've never seen anyone who cared as much for so many people and showed that caring so well. You have always been here for me whenever I needed you and whenever I don't. You are such a big part of me now.

I have been trying to express myself verbally to you but nothing forms in my mind until you are out of sight. So here I am with my best friends, pen and paper. I have read over what I have written and it does not look right. I said what I meant and I meant what I said. Let me offer you a poem:

The Man Who Does Nothing Very Well

Working with Emotions of Fire,
He watches us burn and glow,
He sees our embers as we really are
Just Angels in the Snow

Genevieve

He could always remember exactly when it began: the third day of his fresh-man year of high school. Sitting next to him in his second period algebra class was Nate, jock extraordinaire and football player/star. "Nate of the bulging biceps and recessed forehead; Nate is a Neanderthal," George his best friend liked to say. After only three days Nate had firmly established the routine of copying off his home-work anytime Nate had not completed an assignment. On the third day when he tried to cover his paper during a quiz, Nate told him in no uncertain terms that if he did not uncover his paper, Nate would remove his teeth from his braces so that he would not need the services of an orthodontist anymore. He shrugged and removed his hand to let Nate copy his quiz, telling himself that he wasn't that con-cerned about the ethics of cheating in a math class anyway, while feeling equal part real fear and profound embarrassment.

It began when he went home that afternoon. He went up to his room and lay in his bed. When he recalled Nate's cheating, tears filled his eyes, but he wasn't sure if they were tears of rage, or hurt, or shame, or fear, or embarrassment. He tried to think of something to do about Nate. He fantasized an idea. Maybe on the next quiz he would put all the wrong answers, and then change them at the last second as he was turning the paper in. He closed his eyes and pictured it. He could easily write down a 17 and change it to a 19 at the last second. He pictured going through a whole test and changing each answer at the last second. He imagined the look on Nate's face.

"There wouldn't be anything he could do; he couldn't admit he did badly because he copied my test," he thought to himself with a glee that was terrifically comforting. He just lay in bed and pictured it over and over. Even his mother noticed that he was in a great mood at supper. After supper, he called and informed George of his plan. George replied, "I think it is a great plan, but I have one question. Just how many bones in your face do you think he can break when he catches up with you after school?" He decided not to follow through on his plan, but he had found a successful way to cope with high school: fantasizing, specifi-cally revenge fantasizing. That was the beginning.

From then on, every day he would come home and spend the time between school and supper lying in bed day dreaming some sort of revenge against another student in a class. At first, Nate was the subject of all of his fantasies, but Nate apparently could not even copy very well, as he flunked and was transferred into a lower level math by the end of the first grading period. Other students took Nate's place in his fantasies, including his entire third period class after they laughed when George nominated him for Student Council. There was a girl in his social studies class who teased him because his pants didn't match his shirt. There were many others. Every class produced at least one victim.

His routine became very comforting. He would come home, retire to his bedroom, reminisce over the insults of the day, and imagine a scenario for revenge. He would imagine clever retorts that would devastate the ego of some tormenter and cause the whole class to laugh uproariously, seduced by his rapier wit and superior intelligence. He would smile, giggle, and occasionally laugh out loud, sometimes for hours, after school. Soon these bouts of fantasies became the highlight of his day. Although they began to creep into his class time, he still preferred the after school daydreams, private and uninterrupted. This became his coping mechanism; his way of dealing with what he came to view as the awful grayness that was high school.

There was playfulness in these early fantasies. He would target a specific student, one who had hurt his feelings, humiliated him, threatened him to some extent, or just made him mad, and he would visualize some retribution with a humorous twist usually in the form of a sarcastic remark, but he was not above picturing a well-placed pie in the face or a tack on the seat. However, by the middle of September these types of fantasies began to lose appeal, became boring, and without conscious choice, his day dreams developed violent themes. Sarcastic remarks became tripping students; tripping students became punching them; punching them became beating them; and by November, he would picture blood spattering on the walls and covering his fists as he would continue to pummel the chosen victim.

He was content to carry on like this for several months. He would reluctantly drag himself to school. He would spend the day gathering ammunition for his afternoon date, the center of his life. He'd lie in bed and beat some fellow student to a bloody pulp, smiling in rapture. Things might have stayed that way except for a simple, singular event that went unnoticed by anyone at the time. Late in March, one of the jocks, a basketball player this time, walked to the front of the classroom, strutted would have been a more accurate description. On the way back to the desk, he winked at a cheerleader in the front row and they exchanged a high-five hand gesture. "I wish I had a gun to shoot him," he thought, and that afternoon he fantasized over and over how the cheerleader would respond if she had been splattered by a bullet penetrating the jock's chest. He had found a new fantasy that thrilled him.

Soon weapons became a mainstay of his fantasies. Now he would stab someone in the cafeteria line or in the hallway between classes. He went through a razor blade phase. He visualized unbelievable damage with a razor on a stairwell. At *one point he pictured an attack with a bow an arrow from the top of Hub into the cafeteria. And for several days he fixated on bombs well placed: in the library, in the cafeteria, and, his favorite, in a pep rally.*

But guns were the most fun. He pictured standing at the hallway and pulling out a Colt revolver and taking target practice. What quickly became his favorite fantasy was to pull out the revolver from his jacket as he sat in the back of his English class. He would take his time shooting everyone and they would squirm and scream and beg for mercy, but mostly they would just bleed.

It took most of his freshman year for his fantasies to become violent, but in less than two months he settled on his final vision of annihilation: standing in Hub with a machine gun and mowing down all of the upperclassmen. He wasn't quite sure when, but sometime early in his sophomore year, his fantasy became a plan, but it all began that third day of his freshman year.

CHAPTER 3

PARADOXES NEVER LIE

Angels in the Snow. Whenever Harmon thought about Genevieve's phrase, he thought that it was the perfect metaphor for Homeroom. Harmon never felt that Homeroom's accomplishments were due to his skill as much as they were a testimonial to the power of the communication between students, the power of the gentleness within students, the power of the grace among students. High school students have a terrible reputation because there is so much pettiness and so much cruelty in adolescence, and as they become adults, they remember that cruelty so vividly. However, the memory is often greater than the reality. Much of the remembered cruelty is fantasized projections, and the acts of kindness, equally valid and equally frequent, are too often forgotten. Harmon found witnessing those acts of kindness, those angels in the snow, to be the most rewarding aspects of Homeroom. Genevieve and Wendy were such angels, but when he thought of them he was quickly filled with images from another Homeroom, one filled with contradictions and questions yet, in many ways, the quintessential Homeroom. This second Homeroom brought a great sense of comfort to Harmon, greater perhaps than any other Homeroom. In Genevieve's Homeroom, Wendy was the recognized leader, the identified angel, while this other Homeroom's leadership was never clear, more mysterious and unspoken than direct. During that year, Harmon thought of this Homeroom as Randi's Homeroom, but later he came to believe Shannon provided the core of that Homeroom. Yet, when all was said and done, Kirk provided the most indelible image. In other words, this Homeroom seem to center upon one girl but revolved around another girl, yet a quiet, incomparable, giant of a man-child punctuated the impact of this Homeroom, and all with very little awareness by Harmon. After many years of trying to make sense out of what he witnessed, Harmon was, in the final analysis, still not sure who the angel was. To an objective observer, this ultimate Homeroom, with the usual assortment of typical and atypical West Side students, was just like any other Homeroom, and paradoxically, it was like no other Homeroom.

The tone of this Homeroom was set early in the semester when Shannon revealed an aspect of her life that stunned everyone else in Homeroom. Shannon was a transfer student completing her senior year of high school. She was not a typical West Side student. She was slightly overweight with large hips and bosom. Her chin was slight, and with her overbite, it appeared to be nonexistent. Her hair was short and well kept. Her wardrobe, whether skirt or blue jeans, centered on a letter jacket from her last school that she always wore. The jacket was marked with athletic and academic recognition. She had transferred from a small rural high school where she had been the star basketball player as well as an honor student, ranked number one in her class. She was making very high grades in Harmon's class, but he noticed that she never seemed to smile. He invited her to join Homeroom, and she did.

In Homeroom, like class, she was mostly silent and spoke only when spoken to. The first notable exception came early in the year. The group had been discussing the cliquish nature of West Side when Shannon expressed her viewpoint. "I've been in three schools, and West Side is the coldest one." There was something very flat in her voice when she spoke. Harmon had heard other students make the same observation with great emotion. Shannon just described her experience without any emotion. Her tone had the effect of giving her words more credibility. She was not asking for a response, certainly not pity. She was just painting a picture, an accurate one.

"Until I got into Homeroom, no one ever spoke to me. I mean, it was like I was invisible in all my classes. I thought, God, everyone in this school must be the biggest snob. Everyone was just so hurtful to each other, you know? I mean like all I could overhear people say to each other were teasing and insults. I thought, man, this is one cold place. You know, at all my other schools, kids would go out of their way to say hello and welcome me. I know they were all really small schools, like half the size of West Side, but still. I was so lonely it would hurt. I thought everyone hated me and I didn't know why or what to do. I have a baby, a little girl, Susan. I call her Swoozie, Swoozie Suzy. Anyway, when the teacher ain't teaching nothing or when we are just doing homework, sometimes I just picture Swoozie. I picture her smile; it helps. I mean, I can put up with things, you know?"

She just let the fact that she was a mother slide into the conversation. There was no attempt at fanfare or anything. Her daughter was just a fact, and although a reality that had a riveting effect on the rest of the group, for Shannon, a reality that was just one more aspect of her life. Everyone was stunned. At West Side, abortions were more common than pregnancies. Shannon sensed the amazement and was embarrassed. She continued to be forthright and honest as she told the group about her motherhood in her usual matter-of-fact way. That her tone was lacking in self-pity was part of the reason for the impact of her revelation on the group, but even more powerful was the growing awareness of what the reality of being a full-time mother while attending high school meant.

"I have to get up at 5:30 every morning to get Swoozie ready for nursery school. You know, dress her, feed her and all that. I have to leave the house by 6:30 to have time to walk to the nursery school before I can start walking to school. I get here before class begins at 8 o'clock, but it ain't by much."

One of the other students seemed incredulous. "You walk to school? Each Morning?"

Shannon just shrugged. "Yeah, it's not that far really. As the crow flies, you know? I mean I live about a mile from school, to the east. But the nursery school is another mile south of my house. You know, it's not so bad since I got the stroller. When I had to carry Swoozie and her diaper bag, the last half-mile was torture. Especially after school. Going home."

Everyone sat in silence. They could not imagine walking to school everyday. Harmon spoke. "You have not been absent all semester."

"Yeah. Well, I like school. It has always been my thing, my escape. I mean, my family is like…lets just say that if you look up dysfunctional in the dictionary, you'll probably find a picture of my family."

"Why don't you buy a car?" someone asked, displaying an ignorance that everyone found irritating.

"Shannon just rolled her eyes. "Cars cost money, which is something my family don't have much of. I mean, I had to get state welfare to help with childcare or I wouldn't be able to go to school at all. In fact, there are two nursery schools on my way to school, which would make life a lot easier for me, but one doesn't take infants and the other won't take welfare money. Momma's a registered nurse. She makes an okay income, but there is too much month left at the end of the money, if you know what I mean. When we left Daddy, we were just glad to get out. We didn't have diddlysquat when we got here. Daddy had the checkbook, not like there was a fortune in it. But the only money we had was some cash we managed to squirrel away before we left. She had to find a job right away. It was definitely the right thing to do, leaving Daddy. But it's been hard. She should have done it years ago."

At that point the bell rang for the next class. Everyone sat still. No one knew what to say or do. Shannon took charge. "I didn't mean to get you all bummed out. I don't want you to miss class or get a tardy. I mean, it's my life. You know? That's all. It's just the cards I've been dealt. Come on, we all got classes to go to." She stood up and led the way out the door.

She hadn't asked for pity. She had just described the way things were. Nothing had changed nor had she asked for any changes to be made, but she never walked home again the rest of the year. Someone from Homeroom always gave her a ride. Someone would always be traveling coincidentally in her direction. On rainy days and cold days in winter, someone would always pick her up in the morning. In the early spring, when Shannon was absent three days in a row, several of the girls in Homeroom called and found out that Swoozie was sick. The girls got all of Shannon's assignments; one of them even skipped school to stay with Swoozie so Shannon could take an important test in one of her classes.

Everyone in the Homeroom grew to admire Shannon's ability to adjust and accept adversity without asking for pity or help, although pity and help seemed to be appropriate responses. Shannon seldom talked in Homeroom and she never started a conversation. However, looking back, Harmon came to believe that Shannon was the leader of that particular Homeroom, but at the time, Randi seemed to occupy that role. Randi's impact was more visible.

Randi was a sophomore, which was rare but not unheard of in Homeroom. Allison had referred Randi to Homeroom because of Randi's confused home life. Randi lived with her aunt in the West Side attendance area, although both of her parents were still married and living together on the other side of town raising Randi's siblings outside the West Side attendance area. The reasons the aunt gave for the living arrangements were rather vague, and Allison felt that there was more to the story. She felt that Randi might benefit from having Homeroom to help her adjust to a new environment, but Randi didn't need any help adjusting. She was passing all of her classes and she was making friends. In fact, she had a date the first week of school, which was rare but not unheard of for a sophomore, even beautiful sophomores, and if there was one thing Randi was, it was beautiful. She was of average height but that was her only average feature. She had rich, black, wavy hair that could only be described as luscious. Past shoulder length, her hair caught the light and reflected it back in a heightened way. She would tilt her head or flip it back, and the hair would appear to dance. Her eyes were even more captivating. The darkest of blue, her eyes would dart around the circle of students in Homeroom warming everyone they crossed, and when they settled on a person, they became hypnotic. They penetrated without seeming intrusive, as if they were saying "I am looking at the single most important thing in my universe at this moment." She seldom wore slacks or jeans, and her skirts emphasized her shapely legs and even, healthy tan. Her entire wardrobe was rather form-fitting and her natural curves were aptly displayed but not in a conspicuous way. Her blouses were neither low cut nor were her skirts so short as to violate any dress code. She just looked very healthy and comfortable inside of her body.

She did seem to have difficulty sitting still, as she was always squirming in her seat. She would sit on her legs and then lean forward on her desk, followed quickly by a change to a position with both feet on the floor. She would stretch and even pop her own back. She radiated an innocent sensuality that was irresistible to the males around her. Her behavior might have been construed as seductive if she hadn't lacked guile. She didn't seem to be aware of her effect on others, at least, not consciously.

Everyone in Homeroom, including Harmon, found Randi to be quite charming. She was a conscientious student who made it clear that she was committed to her family and had high moral standards. She made a point of proclaiming her virginity, and she rejected more dates than she accepted because she found "most of the guys at West Side were obsessed with beer". She would often determine the subject in Homeroom, but she was also comfortable following someone else's lead. She was compassionate toward the others in her Homeroom and had a sense of humor that was often self-deprecating. She seemed to be the cohesive force in her Homeroom.

Allison did not completely share Harmon's admiration of Randi. "For a girl who is new to the school, she is just too popular," Allison said. "She may be all virginal and moral like she says, but there is a sensuousness that she exudes that guys pick up on. I mean, I'm not saying that she is sexually active, but the guys I hear talk about her, usually have their collective tongues hanging out when they mention her."

Harmon was shocked by Allison's reaction. "I can't believe you're saying that. She can't be blamed for the way she looks. I mean, if a guy gets turned on by a girl, it hardly seems fair to blame her. I think you are misjudging her."

"I think you are misjudging me," Allison responded. "I'm not saying that she is responsible, or that she is a tease, or that she is anything but what she says she is. What you see may be completely accurate. It probably is. But there is something missing. I can't help but feel that there is more to her than what we see. I basically trust all my kids, and I trust her. I don't even know what I'm trying to say. Maybe what I'm talking about exists on some unconscious level."

"Unconscious level? What are you talking about?"

"I don't know. But there is something that bothers me and I can't quite put my finger on it. Why is she living with her aunt? Her parents are still married, still raising her brothers and sisters. Academic reasons? I don't think so. She is a good student, but not that good, and this is a good school, but not that good. Look, I don't want to ruin your relationship with her. Go with your own instincts and ignore me."

"Forget what you just said? Like when the judge tells the jury to disregard what the witness just said."

"Well, don't let me poison you, anyway. I could be wrong. I was wrong one other time this decade. My advice is to disregard my advice."

"Which advice is that?"

"You know, on the subject of Randi."

"I'll take it under advisement."

In October, the discussion turned to the upcoming Homecoming Dance. Until that time, Shannon had not said a word since the first acknowledgement of her parenthood. Betty was trying to convince Randi that she should go to the dance with Glen instead of Charles. "Look, Charles is a real Neanderthal. He just wants a trophy. He's never had a girlfriend for more than two hours for Chrissakes, and it ain't by accident. You need to go with Glen. He's a real sweetheart. He likes you. He's kind and gentle. He's.."

"A wuss. That's what Glen is, a wuss." Randi interrupted Betty but not in a rude way. "I hate guys who are too nice. You know what I mean? Where's the challenge?"

"He is a nice guy."

"Right, and boring. Glen is sweet and boring. He is nice and boring. Did I mention that he is boring? Charles is dangerous. He needs a little taming."

Kirk, another boy in the group, spoke out. "I have never understood this. What do you want? I mean, what do girls really want? Do you want us to be nice or do you want us to treat you badly? It's like if a guy is nice, girls don't want anything to do with him; they don't respect him. The message is that guys should be jerks to attract a girl. I mean, is that really what you want? Are you only attracted to guys who will hurt you?"

"I know it sounds stupid." Randi looked down and tried to find the words to explain herself and her entire gender. "If a guy, you know, buys me flowers and tries to be too nice, I don't respect him. It's like he needs me. I can't stand when they say they love me. I mean, come on, love? It may be stupid, but..."

"It sure is stupid." Shannon said in her usual matter of fact tone of voice. She wasn't making a judgment as much as a description.

"What?" Randi asked more as a reaction to the fact that Shannon said something than as a reaction to what she actually said.

"It is stupid. Like my Momma and Daddy. Momma was a smart girl. You know, she became a nurse. She put herself through nursing school while having us three kids and coping with Daddy. You can't be stupid and do that. But it's like she had some cogs missing when it comes to Daddy. Like what you were saying. I mean, my Daddy is an outlaw, you know what I mean? He's a drunk, a doper, a criminal. When my Momma met him, he was a biker. He would have been a Hell's Angel except he couldn't measure up to their standards. Everyone in the little towns we lived in was afraid of him. We moved around a lot to keep him out of trouble and because, I swear to God, there were petitions to get us to move. He was, still is, a scary guy, you know?"

"Momma was just hopelessly in love with him. I mean, it was the screwiest thing in the world. Here she was this bright, responsible woman, who was just weak-kneed around him. No one could understand the attraction, not even her own mother. I mean, here she was in her junior year of college when into her life rode this hairy, dirty, biker dude with tattoos, a major drinking problem, and all that horsepower between his legs. Momma just melted. I've talked to her about it."

Shannon looked around the room, and like before, everyone's attention was riveted because her words were so compelling. She was not the least bit self-conscious. To her these were the details of her life and not particularly astounding. The rest of the group knew no one like her father, and they found her story to be amazing. In Shannon's mind, she had taken a small step from talking about the typical female attraction for a rebel to telling about her parents' courtship. However, she had just teleported the rest of the group into a Quentin Tarentino movie, transported them into some alternate universe that they had only glimpsed in the past but had never really entered. Her father was a real person, but he was unlike anyone they had ever encountered.

"Everyone, especially my grandmother, thought Momma just wanted to reform Daddy, like he was some sort of senior class project, a research paper that offered more challenge than most. But Momma never had any illusions that she was going to change him. She thought having kids might slow him down a little, but she didn't hold out much hope."

Shannon hesitated, searching for the right words. She looked around the group. "No, that's not even right. She didn't want to change him. He was a force of nature and that's what she found so attractive about him. He wasn't going to change for nobody or nothing. And he treated her like dirt." She slowly shook her head back and forth. "I mean, he'd cheat on her, hit her, steal from her, humiliate her in front of her family, and she just took it and would ask for more. I saw some of it growing up, but I heard about even more from my aunts and cousins. When people asked her why, she would just say, 'I love him.' He had some weird power over her. What I think is he just turned her on, you know? He was the only one who could set her on fire."

"I have a lot of respect for my Momma. How many people do you know who work their way through college and scratch their way through nursing school with no, I mean, not a lick, of support. Her parents thought she was stuck-up for even trying. They'd accuse her of thinking she was better than them, you know? It couldn't have been easy. She got through with sheer determination and will power, but she had none of these when it came to Daddy. She made it through; it took her two extra years because she had me and J.J.. When she finished, she went to work in a small town. Daddy was big into drugs and she thought that he'd have a tougher time getting any drugs in a small town. She'd work in little hospitals, doctors' offices, and nursing homes. Wherever. She'd work for awhile then we'd have to move because of something Daddy would do. We were just barely hanging on with money."

"Daddy didn't help much. Sometimes he'd have a job, but nothing for very long or that paid very well. Usually he'd get drunk and get fired. What Momma hadn't counted on was how much more he'd drink if he didn't have drugs. On drugs, he was pretty bad, but drunk, he was horrible. He was what you call a mean drunk. We moved around all over the country hoping it would get better, and frankly, hoping that they hadn't heard of us before we got there. We did this for eight or nine years. But it kept getting worse and worse. He started hitting the boys; otherwise I think we'd still be with him. At first when he started hitting them, we tried to ignore it. But Daddy broke J.J.'s nose, and when he damn near knocked junior unconscious, Momma couldn't ignore it anymore. She knew we had to leave or she would have to start making funeral arrangements. Six months passed before she had enough money squirreled away. We left one day after school. It was two days before school let out for the summer. I was exempt from all of my final exams. I was pregnant and was due any day. Momma knew we needed to leave before I had the baby. We never told Daddy. We just left. We hadn't been gone a month when Daddy was arrested for attempted manslaughter. He beat up some guy real bad in a barroom fight. We found out about it after Swoozie was born, and if it hadn't been for Swoozie, I swear, Momma would have gone back to help him."

"I remember driving out of town the night we left. The car was all loaded up with everything we had. I drove because Momma cried for four straight hours. I could barely fit behind the steering wheel. Like I said, I was due any time. The boys sat in the back seat with luggage and a television between them. They didn't know until we were on the road that we weren't coming back. They didn't know whether they were happy or sad. We all sat like that, no one making any sound except Momma crying for four hours. The pavement rolled under our tires. The sun went down. The headlights on the other cars would dart across the windshield, and it felt like we were in some weird episode of the Twilight Zone."

The entire Homeroom sat in silence for the rest of that period trying to imagine what that car trip must have been like.

Shannon remained silent the rest of the semester, but when spring semester began she reenrolled Homeroom. In fact, everyone came back in the spring. Of the other students in Homeroom, three were girls. Betty was a senior who was having trouble deciding on a college. Elizabeth couldn't get along with her stepfather. Vicky never had a problem or a single serious thought. There were also three boys. Austin, a near dropout, was hanging on until graduation. He had problems academically, but he was relatively well adjusted. He worked at Pizza Palace and liked his job well enough to want to become a manager. He had a vocational direction. Derek was an honors student who enrolled in Homeroom because he liked psychology class, but he soon discovered that he was less interested in real people than in the theories. And then there was Kirk.

Kirk was tall and husky, probably 6'4" and 240 pounds. He was built like a football player but he had no interest in athletics. All through junior high school, the coaches had tried to pressure him into playing, but he had a firm enough sense of self to know that he was not a football player. In high school he grew his hair, which was shoulder length by his senior year. By now all his teachers were convinced he was a drug dealer, especially when the coaches used phrases like "wasted potential". In truth, he was neither an athlete nor a drug dealer; he was a magician. His interest in magic started in junior high school. At first, magic was just a hobby, but by senior high, he had joined a magician's union and was earning money on weekends at birthday parties. By his senior year, he was the one of the most prominent magician in the area and had quite a lucrative act. He had earned enough money to pay for his college education, and he planned to continue in college. His act was very professional and he was booked for the entire summer at nightclubs and a variety of resorts. Off the stage, out of his tuxedo, he looked like a giant, a thug, or a loan collector from the Mafia. He could have won an award for the most deceptive first impression because in reality, he was a gentle, sensitive, and a genuinely kind individual. He was the editor of the school literary magazine, to which he contributed many of his poems. His poetry was more philosophical than sentimental. His poetry lacked the emotional gushing so common to most student poetry, "emotional diarrhea" as he described it. Yet it was far from cold and intellectual. His poetry was as difficult to describe and categorize as Kirk was. Harmon told him that he was a paradox, and he liked that description. "Paradoxes never lie," he said in a statement that was as philosophical and insightful as it was humorous. Vicky described him as a big, cuddly teddy bear, and that was as good a description as any.

During the spring semester, a pattern slowly began to emerge, a pattern that Harmon recognized only years later in when reflecting on this Homeroom. At the time everything seemed to flow so naturally. Most meetings would begin with someone bringing up a subject. Sometimes that someone was Randi, but often someone else would initiate a topic. Almost always there was some sort of approval of the topic by Randi before the group would turn their full attention on a subject. Shannon would nod and listen, but she seldom had anything to say or add. However, when Randi would introduce a subject that was personal, involving her own self-disclosure, Shannon would add details from her own experiences. On the surface, her comments seemed to be unrelated, but in retrospect, Shannon's stories punctuated and brought meaning to Randi's stories. Shannon had created an extremely subtle and poignant connection with Randi. Only Shannon was aware of her effect on Randi. Harmon didn't notice this relationship until later, and he was never quite sure if either Shannon or Randi was aware of it. Still he came to see this Homeroom as a multi-layered, subtle, unconscious, communication from Shannon to Randi, and, perhaps, a life-altering communication.

The topic during one meeting was family and responsibility. Randi was the oldest of seven children. She was complaining about being a part-time "mother" as well as an older sister. "I don't feel like I've ever had my own child-hood. I mean, all my life I've had to change diapers and feed kids. I'm the one Mom and Dad expect to be responsible. The others have chores but they never do them, and nothing happens. If I don't do my chores, the whole family falls apart."

"I've always been the adult in my family, too," Shannon began. "Sure, Momma was the nurse and all, but at home, she gave-in, caved-in really, to Daddy about everything. Daddy was just a big spoiled brat. I swear he was worse than any of the kids. By the time I was ten years old, I was organizing all the household chores and cooking most of the meals. At least I was thawing the meat and helping Momma cook when she got home. I had to remember to put the meat down or we wouldn't have supper. I don't know when I stepped over to actually cooking. I mean, I felt sorry for Momma. She was always tired from working, sometime two jobs. Daddy was just demanding or drunk or both. I was always doing housework or schoolwork. School was my only escape. I wasn't like the other kids. I didn't watch television, at least not much. Daddy controlled the set and I couldn't watch what I wanted to watch, so I'd just study some more. If I was in my room doing schoolwork, I didn't bother him. And he didn't bother me."

"What about the boys?" Kirk asked.

"They'd play outside, or go over to a friend's house, or play quietly, or get hit."

"Did your mother ever call anyone?" Harmon was asking, but he could tell from Shannon expression that she didn't understand the question. "I mean, did she ever report him to the authorities? The police? Welfare?"

"Like Child Protection Agency?"

"Yeah."

"No. We never did, but the neighbors sure did. It got to the point that they would make weekly visits. The last house we rented had a fourth bedroom. The boys wanted to have separate rooms for the first time, but Momma joked that we had to keep one room for the live-in form the Child Protection Agency. They knew us well. But Daddy never crossed the line, or at least we never thought he did, so we never really told on him. Besides, I was doing so well in school and the boys were both passing. The agency didn't think there was enough evidence to break up the family. They never helped us at all. They did manage to keep Daddy pissed off, though."

Harmon tried to summarize what she had said. "You just kept going to school, making good grades and raising your brothers."

"Yeah. I was the responsible one. Someone had to be. I never got in any trouble. I swear I was born an old lady. I never did anything irresponsible. Well, except for Swoozie. I did one thing irresponsible and it was the best thing that ever happened to me, to the whole family. There's a lesson there somewhere, but I'm not sure what it is. I know this: Momma would never have left him if I hadn't gotten pregnant. I mean she talked about it, but…"

"So in some ways your irresponsibility led to an even more responsible choice," Harmon said.

"What? Oh, I see what you mean. No, it wasn't like I chose to get pregnant to save the family. I've never told you who the father is, have I? This is hard for me to talk about. I haven't told many people about this." Shannon hesitated as she looked directly at Randi. "I mean, I'm glad I have Swoozie, and I wouldn't want to change anything. She makes me so happy and she gives me a reason. You know what I mean? You have to understand that."

Shannon broke eye contact, and looked around the group. Her voice was beginning to crack, and she looked like she was about to cry. She took a big breath and managed to control any tears. When she began again, her voice was normal. She seemed to direct her remarks to the whole group or, perhaps, she was talking directly to Randi. She looked around the room and when she could see that everyone was listening and supporting her, she dropped her gaze onto her desktop and spoke in a very controlled even voice. "I love my daughter, but I am so ashamed."

Kirk offered verbal reassurance. "It's all right. These things happen."

For the first time, Randi was sitting rigid in her desk in perfect posture. The color had left her cheeks.

"You don't understand, it was like I was becoming my Momma. After all these years of being disgusted by her, I was turning into her."

Randi broke the silence, "Is your Daddy the father of your daughter?"

"No. No. Nothing like that. Daddy's not the daddy." Shannon giggled and the nearly unbearable tension left the group. Harmon found himself breathing again. "No. I can see where you got that from what I was saying. You must have been thinking…No. No. The father wasn't that bad, on second thought, maybe he was. Let me tell you the story. I was nearly seventeen. I never had a boyfriend, never had the time. I had a few dates, school dances, stuff like that. I went on a church hayride one time. That where I learned to French kiss. Anyway it was the fall of my junior year. I was a big basketball star, and would have been valedictorian, feeling pretty full of myself. I went to a carnival with a friend of mine, you know, one of those traveling carnivals. Well, we rode the ferris wheel and the guy running it started flirting with us. At first my girl-friend thought it was fun to flirt with this greasy carnival worker, but she soon grew bored. I didn't. I ended up riding that stupid ferris wheel all night until they closed. Then the guy—I never knew his name—took me to his trailer. He offered me a beer, but I don't drink. Instead, we had sex."

Shannon stared at her hands and didn't say anything else. Someone broke the silence. "Rape?"

"No. I wish I could say it was rape. That would be easier. The truth is…Well, do I look like someone who could be easily raped? Hell, I was bigger than he was and probably stronger, too. He couldn't have raped me. I mean I could have stopped him at anytime. He just kept doing things and I lost the ability to stop him. No, that's not really accurate. What I lost was the desire to stop him. I mean, we had sex three or four times that night. The next morning we did it again, and I came back the next two nights for repeat performances each night. Finally the carnival left town, and I've never seen him again. I don't want to see him again. But I have a new understanding of my Momma. And I know there is a part of me that I have got to watch real careful. I won't let myself get in that situation again. I mean, I deserve better. Like Momma I have a weakness in me, a sickness, and I can't afford not to watch it very carefully. You can talk abut your rebels, your 'dangerous Charles', but for me, I'm not messing around with anyone that ain't gentle and kind and nice. A guy is going to have to respect me as much as I respect myself, and I have a lot of hard-earned self-respect now."

Once again, Shannon's words produced a silence of awe. No one could add to her story, but everyone felt the truth in her revelations. After each of Shannon's disclosures, the group did not know how to respond yet their collective respect for Shannon continued to grow.

The denouement for this particular Homeroom came early in the spring in a series of disjointed, random discussions. Once again, Shannon provided the most dramatic moments, but Randi provided the impetus for the intensity. Betty started by talking about her stepfather. Derek added a clever anecdote about his stepbrother. They were both complaining about their extended family arrangements. This led to a general discussion the merits of being an only child. Austin displayed the most bitterness towards his siblings. "You know how they say, God couldn't be everywhere so he invented mothers?" Austin asked. "Well, I believe Satan couldn't be everywhere so he invented older brothers."

"At least you have a real brother." Betty whined. Betty always seemed to whine whenever she said anything. She had that kind of voice. "I'm stuck with these strangers, two step-brothers, and they don't come any stranger. I don't like them, and they don't like me."

"I really miss my brothers and sisters," Randi sighed. "I miss them a lot."

"How come you don't live with them?" Austin innocently asked, but he was asking a question to which Harmon was particularly anxious to hear the answer. Harmon had refused to ask because he didn't want Homeroom to be intrusive. A respect for Randi's privacy was not a concern for Austin. He asked because he was curious.

Randi looked down and hesitated. She was uncharacteristically somber. The sparkle in her eyes seemed to have dimmed.

Harmon spoke out to comfort her. "Remember, one of the rules in Homeroom is that you don't have to answer any questions you don't want to answer. We are not about probing."

She nodded, but she didn't say anything. Harmon sensed the discomfort her ambivalence was causing her and he tried to reassure her. "If you want to talk, we will listen. I will remind everyone about the rule of confidentiality."

She looked up and spoke very rapidly as if she were trying to spit the words out and remove once and for all. "My Dad and I don't get along. He hits me. The last time, they made us all go to family counseling. We went to our minister, and he, the minister, felt that it would be a good idea for me to leave for awhile. So they sent me to my mother's sister for this year. Dad is going to a psychiatrist and I hope to move back this summer."

There was a collective sigh from the group, more as an expression of awe than relief. She had blurted out a lot of information, but there were a number of questions raised by her revelation. Kirk spoke for the group. "What do you mean he hits you? Does he beat you? Is it child abuse?"

Randi returned to a normal speech rhythm. "They seem to think so, but I'm not sure. Abuse doesn't seem to be the right word. He doesn't beat me. But I make him mad and he…hits. He lashes out. Usually, he just hits me once, but that last time he hit me several times and I had to go to the hospital. I had a concussion." She looked around the group and saw expressions of horror on the faces. A feeling of panic engulfed her. "It wasn't from the hit. The concussion. He didn't hit me that hard. They were more like slaps. When I fell, my head hit the fireplace."

"How long has this been going on?" Harmon wanted to know.

"The hitting? About two or three years. Since I was twelve or thirteen. When I started growing up. He never hit me before."

The other kids expressed support for Randi and were repulsed by the father's behavior, but Harmon was still curious. There were details missing from her story. "What about the other kids? Does he hit them?"

"No. Never. Only me."

"Why only you? I mean, how come he doesn't hit the other kids?"

Her eyes darted around the group and she seemed to be demonstrating guilt feelings. "I don't...know....why." She began to stammer, which she had never done before. "No one...seems to know. I mean, he...I..there is just a chemistry..or something. He gets mad at me, and none of the other kids can make him get that mad. I'm the oldest, maybe that's why. I mean, I'll stand up to him. Maybe that's why. I don't know. All the people we've seen, you know, counselors, social workers, child welfare—nobody knows. It is a mystery."

"Was there sexual abuse?" Harmon asked but he wasn't sure he wanted to hear the answer.

Her eyes flashed at him and fixated into an intense glare, "No. There was never any sexual abuse. My Dad is a good man. No. Nothing like that. He would never...I would never. No. Nothing sexual."

More definitive and emphatic than it needed to be, her response had the opposite effect on Harmon than she intended. He wasn't sure what to say next, when Shannon broke the silence and effectively stole the attention from Randi, rescuing her, as it were. "It was just the opposite in my family. Daddy never hit me. When the beatings began, I was immune. I was just worried sick about the boys."

Everyone directed his or her attention toward Shannon while she continued to stare at Randi. Shannon talked to the whole group, but her eyes never left Randi as if Randi were the only audience she cared about. "When I turned thirteen, Daddy began to notice me in a special way. Hell, who am I trying to protect? Once he tried to rape me."

With that sentence, the rescue of Randi was complete and the group's attention was riveted onto Shannon and off Randi.

"He started saying things at my birthday party. 'You're getting to be a little lady now.' 'My little girl is all grown up.' 'Big boobs.' That was his most direct compliment. I was really uncomfortable, but my Daddy had a history of saying stupid things. Momma would just roll her eyes and tell him to shut up. I just blushed. Then he said I needed someone to teach me about the facts of life, show me how to be a real woman, teach me. I didn't take him serious, but I still felt really creepy."

Shannon maintained eye contact with Randi while her voice lowered and the cadence slowed. "One night, we were alone. Momma had taken the boys to a movie or something. No, I remember, it was open house at school. It don't matter. Daddy had been drinking all afternoon. Momma had been paid that day and he had drinking money. He started saying things to me. He was gonna teach me to be a woman, all that crap. He tried to grab my breasts but tore my blouse off instead. While I was yelling at him and trying to cover myself, he tore at my bra. He used so much force; he bent the hooks and pulled the bra all the way off. Then he tried to rape me. I mean, he hit me, ripped my skirt, tore my panties, and everything. I was naked, essentially. He beat me on the thighs and got my legs apart. I was crying and yelling at him to stop, but I don't think anything I could have said would have made him stop. He was carrying a bottle of whiskey in his left hand and still drinking from it. He hit me in the head with the bottle a couple of times. I was bleeding from the temple. I was hysterical, but whenever he tried to pull his pants down, I'd manage to scoot away from him. He would stagger after me, grab me and knock me down. This happened several times. I'd scoot away; he'd take a swig of whiskey, and chase me down. At one point I managed to get off the floor and tried to run out of the room, but he knocked me down and fell on top of me. He had me pinned down and he was between my legs. He had managed to get his pants down. And then, he passed out. He just passed out."

There was a long pause, as if Shannon tried to picture the exact scene, or maybe she was giving Randi time to picture it. Either way, she continued to stare at Randi. "I lay there a long time; at least it seemed like a long time. Blood flowing down my face, Daddy lying on top of me, his head pressed against my breasts, I lay there catching my breath, thinking, trying to make sense out of what just happened, and trying to figure out what to do next."

Mentally everyone tried to guess what she did next, but it was an impossible task. Nothing seemed appropriate.

"What did you do?" someone asked.

"I took a bath, cleaned myself off, put on a Band Aid to stop the bleeding, and threw away the ripped clothes. I left Daddy passed out on the floor. By the time Momma got home, I was calm and clean," she said in a voice that was strangely cold and composed.

The group sat in silence. Each person had a different mental reaction to Shannon's story. Some tried to picture the scene, some tried to put themselves in the scene, and some tried to figure out what they would have done. No one felt comfortable with his or her thoughts and they all broke the silence at once.

"Did you tell your mother?" "Did you call the police?" "Did he ever try again?" "What happened when he woke up?"

Shannon remained cool; her eyes still fixated on Randi. "While I was bathing, I did a lot of thinking. I remember at first crying and hurrying around, but once I locked the bathroom door, and got into the tub, I became real calm-like. I started thinking about the whole situation like a logic problem, you know syllogism, is that the right word? You know, if this is true, and that is true, then there is a logical conclusion. If I follow one course of action, what will the results be? I knew if I told Momma, she'd take his side, probably blame me, and nothing would happen except Momma wouldn't trust me again. I'd become one of the enemy, one of the forces trying to come between her and him. If Momma is irrational when it comes to Daddy, if Momma has some kind of weird loyalty that I don't even begin to understand, then if I tell Momma, I will lose. Momma will turn on me. If I tell the police, and if they conduct an investigation, then my family will be torn apart, and everyone will blame me. Beside, there was no evidence; there was no real crime. I was still a virgin. Daddy would claim he didn't do anything. Hell, he might not even remember it. He never did mention it to me, and I sure as hell wasn't about to bring the subject up."

"As I sat in the tub, I realized that this was my problem. No one was going to rescue me. I would have to solve the problem myself."

"What did you do?" Randi asked.

"I took care of the problem."

There was a matter-of-fact coldness in her voice that made the group shudder. No one spoke or even moved for several minutes as if the weight of her words left them powerless. They all sat there like a big balloon that had all the air sucked out of it. No one knew exactly what she meant, and no one was sure they wanted to know.

Shannon waited for the full impact of her words before she began. "The next morning, I asked, no make that I made, Momma enroll me in a karate class. I went two nights a week and I was a brown belt within a year. I made sure Daddy knew about the class, I even begged him to go to a couple of my tournaments. I also bought a switchblade knife with a six-inch blade. They are illegal, but I had one anyway, and Daddy knew it. I'd make sure it was in my pocket and that Daddy saw it anytime we were alone. I never said anything to anybody about that night, especially not to Daddy, but he never bothered me again."

Harmon was as profoundly disturbed by the solution as the problem. He felt that he had to ask. "Would you have used the knife if he had he tried something?"

She answered with a steely-eyed stare, but that was not enough of an answer to satisfy him. "Really? Would you have used it?"

"Really? Probably not. I can't really imagine using the knife. But I didn't need to. That's the whole point; I didn't need to use it. Having it was enough."

As Shannon was talking, a subtle change came over Randi. Her jaw was clenched and her hands were in fists, yet there was the faintest of trembling and her eyes looked pained. There were tears in her eyes but they never flowed down her cheeks. She was taking deep, slow breaths.

Concern about Randi was interrupted by a shriek from Vicky. "It's like what happened to me except completely different." She was gasping for air and the babbling confusion of her statement was overtaken by its intensity. "I mean, it wasn't as bad, and it wasn't my father, but…"

Someone handed her a tissue because it looked as if she were going to cry. She never did cry, but she continued to talk in hesitant bursts, waves of pain. Everyone sensed that she was talking about something terribly important to her, something she had been struggling with for a long time. "At church…there was a lock-in. You know, an all-nighter. Me and this junior deacon…we were the last ones awake…we were talking…everyone was sleeping…on the floor, all around us…we were on our sleeping bags….too hot to be in them……I drifted off to sleep…on my side facing him….then I felt something…I kinda woke up but kinda didn't, you know what I mean? I wasn't really awake, I wasn't sure what was happening." She stopped long enough to catch her breath and try to compose herself. "I've never told anyone this; you have to promise not to tell." She didn't wait for an answer; "He had his hands up my blouse…under my bra. I was just drowsy enough…it took me awhile to realize I wasn't dreaming. When I opened my eyes and started to talk, he just said "Shush." I mean, he wasn't mean or anything; he just didn't want to wake anyone. I was shocked, but I didn't stop him. In fact," her voice cracked as she lowered it to an almost inaudible level. "I was enjoying what he was doing. I mean, if I hadn't fallen asleep, I would never had allowed him to touch me, but by the time I was awake, I was really getting into it. I just closed my eyes and enjoyed the feeling. Then he moved his hand down toward the top of my jeans and started to, you know, slide his hand down there. I whispered no and started to cry. He stopped immediately. He got up and walked over to the other side of the room. He never said anything; he never talked to me again. I just lay there trembling. I felt so….dirty and so guilty….and so…incredibly hot, and, you know, turned on."

Harmon glanced at the clock and knew that the bell was about to ring. He knew that there needed to be a point of closure before everyone could go to the next class, but he wasn't sure what to say. As is turned out, as it usually turned out, Harmon didn't have to say anything. The rest of the group responded without his help. Shannon and Randi both directed their energy and attention to comforting Vicky. Betty tried to ease Vicky's sense of guilt. The boys were even more comforting, insisting that the junior deacon was the guilty one. They assured Vicky that she had done nothing wrong. The bell rang and everyone went to class. Vicky felt relieved and had resolved an issue that had been plaguing her since it had happened. Shannon hadn't really resolved anything, but then her solution was already implemented. Harmon hoped that there had been some benefit to Randi in surfacing her issues, but he wasn't sure if anything constructive had resulted.

Looking back at that meeting of Homeroom, Harmon felt unsettled. But that's the way Homeroom is, he finally concluded. Sometimes there is this profound intensity and sometimes there isn't. Quite often, the intensity is followed by superficiality, almost as a reaction to any depth, as if any serious revelation provokes a kind of fear. This Homeroom never became intense again. The disclosures from Randi, Shannon and Vicky took place three weeks before the prom. The next two meetings were focused on who was going to the prom, what the plans were, where to rent a tux or buy a dress. The post-prom Homeroom meetings were equally as mundane. When the semester finally ended and the Homeroom ended, there was a sense of relief for Harmon. The end was anticlimactic. Harmon would have seen the end as evidence that Homeroom had a very limited impact except for two events associated with this Homeroom.

First there was the private conversation with Randi just before school ended. Harmon was sitting at a desk monitoring an empty hallway during final exams, when Randi approached him.

"I'm moving back home. Today is my last day at West Side."

Harmon nodded. He looked to her for clues on how to interpret her message. "Is this a good thing or a bad thing?" he finally asked.

She shrugged and ignored his question. "You know that day in Homeroom, when Shannon told us about her father? It made a big impact on me. I don't know. It was really weird, but when she was talking, it all became clear to me. You know? Does that make sense?"

Harmon nodded, but it was a nod of acceptance rather than understanding. He really didn't know what to say, but he sensed a note of confidence and certainty in Randi's tone that comforted him.

"I had been waiting for someone to cure my dad, someone to change the way things are. I even agreed to leave home for a year, but I hadn't thought about what I wanted. You know? I hadn't thought about what I needed. Shannon made me realize that I have to rescue myself."

"So what are you going to do?"

"I don't know exactly. But I'm not going to be a victim anymore."

"I don't know if I'm comfortable with using Shannon as a role model here. I'm not at all sure it is a good idea to buy a knife."

"Me either. I mean, that's just not me. I think that was Shannon's whole point. Those things worked for her, but do you think I could intimidate anyone? No, I've got to find my own solution. Hopefully it will be with my family, with my father. But with or without them…"

The hallway began to fill with students leaving after their tests, and Randi never finished her sentence. Harmon would remember her that way, as an incomplete thought. He never saw her again, and he never knew what happened to her when she returned home. He liked to think that his confidence that she would work things out was well-grounded optimism rather than an illusion.

The second event from this Homeroom that led Harmon to develop a faith in Homeroom developed from an image, not of Randi, nor Shannon, but Kirk. One of the more pleasant customs at West Side was the elaborate ways boys had developed for asking girls to the prom. Sometimes these requests were quite creative as well as entertaining. For example, billboards have been rented, and singing telegrams have been sent to classrooms bearing prom invitations. Boys have come into classrooms and got down on their knees to ask girls to the prom. They have persuaded teachers to give tests with fake answers regarding prom dates. Students have been called into the Dean's office under the pretense of being in trouble only to find out they were victims of a hoax to get a date for prom.

Kirk performed part of his magic act before the student body at the Senior Talent Show a month before the prom. He got several volunteers from the audience, including Shannon. He produced a dollar bill and had Shannon write her name on it. Then he tore the bill and made it disappear. He went on with his act, performing several other tricks involving other props, including a tennis ball. Finally, he shook the tennis ball and said, "I think there is something in this ball." He gave the ball to Shannon and told her to cut the ball open with the pair of scissors he supplied. Inside was the original dollar bill with her signature. He said, "Turn it over and read out loud what it says on the back."

She blushed and looked around the auditorium, but read out loud, "Will you do me the honor of letting me escort you to the senior Prom? Love, Kirk."

Everyone in the audience gasped, which was followed by a loud wow and a tremendous roar of applause. Harmon felt a lump in his throat as Shannon nodded yes.

Kirk and Shannon went to the prom, and the next day instead of going to the lake with a group of people, or staying in a motel to drink, or any of the other things kids did that year, Kirk took Shannon and Swoozie to the zoo. They continued to date the rest of the year. In fact, Shannon changed her original plans and enrolled in the same college as Kirk. To Harmon, the most indelible image from that Homeroom was at graduation. Shannon, still in her graduation robe, was carrying Swoozie who was wearing her mother's graduation cap. Kirk was holding her hand as they walked down the hall.

Harmon lost touch with Kirk and Shannon over the years. They did enroll at college together, and he knew that the chances were slim that they remained together. Perhaps she got bored with him and left him for another carnival worker. Maybe he discovered that he didn't want to be a father to Swoozie after all. Harmon never knew. But he liked to think, perhaps, needed to believe, that they worked things out, eventually married, and were still together. He still pictures them in graduation robes, carrying Swoozie, holding hands, and he imagines an iridescent glow, a halo over each of their heads. To Harmon, the most enduring image from that Homeroom always causes him to sigh, "Angels in the snow."

As he walked the 70 paces down A Hall from the stairwell on the second floor toward the Hub, he knew no one would notice him. As usual, there were 12 people in the hall, mostly girls although there were three couples. One couple was sitting on the floor pretending to do homework, one couple was giggling, laughing and flirting while standing in front of an open locker, and one couple was kissing oblivious, to everyone around them. The rest of the inhabitants of A Hall were carrying on their usual conversations, too self occupied to notice him. He thought there might have been an outside chance he would catch their attention if he had worn a military camouflage jacket or the cliché black trenchcoat. He thought he needed to wear something long enough to cover the gun, but after weeks of practice, he discovered he didn't need anything long, just baggy. He settled on a big, baggy football jacket. He tore out the lining so that there was even more room, room for the strap around his right shoulder and the gun which he could carry across his chest under the jacket. There was also room for the ammo belt over his left shoulder and across his torso. The ammo belt was really an old carpenter's belt, but he had it rigged with clips of ammo so that he could pull them out and fit them into the gun as quickly as he dislodged an empty cartridge. He could do it in less than one second. No one could see any of this as he walked down the hall toward the Hub and his rendezvous with gore. He liked the way that sounded: rendezvous with gore. He rolled it over and over in his mind as he continued his pilgrimage. No one noticed him; he smiled. Soon, soon they would notice him, but then it would be too late.

He reached the end of the hall and looked around to see where everyone was standing to recheck the efficiency of his planned shooting pattern. There was a good crowd, between 190 and 200. The Vice Principal was standing in D Hall by the railing overlooking the cafeteria; he wouldn't be a problem. There was a group of 15 or so juniors on the left standing closer to the stairs than usual; they would be the biggest challenge. Some of them might even react fast enough to make it down the stairs; but he was sure most wouldn't. The rest were scattered, as usual, randomly in the Hub. The largest group, opposite him, as always, was the seniors, and in the middle was the Senior Class President with wavy blond hair and a scruffy but fashionable beard. Hanging on his left shoulder was his girlfriend. She stretched on her toes to give him a kiss when the first bullet hit her on the side of her head. She never knew what happened, but the Class President had an instant of recognition as he turned toward the gun, before he took a bullet right below his left eye. By then the blood began to splatter on everyone and screams were followed by the smell of blood and the smoke from the gun. He emptied his clip into the crowd. Quickly changing clips, he pivoted toward the left and took down the juniors, only two of whom had actually started toward the stairs. Next he eradicated the Vice Principal, followed by a quick sweep of the Hub before he turned his attention toward A Hall. By then several of the girls in A Hall were screaming and trying to run away toward the stairwell down the end of the hallway, but it was too far and he easily mowed them down before they were even halfway down the hall. The couple that had been kissing did not even have time to realize what was happening, and he cut them almost in half with a deluge of bullets across their waists. The girl who had actually been studying stupidly raised her booking an attempt to hide or protect herself, but the shots formed holes in the pages and the blood spattered on the locker behind her. He spun around in a complete circle, changed clips again and looked for evidence of any survivors.

He moved over toward the juniors by C Hall and shot the few who were still moving, although twitching would have been a more accurate description. He turned and slowly made his way down the hall toward D Hall, shooting anything that moved, even the bodies that didn't move, just because he could. He stood at the end of D Hall and looked back over the carnage of dead bodies, the results of his carefully planned handiwork. He changed clips again and sprayed the corpses, making them flop about in one more macabre dance.

"Who's better now?" He shouted, and then he turned to go downstairs.

CHAPTER 4

TOGETHER AGAIN FOR THE FIRST TIME

"So what?" Harmon thought to himself. He wasn't comfortable going to the Board and telling them about "Angels in the Snow." He doubted they would appreciate or even understand. He was pretty sure they wouldn't be impressed. He doubted that the stories of Wendy, Genevieve, Kirk, Shannon, or Randi would provide sufficient motivation for the Board to continue Homeroom. He didn't think there was enough tangible gain. He needed concrete evidence of benefit for the student body.

However, in the past whenever he had tried to assess the benefit of Homeroom, he was surprised that the feedback from students always exceeded his own evaluation. Something transpired that was beyond his ability to analyze. There seemed to be a loyalty to Homeroom from the students that transcended anything actually accomplished from Harmon's perspective. Homeroom seemed to meet needs of the students, but Harmon was never quite sure what those needs were.

Whenever he asked students to identify the greatest benefits of a Homeroom, their first answer was that Homeroom provided an opportunity to get to know people they would not have known otherwise. Because the Board seemed to be the main instrument for the Cult of Uniformity, Harmon feared that they would not place much value on that benefit. He thought that the Board probably operated under the great delusion that a high school was some sort of social melting pot where all the different classes and types of students mingle together, when, in truth, high school is a closed society. People tend to stick with their own kind. Inter-clique relationships are frowned upon, if not actually forbidden. The cliques that do exist usually center on activities that determine, in part, the student's identity. Therefore, the jock associates with other jocks and athletic supporters, so to speak. Socials, or preppies, dress alike and hang out at the same parties in preparation for their future fraternity beer bashes. The members of the band tend to congregate with other band members. The honors students are either intimidating to the other groups or are just excluded for general nerdiness. Everyone rejects the freaks, druggies, greasers, outlaws, or whatever terms are currently popular at a particular school. Add to this mixture racial and ethnic diversity, and one has a closed social system without a great deal of mobility. Of course, there are a few exceptions—a jock who makes good grades and is a member of the honors group, a cheerleader who dates a bassoon player, a drill team member who dates someone of another race—but these are the exceptions rather than the rule.

There are a few unifying factors, alcohol, and particularly beer, being the most evident. Another source of continuity is provided by the economy. At West Side, and probably most other high schools, one can too accurately predict to which group a student belongs by looking at the income of the parents. Instead of providing a place for the poor and rich to be equal, schools often provide a means of cementing the advantages of financial wealth. The doctor's kid tends to make the best grades and the children of blue-collar parents enroll in shop classes. If one thinks of high school as a mixing of the races or cliques, one doesn't remember the reality of one's high school experience.

Homeroom is a deliberate deviation from this social rigidity, and that has always been one of its attractions to the students. Harmon always thought of two particular couples as examples of the power of Homeroom to introduce diversity to a conforming, rigidly stratified population: Emily and Linda, and Bruce and Missy, more angels in the snow.

EMILY AND LINDA

Emily was the president of her senior class. She was very personable and charming. She was what they used to call "polished". She planned on attending college on the West Coast because she was going to channel her people skills into television journalism and wanted to be near the networks. Her grades, her SAT score, and her resume had earned her several scholarships. She had earned the prestigious Bellamy Institute Scholarship for Citizenship, which was determined in part by the initiation of service projects. Emily was instrumental in the creation of several projects for the National Honor Society involving home repair for elderly in the poor, racially diverse section of the town. She was also involved in an anti-drug program. She organized high school students to go into the junior highs and elementary schools to lecture on the dangers of drugs and to instruct students on the refusal skills needed to avoid drugs. In the high school itself, she managed to eliminate much of the hazing and active hostility between the classes. For example, she was responsible for stopping the practice of having cheer competitions between the sophomore, junior and senior classes at pep rallies. She tried, unsuccessfully, to get an AIDS awareness assembly for the school. In short, Emily was a preppie with a social conscience and compassion.

Linda, a junior during Emily's senior year and the antithesis of Emily, had been referred to Homeroom because she met the criteria of being an "at risk" student, well on her way to becoming a dropout. Linda had passed only two classes. She was bright enough, but she did not care about school at all. Her wardrobe seemed to highlight the point—flannel shirts, Doc Martens, black nail polish. In most classes she would sleep and certainly would not do any homework. Occasionally she would pass a test, demonstrating some innate intelligence. At the start of her junior year, she realized the folly of her educational approach, and she was smitten by the desire to succeed and do well in her studies in order to graduate and go to college. That feeling only lasted a week or two and produced little noticeable improvement in her grades. She was not hostile toward school as much as she just had other priorities. School was less a hassle than it was an annoying inconvenience. She had other priorities.

Her relationship with her mother was one of those priorities. Deep down inside of Linda there was a love for her mother, but a long time had passed since she had demonstrated that affection. Their relationship had developed into a constant state of turmoil. In fact, warfare seemed an appropriate metaphor. Linda had been kicked out of her house numerous times, and had run away even more often. Between escapes, she fought with her mother over anything and everything possible. Their conflicts were very predictable. With anything her mother would say, Linda would adamantly disagree. Her mother would question Linda's choice of dress for school, and Linda would see it as a major civil rights violation. On the other hand, her mother would see every act on Linda's part as a betrayal and pointless rebellion. They lacked any mutual respect or understanding. That each one blamed the other for the divorce only intensified their hostility. Linda, of course, constantly used the threat of running off to live with her father as blackmail. In fact, she had tried to live with her father on two occasions, but these lasted less than a month each time. The relationship between mother and daughter would have been rather humorous if it hadn't been so bloody, figuratively and literally. When they would argue, sometimes a fistfight would result. The mother had been reported to Child Protection Agency while Linda was in junior high school. When the social worker investigated the report, the mother compared bruises with Linda and asked, "Who exactly was being abused by whom?" The CPA gave up trying to help when Linda reached high school age.

Linda's other priority was her boyfriend, Teddy, another source of discord with her mother. Indeed, Teddy was every mother's worst nightmare. He had a long history of trouble with the law, usually involving fights, and he had served some time in prison for burglary. He had undergone drug rehabilitation twice, but mostly he just drank a lot. A former girlfriend had charged him with assault but dropped the charges before the trial. In spite of his checkered history, Linda had found in Teddy her "soul mate". By her junior year, whenever Linda was missing from home, whether a few hours after curfew or several days, the mother knew Linda was with Teddy. At one point, they lived in his car for two weeks. Linda would break into her house to bathe and wash her clothes whenever her mother was at work. Her mother came home early one day and found them in the bed napping. It was then that her mother got a protective order against Teddy, which accomplished nothing, except to further alienate Linda.

Linda and Emily spent two semesters together in Homeroom during the first year of Homeroom. They developed some affection and mutual respect for each other. They laughed at some of the same jokes; they were critical of some of the same teachers; they thought some of the same rules were petty and stupid; and surprisingly, they shared some of the same feelings about their parents, although Emily had the luxury of having two parents. Their relationship, part friendship and part mutual admiration changed the composition of the school permanently.

During the second semester of the year, sometime in early March, the senior class sponsors the last school dance of the year except for the prom. The Senior Spring Fling, as it was called, evolved into a sort of a prom rehearsal. According to custom, the girls asked the boys, and many prom dates were thereby arranged. The junior girls were not allowed to attend unless invited by a senior girl, and the invitations would go out, anonymously, two weeks before the dance. The rationalization was that the senior girls would have plenty of time to get their dates before the junior girls were allowed to enter the derby, so to speak. The invitations evolved into a competition, a source of embarrassment, hostility, and revenge for many senior girls. Quite often many junior girls would not get an invitation because they had offended a senior girl at some point during the year. Therefore, the invitations became a sword dangled over their heads. To many, the invitations were a friendly, teasing formality; however, every year several girls would not receive invitation and would be hurt by the experience. Usually the girls not receiving an invitation were the girls who were least social, most rebellious or non-conforming. In short, the Senior Spring Fling had become a source of rejection for the most alienated, as if they needed one more chance to be rejected. It was dominated and controlled by the forces of conformity, the "Socials".

During the middle of the dance there would be a promenade of senior and junior couples. Someone would line up all the senior couples on one side of the floor and the junior couples on the other side of the floor in some complicated, prearranged order. While the band would play some song appropriate for the theme of the dance, the couples would march in and around the floor. Then the lines would intertwine around each other and march around some more, like some slow, lazy, giant square dance. Eventually they would march together down the middle of the dance floor arm in arm. At that point, each senior girl sending an invitation would be matched with the junior girl receiving the invitation. Usually, most girls knew who invited them, but sometimes it was a surprise, and, if nothing else, the promenade provided the first opportunity for the juniors to publicly thank the seniors for the dance and the stamp of approval that the invitation had come to represent. It was quite a touching ceremony, if rather contrived.

Needless to say, Linda did not expect to get an invitation, and when she did, she immediately suspected Emily. However, Emily would not acknowledge this fact, as was the custom. Linda decided to go to the dance but was less than enthusiastic. She thought it might be "hoot" to go to a school dance. Linda was not aware of the cost of the invitation.

As president of the senior class, Emily was responsible for organizing the dance and seeing that all the invitations were sent out in time. Emily demanded that the custom be changed so that every junior girl would receive an invitation. This was met by a great wave of resentment and hostility from the other members of the committee. Linda, particularly, was the center of the controversy. Whenever the issue was debated, Linda would be brought up as the perfect example why some junior girls should not receive invitations.

"She'll show up with some biker guy who'll start a fight." "She'll be selling crack in the bathroom." "She won't bathe." "They don't even make formal flannel wear." Even the faculty sponsor of the event agreed with the students. Emily clenched her jaw and responded calmly. "She is a student at this school. The senior class should not be in the business of judging or rejecting anyone!" Through sheer personal determination, Emily forced her will on the committee, and convinced them to alter the policy. Starting that year, the policy was changed so that every junior girl would receive an invitation, and after every senior girl had selected her invitee, the remaining junior girls would be randomly assigned to senior girls. No one would be rejected again. Only the senior class officers, cheerleaders, and other prestigious seniors would participate in the promenade.

Linda was oblivious to all of this. She came to the dance on a lark. She was there for the experience, her only school dance, and she wasn't going to take it very seriously. She wore Doc Martens with a very short dress and plenty of cleavage on the top. Teddy had on a T-shirt made to look like a tuxedo. In the middle of the dance, she went into the restroom and overheard some of the other senior girls talking about her and Emily, and how Emily had insisted that everyone get an invitation, including that "wretched Linda". Later in Homeroom she told what transpired next. "At first I was really pissed off. Like I was some sort of guinea pig in one of Emily's sociology experiments. I ain't seen her at the dance, but I swear I was going make a scene. She was going pay! I figured I'd punch her out in the middle of the frigging dance floor, in the middle of the frigging dance! Then I thought about it some more. I started to chill out a little, and I began to see it differently. You know, this was like the first time anyone at this school had been nice to me. You know, reached out to me. But it was more important than that. This was the first time *anyone* at this school had reached out to anyone *like* me. If I didn't measure up, no one else would ever reach out again. And I thought of Emily, standing up for me, risking her reputation on her faith in me. She didn't have to do that. She didn't have to select me. She could have chosen someone else and still given me my invitation. She was putting her ass on the line for me. Walking her talk! I felt stunned and awed and overwhelmed and a little scared, but more than anything I felt appreciation, a new experience for me. And then the promenade began. Teddy and I were instructed where to stand and move. I went through the motions, thinking about everything, having no idea where I was going or doing. Then we were standing at one end of the floor facing Emily and her date at the other end of the floor. The annoying background music from the band changed, and they played the first few bars of 'That's What Friends Are For'. Talk about cheese! I always hated that song, for Chrissake. But it got to me; you know what I mean? The music swelled, we walked toward each other, and by the time I got to the middle of the floor, I was crying, sobbing. I wanted to say thank you to her, but I couldn't even talk. She looked at me and said, 'Hi. How do you like the dance?' I just hugged her. We stood in the middle of the floor and I cried on her shoulder like an idiot."

Emily went on to college. She graduated recently. She has a job at a television station in a small town in California. She is engaged to a successful lawyer and will get married this June. Linda dropped out of school her senior year but she did pass a high school equivalency exam. She has attended a local junior college off and on the past few years. She had a baby. In fact, was one month pregnant at the Spring Fling. She and Teddy married and tried to make things work out, but, as she said, "He ain't ready to settle down and do the daddy thing". He was arrested and is currently in prison. She separated from him before the arrest and currently lives with her mother. She says she still loves Teddy but knows that they can not "make it" together. The existence of a grandchild has healed the relationship with her mother. Linda looks at her year in Homeroom as a turning point in her life. "You know, this is really weird for me to say, but I feel like I learned from Emily that I can somehow become an adult and fit in, that there is a place in this world, even for me. You know, I've thought about this a lot and I think the only difference between Teddy and me is Emily and Homeroom."

BRUCE AND MISSY

Bruce and Missy were another example of two vastly divergent lifestyles meeting and bonding in Homeroom. They met in Homeroom during a spring semester. Missy was a graduating senior headed for Boston University to major in accounting. Bruce was in what he liked to refer to as his second junior year. He also had had two sophomore years, and he never completed his senior year. Missy was a member of the drill team. She was very personable, cute, and most people liked her. She was a tall blonde and definitely on the attractive end of the scale. She was, in many ways, a typical high school sweetheart, beautiful in a socially acceptable way, intelligent enough to succeed in college, socialized and well graced. In the yearbook she reported, "I like winter, dancing and S'Mores".

Bruce, on the other hand, liked scaring people. He was very tall, maybe 6'3", large-boned, with a weight problem that was hidden by his ever-present black trench coat. There was an air of mystery about him that was intensified by the dark sunglasses he always wore. He never carried a notebook or paper to class, and he always seemed to sleep in the back of the room. He could have easily been elected as the student Most Likely to Become a Serial Murderer. Most teachers and many students thought he was some type of gangster. Before school he could be seen sitting in the back of the cafeteria surrounded by a group of students, but he never interacted with those students; they were around him but not with him. His feet would be on the table, and with his sunglasses, it was impossible to tell if he was asleep or vigilant. Everyone around him played Dungeons and Dragons or swapped comic books. One rumor was that he was hired as their bodyguard, while another rumor was that he was a drug dealer and they were all his pushers.

Bruce was the topic of conversation in the teachers' lounge during his first sophomore year, long before his involvement in Homeroom. At that time, Bruce took to wearing a hangman's noose around his neck as he went to class. He used some sort of string or cord; he never used a real rope, but it was tied in what was unmistakably a hangman's noose. The faculty felt that he was displaying very poor taste in light of the recent history of suicides. He thought it was funny that he got such a rise out of the faculty. Another time, he began the semester carrying a coffee can with a sign on it that said "Charles Manson Defense Fund, (Tax Deductible)". He claimed he was collecting money for his mentor to afford adequate legal counsel for his parole appeal. He did both of these things very quietly and discreetly; he didn't draw a lot of attention, which, was most disquieting to the faculty. If he had been loud or obnoxious, he would have been easy to dismiss as just another disruptive student desperate for attention.

But Bruce was different. He was quiet, almost shy, and yet to most faculty members profoundly disturbing. He enjoyed his image, manipulated it, and played with it, to the distraction of practically everyone. During the first semester of his second junior year, he purchased a very expensive set of realistic looking fangs. Periodically he took to wearing them in class. He would sit in the back of the room wearing his sunglasses and trench coat, not saying anything and not disturbing anyone, while the teacher was lecturing. Then he would slowly smile, baring his fangs. The effect on the teacher was devastating. Seldom could a teacher complete the lecture. Bruce was sent to the dean. He was sent to the counselor. His parents were called. Meetings were arranged. Detentions were issued. Suspensions resulted. Through it all, he would sit quietly and watch the adults "go ballistic", in his words, as a reaction to his quiet smile, fangs and all. Eventually he stopped bringing his fangs to school because he discovered that he needed only to smile and to get the same affect. Some of the teachers became so nervous and anxious about the fangs that the threat of the fangs became as powerful as the reality of the fangs. Bruce had more ammunition in his mission to prove that all adults were crazy. Shortly after the fangs, Bruce was invited to Homeroom.

Missy was in the same Homeroom. Nothing in Missy's background prepared her for someone like Bruce. They already had had limited contact in algebra class. Her first impression was that "Bruce is living proof that even God can make a mistake". She was having difficulty and had to hire a tutor to squeak out a passing grade. Bruce never did any work in the class, never sweated any of the tests, and never passed anything all semester. She was both repulsed by his ignorant behavior and somewhat envious of his lack of anxiety. He was anything but uptight. She had no respect for his attitude yet found it undeniably attractive. One time, the algebra teacher attacked Bruce in front of the class. She started yelling at him for not turning in his homework and for not trying on his tests. "Do you know what your average is in this class?" she screamed, "You are making a 17. A 17!"

He looked up at her and replied, "Your point is?"

"You are not going to pass this class if you don't at least do your homework."

"And?"

"Well, you better get started. You don't have much time left."

"Let me see if I got this right. You think I want to pass your class."

Missy began Homeroom appalled at Bruce's lack of ambition. She ended up respecting his philosophy, while still rejecting it. They debated their various approaches throughout the semester.

"How can you not care about your grades? You will never get into a good college."

"And this is a bad thing?"

"Of course it is. You'll never make anything of yourself; you'll never be a success in life!"

Bruce would just shrug. "Where is it written that you will be a success just because you tried? Like the man says, you work your fingers to the bone and all you get is bony fingers."

"It is just such a shame. Such a waste of potential."

"But it is my potential, and who says I shouldn't waste it?"

Missy didn't know what to say. She just stammered. His way of thinking was too foreign for her.

"Look, Missy," he uttered with a hiss. "I'm sick and tired of this kind of crap. I've been getting it all my life. What makes your future life so damn good? You work and strive and struggle along, preparing for the good life, and then one day you die. Somewhere in between you have kids and suddenly your energy goes into making their life better so that they can work and strive and struggle to have a good life. When does anyone live?"

"It's not like that. I work. But I smell the roses; I enjoy life."

"Oh, really? Your whole life is like being on the drill team. You make sure you take the right steps at the right time in the right direction. You take the right classes, you make the right grades, you go the right college, you join the right sorority, you marry the right guy, you have the right number of kids, you..."

"Oh, just shut up." She interrupted him less with anger than resignation and disappointment.

"You lose your soul by being right so often."

"Oh, please. Give me a break. You think you are so free. Such an individual. Well, what do you want? What are you doing with your life?"

"I live, baby."

"Right. You live. What does that mean? What do you do that is so wonderful?"

He didn't answer. He didn't have an answer. He knew what type of life he didn't want, he knew what values he rejected, but he didn't have any real answers. "I don't know. I just know your life is...fake."

"How dare you! You don't know anything about my life. You know what I do but you don't know who I am. And you. No one knows who you are or what you do. Do you do anything? I mean, what *do* you do?"

He lowered his head, slowly shook it side to side, and barely audibly replied, "I drink."

"And that's better than studying, and dancing, and all the stuff I do?"

"I don't drink anymore." He looked up at her. "I stopped. I'm an alcoholic. I can't make plans because I don't know if I will still be sober tomorrow. But I do know that thinking about the future all the time will drive me to drink. It'll drive anyone to drink. So I live one day at a time. I try not to judge others and I stay mostly to myself because everything seems..." He hesitated, desperate to be understood. "So full of shit. You know what I mean?" He pleaded.

Her eyes moistened, a nerve was touched. "Yeah, I do know what you mean. I get really fed up with the phoniness of everyone around me. Everyone is so preoccupied with appearance."

After an uncomfortable length of silence, Harmon tried to put what they were saying into perspective. "We are all so desperate to be liked and scared to death everyone else is going to find out."

There was something desperate and pathetic in Missy's voice as she directed her remarks to Bruce. "Have you got something better? Anything?" There was a long silence. "I'm waiting."

Bruce never answered.

Variations of this scene were repeated regularly during the semester. Missy argued for the need to make plans and to have order in one's life; Bruce would advocate the wisdom of spontaneity. To him, plans, organization, and an orderly processional in life were the antithesis of freedom and living. She could not understand how he could function that way; he could not stand that she didn't. She asked him one day, "Where are you going to college?"

"I don't know."

"You can't wait for the last minute on that thing. If you don't apply, you don't get in."

"Okay, then I won't go to college."

"How can you just not go to college?"

"It's easy; you don't enroll."

"Don't you want to go to college? Don't you want to be a success in life?"

"Nope."

"How can you say that? How can you be so…so blasé?"

"It's easy. I want to be a success, but only on my terms, not yours. You know, success is a by-product, not a goal. You'll spend so much time pursuing success, you'll never enjoy it."

"But…" She was exasperated, but she couldn't think of anything to say. "I know there is a lot of truth in what you are saying, but there has to be some sort of balance."

"There is a balance," he said. "I don't run out in front of traffic. When I go someplace, I know the destination before I leave. But, you know, sometimes I find other routes and sometimes I end up somewhere else and sometimes it's even better than where I was headed."

Ultimately, Missy was envious of Bruce's approach to life; she wished she could be more like him, and she didn't like that in herself. "You just seem so lazy or indulgent or…I don't know…"

"Abnormal? Sick? Unhealthy?" Bruce countered. "I have heard all of those things before. But it is my choice, not yours. My life is not anyone else's. I have a right to be abnormal, sick, or unhealthy. If you want to join me, party on! Otherwise, leave me alone. Let me be. Don't try to change me!"

Between these exchanges, the entire Homeroom slowly got to see in Bruce a truly unique person. He had a very playful and childlike spirit, with a morose, black side. He told of the Christmas morning he woke up before anyone else in his house and took all the Christmas gifts and hid them in the garage. He went back to bed, and when the rest of the family woke up, he let them think the gifts were missing. "Maybe Santa stole them," he said.

He told how he liked to ride around in the back of a friend's pick-up truck on Halloween wearing a hockey mask and carrying a chain-saw, scaring all the little kids who were trick-or-treating, not to mention the adults accompanying them.

He told of the first time he went into a hospital for alcohol treatment, just after a friend died of alcohol poisoning. He admitted himself for a two-week treatment, and when he came out, his parents were not even aware he had been gone.

He showed his car, which was his corner of the universe, the center of his world. Although it was trashed out with candy wrappers and burger bags and left-over french fries, it also had a half dozen Muppet figures on the dashboard. "Gonzo's my hero," he would say. The cloth on the ceiling of the car had been ripped off, and he had painted a variety of cartoon characters. The trunk of his car was filled with Stephen King books. Having read everything about him and by him, he was an expert on Stephen King, his other hero. He would buy the books at garage sales and every other place he could find them. Then he would give them as gifts to people he would meet.

He told of how he'd had a short story published in a science fiction magazine and had had a children's story, "an urban fairy tale", accepted by a publisher. "But I can't pass sophomore English; go figure."

A recurring theme in his educational history was the open hostility he elicited from his teachers. "They all hate me. That's why I do so bad. My English teacher, for example, me and Mark turned in the same paper. I wrote it and Mark copied it. He got and A; I got an F."

"Are you sure their hate precedes your bad grades?" Harmon asked.

"What do you mean?"

"Well, maybe you have cause and effect mixed up."

"What?"

"Maybe they dislike you because you make failing grades and don't really try."

"No. They just hate me."

"Why you? I mean, do they select you to hate before the first day of class? Do they pick your name from the roll? Is it a random selection?"

"It's my reputation. They hear about me. I'm a threat to them. I scare teachers because I refuse to conform. I don't take their bullshit. I'm an individual, and they can't handle that. Not all teachers. I get along with you, you and Tamsen."

"Why? How are we different? You didn't really pass my class until the last quarter, and then only barely."

"Yeah, but you didn't hassle me. You didn't keep pestering me to do better. You and Tamsen, you recognized that my grade was *my* grade. You respected me. I felt like you cared about me and not just letters on a piece of paper. Every other teacher I've had wanted to save me."

"What do you mean?"

"I can't tell you how many times teachers have called my parents or talked to me after class and told me that I was wasting my potential. They want to know what is wrong, if they can help. I'd just tell them to leave me alone. They wouldn't, and pretty soon they'd start taking it personally, like I was hurting them."

"It's hard not to take it personally, but I can't believe you are describing the teachers in this school."

"You're right. It was mostly elementary school. In high school, the teachers don't care. They just fail you."

"Isn't that what you want?"

"If they would just settle for that. But they still badger and pick on you. They want you to be just like them. And they make every failure seem like such a big thing. And it's always my fault. You know, when I fail a class, it's the teacher's failure as well as mine. If the student don't learn, the teacher ain't taught."

"So when you were failing my class, it was my fault. And when you finally passed, that was my success?"

"No, you're different. I mean you saw that grades and the class were two different things. You knew that I was learning something, or maybe, I guess, you *trusted* that I was learning something."

"The map is not the territory."

"Huh?"

"I try not to confuse what is being measured with what is doing the measuring."

"I don't get it."

"Well, I know that tests and grades are my tools to try to assess what is essentially an internal process for you, your learning. My tools are less than perfect. You may be learning a great deal but it may not show up in high grades."

"Yeah, whatever. All I know is that I didn't feel bad in your class when I would get a bad grade. I didn't feel angry like you were doing it to me on purpose."

"You feel angry when you get a bad grade in other classes?"

"And sometimes victorious like I just got them."

"So you fail in order to get revenge?"

"I'm not going to pass their stupid class; that's what they want."

"You're going to teach them a lesson? By failing?"

"Yeah."

"Bruce, that's stupid. I mean, doing well would be the best revenge. Pass in spite of them. Failing is just stupid."

He hesitated. "Failing is a lot easier and a helluva lot more fun."

At that point Missy jumped in. "I hate grades too. It is like they put up all these hoops you have to jump through: write these papers, use these many sources, put your name in the top right corner, solve the problem this way, this poem means that, that poem means this. Grades don't measure what you learn; they measure how well you can jump. And no one cares if it makes any sense to you. But, damn it, there has to be grades or no one would do anything. And as much as I hate them, I don't know of a better system. I guess that is the flaw in everything you say. I mean, like I agree, but what does it get you? You don't really have any alternative. Grades are stupid, but what do you have that's better? People are hypocrites and superficial, but they are all that we have. Plans are restrictive, but not planning…. sucks!"

They could go on and on like that all year, and mostly they did. Almost any discussion would revert to a philosophical debate between Missy and Bruce. On one hand, Missy would argue for conventional wisdom, the need for mental discipline, and especially looking ahead. On the other hand, Bruce would argue for the necessity of enjoying life, and "letting life happen rather than trying to choreograph it." Some days Missy would seem to be winning but mostly Bruce held the upper hand. His arguments were much more attractive and funny. Besides, no one, except maybe teachers, wanted to hear a rationale for homework.

Everyone was surprised when Missy asked Bruce to the prom. Usually boys asked girls, but with an event as big and as important as the prom, etiquette permitted a senior girl to get a date anyway she could. Some girls were desperate to the extent that they would ask a friend, any friend, rather than limit themselves to potential romantic relationships. Missy wasn't desperate, but she did not have a boyfriend. Most of her dates the past few years had been with guys who had already graduated. She was very pretty and considered quite a catch, and any guy who dated her would be considered quite lucky. She wanted a date who would be able to go to the prom, have a good time, and not try to make more of the relationship than it was. Someone who could handle a relationship that did not conform to a normal definition. She wanted a date, not an engagement. Bruce seemed to be the ideal person. He was open-minded. He didn't need a label. He wouldn't require commitment; besides, there was no one whose company she enjoyed more. She knew him to be a gentleman who only appeared rough. At heart he was tender and kind. His childlike nature was very appealing. But more than anything else, he made her laugh.

Bruce found himself agreeing to go to the prom, a fact he found as startling as any development of that year. What was most startling was his attitude toward the prom. Everyone expected an anti-prom pose, a protest movement, but instead he looked at the prom as a solemn responsibility. He was determined to provide Missy with a rewarding prom. He would not let her down. He would transcend expectations and give her a once in a lifetime experience. He succeeded.

On the Monday following prom, Missy came to school early. She caught Harmon in the hallway and asked to talk. They went into his room and she told him about the prom. "You won't believe the prom I had!"

"What happened? Did anything go wrong? What did Bruce do?"

She got misty-eyed and seemed to focus in the distance. "It was...the most romantic, wonderful, perfect." She looked at Harmon as if he were to complete her sentence for her. "It was unbelievable."

"You had a good time, huh?"

"It was more than that; it was..." Again she uncharacteristically strained for words. "Illuminating. Inspiring. You remember in class when we talked about peak experiences? It was a peak experience. No, you know what it was? It was magical. Yeah, magical."

"Tell me."

"Well, let's see, where do I start? When I asked Bruce out, I thought it could be fun. You know. He makes me laugh. I've been to proms before. I figured with Bruce it would be real different. My friends think he's a psycho. I saw it as kind of a lark. Like doing something really daring and different. But I didn't know what to expect. I tried to make plans with him, but he would always just tell me to relax, that he was taking care of everything. At first this would just make me real uptight, and I thought about just canceling, but I tried to get into the spirit. And it became obvious that he was taking things seriously, so I went with the flow. When I was getting ready, I didn't know what to expect. I started to get all hyper waiting for him. I told my mom that if he showed up dressed really weird, just to tell him I had an emergency and had to leave town. I was trying on different excuses when he picked me up. He was knockdown handsome! I mean, you know, at school he always seems so raggedy with his trench coat and sunglasses. Well he showed up in a tuxedo, clean-shaven, hair well groomed. He did have his sunglasses, but he looked great." She got that far away look again, as if she were trying to picture what he looked like.

"My mom took the customary three rolls of film, and we eventually got in the car to leave. He rented a really fancy car, Cadillac, I think. Everything was flawless. When I asked him where we were going, he would say, "You'll see" which did not comfort me. He took off driving away from the city, out to the countryside, down small farm roads away from civilization. I was getting more and more nervous. Images of date rape flashed through my mind. I mean, how well do I really know this guy? We drove for maybe twenty minutes in the countryside, when he pulled off onto a farm road. It wasn't really a road but one of those paths for tractors. I'm really getting scared when he parks the car. He opens my door and when I protest and ask "What the hell are you doing?" He puts his finger to his mouth and gestures that I should follow him. We walk up a little hill, under the biggest oak tree I've ever seen, and there is a table with two chairs and a meal and wine and everything. He pulls out a chair for me, I sit down, he sits opposite of me, and we eat this wonderful Italian meal, under this huge, Oak tree and watch the most beautiful sunset I've ever seen."

"Wow," was the only response Harmon could muster. "How did he get the food there? How did he find the place? How did he keep the food warm?"

"I don't know. He told me that he drives around a lot, and he found the place one time driving around, but it was off the road, so I don't know. When I would ask him about details, he would refuse to answer. He would just smile and say 'It's like a good magic trick, if you understand how it is done, you take the magic away. Just relax. Enjoy. Experience the magic.' So I did. And did it ever work! We were alone in the middle of a field of some sort of crop. The sunset was breathtaking. As we ate, we stared into each other's eyes and watched the sunset crawl across the field, slowly creeping toward us. We hardly spoke because there was nothing to say as eloquent as what we were doing. When we finally finished, the moon was shining. We walked back to the car. I asked him about the table and the clean up, but he only smiled at me as if to say, 'Stop it. Don't ask.' I put my arm around him. He said, 'Let's go to the prom now,' but I really didn't want to leave this spot. Reluctantly, I got into the car and we left for the prom."

Missy was sitting on one of the desks. She had been sitting on the edge of the desktop, but at this point she moved slowly behind the desk and sat down on the chair. She leaned forward on her elbows, relishing the memory before she continued her narrative. "I wasn't sure what to expect at the prom. I mean, it's not like the prom is exactly what you have in mind when you think of Bruce. I was about half-afraid that he would do something obnoxious. You know, something he would think was clever and some sort of social comment on the evening. But the dinner relieved my fears, mostly. At the prom, he was perfectly behaved. He talked politely with everyone I introduced him to, and he was very funny. He was an adequate dancer. He brought me punch when I asked for some. I don't know how anyone could have been more charming and delightful. By the end of the evening, I found myself feeling proud of him. None of my friends' dates could measure up to him. I was really surprised by all of this. Going into the evening, I thought we would have an okay time; he'd probably say funny things all night. I thought, maybe he might even dance okay. But I was not prepared for how charming he was. I mean, by the end of the evening, everyone was envious of me. They thought I had made the difference in him; I had tamed him. You know high school girls all love outlaws that they can reform through the sheer power of their affection. All my girl friends were jealous of me."

"After we left the prom, we went to several private parties. Most were in the same hotel, but we also went to a few at people's homes. We must have gone to half-dozen or maybe even more. Booze was flowing everywhere. It was impossible not to have a beer or cocktail shoved into your hand as you entered a room. I was really worried about this. You know, with Bruce's background, I didn't want to be the cause of him falling off the wagon. He drank grape juice at the dinner, but I was really worried about the parties. But every place we went, even when a drink was shoved at him, he never took a drink. He would carry the drink around pretending to drink it or he would put it down, but he never drank. I was amazed and when I asked him if it was hard for him and should we leave, he said as long as I was with him, it was easy to refuse a drink. He wanted to spend every moment with me sober."

She stopped and hesitated. She had to clear her throat several times before she continued. "That was the most flattering thing anyone ever said to me because it wasn't just words. You know? He meant it. He stayed sober all evening. You have any idea how many people were sober that night? I tell you none of my friends were. But Bruce was."

She stopped and made a gesture to indicate that she had to take a minute before she could continue. She leaned back in the chair and crossed her legs. "I had a few sips of something at almost every party so I was a little less than sober. Don't get the wrong idea; I wasn't drunk or anything. I wasn't staggering or anything like that. But I felt a little woozie. Well anyway, Bruce said he had one more place to take me before we called it an evening so we left the last party about...oh, I don't know...it was real late. We drove around for some time up and down streets toward the country again. I had no idea where we were headed, and I'd had too many drinks to really notice the route, to really care. He finally parked on some street up in the hills overlooking the city. By now, after the whole evening, I trusted him enough not to question his intentions or sense of direction. We got out of the car and walked through some bushes until we came upon some cement fence, more like a wall. He climbed up on the fence and helped me over. Then he turned and sat on this grassy hill over looking the valley with all the city lights below. I don't know how he found that place because if you didn't know it was there, you'd never stumble upon it. We sat down. There was a blanket there and an ice bucket with some chilled champagne. He opened the champagne, poured a glass for each of us, and made a toast, 'To you and to an excellent prom.' We drank a sip and he threw the rest of his champagne on to the ground while I drank the rest of mine. He put his arm around me and we looked out over the city. I soon realized that we were facing east. He told me that we had shared a sunset and now he wanted to share a sunrise. It was kind of chilly and he put his jacket around me, and we sat in silence watching the sun come up. This whole night he said was like from his favorite movie, and this was like his favorite scene in the movie. 'What movie?' I asked. 'Lady and the Tramp,' he said. So there I sat with his arm around me, feeling very warm and safe with a guy whose favorite movie was a Disney cartoon about puppies. I swear to God, there were tears rolling down my cheeks. I don't think he ever knew about the tears. I mean, we finally kissed, but only after a long time of just sitting basking in the moment, and he never tried to take advantage of the moment. I mean, he never tried anything. There are not many guys I know that wouldn't have tried something. And to tell you the truth, the way I was feeling, he would have met with a lot of success."

She was embarrassed by this last admission. "Don't get me wrong. I don't mean he could have had me right then and there. I'm not some cheap.... thing. I don't have sex all the time. I mean I'm a virgin, mostly. But if ever there was a time when I could have been swept away and seduced by the moment, that was it. But I didn't have to worry about controlling things or getting carried away. He was content just to hold me and watch the sunrise with me. It was exhilarating and very liberating for me. I could totally just feel. And that is just what I did."

She looked up with tears in her eyes. Harmon understood. At least, he said he did. "That is the most touching prom story I have ever heard. But you most have come home really late. Did you get in trouble?"

"No. You want to know what he did? He called my mom and actually went by and met her like a week ago and shared his plans with her. He got her permission for the whole evening. I mean, can you image that?"

Harmon could only shake his head.

"Yeah. You know, I don't do drugs or anything like that, but I can't imagine a drug being a better high than this prom was. I mean, that is the best way to put it: it was a high."

"Doesn't sound like you've come down yet."

"Yeah, I guess you're right." She looked around the room as if to reconnect with the real world. "How long do you think it will last?"

Harmon wasn't sure what to say and he didn't really have an answer, anyway. "I'm not sure you ever come down from real highs. I mean, unlike drugs, real highs seem to change things. You know what I mean? Real highs illuminate; they transform."

"Yeah, I'll never see things the same way. I know I'll never look at Bruce the same way."

When Missy left to go to class, Harmon felt very uneasy. On one hand, she seemed to have had a wonderful, guilt-free, safe prom, the kind you would hope everyone would have, and a truly romantic date. Yet she seemed overwhelmed by it. Harmon feared that her reaction was out of proportion. He hoped she wasn't about to crash harder than she had ever crashed before. He sensed vulnerability, from which she had always managed to shield herself in the past. And he wondered how Bruce felt.

But Bruce was absent on Monday. He was also absent on Tuesday and Wednesday. He missed Homeroom. By the next week, Missy had come down from her prom high; she had returned to reality. Harmon thought at the time, and it was later confirmed, that Bruce's absences were deliberate, and for Missy's benefit. In those two weeks, she studied for some tests, did some homework and hung out with her friends. Reality slowly usurped the romantic images of the prom. She got back to the business of being Missy, and there was little room in her world for Bruce. Bruce instinctively knew this even before Missy became aware of it. He knew it before the actual prom. He went with no illusions. He set out to give Missy a magical prom and he succeeded beyond her wildest dreams, which is why he was content to hold Missy and merely hug her on the hilltop looking over the city. He knew that if they had made-out or anything, the sex would have become the focal point of the night. Eventually she would have regretted it. He didn't want that. He wanted the defining moment to be something she would cherish forever and never regret. His decisions on that night demonstrated profound wisdom and extraordinary insight.

Within the next few weeks, the last weeks of school, Missy came to the same realization: Bruce and she were not a good idea, not a good match. However, that awareness led only to an even greater appreciation for him and for the prom he had given her. On their last day of Homeroom together, she gave him a warm fuzzy. "Bruce, I want to compliment you for something very rare." She started with a slight crack in her voice. She was holding back tears successfully but with some effort. "There are lots of guys out there who will date me, and probably a few who would agree to be my boyfriend if I wanted them, but you…you are the only boy I know who is," she hesitated trying to find the right words before speaking, "big enough, strong enough to be my friend. I can't tell you how much I have come to appreciate that."

Bruce swallowed to suppress the lump in his throat.

She continued, "I don't know if you will understand this, but I hope you think about it until you do understand. I know you are an author and write stories and stuff. I think you think your greatest work of fiction; your greatest creation is **you**. Well, you're wrong."

Bruce looked up.

She didn't blink. "I know you Bruce, I have seen you, I know who you are, and the part of you that isn't fiction, the real you…that is your greatest gift. And I can't thank you enough for sharing it."

He was trembling but, with great effort, he was restraining any reaction, any show of emotion.

"Look at me," she pleaded maintaining eye contact. "The reality of who you are is greater than any image you have created."

There were several moments of silence as Bruce's shoulders scarcely heaved. Finally, barely audible, he whispered, "Thank you."

Missy went on to graduate. She enrolled in college and is probably nearly finished by now. Bruce never did graduate. He was back at school the next year, but he never enrolled in another Homeroom. By then, Harmon had heard more details about Bruce from his teachers, friends, and Allison; the blanks that were filled in did not paint a flattering picture. The less one knew of Bruce, the better, it would seem.

In short, everything Bruce told Homeroom was a lie, plain and simple. First, he had never published a story. His English teacher maintained that it was doubtful that he had the language skills to write a competent paragraph, let alone a short story. Stephen King might have been a personal hero, someone with whom Bruce identified, but the source of his identification was King's learning disabilities rather than his creativity. Bruce never overcame whatever obstacles prevented his intellectual growth. Second, his self-commitment for alcoholism was a fabrication. He had been hospitalized but it had been for depression, and his parents had done the referral. Third, there was some truth in the statement that he was an alcoholic; the lie was that he was in recovery. He had never stopped drinking. He really did stay sober on the night of the prom, but that was the exception rather than the rule. He drank regularly before and after the prom. In fact, the three-day absence after the prom, that Harmon thought was due to Bruce's wise withdrawal from Missy, was in reality due to a drunken binge. For Bruce the prom had been a bittersweet experience and he chose to drown his sorrow, to self-medicate in a river of booze.

When he first learned these facts about Bruce, Harmon despaired. He questioned the validity of Homeroom, and the validity of his involvement in the lives of students. What good was Homeroom? What good was he? Then he had second thoughts and began to see it differently. In the light of the truth, Bruce and Missy's story, in some ways, became even more poignant. Bruce's sacrifice on prom night really was a sacrifice. He did stay sober for Missy, and it was for her. And Missy gave Bruce something no one else had ever given him; she touched him. Missy's last words take on new, richer and deeper meaning in the context of the revelations, "I know you, Bruce, I have seen you, I know who you are, and the part of you that isn't fiction, the real you...that is your greatest gift. And I can't thank you enough for sharing it....the reality of who you are is greater than any image you have created."

Bruce gave Missy the prom, but Missy gave Bruce something much greater; she gave him human contact. And human contact is good. It happened in Homeroom, because of Homeroom, and maybe Emily was Linda's angel, but Harmon was never quite sure if Bruce was Missy's angel or if Missy was Bruce's angel, or if there was somehow, someway, something angelic conjured up between them.

The intensity of his hatred toward everyone and everything associated with West High School surprised even him. He wasn't even sure of its origin. He wasn't sure if it was rational, but he didn't care. His hate transcended logic. He knew it was deep and cold and true. Nothing this intense could be false. It was some primal truth calling out to him and even if he couldn't articulate it, he had no difficulty conjuring up images to support his rage. Any list of images started with those damn Homecoming mums and garters. On the Friday of the Homecoming dance, the girls would come to school with their mums pinned to their chests and the boys wore corresponding garters around their arms, and each year they became more and more elaborate. The girls' mums were huge, hanging to the floor with ribbons, plastic symbols, stuffed animals, cute names, anything that would serve to identify the couple and the year. Then there were the damn cowbells. Their size, tone, and loudness indicated the popularity of the couple. The overall effect of the mums and garters was complete disruption; nothing was done in any class. No teacher tried to compete with the incessant clanging of the cowbells. Teachers hated the mums, but the students who didn't receive mums hated them even more. To those students, the mums were not just a symbol of their unpopularity; they were a physical proof, a tangible demonstration of a lack of respect and caring for them both by other students and by the school itself. It was a statement that they were not welcome. Not to receive a mum or a garter was a testimonial to your value, to your worth, and it explained why the absence rate was four times higher on Homecoming Friday.

But there were other things on his list of things he hated about school. There were the class favorites every spring: Most Beautiful, Best Sport, Best Personality, Most Likely to Succeed, Most Talented. Every first period class would nominate the candidates and the student body would vote during lunch period, and yet one could predict the winners with amazing accuracy. It was the same five kids nominated in each category each year. An outsider could look at the yearbook and get the impression that there were only twenty students in any given class; they were the class officers, the class favorites, student council officers, the star athletes, and the cheerleaders. The rest of the student body, as many as 2,000, provided background, the template for their celebrity, fodder for the ones who mattered.

Even the Student Council, which had the reputation for being a fair and equal representation of a wide range of students at the school, was just a big farce. There might be different people nominated, but the same ones were always elected. During the first semester of his freshmen year, he and George would laugh and make jokes about all the injustices that called themselves "student elections", but when George moved, he was left alone and the jokes weren't funny anymore.

The teachers made the situation worse. The faculty knew who should win the elections, who should make the best grades, who should be given the benefit of the doubt, who could be trusted, who fit in and who did not; they knew who was a winner and who was a loser. They certainly weren't going to do anything to disturb the social structure. A cheerleader could turn in a paper late without a penalty, a football player could be caught copying a homework assignment without consequence, but anyone who would choose to go to the cafeteria during a pep rally would be looked upon like a leper, void of any redeeming social qualities. "Don't you have any school spirit?" he was asked, as if school spirit were a worthwhile trait to have, worth selling your soul for, your identity, your individuality. Any breach of school spirit was treated like a crime against nature, a much greater crime than cheating or fighting, violations that those with school spirit could safely commit with regularity.

Then there was Good Life, the Christian organization. It met off campus and could not officially advertise in the building. The members all wore T-shirts proclaiming their faith on the front and announcing the meeting time on the back. Apparently the students could go around the cafeteria inviting students to the meetings. And everyone was invited. One did not have to be a hypocrite to be a member of Good Life, but hypocrisy certainly did not hurt. Some of the biggest drunks attended regularly, and Good Life gave many people one more place to feel better than everyone else, one more place to practice blatant judgementalness.

These countless, daily indignities were more annoying and silly than enraging but, when he thought about his anger, he remembered an evening shift at McDonald's.

Although he was working a four-hour shift with his eager-beaver shift manager, he was in a good mood when Ben walked in with his girlfriend. Ben was in his math class. Ben, a student council officer, was headed to college to be a business major and was destined to be in one of the best fraternities on campus. Despite all of this, he liked Ben and thought they had a relationship approaching something like a friendship. The day before, Ben had asked him for some help on a math assignment, but none of that seemed to matter as Ben approached the counter with a girl at his side; Ben did not acknowledge him.

"I'd like two cheeseburgers and two chocolate shakes, please," then he turned toward his date, "I mean two McCheeseburgers and two McChocolate McShakes." The girl absolutely guffawed at Ben's display of wit.

"Would you like some fries with that?" he asked, as he had been instructed by his manager to ask.

"Did I say I wanted some fries?"

"No."

"If I wanted fries, I would say I wanted fries. Do you have to, like, flunk an intelligence test to get hired here or what?" This was followed by more laughter by the girl.

He didn't mind being the butt of a joke, being laughed at; he minded being treated so dismissively by someone who less than 24 hours earlier needed his help in math class. The only thing that had changed was context, and he hated that he was now in the context of being Ben's servant. Ben knew what the proper relationship should be, and now that they were out in the real world, Ben would demonstrate the proper dominance. Ben was big; he was small. Ben was important; he was not. Ben was the customer; he was the guy behind the counter. Ben would condescend and insult; he should take it. Ben had the girls; he had none. Ben had the student council office; but he had the bullet., Tonight when he would fantasize shooting everyone at school, Ben would be his first victim.

Whenever he thought about all these images of insults and humiliations, they never seemed to justify the intensity of his feelings. There was something else, something that gnawed at him, something deep inside that festered like a deep sore. It wasn't just that they won the elections and ruled the classrooms; it was that they believed they <u>should</u>. What he hated more than anything else was their horrible attitude of superiority and the sense of entitlement that resulted. They all felt they deserved every election they won, every honor they received, every accolade bestowed upon them. They seemed to tower over the little people that surrounded them, and they viewed it that way. The rest of the school existed to provide some sort of background for them, an audience for their personal glory. And that attitude was what he hated. Their contemptible and unrelenting arrogance; they really did believe that they were better than everyone else. More than anything, he wanted to wipe the smug smiles off of each and everyone of their faces, but he would settle for just wiping their faces off.

CHAPTER 5

THE SUBJECTIVITY OF DISTANCE

As Harmon continued his journey to Allison's office, he tried to organize his thoughts for presentation to the Board. "Angels aren't going to work," he thought. "We can eliminate that option."

He began to formulate a plan for his presentation. He had two main arguments in defense of Homeroom. First, Homeroom brings together people who wouldn't normally come into contact with each other, for example, Genevieve and Wendy, Emily and Linda, and Bruce and Missy. This is a good thing because it expands students' perspectives and experiences. A second point would be that Homeroom serves as a sort of little-known crisis center within the school, a place to give students a time-out in times of emotional crisis, a place to refer students in times of emergency. "A place for angels to spread their wings and weave their magic" he thought, knowing he would never let himself speak those words out loud.

COLLIN'S STORY

During the third semester of Homeroom, Harmon saw Allison in the cafeteria line at lunch. "I don't see you here very often. What's the occasion?" Harmon asked.

"You eat here everyday?" she replied.

"Sure. Best meat-like substance in town. Try their chicken fried steak; it's covered with a unique taste treat, a non-dairy cheese product, spreadable gravy that is neither gravy nor cheese. Like the Osmonds, a little bit country, a little bit rock 'n roll."

"I'm sold."

"What is the occasion?"

"What do you mean?"

"Why have you graced us with your presence today?"

"I've just had a rough morning and needed a nutritious lunch,"

"But you settled for the cafeteria instead."

"Yeah."

"Well I hope it wasn't anything too serious. If I can help…"

"You know, maybe you can. You have a Homeroom last period today, don't you?"

"Yeah."

"Well, I've got a kid I want to send you."

"Sure, it's a small Homeroom. We can use another member. Send him to me. I'll give him a permission slip and tell him about the program."

"No, I don't mean all the time, just for today. I just want to send him for this one day. He has a class, probably an honors class, but I think the teacher will let him go this one time. I think you, Homeroom, might be able to help him more than I have been able to."

"What's this about?"

"I'll let him tell you if he decides to come. I'll see him right after lunch and if he decides to come, I'll send you a note."

"What is his name?"

"Let me see how he responds to Homeroom first."

Collin appeared last period. He introduced himself and took a seat as the rest of the group filed in. He was tall and rather gangly. His hair was shoulder-length and very curly. He wore a plaid flannel shirt with a dark blue T-shirt underneath. His fingers were very long and almost delicate. Although he was sophomore, his reputation had preceded him. He was considered somewhat of an eccentric genius. On first impression, he appeared to be one of those "stuck-in-the-sixties" kids. Harmon told the group that Collin was there because Allison suggested that he should talk to us about something that was bothering him. Harmon told them that he had no idea what the subject was, but that if it was okay with the group, he would let Collin take over. They all agreed, and Collin started to tell his story.

"Last night. No….well…where should I start? I got this friend, Jeff. Jeff is kinda weird. Always has been. I've known him since like second grade. He goes to St. Andrew Catholic School. Well, he's been into drugs lately. I don't know what. Despite what a lot of people think, I don't do drugs, and Jeff doesn't do them around me, but he's into it. His dad thinks drugs are the whole problem, but I'm not so sure. It's hard to tell. Lately, he's been skipping school and staying out late and stuff. He has always been a good student, weird, but a good student." He caught the irony of what he had said as he looked around. "Like me, I guess. Anyway, this drug stuff is all new to Jeff. Last two months maybe. Lately he has been talking weird. I mean, weirder than usual. I mean, he has always been…" He looked around the group, saw that everyone had fixated on him, and tried to find the right word. "So…so…abstract. You could always get him to talk about reality, you know? What's real, where does the mind end, you know? Stuff like that. But lately he has seemed so much more intense."

He stopped and no one moved or said anything. He seemed to be gathering his thoughts, or strength, to go on with his story. "More intense and paranoid. He's said some really strange shit lately, you know? Like about life on other planets and the solar system inside his head and the plot to quiet him. He's been seeing a doctor, a psychiatrist, but he won't take his medicine. He thinks its part of the plot. His doctor talked him into going into a hospital. I can't even imagine how he did that. But when he got home and started getting ready, he changed his mind. He ran out the back door, down the alley to my house. He wanted me to hide him and help him run away. I talked to him for awhile; my mom fixed him a sandwich. My mom took me aside and told me she had called his father while he was eating. She told me that we had to help get Jeff to the hospital. When his father got there, I blocked the back door. The father took him, literally dragged him out to the car. Jeff was crying, but he really stopped struggling after he saw I wasn't going to help him. He gave up, sort of caved in, if you know what I mean. The last time I saw Jeff, he was looking at me out of the car window with this hurt look on his face. 'I thought I could trust you' was the last thing he said to me." At this point, Collin's voice did not reveal the intensity of his emotions.

"Maybe I shouldn't have done it; maybe I should have helped him run away."

"Where would he have gone? What would he have done?" Lilly was the first member of the group to speak out. She spoke with a decisiveness that seemed at odds with the account.

Collin dropped his head. "I don't know. Probably gone into the hospital anyway. But, he still would have had a friend instead of being all alone and feeling betrayed."

From the other side of the circle, Frank spoke out; "You did the right thing. If you'd have tried to help him, he could be lying in a ditch somewhere. Who knows? At least he is safe."

"You didn't really have a choice," Linda added. "If you'd helped him escape, you'd be in trouble, probably with the law as well as with your parents and his parents. Plus, if you have doubts you did the right thing today, imagine how you would feel if he was out there tomorrow without help. No, you really had no choice; you had to do what you did."

Collin listened and he seemed to be feeling a little better, but he still seemed a long way from being comfortable. "But you didn't see the look on his face. I don't think he'll ever trust me."

"Which would you rather have?" Lilly had a way of putting things into perspective. "Your friend's trust or his safety? I mean, would you rather have him hating you and alive or trusting you and dead? He'll eventually see that what you did was for his best interest. He will appreciate what you did." She hesitated for what seemed like a long time before she added. "Believe me, I know."

At that point, everyone turned to face Lilly with looks of expectation. "When my parents put me in drug rehab, I hated them. I didn't want to go. I tried to run away. I was sure I would be better off on my own. Leave me and my drugs alone. We'll be fine. I even had some romantic image of being a prostitute in LA paying for my drugs while I waited for Richard Gere, you know like in <u>Pretty Woman</u>. But after two weeks in rehab, I felt differently, and by the time I left, I was glad, I mean *glad* that they had done what they did. You know, I now look at that as the first sign that they actually loved me. Your friend will feel that way to, eventually."

"The same thing with my sister." Wayne spoke out. "She was diagnosed with anorexia. She was going to die. She was into denial big time when she went into the hospital; she refused to say she had a problem. And she hated my parents for making her go. But when she came out, well really after a year of family therapy, now she's glad."

Paul was in this group and he even added his testimonial. "Me, too. When I went into the hospital, I just wanted them to leave me alone. Just let me die. But I'm glad they didn't."

Harmon tried to make some sort of summary on this issue. "I guess no one wants to admit they have a problem; no one wants to go into a hospital. In fact, if you think about it, how would you have felt if he wanted to go into the hospital, if he had gladly taken the plunge? Wouldn't that have bothered you more?"

Collin barely acknowledged what Harmon had said; it wasn't a useful statement, but he did respond to almost everything the students were saying. Harmon realized that Collin needed peer support more than any adult intervention, which was why Allison referred him in the first place. So he shut up, sat back, and watched. Almost everyone had a relevant story, but the most powerful story came from Frank. "We had to do the same thing with my little brother. I knew he was drinking and doing some drugs. My parents were in the dark. Man, I could see he was losing it: bad grades, not bathing, change in friends, depression, the whole nine yards. He was like in seventh grade. My parents thought it was some kind of phase. I had problems in seventh grade, too. Who doesn't? After I told my parents the whole truth, when he found out I was the one who told them the truth, he came at me with a knife. They put him in the hospital, drug rehab. He swore he was going to kill me when he got out." Frank stopped, realizing he had revealed more that he had wanted to say. He began to blush.

"What happened?" Collin asked.

"He tried to kill me, but I killed him instead."

Everyone gasped.

"I'm joking. We're best friends now. He just had to sober up to realize what he was doing to himself. Now he's back home and does no drugs. In fact, he's found religion and he's a born-again Christian. He is trying to save the whole family. I may have to kill him after all."

Harmon did not see Collin again until his senior year, when he took Harmon's class. Harmon asked him how Jeff was. Collin told him that Jeff had enrolled in a private school in Minnesota after leaving the hospital, and, as far as he could tell, Jeff was doing well. Collin thanked Harmon for Homeroom that day. It helped him more than anything else had. The kids gave him a perspective that Allison couldn't provide. He left school that day feeling better.

MEGAN'S STORY

The quintessential Homeroom moment came because of a referral from Mr. Tamsen, the advanced-placement chemistry teacher, early in the history of Homeroom during one of those meetings scheduled during a lunch period. B lunch was beginning and the students were eating their lunches while putting the desks in a circle, when Megan appeared with a note from Mr. Tamsen that said she needed to be in Homeroom today. Harmon was surprised that anyone in the faculty knew about Homeroom and was flattered that Tamsen had sent her. Megan was actually the first referral, and Harmon was anxious to satisfy any faith put into Homeroom.

Megan took center stage and everyone listened to her. Her eyes had the tell-tale puffy redness of recent tears, and she was obviously still very disturbed. Her hands were busy, and she alternated between staring straight ahead and darting her eyes to everyone in the circle. "My first period class is health here at West, but I have second period at East High School, A.P. World History, and fourth period here, A.P. chemistry. I don't have a third period class. Usually I grab lunch at Burger King on the way here. I have like twenty to thirty minutes to make it here in time for chem. Well, anyway today I was running late from first period so I got to East a little late. I was walking down the hall toward my class with my head down trying to figure what I'm going to say to my teacher, when this guy like brushes against me as he goes into his classroom. I barely notice him except I notice he has something in his hand. I take a step and it registers—he has a gun in his hand! I was grabbing the door handle to go into my class when the shot rang out. Like an explosion. I mean, it sounded like a cannon echoing down the hall. I guess it was more like a small cracking sound. The next thing I notice is his body flopping out of the room. It lies real still in the hallway with a small puddle of blood forming around his head. The blood is coming from a small, dark, smoking circle on his temple. I notice that the puddle of blood is bubbling, which seems odd to me. A girl comes running out of the room screaming, with blood splattered all over her face and shoulders. I think she was screaming. I didn't hear her voice. I didn't hear anything. She runs down the hallway away from me."

"I step into my room numbly. One foot in front of the other, automatically. The way you walk when you are in a daze. I wasn't thinking. I wasn't sure what I had just seen. I wasn't even sure if I had really seen what I had just seen. The rest of the class was milling around sliding desks and passing books back and forth. The teacher was standing in front of the class directing traffic. She smiles at me as I enter the room and I start looking for my desk. It all seems so, so…unreal. The teacher says 'Hi. What's the commotion in the hall?' I mean, it is all so weird. It is like all of this happens at the same exact instant. This guy bumps into me, I notice a gun, I reach for the door, I hear a shot, I see a dead body, I see a girl scream, I come into class, and the teacher says hello. No one else seemed to have heard anything. Time has like altered. Before I could answer the teacher, before time becomes normal, the intercom sputters and the principal announces that there has been a serious incident on the third floor and all classes will stay in their rooms until further notice. All of the kids looked around to see what to do. The teacher told them to sit down, and every-one turned toward me. 'Some guy just shot himself in the head. I think.' And then no one spoke and there was this really eerie silence, and now time became stuck. It was like time didn't move or change. We were stuck in this same moment."

"Eventually, they let class out. By then, I guess the word got around the school what happened, because when I left it was lunch period and I saw everyone sitting in the cafeteria. No one was talking. There was only this kind of eerie sound of plastic forks and knives scratching on the Styrofoam plates. Time was unstuck, but somehow altered. Everyone seemed to be moving in slow motion."

Harmon knew that the incident she was describing actually happened. An emergency memo was sent third period informing the teachers of the tragedy at East High School. The staff was anticipating repercussions; Harmon just didn't expect them to be so soon or so direct. He wasn't sure if any of the stu-dents had heard anything, and he couldn't tell from their silence.

Megan continued to talk. "I came to school and went to my chemistry class because I didn't know what else to do. Allison isn't in her office; she is over at East High to help. I tried to just sit in class and be a student, but I kept…" She looked up at Harmon and the tears started again, as her voice went up in pitch and her shoulders started to shake slightly. "I kept…I kept…. I kept picturing the bubbles in the blood. I don't know why. Just those damn bubbles. I started to cry and shake, and mostly I've been crying and shaking ever since. Mr. Tam-sen sent me here because he knew I didn't need to be in class and there really wasn't anywhere else to go."

The tears had slowed down and her shaking had stopped. The students asked her questions for a few minutes: who, why, what class, and so forth. She tried to answer but she had only rumors and incomplete information. They listened to her tell the story one more time, which seemed to comfort her. However, the image of the bubbles in the blood would disturb her so pro-foundly that the crying would start again. A point was reached where all the questions had been asked, and Megan was exhausted from crying and talking. Everyone sat in an uncomfortable silence. Harmon was sure every student was identifying with either Megan or the suicide victim. As they sat and thought about how the tragedy related to them, Harmon tried to think of something to say. He felt that the silence needed to be broken, having lasted much too long, but he couldn't think of anything appropriate to say.

Finally, Wally, a big, strong, scary-looking guy with long hair, wearing a black T-shirt but with the personality of Winnie the Pooh, broke the silence. He turned towards Jenny, "Ask me if I'm an orange." She looked at him with a look of bewilderment, "Are you an orange?" "No," he replied. The entire group burst into laughter, the kind of laughter that starts at your feet and shakes through your entire body, the kind of laughter that comes only as a relief from great stress and turmoil, the kind of laughter that comes in waves, ebbs and flows, and regains strength to begin again. They laughed like that for several minutes. When they would stop for a brief moment, the laughter would overcome them again and take over even stronger than before. They sat there the rest of the period roaring in laughter over and over at a joke that at another time, under a different circumstance, no one would even think funny. They didn't feel they could stop, and no one really wanted to. And Megan laughed the loudest and the longest.

MATTHEW

Loneliness is an underreported fact of life for many students in a modern day high school, and there is no loneliness more profound than loneliness in the midst of a crowd. The sheer numbers emphasize the isolation. According to theory, during adolescence, peer groups provide a value system or a sense of identity. This may be true in junior high school, but in high school, the main purpose of a peer group is to protect against loneliness. The student who does not have a group to hang-with is alone in a very fundamental, profound, and terrible way.

Many students do not fit into an identifiable group. They are different in some basic way, which causes them to be estranged from those around them. Sometimes there is choice in their alienation, but often there is no choice. They may dress differently, or think differently, or act differently. There is an almost unlimited list of reasons for social rejection. For a student who is profoundly alienated, high school has little to offer but pain. At West Side High School, Homeroom provided one of the few comforts available to these students. Homeroom was a life raft for people drowning in loneliness, and Harmon hoped that the Board would be persuaded to put an alternative to loneliness as a high priority.

Matthew was an emergency referral to Homeroom. Matthew was weird. In many ways, he was the most enigmatic student ever enrolled in Homeroom. Harmon never understood him, and somewhere about Matthew's junior year Harmon gave up trying. Harmon watched him in Homeroom for four semesters, as he would sit and fidget, bounce his feet, and play with rubber bands or pencils or whatever he could get his hands on. He was the only student who ever brought paper and pencil to Homeroom and would put them on the desk in front of him as if he were going to take notes. Sometimes he would talk very softly and sometimes his voice would boom, and there was no discernible connection between the volume and the subject matter. Sometimes he seemed in a rage over something but inattentive at the same time. Often when he talked, he seemed to be throwing out bait to see if anyone would pick it up. At other times, it seemed that his emotions were so powerful he couldn't deal with them except by shrouding them in mystery. No one knew if he was a clown or a tortured soul, or both.

Matthew transferred to West Side during the second semester of his sophomore year. He was handsome but slight in stature. His complexion was dark, as if he were well suntanned. His hair was curly and very black. It was impossible to guess his ethnic origin, and he would not reveal it, although he challenged others to guess what it was. Apparently his family was originally from a small Central American country. The family, composed of Matthew, his natural mother, and his stepfather, had just moved from California to the West Side attendance area. His mother was, according to Allison, "knock out beautiful". She was very successful in the financial community. His stepfather either did not work or was enrolled in college; it wasn't clear.

During the first two weeks of the semester, Matthew became a discipline problem in his classes. Allison talked to him on several occasions and then referred him to Homeroom. Only Trey, a senior with experience in Homeroom, and Harmon talked to Matthew on his first day in Homeroom. An assembly was scheduled and all of the students were there except Trey and Matthew. When Matthew sat down, his hands were twisting a rubber band, and Harmon sensed his nervousness and tried to relax him.

"Hello, Matthew. I understand you might be interested in Homeroom. We will answer any questions you have about Homeroom."

"Questions? I don't have any questions. They tell me to go here and they tell me to go there and now I'm here."

"Well, this is purely voluntary and if you don't want to be here or if you feel uncomfortable...."

"I go to my class; they tell me where to sit. I have to do this and that."

"What are you talking about?" Trey asked. Trey was a very bright student with impressive people skills. He listened well, and communicated that he listened. He was sitting on the edge of his chair, facing Matthew, staring intensely.

Trey always hung onto every word said in a Homeroom, and he was trying to do the same for Matthew, but he was experiencing as much frustration as Harmon was.

"You sound like you are really mad," Harmon said.

"Mad? No, I'm not mad. How would you like being told everything and never getting to do anything yourself?"

"Who is telling you to do everything? What are they telling you?" Trey asked.

Matthew stared at him, "Everybody. Everything."

"What are they telling you?"

"Like I said, where to go, what to do, everything."

He was stretching his rubber band this way and that, desperately. "You seem really nervous. How can we help?"

"You can't. No one can. I don't need help."

"So why are you here?" Trey asked.

"Because Allison told me to come. She told me to talk. Talk. Like that will help. So I come. They tell me and I do."

"What would you like to do?" Harmon asked.

"It doesn't matter what I want."

"You sound really angry and bitter and you seem so tense with your hand and the rubber band."

"Okay, so I can't play with the rubber band either. Okay." And with that he hurled the rubber band across the room.

"No." Harmon got up and walked over picked up the rubber band and gave it back to him. "I didn't mean you couldn't play with it. You just seem so tense and I don't know what's bothering you. I'd like to know."

"I'd like to know, too," Trey echoed.

"Bothering me? Oh, nothing really. Just one day I come home from school and they tell me I'm moving here. No asking, no warning, just up and move."

Trey asked him about his old school, "Where are you from? Did you like you old school? Was it better?"

"I hated it. I wanted to leave it as soon as I got there. It was like…I mean, how would you like it if you were afraid all the time?"

"What were you afraid of?"

"Nobody likes new kids. This one guy was trying to scare me. I didn't throw him through the window, but I still got suspended. They told me I couldn't go to school for five days. Then I had to go back. Everybody, nobody would talk. One guy, we played Nintendo. They flunked me."

Harmon looked at Trey, and he looked back. Neither of them knew what to say next. Harmon tried to replay what he had just said and finally he tried to pick up on the fear element of what Matthew had said. "Do you feel frightened at this school?"

"No."

"Well that seems to be some progress."

Matthew was quiet, and he temporarily stopped stretching his rubber band.

"Have you met anyone? Have you made any friends?"

"No."

He continued to sit quietly, and then he slowly started twisting and pulling on the rubber band again. When the pulling reached a certain level of intensity, he started talking again. "No. No friends. Of course not. Who would want to be my friend? I can't do anything. I can't go anywhere. Where am I gonna make a friend?"

Trey spoke up. "You could go to a school dance, or a basketball game. You could call someone up and ask about homework. You could..."

"No I can't."

"Why not?"

"How will I get there?"

"I know you don't drive, but none of the sophomores do. There are ways."

"Right. What do you know?"

Trey was beginning to get mad. "Ask you parents for a ride for Chrissake. Walk. Ride a bike."

"Yeah, right."

"Do you want to do anything or do you just want to complain?"

"I told you, it doesn't matter. My stepfather won't take me any place. My mother is never home, and when she is, she wants to know exactly where I am at. I can't do anything until she gets home, and she works late every night. I hate sports. I don't do homework."

"So what do you do? I mean, after school."

"Nothing."

Trey wanted to know and was not satisfied with Matthew's answer. "No, really, what do you do? You have to do something."

"Nothing. I do nothing."

"You must do something."

"No, I do nothing."

The jaw muscles in Trey's face tightened, and he was about to lose control. "No wonder you take it out on your rubber band."

When the bell finally rang to end that class period, Matthew bolted out of the classroom down the hallway. Trey lingered. "Something is really bothering that kid!" Trey offered.

Harmon nodded in agreement. "You got any idea what it is?" he asked.

"I have no idea."

Allison wasn't much help. She had sent Matthew to Homeroom hoping that it would reveal something about his problems. "There was some hint of trouble in his last school, but the officials are vague about the details. All I can get out of them is that he had a fight once."

"I see him in front of me filled with all these intense, pent-up feelings, but I can't figure out what is producing it. I can't even get a handle on what the feelings are exactly."

"Rage seems most accurate, but usually rage is directed at something, and Matthew doesn't seem to have a target for his rage."

"Or has too many different targets."

For the next year and half, Matthew continued to be an enigma. His attendance at school was perfect and he never missed a Homeroom. His warm fuzzies were always bizarre and irrelevant. They weren't insincere or undeserved; they were just random. For example, once he complimented a girl in Homeroom for her good penmanship, although no one could figure out when he had ever seen an example of her handwriting. Sometimes he was more agitated than at other times, but soon most of the other kids developed a tolerance for him. "That is just his nature," they seemed to say. He mostly listened to the other students and would occasionally respond in varying degrees of congruency. Sometimes his responses would be so completely off the subject, that the whole group would be caught off guard. He seldom initiated a subject, and even when he did, he never revealed anything personal.

One semester a recurring topic was his Sunday study time. According to Matthew, his parents made him stay home every Sunday from noon until eleven o'clock at night doing his homework and studying in his bedroom. His grades actually dropped during this time period. He was convinced that the more he studied, the worse his grades were. "If I don't study or do homework, my grades get better. The more I study, the worse they get," he would say, with a look of delight on his face. Efforts by Harmon to get him to see any role he played in his grades were met with resistance and frustration. He did not believe he sabotaged himself with his grades. He did not believe he did worse to hurt his parents. He did not believe that doing poorly while trying to do well, and doing well when not trying at all made no sense. He seemed to take some pleasure in living a paradox, but he refused to acknowledge that he was playing a game.

There were times during his involvement in Homeroom that Harmon wanted to give up on him. He was extremely frustrating. One of the students, after one session, summarized Matthew, "I don't know if it is just me, but when he talks, I never understand anything he says." His whole communication style was contorted. He spoke to conceal rather than reveal. Harmon lost patience and stopped trying to understand or make sense from his ramblings. Harmon realized that when Matthew said something like "I can't go to the show on Friday night", he meant something quite different from what other people would mean. During his senior year, he did get a car, and he enrolled in a work program. He still enrolled in Homeroom, but could not attend regularly. During the second semester, he did not even enroll. He seemed much happier by then. In a typical gesture for Matthew, he came to see Harmon the day before graduation, "I just wanted to say thank you for your...I mean Homeroom was.... here is a gift for you." He handed Harmon a stick, a four-foot-long stick.

"Thank you." Harmon said, "This is a really nice....stick."

"No, it's a walking cane."

Harmon looked it over and ran his hand over it. "No, it's a stick."

"Well, maybe. But it's really a good stick."

Harmon told Allison about the stick and she laughed, but she had no more insight regarding Matthew than anyone else. No one ever really got a handle on who he was or what he was about. "I don't know if this explains anything or not," Allison offered, "but I saw his SAT scores. He had a 790 on the math part and a 200 on the verbal part."

"Well, I knew he was better in math."

"You don't understand. His math score was almost perfect, 790 out of 800. But his verbal skills could not be worse. You get 200 for putting your name on the paper."

"Are you saying that his problem was that he was...what?...learning disability? Language impairment?"

"I don't know. Maybe."

"No, I don't think so. I mean, that might be part of it. Maybe even a big part, but there was something else, something more."

Two years later, Harmon found a note from Matthew stuffed into his mailbox at school. The letter was stamped but not mailed. Harmon did not understand but he wasn't surprised that Mathew didn't stay to talk to him in person.

Matthew was moving to New York. In his rambling, one-page letter, he changed topics several times and returned to complete thoughts in a random fashion. After reading it several times, Harmon realized it was a thank-you note. In part it read:

"Homeroom was a positive experience. It let me feel <u>not</u> lonely. If only for a small/short amount of time. It helped me to look at my own demons. Even though I didn't bring up all the crap that happened to me in my life. Now I'm in therapy. Since last year. I believe that if it wasn't for Homeroom, I probably would have resisted getting help with my problems."

In the back of Harmon's classroom, on the left-hand side, there is a bookcase. On the top of the bookcase, there is a four-foot stick. Students want to know what the stick is for. He tells them it is a snake lure, that it catches snakes. If they ask, how it works he tells them, "Not very well".

PAUL

No other student attended as many Homerooms as Paul. During his three years in high school, he was in at least two Homerooms each semester, sometimes even more. Paul first enrolled in October of his sophomore year. His mother had requested that he enroll in Homeroom because he did not know anyone at the school. They had learned about the program through Allison. He was the only male in his first Homeroom, and most of the time was spent trashing males. Paul didn't seem to mind. However, by graduation he had seen the complete range of personalities that Homeroom covered. He experienced the full spectrum of Homeroom's diversity. Yet he never offended anyone nor was he obtrusive. He was easy to take for granted because he had a gentleness that everyone came to appreciate more and more during a semester. He interacted with numerous individuals from all the different backgrounds West Side presented, but no one ever said anything bad about Paul. He connected with people with softness and gentility, but not without impact. He was particularly effective in expressing empathy and understanding for females, perhaps because of his parents' divorce. He had been without a father for most of his life, and he said once that the only thing he remembered about his father was the pain he left behind.

Paul had transferred from a small, fundamentalist religious school, the type of school that would take a great deal of searching to find. In Homeroom, Paul had listened to people talk about drug and alcohol use, sexual activity, while Paul himself had come from a very strict religious background. However, not once did he ever say anything judgmental of others. He clearly rejected the values that some professed, and he never compromised his own morality, but he never passed judgment or made anyone else feel defensive. He managed to convey understanding and empathy for others without judging. His previous school expressed his personal values while his new classmates lived a lifestyle he often found morally repugnant, yet he never voiced any conflict between his public image and inner conscience. He exhibited the spirit of his religion rather than the letter of the dogma; he saw the forest instead of the trees, so to speak. Understanding and compassion were more at the core of his belief system than was judgment of others.

Perhaps his open-mindedness could be understood, considering why Paul had transferred from his school. Most of his classmates at the religious school were critical of him, and they decided that Paul was too effeminate for their liking. He was called "queer" and "homo" and all the usual offensive names given to homosexuals. Paul could have handled the name-calling had it not escalated into a divine mission to cure him. The entire school, including the headmaster, took on Paul's salvation as a mission. The more Paul would deny being homosexual, the more effort they would spend on his conversion. Like some bizarre, modern-day witch-hunt, the homophobic crusade had inertia. Despite the fact that there was no evidence to support their accusations, despite the fact of his continued denial, despite the fact that the headmaster eventually came to believe Paul and tried to stop the students, the intensity increased. A petition was signed asking to ban Paul from using the restroom. Rumors spread, and everything was used as fuel to fan the fires: for example, if Paul made a good grade on a history test it was because the test was about Alexander the Great, a known homosexual. His notebooks reflected a homosexual obsession with neatness. The attacks were as absurd as they were intense, and although he wanted to wait them out, they showed no signs of waning. Everything he could think to do was taken as proof of the allegation. "Denial is the first sign of homosexuality."

Eventually, the accusations took a really vicious direction. They began to ask, "If Paul is gay, why is he enrolled in our school? He must have some secret agenda, an agent of some insidious plot." Within one month, Paul ceased to be seen as a productive member of the class. The school moved from seeing him as some poor, little sick kid who needed their help to "a threat to the continued existence of our right to worship as we please". The last phrase was an actual quote from a letter sent to all the parents. When Paul's mother tried to talk to the other parents about the injustice being done to her child, she was treated either as a poor, misguided innocent, too naive to realize the truth, or as the source of Paul's perverse nature, the author of the plot. The headmaster realized the truth too late. The schools perceptions had become the "truth". There was no hope that the situation was going to improve. Even the students who believed him were reluctant to work with him on church projects or in Sunday school.

The church and the school had been very important to Paul. They had provided the strength and direction he needed to cope with his parents' divorce. They had helped him to come to terms with his father's infidelity and immorality. Paul's spiritual quest to know and do the right thing had led him to reject anything resembling his father. He did not want to be guilty of causing another person the pain his father had caused his mother. When the church and school turned against him, he was left adrift and alone. There was no one who could make sense out of his predicament. He prayed. He read the Bible. But each night, he was alone and felt abandoned by his faith. He began to wonder why he was accused and why no one believed his denials. Did they know something he didn't know? Could he be homosexual and not know it; a concept he considered abhorrent? He began to feel guilty, and confused. When the pressure became unbearable, he took a razor blade to his wrist. His former classmates took his suicide attempt as proof of their accusations. When he left the hospital, his mother transferred him into West Side High. She hoped Homeroom would provide some healthy connections with other students.

In Homeroom, Paul's sexual preference was never a subject. He never talked about his experiences at his old school. He made only one reference to his suicide attempt and that was in the context of helping another student.

Paul's mother talked to Harmon at graduation and for the first time revealed the history preceding her son's enrollment at West Side. She expressed a great deal of gratitude for Homeroom. "Before Paul went into the hospital and while he was there, I felt like I'd lost him. Now, I've got him back."

"I didn't do anything, really." Harmon said humbly, but accurately, he believed.

She brushed away a tear. "Well, let me tell you what you didn't do. Paul has six friends, true friends, really good friends. He has another dozen acquaintances that he can hang out with sometimes. And as we were discussing last night, he realized: all of his friends and acquaintances, he met in Homeroom."

That night, as Paul walked across the stage and to get his diploma, Harmon realized that the journey across the stage was not the same distance for everyone. As Paul walked off the stage, he smiled at Harmon and gave a thumbs-up sign.

*Early in his junior year he settled on the one fantasy that was the most reward-
ing, which is to say it produced the highest body count with the most personal
face-to-face violence. The use of bombs planted throughout the school would kill
more, but the destruction would be too impersonal to be rewarding. He wanted to
experience the deaths; he wanted to rub his face in the gore, to viscerally experience it. That was the rewarding part. Bombs just wouldn't cut it. He settled on
shooting his victims in the Hub.*

*He dreamt it, he fantasized it, and then one day he took what he considered a
simple step; he made a plan. The decision to actually act on his fantasy was made
dispassionately. It came to him one evening after supper, between homework
assignments. As soon as he decided to start work on his plan, he made a simple,
short working outline of tasks to complete in order to implement his strategy:*

I.   Gather data to determine best route & time

II.   Select & purchase the best weapon

III.   Practice with weapon (target practice?)

IV.   Determine money needed and make plans for funds

*Under each topic he quickly listed a half-dozen questions and details. He
quickly realized that his project was going to require a great deal of time and work.
At that point, his adrenaline began to surge and he started to feel excitement, so
much so that on that first night he actually got very little sleep as he filled several
pages with plans and questions and directions for further research. Later he got a
notebook for each phase of his project.*

*One notebook was marked: WEAPONS. He gathered articles from magazines
and from the internet on various automatic guns. He organized them based on
size and power and price and difficulty in obtaining. In another section, he organized ads for weapons from newspapers, magazines and local gun shows. He
searched the internet to find other gun shows in adjacent communities, looking for
cheaper and better prices.*

*Another notebook was labeled ROUTE & TIME. His statistics class proven to
be invaluable in this task. One assignment was a long range project of gathering
data of some type and analyzing it. He chose as his project the traffic pattern in the
hallways of West High School. He got permission from his teacher to leave all his
classes early and count the number of students in the hallways between classes
each period and the direction they were traveling. It really only took six days to*

gather all the data, one day for each major hallway spinning off from the Hub both upstairs and downstairs.

By October of his junior year, his plan was beginning to shape up and the more it came together, the more excited and thrilled he became. After looking at all the traffic data, he settled on doing the shooting right before classes would start in the morning. The Hub would be nearly filled with upperclassmen. There would be other periods with higher density of students, but at those times, the students would be moving, classroom doors would be open, and they wouldn't be in the middle of the Hub. The kill rate, he deduced would actually be lower at those times even with the higher number of bodies available.

In the notebook marked WEAPON he put his search for a weapon. He looked at many guns, but the weapon he kept returning to was an Uzi. It was not a large weapon. He did not need a large weapon. It was not a particularly accurate weapon, but accuracy was not something he needed. He needed something that delivered a powerful caliber very quickly, and in that regard the Uzi was the best. It was also the cheapest. Automatic weapons were illegal which only meant that they were going to cost more. There were more than a few used Uzis on the market driving the price into an affordable range.

He went to work at McDonalds to finance his project. It took five months at McDonalds to save enough money, and during the same five months he searched the internet, until he found a gun show where he could buy an Uzi. Early on a Saturday morning, he took a bus to a gun show in another city and bought an Uzi under the table from a contact he made on the internet. He had to work one more month for funds to purchase enough ammunition to kill everyone in the school five times. He immediately quit McDonalds.

He did one target practice only, deep in the woods on the outskirts of town. He shot one magazine, one clip into a group of trees to get the feel of firing as rapidly as possible at close range but with targets at varying depths. He didn't do any more target practices because of the cost. Also, he feared that if he made too much noise he might draw attention and be caught, but the main reason was less complex. He was satisfied with the results. He knew he would not have to be accurate as long as he was rapid. At home, he did practice changing magazines as quickly as possible. He stood in front of his mirror and dropped a clip from the Uzi and loaded another one over and over. He tried various ways of carrying the magazines including in his pants, and pockets, until he settled on a carpenters belt; he could load nearly a dozen clips onto his belt, strapped across his shoulder to his hip with easy access. He had one modified magazine that held 100 rounds, four that held fifty, and the rest held twenty. He briefly toyed with the idea of getting a sec-

ond gun, but he gave up that idea after he realized that he could get off more shots by changing magazines faster than he could by having two guns and not being able to change clips as fast. He would have to be careful with his first 100 shots to make sure that no one could charge him while he was changing his first clip, but after the first one, there should be enough damage near him that no one could reach him in time to threaten him.

His next big challenge was figuring out how to get into the school carrying the weapon and ammunition without being noticed. The ammunition was no problem; he could wear it under his jacket and no one would see it. But the Uzi itself was a potential problem. He thought about carrying it in a box. He figured no one would notice and he would unwrap it at the end of the hallway. But that seemed awkward. Same thing applied to his back pack. The Uzi could barely fit into and it was awkward pulling it out; anything that wasn't smooth might draw attention and threaten his mission. The solution came to him one afternoon while putting on his jacket; it was so bulky. He had one of those big bulky football team jackets. He ripped the lining out of it and tore open the pocket. Now he could carry the Uzi under the jacket with his right hand slid through the pocket onto the trigger. His left hand could hold the jacket closed. When he'd get to the end of the hallway, the left hand would let go, and the right hand would swing the Uzi around, free to fire at will.

His plans were finalized. Now he just practiced, maintained the equipment, and set a date. He decided that a Wednesday would be the best day of the week, and that the spring semester of his senior was the right time, sometime early in May.

CHAPTER 6

TRUTH HAS A MULTIPLE PERSONALITY DISORDER

Harmon finally reached Allison's office. She waved him in, indicating that she would be with him as soon as she completed a form for a student. Her office was as much a place of comfort and warmth to Harmon as it was to the students. The office was small, only about ten feet by ten feet, changing daily in small, subtle ways. On one wall was a corkboard, about three feet wide by four feet high, right above Allison's head when she sat at her desk. On the board were a variety of student pictures, mostly yearbook pictures. There were also pictures of students fishing or camping or working. Cartoons, some drawn by students and some from the newspapers were also on display. There were newspaper headlines describing student accomplishments, and some things so random as to elude any reasonable explanation, like recipes and strange product advertisements. All sorts of things would appear on the board, but nothing ever came down. Each year Allison started with a brand new, empty board. By the end of the year, the board would be filled and Allison would take it home, frame it, and hang it somewhere in her home with the year marked on the bottom.

Her desk was turned to the wall away from the door. Students would sit to her right, and she would swivel in the chair to face them. Her desk never came between her and the students. When she did have to work on her computer or have to do the paper work on her desk, her back was to the door but she could see, by a reflection in her computer screen, anyone at the door. Along the wall to the side of the doorway was a bookcase. Psychology books and counseling texts filled one shelf, along with yearbooks from previous years, guidance manuals, vocational journals, a DSM Manual and comic books. Collections of cartoons, The Far Side Gallery for example, took up an entire shelf. The bookcase was a motley collection showing Allison's wide range of interests and tastes, which summarized Allison herself, a little something for everyone. Above the bookshelves, were about a half-dozen framed documents—diplomas, counseling license, recognitions from the PTA, a certificate from suicide crisis center, and three consecutive certificates of recognition for being named the Most Influential Teacher by a Top-Ten graduate. To her right, across from the corkboard, there were two wooden chairs, and one waste paper basket which could be used as a chair when the office was crowded, although Harmon was the only one who ever used it for that purpose.

The student, his form completed, left the office, and Allison turned to face Harmon, giving her complete attention to him as she did for anyone who was sitting in her office. Harmon liked Allison a lot, but he respected the job she did even more.

"So what's the story with the Martins?" he started off.

"Their son Peter has been having some difficulty, 'academic difficulty'. So they are thinking of transferring schools."

"Academic difficulties?"

She raised her eyebrows. "I think that might be a euphemism. I think he's into drugs, and they want to make sure he has new friends. I gather that in the past they haven't felt that the schools have been responsive to his needs, or perhaps, more accurately, their, needs. They think he needs to be challenged more but that at the same time he needs an atmosphere more user friendly."

"So we are to teach him, stretch him and be his friend."

"That about sums it up. Let it be a challenge."

"Mrs. Martin looks like she might be a card carrying member of the Cult of Uniformity."

"No, I don't think so. More like victims of the Cult."

He pretended to play an invisible organ as he hummed horror movie music, "Dum, dum, dum, dum."

She joined him on the chorus. "Everyone is a victim to the Cult."

After they both laughed, he said, "He reminds me of Raymond."

Allison wrinkled her face at the mention of Raymond. "I don't think they are at all alike; we are at least assured that Peter is completely human."

"Oh I didn't say they were alike, which is what makes me think of Raymond."

"I can't believe he graduated last year, I mean, before someone killed him."

Raymond was one of the few students with whom Allison did not seem to bond. She didn't exactly dislike Raymond, but he would never make her list of favorite students, but then, not many people were fond of Raymond. In fact most people actively hated him. Raymond was good at generating negative reactions, perhaps even a genius at doing so. Harmon, of course, enjoyed him immensely. During Raymond's sophomore year, several different teachers asked Harmon to enroll him in Homeroom to get him out of their classes. Although he was flattered to receive a faculty referral, he soon realized that the referrals were not so much testimonials to Homeroom than they were desperate attempts to remove Raymond from their classrooms even if only for one day per week. Raymond was disruptive in ways that confounded even the most experienced teacher; he was extremely bizarre.

The German teacher, for example, reported, "One time I passed back a test, and Raymond jumped up from his desk and yelled, 'There is a God after all!' He'd made a passing grade, for Christ sake. No one in class thought he was funny. No one laughed. They all thought he was crazy."

His geography teacher, after one lecture, asked the class if there were any questions. "Raymond raised his hand and politely said, 'What is reality? Is there a life after death?' It was so random, so inappropriate, so weird; no one laughed."

His math teacher added, "He is always saying these weird, inappropriate comments that no one thinks is funny. The whole class hates him."

His English teacher found him walking the halls during third period, trembling, shaking almost uncontrollably because he couldn't get his locker open and was going to be late, for class, a class for which he never did any homework. The vice-principal had called him in the office twice for fighting. The first time he had slapped a girl. The girl had called him stupid in class. He waited until after class and the bell had rung. When he was sent to the dean Raymond said, "I didn't think that the teacher had any jurisdiction if an altercation happened in the hallway after her class was over". In the other fight, Raymond was shaking and hyperventilating so intensely that he could not actually hit the other student. He ended up trying to kick him and falling on his own face. In light of all of these reports of Raymond's troubling behavior, Harmon immediately enrolled him in one of the Homerooms.

Appearance wise, Raymond looked like a throwback to the forties. His hair was long and wavy but stuck straight up. He wore shirts with the collars all flattened on his neck like wings on a dead bird. He did wear jeans but they were always too long and he would roll the legs up into cuffs the way elementary school kids did. Sporadically he seemed very bright, as evidenced by his achievement tests, but his grades were, at best, borderline. Usually he failed one or two classes each grading period. He would alternate which classes he would fail and by the end of the year he would manage to have a passing average in every class. He had a peculiar sense of humor that centered on puns and off-the-wall comments. The other students either did not get his jokes or did not consider them funny or both.

As intelligent as Raymond seemed to be, he completely lacked any social skills. The fact that no one laughed, liked or even tolerated his jokes never once stopped him from saying them. He would blurt out jokes and comments whenever they would spring into his consciousness, regardless of the setting. Teachers and students were unanimous in their rejection of his comments, but that never thwarted his resolve. Raymond could not understand why anyone was mad at him, and at the same time, he became rather paranoid, which may have had some basis in reality. His belief that everyone was picking on him prevented him from realizing that there was any connection between his behavior and the way people responded to him. He was the victim, so he thought, of random acts of hostility. In all his classes, Raymond became the scapegoat for classroom frustration.

On one hand, Raymond often deluded himself into thinking that the other students liked his jokes. Their moans to him were signs of approval. On the other hand, he saw their overt hostility as proof that they did not like him, and he was right. He had this strange double-think; he thought everyone laughed with him while he felt that everyone hated him. His paranoia, not exactly delusional, developed into a sort of self-fulfilling prophecy. He seemed to have alienated every classmate at one time or another. For example, he began hanging out in A 216, Harmon's classroom during lunch. Several other students were coming to the room to eat their lunch, also. At one time or another, as many as half a dozen students were hanging out during lunch. Raymond would often spend the entire lunch period pacing up and down the rows of the classroom. By the end of the semester, he had driven off most of the other students. One girl, who would come consistently, was a very gentle person, quite timid actually, and soft-spoken. Sometimes she would bring a guitar and sing, gentle, peaceful folk songs, to herself mostly. Raymond would listen intensely.

He loved her music, but he would irritate her by making requests and interrupting her songs. One day he was pacing through most of her repertoire, when he finally stopped within six inches of her and just stood watching her, grinning through two or three songs. Finally, she could not bear it any longer and she looked at him with her beautiful dark eyes and softly said, "Raymond, if you don't get away from me, I'm going to break my guitar over your head." He laughed uproariously, never realizing that she meant it, and that she was genuinely upset by his behavior.

Harmon tried to get Raymond to see the connection between his behavior and the rejections he received from the other students, but he could never accept it. Raymond was the only exception Harmon ever made to being nondirective in Homerooms. On several occasions, Harmon was very directive with Raymond but with little constructive results. Raymond never seemed to respond to Harmon's efforts. However, there was something resembling growth in Raymond. The first year in Homeroom, he could neither give nor receive warm fuzzies. When the time came to share them, Raymond was mute. By his senior year, he was very adept at giving them. His compliments showed insight and sensitivity that he didn't reveal anywhere else or at any other time. He had gained some social skills. After his graduation, Harmon received a letter of thanks from Raymond's mother. Raymond's sophomore year had been his last chance, and his parents had been about to institutionalize him when he first enrolled in Homeroom. In her letter, his mother stated that Homeroom was all that stood between Raymond and an indefinite stay in a mental hospital. She said that Homeroom had made a positive impact on his life. Allison was not quite so sure. Even if Raymond hadn't exactly alienated Allison, he had managed to push her far enough away that she felt relieved when he graduated. She did not expect him to come and visit her after graduation.

"I always looked at Raymond as proof that birth control should be retroactive." Allison began with that look that indicated she was serious. "I don't want to reminisce about Raymond, as rewarding as that might be. I need an update on Cindy."

Allison did not usually ask about a student. Usually it was Harmon who did the asking. Cindy had been the source of many discussions between Allison and Harmon, but he knew that Allison's question was an indication of something serious.

Cindy, a senior, had been in Homeroom since the spring semester of her sophomore year, when she had enrolled at the urging of Mrs. McKinney, an English teacher. McKinney knew about Homeroom, and she felt that Cindy had much to offer the program. McKinney had known Cindy in junior high and was aware of the remarkable transformation she had made in high school. Harmon interpreted this to mean that Cindy had matured out of the developmental malaise known as junior high school and invited her to join Homeroom. Harmon's first impression of the sophomore Cindy was that she was very pretty, very peppy and very short. She only stood about 4'1" and weighed maybe 80 pounds. She had very short blond hair that was cut almost like a boy's. She approached everything with a bubbly energy that was contagious. She soon became one of the most visible members of the sophomore class. Her favorite expression, which she used with incredible frequency, was "wowzer". In her first Homeroom, one of the other girls described her as a living aloe vera plant, "very soothing, very healing and very cute". She was in effect a pixie, a real life Tinkerbell.

But she was more than cute. Cute is quick and superficial. Cindy touched people; she touched some people deeply, and she touched people in profound and unique ways. For example, she had one class with Raymond and while everyone else picked on him, she alone stood up for him. One day even the teacher was picking on him. "No one thinks you're funny," the teacher said to Raymond. "No one even likes you." Cindy stood up in front of the class and said, "I like him; he's my friend!" She could say something like that and the rest of the class would be put on notice. The next week she even had a valentine delivered to Raymond during class. Raymond, being Raymond, never said thanks or realized the social risk she took in sending him the valentine, but the student body and Harmon were awed at her ability to stick up for a social leper like Raymond. In a school where being unpopular was a crime, Cindy was not afraid to be a friend nor would she avoid the risk of being unpopular. That first year, she referred three other students to Homeroom, and she seemed to be instrumental in preventing one suicide attempt. Very quickly Allison saw Cindy as a foot soldier in the war against the Cult, the first line of defense. Harmon was convinced she was an Angel in the Snow.

But during her junior year, a darker side to Cindy surfaced, and in some ways, she was even more impressive as it became clear that there were obstacles she had overcome. During one of her Homerooms the subject was sex education. Cindy reported, "You want to know where I learned about sex? I'll tell you. I was seven or eight. School got out early because of some teacher meetings or something. I walked home and found my dad in bed with some other woman. I walked right in the middle. The woman was screaming, and when she saw me, she screamed differently, if you know what I mean. Dad jumped out of bed and pushed me into the other room. He leaned over in front of me and was yelling that I couldn't tell Mom what I'd just seen. Now I'm about two feet tall and all I can see is his private parts dangling in front of me as he's yelling at me. I'm crying, the woman left, and I asked Dad questions while still crying. Dad didn't know what to say to me except to try to make me promise not to tell. He promised me an ice cream cone, and I finally calmed down. He never explained anything to me, but the images taught me a whole lot more than I wanted to know, and I became an expert on sex to all the other kids throughout grade school. I never told on Dad, but Mom discovered him in the same situation a couple of months later."

The group didn't know whether to laugh or cry. Somebody said something to convey empathy, and Cindy continued. "Actually that was one of my more pleasant memories of Dad. Dad is a drunk. I've seen him drunk more often than I've seen him sober. Mom would go to work early in the morning, and he would come home all tanked up from a binge. He'd wait until she left for work before he'd come home. So usually I helped put him into bed before I left for school in the morning. More than once, I had to clean up his vomit before I left. That was first and second grade for me. When she finally caught him cheating, we left. That was in third grade. We moved here. Divorce, no child support payments ever made. I haven't talked or seen Dad for what, seven years? I take that back, he has called twice. Both times he wanted money to get out of jail."

The group was stunned. Harmon was stunned. No one had any idea of what to say next. Cindy finally broke the silence with her customary, "Wowzer! Don't go getting all serious on me. I've learned a lot. My childhood wasn't so bad. My mother and me got real close. We are bestest friends."

The last statement was not completely true; their relationship was not without troubles. Her mother seemed to be the exact opposite of Cindy, "the anti-Cindy" as one of her friends called her. Her Mother hated schools and education in general. To her, school was the enemy and she could not understand how Cindy could have anything resembling school spirit. While Cindy was always cheerful and full of energy, her mother's defining characteristics seemed to be bitterness and laziness. "Her career ambition is to be declared disabled so that she won't ever have to work, and she's pretty pissed that she hadn't succeeded ye." Cindy once confessed.

The negative side of their relationship became clear in March during Cindy's junior year. Cindy startled Homeroom that particular day by announcing that her mother had beaten her up the night before. She said this with a smile on her face and with her usual "Wowzer!" The group had been talking about relationships with parents so her comment was germane to the discussion, but it still seemed odd.

"What happened?" someone asked.

"Mom has been transferred to another store on the other side of the city, a 45 minute commute through traffic. Last night she says she was tired of the trip, and we'll be moving. So I says I don't want to move. Why, she says. I says I like my school, and she hits the ceiling. She says I'm selfish and that a school is a stupid thing to be loyal to. We start screaming at each other. She hits me in the face. I hit her back and we're duking it out." All of this was said with the same cheery facial expression and effervescent tone of voice as all her other stories, but no one thought she was saying anything funny.

"What, what happened next?"

"She hits me and I kind of kneel down and then she jumps on me. I mean she is like sitting on me, screaming and banging my head on the floor. Nathan shows up then; we were going to a church meeting. He pulls her off of me and stands between us. Nathan ends up crying and trying to settle her down. We didn't go to the meeting. We sat out in front of my house and I cried in his arms until, well really, until this morning. When Mom left for work, I went in and got dressed for school. Nathan is so wonderful! Wowzer! He comforted me and let me cry. His dad is a real successful lawyer; he is going to check on me becoming an emancipated teenager."

"What about your mother?"

When the words hit Cindy's ear, Harmon briefly caught a glimpse of a Cindy he had never seen before. "That frigging bitch! If she ever touches me again, I'll kill her! I frigging mean it. She ain't gonna ruin my life. She says I'm stupid to stay at this school. She ain't never had no school spirit. She don't understand. Well, I've come too far to give this up; she's frigging out of her mind if she thinks I'm leaving for her job!"

Her language and her intense rage, along with her lack of grammar, was startling. If Harmon had suddenly seen a glimpse of the real Cindy, he was aware that it must have taken a great deal of effort for Cindy to suppress the passion he had witnessed.

The next week Cindy was back to her usual self, and when asked what happened with her mother, she shrugged. "Nathan is going to lend his car to my mom, for the rest of the school year so she can make it to her job. He has a Beamer, you know, BMW. Wowzer! Her car was the real problem." Harmon didn't know what to think. He wasn't sure whether the problem itself or its resolution was the greater shock. Harmon was dumbfounded. This would become a common reaction to Cindy over the next couple of years. He did not know how to process the whole situation or what part was even the most amazing to him—that Nathan, a senior in high school, would sacrifice his car for the benefit of his girlfriend's mother, or that his parents would allow it, or that Cindy's mother would actually accept the offer.

Another time during her junior year, Cindy revealed more about her past. She stated, "I was in ..umm..some trouble in junior high, and since then..well, my mom has to ..sort of keep tabs on me."

"I don't understand." Harmon sought clarification.

"Well, it was a long time ago and I don't want to go into details. Let's just say that it was part of the court deal that my mother has to report, you know, my comings and goings."

"What did you do?"

"Just the usual junior high stuff, you know. I drank and did drugs and all that junior high stuff."

"Junior high stuff?"

"Well, I got into some fights, a little vandalism, too. But it was four years ago. It will be five in August and the probation will be over. I don't do that kind of stuff no more. I really cleaned up my act in high school. I've never been suspended or even had a detention. My grades are good. No, great! I'm going to graduate with an A average. Except math. Wowzer! I don't know if I can get through calculus!"

Cindy had revealed all that she was going to reveal. The conversation was over. Even if she was a little guarded, she seemed to have made some major adjustments and turned her life around, and Harmon could not help but be even more impressed. At that point, Harmon discussed Cindy with Allison, and they both were impressed by the way Cindy had overcome her past. However, later that spring, Harmon's favorable view of Cindy was shattered.

Raymond had insulted and embarrassed Cindy with some remarks in speech class. Two days later, she hid in the hallway and jumped Raymond, breaking his nose. Undoubtedly Raymond had done something to provoke her; he could be awfully annoying. In fact, all the other students took Cindy's side. What bothered Harmon was not so much that Cindy had lost her temper, or even that she had resorted to violent behavior; it was the fact that she was so efficient. There was something very calculating and secretive about the attack. She had apparently waited for him in a hallway when no one was around. She struck swiftly and quietly and no one could ever prove she had been the assailant, although no one ever really doubted it. Cindy never received any punishment or discipline for the attack because no authority could ever prove what had happened, and Raymond, uncharacteristically, refused to incriminate Cindy. The general feeling was the Cindy had done the deed, but there had been no witnesses. In Homeroom, Cindy never denied the attack. But when Harmon expressed that he really thought that the attack was wrong, she became defensive and changed the subject to Raymond's behavior. The episode caused Harmon to question his views of Cindy. The high regard he held her in during her sophomore year was diminished. When Allison asked about Cindy, his first inclination was to avoid the subject, but he and Allison had discussed Cindy too many times during the past few years for him to be able to ignore the subject.

"Well, to tell you the truth, Cindy is a mystery to me, the depth and width of which continues to grow for me. She's still in Homeroom, but I'm not at all sure she is getting anything from it. On the first day when I asked everyone what they expected to happen in Homeroom, she said, 'Nothing'. She said it in such a cold, dispassionate way that the whole Homeroom was off to a negative start. Later, I asked her what she meant, and she said she was just trying to say that she didn't have any expectations and was willing to let Homeroom develop, 'Go with the flow', as she put it. But I wasn't convinced. Currently she's doing crossword puzzles during Homeroom. I don't know why she continues to come, but she never misses."

Allison responded in a flat tone. "The crossword puzzles are from her SAT class. Her teacher said that crossword puzzles were a good way to increase her vocabulary for the SAT. She takes every little hint from her teacher as if they were biblical. She wants to double her SAT score."

"That figures. She says her SAT scores are a little too low for Stanford."

"Her SAT scores are a little to low for any college. She will be lucky to be accepted anywhere, and if she doesn't pass the state math proficiency exam, she won't be graduating. She's flunked it three times."

"I thought she was in calculus."

"Is that what she said? She is in remedial math."

"But her GPA is above an A average."

"Yeah. If she gets in to college it will be because of her grades. She is a hard worker. She is an example of something I used to think didn't really exist: an overachiever." Allison was shaking her head as she spoke.

"That makes some sense. When she took my class, she made an A because her homework grades were so high, but I don't think she ever really passed a test."

"Did she do her homework? I mean, was it her work?"

"Yeah. I think so. Well, I don't know for sure. No, at least, most of it was her own work."

"Most?"

"Maybe some. It is hard to monitor something like that."

"Yeah. I know, especially with Cindy." Allison dropped her head slightly, and Harmon could sense something was really bothering her, something out of the ordinary.

He wasn't sure what to say, so they sat in silence for a few minutes. Allison still had that far-away look.

"You know," he started, "when she was a sophomore I thought she was really someone special."

"I nominated her for the city council student representative."

"Every once in awhile, there are moments, when she seems just as impressive. But the moments seem farther and farther apart."

"Oh?"

"Well when Alicia died, Cindy really helped some students cope. I saw her giving support and comfort to several people and not only in Homeroom. The district sent in all those support experts to help the student body deal with the loss…"

Allison nodded slowly. "The emotion police. It's district policy whenever there is a trauma, like Alicia's death, they are sent in to help the student body cope. They really are highly trained and good people."

"Yes, but Cindy was in all their support groups helping students. She was a great comfort. I even saw her in the hallway comforting Coach Monroe," Harmon added.

"Yeah, she was great, and she missed all of her classes for almost four days. She managed to convince her teachers that she was up late talking to students each night for over a week. The teachers gave her a lot of slack, and she used it. Only, the experts left the campus after two days saying that the student body was coping as well as could be expected. All the vulnerable students had made emotional contacts. Alicia had been very religious so most of her friends went to church, and that helped. No one can figure who Cindy was talking to each night. If there was that much unexpressed grief, I think I would have known."

Harmon wasn't sure whom he was trying to convince, but he found himself defending her. "Maybe she exaggerated and maybe she lied and maybe she didn't help that many people, but she did help. She did make the situation better, not worse."

"I know, I know. That's what so hard. She's not a bad influence in this school. If anything, she has brought a great deal of cohesiveness to the student body."

"I mean, she was elected cheerleader and student council officer."

"With more votes than anyone in school history," she said.

"She has a big following. Every type of student likes her."

"Some of that is due to her junior high school history. All the druggies did drugs with her and they see her being a cheerleader as some sort of validation."

"Better living through chemistry." Harmon sighed.

"The same is true for her student council election. I was surprised that she wasn't elected Homecoming queen. Has she ever talked to you about the student council?" Allison asked.

"Just the typical Cindy thing. Everyone was jealous of her popularity. No one liked her."

"Did she tell you she was kicked off?"

"No."

"She missed all the regular meetings. She would call meetings for her committees and then never show up at the meetings. That happened several times. The sponsor talked to her about it, the other officers talked to her about it."

"But in typical Cindy fashion, she thought that they were attacking her." He could picture Cindy retelling the story.

"You think so?" Allison wondered.

"Yeah. I've seen that side of her. If someone is critical of her, she sees it as a personal attack. When I told her I thought her hitting Raymond was wrong, I didn't think she would ever talk to me again or join Homeroom again this year."

"She didn't show up at the football game with East High."

"Didn't show up?" Harmon was dumbfounded. "That's the biggest game of the year against the arch rival? You're kidding."

"Her mother bought her tickets to a rock concert."

"A rock concert?"

"REM. They don't tour that often. The tickets were hard to get. Mother had tried so hard. It would crush mother. Ya da, ya da, ya da."

"Well, to tell the truth, I've always had difficulty seeing her as a cheerleader. She told me last year during tryouts that she wasn't going to let cheerleading define her and dominate her whole life."

"The rest of the cheerleaders and Mrs. Larkin have about had it with her. She misses practice regularly. Her latest excuse is play rehearsals. She tells the drama teacher that Mrs. Larkin doesn't want her to be in the play. She tells Larkin that she'll be cut from the play if she misses a rehearsal. She's in one scene and has one line. Larkin and the drama teacher don't talk to each other or they would find out that Cindy is playing each one against the other."

"Allison, what are you telling me? I know she has a tendency to exaggerate and to interpret things in a questionable way, but I think she just sees things in a warped sort of a way. I don't think she lies as much as she just…..sees things in a self-serving way."

"Maybe you are right," Allison said as she looked down at her hands in her lap. She cracked her knuckles. "I hope you are right. I want to think you are right, but have you seen her Honors and Awards Form?"

"You mean that thing all the seniors fill out to inform the school about scholarships and awards they've received?"

"Yeah. Well she has listed over $200,000 worth of scholarships."

"How much does she really have?"

"Maybe $2,000 from a grocery chain, and she qualifies for some student loans. She applied for this scholarship from the grocery store when her mother worked for them. Her competition was other clerks and children of employees. Very few class officers and cheerleaders to compete with. Then she later applied for loans when her mother was unemployed and qualified for them. The best of both worlds," Allison said as she looked around the room.

"A lot of students exaggerate and make outlandish claims on those forms. Todd claimed a $50,000 scholarship from Yale for General Coolness."

"The only scholarship Yale would give Todd would be a scholarship to attend Harvard."

"Well, you know what I mean. It is a joke for most of them."

"There is a difference. Cindy has never retracted her claims. I think she wants people to believe them."

"Or maybe she wants to believe them." He made direct eye contact with Allison.

"Or maybe she needs to believe them." She returned his eye contact. "She told me that state university lost her application, that she was rejected by mistake. She said the registrar apologized to her for the mistake but that it was too late to affect her admissions this next year. She was promised a scholarship for next year. Truth is, she can't get into the state university. Her grades aren't high enough to cover her low SAT scores."

"So is she lying to us, or is she delusional?"

"Well, I don't know, but have you noticed that with every part-time job she has had, she ends up being fired because the other workers were jealous of how well she was doing and how much the boss liked her?"

"Her sophomore year I believed her." Harmon sighed as he lowered his head and stared at the floor.

"Her junior year I believed that she needed to see things that way." Allison's voice trailed off in resignation.

"And now you think maybe she is just a liar, plain and simple?"

"Not plain and simple, no. Nothing about her is simple."

Allison sighed and gazed looking over Harmon's shoulder at the wall to his left. Neither knew what to say next, but they both sensed that closure had not been reached. Harmon broke the silence. "She still has a lot of people who believe in her."

"Yeah, I know," Allison said. "Like her boyfriends. She never seems to have difficulty attracting them."

"Yeah, but each one is younger than the last. Nathan was a senior while she was a sophomore; Freddy was a junior when she was a junior. Now this guy Bernie is a sophomore, while she is a senior."

"And their GPAs seems to get lower each year." Allison shrugged her shoulders.

"Each one seems more and more desperate or clinging or something. I gather this Bernie has never dated anyone else before."

"Somehow as a senior, a cheerleader you'd think she would be attracting a more popular, or visible element. I've asked some of the guys why they don't ask her out, but I don't get any consistent answers."

"She scares some guys."

"Yeah, some, but she also says no to a lot of guys that other girls would say yes to."

"You think she's afraid of them?"

"You know, about those boyfriends of hers, she was the one that broke up with each of them. I never could understand it. Nathan, for example. He was great for her. He would do anything for her. I think he still would. I mean, how many guys would give their car to their girlfriend's mother?" Allison added.

"Did you know that Freddie's dad paid for all of the college applications she sent?"

"I didn't know that. Are you saying that you think she only uses these guys?" Harmon responded with doubt in his voice.

"She uses them, but I don't think it is that simple."

"Allison, I had reached some sort of compromise in my dealings with Cindy. I had come to see her in some different light, but what your're telling me is....beyond anything I had thought of her."

"Yeah, normally I wouldn't go into details like this. It is kind of a breach of confidentiality, but I was hoping you could share some light on her. I fear that we might be coming to some sort...of denouement."

He was stunned, "What do you mean?"

"She seems more desperate the closer she gets to graduation. I think we have fulfilled some sort of....some need for her, and I'm not sure she can deal with its absence. I'm afraid that Cindy seems to have lost whatever grasp she had on things."

He thought that over. "I don't know if I can shed any light on anything. She really hasn't talked about much in Homeroom this year. She's shared a few battle stories about junior high. I take that back. A couple of weeks ago, she cried in Homeroom. Come to think of it, that was the only time I've ever heard her cry. Let me see if I can remember the circumstances. Oh yeah, she was talking about her boyfriend's family. They blame her for his bad grades and the fact that he is smoking. She was saying that the mother gossips behind her back and makes up stories."

"How did the group respond to her?"

"They were very supportive. They told her that Bernie's mother was wrong not to realize what a special person she was. That's when she cried. "I'm not a bad person," she said."

Allison nodded, "Let me tell you the other side of the story. Bernie's mother called me and wanted to talk about Bernie and Cindy. She does not blame Cindy for Bernie's grades or for the smoking. She does object to the sex; mothers are like that. She came home for lunch a few weeks ago and found them in bed. She wanted to know how they got out of school and if this is a regular thing. Cindy is a teacher's aide for Miss Winslow, the space cadet. Apparently, they have been meeting daily for the entire semester."

"What does Cindy get from him?"

Allison just looked at Harmon.

"Okay. Dumb question."

Harmon wasn't really shocked or surprised. He had guessed Cindy had been sexually active in junior high school and he had thought she might still be, but he was not prepared for this level of activity. He remembered once during her sophomore or maybe it was her junior year she revealed that her hero was Marilyn Monroe. "Wowzer!" she had said. "I identify with Marilyn Monroe, a slut with class." It was funny at the time. Her recent words and tears took on new meaning also, "I'm not a bad person," she had said.

"You know, Allison, this conversation is really depressing."

She nodded, but he was the first to speak, "Were we that stupid two years ago, or has she changed that much?"

"Both. Maybe."

"You know for a long time now, she has suffered a crisis of credibility as far as I'm concerned, but I've never known how to deal with her. First of all, I've never been sure if she just exaggerated things on purpose or if she just saw things in self-serving ways. From what you are saying it is hard not to see her as being malicious. But I'm not sure how in control of her deceptions she is."

"I know what you mean. Is she aware of how dishonest she is?"

"I guess to me the question is does she have a choice? Could she face reality if she had to, or is fabricated reality her only defense?"

"I don't know. Maybe both," Allison hesitated. "Maybe it's some of both."

"What do we, I do? I have never figured out how to deal with lies. I've told you before; this is the biggest weakness in Homeroom. And Homeroom is not really about confrontation. Should I continue to give her support even though she doesn't deserve it? Deserve is the wrong word. Warrant. If I don't confront her and continue to just give emotional support, am I not enabling her?"

"How would you confront her? How could you?"

"Good questions. Most of her deceptions would require somebody playing Sherlock Holmes to discredit them. Then some of them would require breaching confidentiality. For example, I can't tell her what Bernie's mother said, and even if I did, she would just say that the mother was lying and I have no concrete proof. You see what I mean?"

Allison was nodding the whole time Harmon spoke, and then she added, "Usually, in the past, when I've had students who lie to me, I approach them by asking for their help. I say something like, 'I really have some difficulty understanding why you would feel a need to lie to me like this. Can you help me?' Usually that works, but when I've attempted to talk to Cindy like that, she refuses to acknowledge any dishonesty or deception. The fact, that she is so adamant in her denials is why I question if she knows what is true or not."

"So what do I do?"

"Actually I was hoping you would provide some answers for me."

Suddenly Harmon was thrust into a new position, one of counseling the counselor. He knew Allison respected him, but he was always the one needing guidance, not her. This role reversal was a little unsettling. He wasn't sure what to say, but he tried, "I don't see confrontation as having much likelihood of success. She might need confrontation, along with some extensive therapy. But we can't really provide either."

Allison nodded, but said nothing.

Harmon continued to speak, "Cindy's needs are greater than we can provide. That sounds cold. But when she entered this school, she was the classic 'at risk' kid. Her chances of completing high school, not to mention succeeding, were slim. Now she is going to graduate and go to college. And she will have a good academic background. All these other issues are beyond our ability. Not that she doesn't need help. I have told her more than once, and I bet you have too, that at some point I think she needs to see a professional therapist. She agrees but says she can't afford it right now."

Allison nodded and sort of looked away at the same time. She looked rather misty eyed, but her body language indicated resignation more than sadness. She stared at the wall for what seemed like an awfully long time before she spoke. "When I was in graduate school, I worked with this one girl who had a lot of potential. She had a creative, bright mind, but was on her way to becoming a dropout. I worked with her a whole semester, but in the spring, she got herself pregnant and dropped out. I was devastated, and I talked to my mentor about it. He was very understanding and tried to comfort me. He said that you can't live other people's lives for them. He told me that the real problem with this job is that you can't stop people from doing self-defeating behaviors; no matter how hard you try. Caring doesn't guarantee success. He said all those counseling clichés that I'd heard before, knew they were true, and yet didn't understand them emotionally. Then he said something that really did make a difference. He said, "Sometimes being a counselor is like being a parachute, you just slow the descent." I can't solve all the problems my students bring in here. Sometimes I just slow down their fall."

A silence hung over the room for a few minutes as the emotional impact of what she had said settled in. Then he broke the silence and the mood. "That's it? Frankly, Allison, I was expecting more from you."

Allison raised her eyebrows in a gesture of resignation. Then she laughed and changed the subject. "Why are you here in the first place? What did you come in here for? What do you want?"

"Well, I just met with Randich. He informed me of the fate of Homeroom. There won't be any next year."

"Budget, right?"

"Yeah."

"I can't say I'm surprised, but I am disappointed. Is there anything I can do? Do you want me to talk to him, or write a letter, or get some parents to write?"

"I have one chance. I'm supposed to make a presentation to the Board; prove that Homeroom should be continued. Got any ideas of what I should say or how to should say it?"

"It's hard to assess Homeroom. I know it is doing a good job, but it is hard to articulate what it accomplishes. Well, the thing is, you see," Allison said in a halting fashion that was uncharacteristic of her, "you have to think like a trustee. The only things those people respect are numbers. If you can't count it, it ain't real." She lapsed into her garage mechanic voice. "You got your basic Homeroom, and the trouble is you ain't got nothing to count. You give me something I can count, that I can add and subtract and maybe even divide, and your talkin' real data. If you're looking at a 50 or 75 or over a hundred, doesn't matter what your counting, but the bigger the number the better—you give me something with a 1500 attached—it doesn't matter what—you're lookin' at Homeroom for another two, three years. Seriously, the board needs to justify its actions and numbers are the only tool they have. And let's face it, especially in our community, there are a whole bunch of people whose only reality comes attached to numbers. You know, the only things they respect are measurable."

Harmon smiled, "The Cult of Uniformity strikes again. But how do you measure something like Homeroom? I mean, it's hard to say what it does, and even harder to prove it. You know, like I think we've made a difference concerning suicides, but I can't tell you how many people didn't commit suicide because of Homeroom."

"I think it makes a difference in drug and alcohol consumption too, but you can't measure how much wasn't drunk or snorted."

"Exactly. How do you measure a non behavior? And how do you put a number on loneliness? How do you convince people that loneliness has been affected?"

"Or that affecting loneliness is a worthwhile goal? The Cult of Uniformity might have trouble buying into that one."

"What are the objectives of Homeroom?" Allison asked.

"I don't know."

"What do you want to see change when a student finishes a Homeroom?"

"It beats me."

"What do you want to accomplish?"

Harmon sat in silence.

Allison couldn't understand his silence. "How do you intend to prove the value of Homeroom if you don't know what you are trying to do? As far as that goes, how do you even know if Homeroom works if you can't define working? I mean, what would you measure if you could measure anything?"

Harmon hesitated, staring at the floor before carefully, slowly, and deliberately he answered, "I don't want to frustrate you, and I'm not trying to play some coy game. It's not that I'm incapable of articulating any direction. But I can't tell you how much I really reject the kind of thinking you are advocating; it's like a page from the Cult of Uniformity Manual. It's not so much that I don't have an answer as it is that I reject the question."

Harmon looked up at Allison, and if she didn't realize he was serious before, she now realized his seriousness by the intensity in his eyes. "I purposely do not have an objective for Homeroom. I don't want to have an objective for Homeroom. I want Homeroom to free people from other people's objectives, including my own."

To his embarrassment, he found his voice gaining volume with every statement. He tried to return to a quiet decorum, but his passion was greater than the success of his efforts to control his emotions, and he became even more definitive as he spoke. "My only objective is to have no objectives. I don't want to pre-establish any goals for the students. If anything, I want them to come up with their own objectives. I want them to author their own changes."

"But you have to have some sort of idea of what you want to accomplish. You can't just…" She left her thought unfinished.

"Can't just what? Relate? Why not? Maybe, just maybe, the best thing I can do for my students is not to select the course of their life, but rather respect their own ability to make those decisions. You know the old saying: "You are free to change, only if you are free to remain the same". I believe that. I don't want Homeroom to be an instrument of change as much as I want it to be an opportunity for students to direct their own change if they choose to change, heavy emphasis on choose. In the meantime, my efforts will not be wasted on getting them to live up to my expectations, fulfilling my sense of who they should be. I'm not qualified to make those kinds of decisions even if I wanted to. I mean, who is?"

Allison was shaken by the intensity of his remarks and seemed momentarily stunned, but she quickly regained her composure and continued to push for a focus to Homeroom, "You are going to have a hard time getting the Board to buy into a program that just lets kids…hang out. I mean, what is that? You have to have some sort of goal for them. I mean, how can you not have some sort of goal? You can't tell me that if you have a kid on drugs, you don't want him to stop using? Well, that is a goal!"

He sighed, a very long, defeated sigh. "Let me put it to you another way: the best way to get a student to stop using drugs is to recognize his freedom to make those choices. In my opinion, my humble opinion—I don't have experience in a therapeutic mode, only in a school setting—the worst thing you can do is try to force him to change because then he will become defensive and come up with a million reasons to support his continued use."

"I realize that my approach may not be appropriate in a rehabilitation setting, dealing with addicts or alcoholics or any of the hardcore drug users. Incidentally, I haven't seen too much evidence that anything else works. I mean what is the failure rate for those drug programs? It seems like there are two or three failures for every success, and usually the successes attend more than one program before they succeed."

"Anyway, conceding that my approach is not always the right approach for the hardcore drug user, I'm not dealing with that kind of population. I don't have any crackheads in Homeroom, no heroin addicts, no gang members, and if some drink too much, it is still debatable whether they have arrived, or are even on their way, to becoming alcoholics, and I would argue that my approach is best for avoiding traveling down that road."

He knew he was becoming too passionate, and he wanted to move in a more intellectual direction, less emotional. "Look, since the start, Homeroom has been guided by the nondirective model of teaching. The creation of a psychologically safe environment is the only identified goal. Learning objectives, as usually stated, are not the goal. That would be Cult thinking. That students will discover their own objectives is the primary assumption of Homeroom. Therefore, Homeroom was created without any learner outcomes in mind. Homeroom attempts to create an environment that manifests the three characteristics that Carl Rogers theorized as necessary for a psychological growth: empathy, unconditional positive regard, and genuineness on the part of the teacher. I just try to create, no, allow these traits to exist with the belief that the students then will be able to identify their own personal goals. I want to communicate that I have no preconceived notion of the direction in which students should grow or how they should 'be'. To create an objective research instrument to evaluate Homeroom would require defining the learner outcomes, which would be the complete antithesis of Homeroom."

Harmon thought about saying that he wanted to create an environment where he could nurture angels, where he could watch them spread their wings, where he could see them spring forth from students and take flight, but he was pretty sure Allison would not understand and she might even think that he was crazy. He decided to continue to talk rationally. "Homeroom is designed to impact the subjective perceptions of the students. No other criteria have been articulated. If the students value the experience, then there was value by definition, and the program has met its stated goals. The student perception of the program is the primary concern."

Allison was impressed by Harmon's ability to articulate Homeroom's direction. She was also surprised. Most of the time, her exchanges with Harmon were casual and clever. She sometimes forgot the intelligence behind his actions. He might be a jester, but he was not a fool.

Harmon feared that he had been too emphatic in his defense of Homeroom. He felt a need to apologize before continuing. "I'm sorry if I sound hostile, but I believe very strongly that we'd all be better off if we stopped trying to help students so much and started putting more energy into communicating with them. Let's listen to them rather than always talking at them.

"I mean, I'm not saying that my approach is the only approach. I'm not even sure that it is always the best approach. I'm sure there is sometimes, perhaps, maybe, a need to be directive and give competent advice. But I think advice, even the best advice, needs to be presented in a context of listening. And there is a need, or at the very least, room, for my approach, too. I have a gut feeling that Homeroom accomplishes more than it attempts."

Allison looked around the room. She squirmed and readjusted her seating. "I don't disagree with you," she said, "I really don't. I am on your side. I think you know that. You are going to have one difficult time convincing others. Your way goes against everything everyone else believes. You speak a different language than the Cult. You walk on a different landscape. How can you convince the Board to see the wisdom of your way? They want, they <u>need</u> evidence."

"I know," he said.

CHAPTER 7

EVERYTHING WORKS SOMETIMES

"Have you thought what tonight is going to be like? I mean, have you ever attended a Board meeting?" Allison asked, with a change in tone that rattled Harmon.

"Not recently."

"You are meeting the enemy on their turf."

"I think I can handle it."

"You are leaping into the jaws of the Cult without a safety net."

"Oh, Master of Mixed Metaphors, what is your point? How bad can it be? The worst that can happen is they turn me down, right?"

"I hope so. You are probably right. But right now, the Board is really a....battle zone. I wouldn't want you to be some sort of...collateral damage, as they say."

"Well, I know there is a lot of divisiveness, but that's pretty common these days," Harmon observed. "It seems like the boards in all the districts around us are just as messed up, just as much at odds. The power is no longer held solely in the hands of a superintendent. Instead there is a power vacuum that various groups fight over. We had one superintendent for forty years. Now we've gone through five different superintendents in the last seven."

"Don't forget, the demographics of our district have changed dramatically," Allison added. "Ten years ago, over 97% of the student body was made up of the white middle class. Today close to 50% of the students enrolled are members of minority groups. The economic level has dropped considerably, too. Last year, for the first time in the district's history, a significant number of students qualified for federal lunch programs. There are some 60 different languages reported as the primary language spoken in the homes of students. The special education department has come under scrutiny from the state. The attendance rate has been seriously impacted by the influx of what some people call "migratory students", here one semester, gone the next, and back the one after that. All these changes have been seen least at West Side, which causes some people in the community to view West Side as the last bastion of the way things used to be. The results are that the district has become a battleground among various pressure groups, and the role of superintendent has become more that of a political juggler than educational leader. Our current chief, Dr. Harrison W. Spaulding, fits the role perfectly. He manages to keep everyone relatively happy, or perhaps better put, he disperses the dissatisfaction equally. The district survives and continues to run smoothly, but there is no direction. It has become reactive rather than proactive and we bounce around slowly, making some sort of movement that may or may not be called progress."

Harmon wasn't sure why Allison felt a need to inform him on the history of the school district, but he listened as she went on. "To his credit, Dr. Spaulding looks like a great superintendent. He is tall and muscular, with a full head of white hair, which is always immaculately groomed, like a television evangelist. His voice is low and sounds regal. He is quite articulate and his vocabulary is impressive. He sounds profound until one analyzes the content of his communication. Then one notices an alarming lack of substance. He is a master of public relations. The fact that the district has maintained such a reputation for excellence is due to his ability to milk publicity out of any positive recognition while minimizing any negative showing. I am never sure if Spaulding lacks vision or backbone, but the results are the same, a kind of uneasy balancing act with the warring factions of the Board."

Harmon nodded and responded, "I always felt that the continued achievement was proof of the illusory power of the Board and superintendent. Things went on in spite of their best efforts to screw them up." He thought about what he had just said and added, "Right now their power does not seem so illusory."

"Spaulding is not unlike the ringmaster of a three-ring circus. I'm not sure I've gained any respect for his performance, but I'm more aware of how difficult his task is," Allison said. "The president of the Board of Trustees is Dr. Carol Henderson. She is a full professor in the education department at the university. She had been an educator for over thirty years, with a Ph.D. for the past twenty. She has more academic credentials than Dr. Spaulding, but she is still called Mrs. Henderson at board meetings and by the press. She is a conscientious educator who keeps up with the latest research. Of all the members of the board, she had the broadest perspective on education. She is capable of providing vision and direction, but she has more experience with instruction than administration and does not initiate any policies."

"Does she belong to the Cult of Uniformity?"

"She probably worships at the altar. She is serving her third term on the Board and is respected by most of the community. I expect that she will support Homeroom only if you can provide some sort of research and/or theory upon which she can rest her support. Research is the only language the Cult respects."

"Which brings us to Mr. Scott Hitchcock."

"Yeah. I know Hitchcock." Harmon rolled his eyes.

"Mr. Hitchcock is the real thing, and you best be careful of him. Be very careful. Hitchcock is serving his second year on the Board. His campaign centered on one issue: he advocated the refusal of federal funds for free lunches. He maintained that accepting the money would give the federal government too much power over local policy and curriculum. Hitchcock became the champion against the bureaucrats and the power brokers. He rode a wave of anti-establishment feeling to victory. Shortly after the election, the true nature of his agenda began to show. Although he's always denied it, and there is little proof, he meets all the criteria of being a 'stealth' candidate, which is to say he represents the fundamentalist, religious right, extreme conservative viewpoint, but without announcing his affiliation during the campaign. He denied such a connection, thereby avoiding the charge of sneaking into the election victory under false pretense. Whether he has an official relationship with the religious right or not, his position on a variety of issues is consistent with their agenda."

"Yeah, I know all that," he said, "but there is only one of him. He is not the whole Board."

"Keep telling yourself that. In the 20 months that he has served, Hitchcock has not really initiated any programs. Mostly he has opposed everything the superintendent has suggested, and he's voted against everything."

"I am aware of Hitchcock," Harmon replied.

"I think Hitchcock is more dangerous than we give him credit for being. I don't think he is the joke everyone likes to see him as." Allison said.

"Thanks. I had been a little worried, but now my anxiety has reached classic proportions. Paranoia maybe the word I'm searching for."

"I'm serious. Watch out."

"I will, but one question."

"Yeah."

"What am I watching out for?"

"I don't know."

"Gee, thanks."

He stood up and nodded as left the office. Harmon realized that he still had 10 or 15 minutes before his next class. He needed to digest the events of the past forty minutes: the cancellation of Homeroom, the revelations about Cindy, and Allison's warnings about the Board. He found that a cup of coffee often helped at times like these so he headed for a place he usually avoided, the bastion of the Cult of Unifomity, the teacher's lounge.

The teacher's lounge at West Side High is a large, rectangular room. The room was originally the library. Bookcases still cover the lower portion of the wall below the windows and make up the longest side of the room. There are books scattered about these cases, mostly randomly discarded textbooks, ungraded papers, and notebooks. Across the room, between the two entry doors at each end of the room, are a sink, a candy machine and two soda machines. This year there was a choice between Coke and Dr. Pepper. In the past, the Pepsi distributor was more user-friendly, and there was a Pepsi machine where the Coke machine now stood. Many teachers were glad with the return of Coke; it doesn't take much to make teachers happy.

In the front of the lounge are four parallel tables, each big enough to seat eight. Behind them, closer to the windows, are five square tables. The table furthest right has a phone strategically located to guarantee no privacy. Another square table has three computers, while another has two different grading machines. A fourth table has loose leaf papers and booklets from the administration on district policies. One lone table, way in the back of the room, is for smokers.

The room used to be divided in half by an invisible wall between the smokers and nonsmokers. Several years ago, the smokers outnumbered the nonsmokers, and the lounge reeked of tobacco. The nonsmoking group has grown both in number and power, and two years ago there was a movement to make West Side a smoke-free environment. Although the movement hasn't yet achieved complete success, the territory for smokers has been scaled down to one table, at the rear of the lounge, next to an open window. The result is that fewer teachers smoke, and those who do are isolated to some sort of remote, frigid Devil's Island. Still there are a few hard-core civil libertarians who refuse to be coerced into a healthy lifestyle. On this day one solitary smoker, Ms. Phillips, the economics teacher, was sitting at the smoking table grading essay tests.

At the front table were three teachers: Mrs. Bryce, a math teacher, Mrs. Carmine, an English teacher, and Mr. Madison, a biology teacher. Harmon had never spent five minutes around Mr. Madison without wanting to choke him. He was obnoxious and opinionated, a combination Harmon found toxic. Harmon didn't mind Madison being opinionated if he could count on him to be consistently wrong. Unfortunately Harmon found himself agreeing with Madison more than he liked. Harmon poured himself some coffee, sat down at the table, and preceded to contemplate the cup. The teachers were immersed in a conversation about students wearing caps in class. The volume of the discussion and level of animation indicated that the conversation was intense, although no one seemed to be voicing an opposition to the main thesis that caps were a terrible thing for students to wear in school, a threat to civilization as we know it.

"I do not tolerate them in my class," Mrs. Carmine was saying.

"I got one of those, you know, poster things." Madison was trying to explain his contribution to the issue. "The one that has a picture of a cap in a circle with the line through it, like Ghostbusters."

"I've got quite a collection of caps myself," added Mrs. Bryce.

They all stopped at once and stared at Harmon. He'd seen that stare before. They hurled their collective gauntlet down at him and waited for him to pick it up. He didn't feel like arguing. "You know," he said, "a lot of schools are banning caps because they are used as gang insignia." He could tell that didn't satisfy them, it was not a strong enough condemnation. "Of course, we don't have much gang trouble at West Side, but you wouldn't want to wait for a problem. You know, you gotta be proactive."

Carmine responded, "Well, I don't care if it's gang-related. Caps in class are just rude."

"Yeah." Madison added. "Besides they use them to hide cheat sheets."

"I just hate that you can't see their eyes." Bryce completed the round.

Harmon didn't really see caps as a major obstacle to the intellectual growth of students, but he was not particularly fond of them either. To him, caps just seemed to boil down to a value judgment by the faculty. They just don't like caps in class. Gang insignia was an excuse, not a reason. The gangs would find other things if caps were outlawed. To say that students use them to cheat was ludicrous. Still, he didn't really have a problem with their opposition to caps. He just wished they wouldn't cloak it in such absolute terms. If you don't like caps, say so and ban them in your own class. He was not convinced that there was a need to establish a consistent policy. The cure seemed to be more problematic than the disease. He was, however, more than a little concerned about the direction in which the school would be heading if the faculty started arbitrarily deciding what styles were acceptable and not acceptable. Next they'll ban earrings on guys. Then beards. Long hair. Some teachers don't like jeans. T-shirts. Short skirts. Long skirts. He had heard teachers propose bans on all of these, in some form or another. Pretty soon a school would be a place where it was not safe to be different, the ultimate victory for the Cult of Uniformity. They probably knew the inclination of his thinking, which is why they turned to him expectantly. He just didn't want to get into it, so he sat and nodded a tacit agreement.

Mrs. Bryce commented on the rarity of his presence in the lounge. "You're kind of a stranger down here. What's the occasion?"

"I just had a few free moments. I had a meeting with Randich."

"Our illustrious leader," Madison offered. Once, a long time ago, Madison had said something nice about a principal, but no one can remember when it was. "What did he want?"

"It was about Homeroom."

"Did you have to explain it or only spell it for him?" Madison asked in his usual condescending way.

"I have to go the Board and defend it."

"If you are going to the Board, be sure to use crayons in your presentation," Madison added continuing his string of consecutive statements without adding anything constructive.

"Whew, I don't envy that job," Mrs. Carmine added.

"What exactly is Homeroom? Is it two words?" Madison asked without any awareness of the irony he had just demonstrated. All the other teachers nodded.

"Homeroom is sort of like a support group for up to ten students, meeting once a week. We talk about various issues. Uh, I never—make that seldom—get kids out of academic classes. That's why you don't know what it is. It's kind of a badly kept secret."

They looked at him as if he were speaking a foreign language.

"It's an anti-drug, suicide prevention program, sort of."

"Oh," Madison said, and Harmon was sure that the next thing out of Madison's mouth would make the hairs on the back of his neck stand up. Madison didn't disappoint. "It's one of those programs."

Harmon took a slow drink of coffee, washed it around in his mouth, trying to compose himself before responding to Madison's pronouncement. "One of <u>those</u> programs? What does that mean?"

"Oh, you know, where everyone sits around wallowing in self pity. These kids don't need that; they need to get on with life, a little less pity and more self-discipline."

"Does it work?" Mrs. Carmine asked.

"I don't know." Harmon certainly didn't want to go into the details as he had with Allison. "Hard to tell, but yeah, I think it works. Anyway, that's what I've got to convince the Board."

"Well, if I can help." Mrs. Bryce startled Harmon with her offer. "You let me know. I know it works. I used to teach in junior high, and you got that girl, Cindy. Well, I used to know her in junior high school, and oh dear, she was something. She got my vote for most likely to commit homicide. That program has really made a difference for her."

"I think Homeroom can be a real powerful program. I knew a few students have been really touched by it." Harmon decided to try out his working defense of the program. He explained that Homeroom brought people together that wouldn't normally contact each other, that Homeroom was an antidote for loneliness, and that Homeroom had functioned as a crisis center on more than one occasion.

Mrs. Carmine and Mrs. Bryce both listened and seemed to validate his assessment, but Madison, not surprisingly, scoffed. "Good luck trying to sell that to the Board."

"You have my sympathy." Mrs. Carmine offered. "You will have a difficult time proving the benefits of a program that tries to prevent something."

"Besides, everything in education accomplishes its opposite." Madison's indictment was followed by the type of blank looks that indicated no one had the slightest idea what he was talking about. "Let me put it this way. I've been teaching a long time and I think the whole profession is run by idiots. We develop reading programs, and the illiteracy rate grows. If kids can't learn to read in nine or ten years, we think one more year of instruction will suddenly work. Creative thinking programs prevent creative thought. We develop drug programs, and drug use increases, only now we have kids who think they are sophisticated enough to know what they are doing."

Carmine picked up the baton. "Remember the Correlates of an Effective School? We worked all semester, three or four in-service meetings, formulating our "Mission Statement", and we finally got it all together and refined and perfected it, and no one, not one teacher that I ever talked to, made even the slightest change in their lesson plans because of it."

"What about PETL?" Bryce asked the question but they all shook are heads. "Don't you remember? Madeline Hunter? The ultimate model for teaching. Our evaluations are based on it. Anticipatory sets?"

"Oh yeah, Paddlin' with Madeline," Madison responded.

"Yeah, well we all had to have certification in Hunter's model of teaching. We'd get the lessons and then everyone would go back in their classrooms and teach the same damn way until 'dog and pony time', you know, evaluation."

"It's like our attendance policy," Madison liked to bring this up to support his thesis. "We used to have an attendance rate over 97%. We decided to try to increase that, so we established an attendance policy: no one could get credit for a class in which they missed more than three classes in a semester. That was immediately interpreted by the students to mean that they had three free absences, thus increasing our absences. Our daily attendance rate fell so we adjusted our requirements. Now they can have up to ten absences, and even then they can get a waiver with a letter from their parents. We have managed to take a student body that was attending at a 97% rate and motivated them into barely a 90% daily attendance rate. If Homeroom works, the Board will never approve it, and if the Board does approve it, you can take it as proof that it ain't worth continuing."

"Finished!" Mrs. Phillips in the back of the room yelled as she stood. Then the bell rang. Everyone emptied the lounge and went back to the sanctity of their own classrooms.

Harmon usually avoided the teacher's lounge, but not for the usual reasons. There is an old saw that good teachers avoid the teacher's lounge, the arena of discontent. Griping is the main activity in any teacher's lounge, but Harmon viewed that as an educational fact of life like low pay, pointless paper work, and useless in-service. He had no criticism of the attitude of teachers expressed in the lounge. There are legitimate gripes and there is no other avenue to vent these grievances. They represent a host of petty, mundane annoyances, and if complaining serves as a catharsis, what is the harm? The right to complain is a compensation for the hard work that teaching demands. Teaching is not an easy job. It requires a constant juggling of intellectual content and emotional awareness. How do you teach the Pythagorean Theorem to a room full of raging hormones? How do you introduce the Periodic Chart to students saturated by the cultural messages of MTV? How do you shape the minds of students who see education as an adversarial relationship? And no matter what the subject, the only consistent thing they communicate is boredom? Often the answer is that you develop a callous facade. There is another old saw that says there are two kinds of teachers, those who are disillusioned, and those who are about to become disillusioned. Disillusionment and cynicism are ways of compensating for a career filled with rejection.

For all the cynicism expressed by teachers toward the system, for all the complaints about the students' lack of effort and desire, for all the curses hurled at parents, principals, and educational bureaucrats—few translate into action. Harmon had seen teachers spew forth venom regarding their lazy ignorant students, and then spend endless hours, on their own time, going over lessons with these same students helping them to learn the material. In all his years of teaching, he had never known a teacher who was not willing to do everything possible to help any student understand any subject. They may sound uncaring, but their actions demonstrate a commitment to their students that contradicts their words. Take Madison, for example. Any criticism of his complaining must be balanced against praise for his actual conduct. He is always the first teacher at school every morning. His room is filled with students before school and after school. He is very patient and explains everything over and over again to any students who seek his help. To those students who don't seek it, but need it nonetheless, he calls parents, he nags students, and he tries to get them to come for extra help. He does everything he can to fill them with the knowledge of his subject matter. His efforts go way beyond his job description. The reality of his commitment shows in his actions and they should speak louder than his verbose cynicism.

But Harmon avoided the teacher's lounge for different reasons. He simply felt lonely in the teacher's lounge, like a leper. He felt like he inhabited a different world because he asked different questions. While other teachers would look at the faces in front of them as relatively empty vessels that needed filling, he saw three dimensional, fully developed human beings. Often, he was the one who was needy.

Sometimes students told him that he cared more than other teachers, which he knew was false. All teachers care about their students, or at least most do, even the ones who don't seem to. They care passionately about who their students will become and that the students learn all the essential lessons. He cared less about what they learned because he had faith that they would learn what they needed to learn. Unfortunately, perhaps tragically, he had more faith in the students' ability to learn than in his own ability to teach. He cared less for what students would become because of his faith in what they were. He knew he was a helpless idealist. However, his was an idealism not born from igno-rance or naiveté. He had been burned by students just as much as the next teacher; however, how one responds to being burned is a choice. He had come to the conclusion that idealism, his idealism, was a more helpful paradigm. Operating from any other starting point didn't seem to help him, or his stu-dents, or the relationship between them. His trust in students might be mis-guided, his vision too narrow, but his faith in students was his greatest strength as a teacher. He believed in his students not because he was stupid, but because he saw trust as the best, most productive starting place for a relationship.

Harmon was not a member of the Cult of Uniformity. He chose to see angels in his classroom. And that was why he avoided the teacher's lounge.

His senior year began. He wanted to run through a few more practices, check out the traffic patterns in the Hub before school a few more times, but he didn't expect any major changes. He knew he was ready. Now he was just marking time, waiting for the right day. He had settled on a Wednesday early in May. He performed in his classes in a perfunctory way. He didn't care, but he didn't want to draw attention to himself and jeopardize his plans. He neither flunked nor did he do particularly well. He was amazed at how easy it was to just slide by in high school. He found that if he turned in his homework, or at least most of his homework, no one noticed him. He didn't do well enough to get anyone's attention, nor did he do poorly enough to cause concern. He told Allison he was planning on going to a junior college after graduation. Beyond his plans were vague. Perhaps a trade school, perhaps the military.

His psychology teacher, Mr. Harmon was a little different. For example, Harmon noticed when he wore his Marilyn Manson shirt on the first day of class. "You a fan of Marilyn Manson?"

"Yeah. I like some of his stuff."

Harmon nodded, "I thought his 'Antichrist Superstar' was really interesting; he has a lot to say."

He nodded but he wasn't sure how to respond; he wasn't sure if he could take Harmon seriously.

"I think Manson has a really bad reputation," Harmon went on. "He isn't half as bad as people think he is."

"You like him?"

"He's okay; I've read some of his interviews."

"You listen to him?"

"No. I can't say that I like his music, you know, he sounds like hail on a Quonset hut. It's an attack on the central nervous system. Although I hear that he did some early covers that are awesome. I hear his version of 'Red, Red, Robin Goes Bob, Bob Bobbin Along' and 'Zip A Dee Do Dah, Zip A Dee Day' are classics."

Then he knew to laugh. Still Harmon teased him about Marilyn Manson without putting him down. That same day two of his other teachers mentioned the shirt but in hostile tones, with one even threatening to have him suspended if he wore it again.

By the second week of the semester, Harmon had invited all of his students to join Homeroom if they had a study hall or gym class that they could miss one day a week. Harmon made a special invitation to him, and he joined. He thought it would be a good way to kill time and he might even get more evidence to fuel his hatred.

CHAPTER 8

NOTHING WORKS ALL THE TIME

Third and fourth period passed, with lunch in between. Harmon felt fortunate that he had a film on the brain scheduled. Filled with gross images, explanations of neurotransmitters, split brain research and all sorts of fascinating stuff, the film would capture the student's attention while Harmon sat in the back of the room and ruminated over all the events of the morning. He tried to organize his thoughts for his presentation to the Board, but the more he thought about things, the more he kept coming back to the one subject paramount in his mind, Cindy. "Why did Homeroom fail to make a positive difference in her life?" Even as he thought the words, he questioned them. Was it really a failure? From watching Allison over the years, he learned that what Homeroom offered students fell short of what Allison offered students in her office. She counseled kids, but what Homeroom did could not be called counseling. Another term was needed for what went on in Homeroom. He had taken counselor education classes and had received his masters' degree, only to decide to stay in the classroom. He was familiar with counseling techniques, and he felt this knowledge helped him in teaching. But in Homeroom, he consciously chose not to utilize any counseling intervention other than active listening. He felt that listening was enough for Homeroom. His understanding of Homeroom's limitations seemed to him to be his greatest asset, but now with Cindy, he wondered if he had been wrong. Simply put, Homeroom was not therapy even if it was sometimes therapeutic. It was a subtle point, and he wondered if anyone else, notably the Board, could appreciate it, or even understand it, and he wondered if he really knew what he was talking about. Sometimes there were no angels in Homeroom. He thought about Sara.

SARA'S STORY

Harmon popped into the counselor's office one Thursday before a four-day weekend to check on a student's grades. Allison called him into her office and shut the door. Harmon couldn't remember her every doing that before, and he took it as a sign that she wanted to share something very important or confidential, or in this case, both. "Do you know Sara?" she asked.

"I've seen her in the halls with a few of her friends who are in my class. I've never really met her or talked to her," he said. His first thought of her was that she was not a very pretty girl, although it was hard to explain why. She had many of the classic features that went along with being pretty, but they just weren't put together in a traditional way. She was quite tall, with dark rimmed glasses. She wore very conservative clothes. Her hair was short cropped and her mouth and eyes seemed slightly too large for her face. Other than that, Harmon had not gathered much of an impression of Sara.

"Well, she needs to talk to someone today, before the weekend, and I thought Homeroom would be the perfect place. She's talked to me, but she needs feedback and input from other students. She'll be in your last period Homeroom."

"An emergency?" He didn't really ask.

"Oh yes!" She said with an emphasis that communicated more than her words.

Harmon agreed, and once again he found himself asking a Homeroom for permission to allow a new student to dominate a meeting, and once again, not surprisingly, the Homeroom said yes and turned their attention toward Sara.

She sat down in the circle directly opposite Harmon. She squirmed in the chair, twisted her hands slightly, and tried to avoid eye contact. Finally, she looked directly at him, with tears welling in her eyes but not yet flowing down her cheeks, she began to speak.

"I talked to Allison all third period; she thought I should talk to you. I...I just need to tell someone...talk to someone, you know?"

"Yea, I think we know what you mean. We'll listen. What's going on?" Harmon asked.

"This guy, Philip, I've known him since like fifth grade. He moved to..that housing subdivision up north...the ..the, you know where Main High School is."

"The Colonial Village?"

"Yeah, that's it. Anyway he moved there a couple of years ago, but we stayed in touch. I don't know, maybe a phone call every month or so. We'd see each other in the summer at a church camp that we both attend. Since summer we've been calling each other...Well actually, he's been calling me, weekly. He was going with a girl that I was good friends with at the camp. Actually, I haven't had much contact with her at all since the summer. Anyway, they broke up a month ago. He's been real postal about it, real depressed."

She said all of this with a certain stilted cadence, very efficient, quick and mechanical. She reached a point where she slowed down and the words came slower and with much more effort. After a moment of silence, she began again, "Well, yesterday I had to go to the library after school. When I got home there was a message on my answering machine. He wanted me to call him. It was important he said. I had to go to the church for a youth meeting, supper was already in the microwave, and I just didn't want to take the time. I mean, lately he's been so depressed; I figured he'd take a long time. You know, on the phone. I was going to call him when I got back, but I didn't. I didn't." She had to stop again, her voice cracking and the tears finally coming. Harmon feared that he knew what was coming next. He was right.

"This morning another friend called me and told me that Philip killed himself last night."

After an audible gasp, everyone sat silently. They looked at her and waited to see what to do next.

"If only I had returned the call..." she said, her voice trailing off. "Do you think it would have made a difference? Could I have stopped him? Is it my fault?" Each question became more pleading and intense. "It's not my fault, is it? Tell me, is it my fault?"

Of course it was not her fault, and Harmon wanted to help her see that, so he prepared to emphasize and paraphrase, restate and reflect, hoping to lead her in that direction, but the students were less patient and more direct. Unanimously they began assuring her that there was nothing she could have done that she was not to blame. Harmon was hesitant to give her assurances without knowing the rest of the story. He was confident that she was not responsible and probably, at best, could have only postponed Philip's decision. However, he was not sure that he fully understood the source of her guilt. He wanted to hear more before trying to assure her. The students had heard enough, and their reassurances seemed to comfort her a great deal.

"I know. To think that I somehow caused this is pretty stupid, and probably egotistical to think I could have done something, but I guess I think that I should feel responsible, you know? I mean, ultimately, didn't we all..everyone who knew him..play a part of his decision? I mean, I might not know what I did, but I've got to feel that there was something, some influence I had. If I wasn't part of the solution, I must have been part of the problem, right?"

Everyone sat in silence at that. No one knew exactly how to answer her. She was still crying, but softly in an almost rhythmic pattern. Her voice wasn't as shaky. "I don't know what to do. Should I call his mother and go by his house? I'm not sure she even knows me. I don't want to be in the way. Should I go to his funeral?"

"What do you want to do?" Harmon asked, feeling a little more comfortable with a topic that he could handle.

"I want to do both, but I'm afraid."

"Of what?"

"I'm not sure." The tears started to flow again. "What if I break down in front of the family? What if I make a scene at the funeral?"

Three students talked at once, volunteering to accompany Sara to both Phillip's house and the funeral.

She looked at them with her lower lip quivering and thanked them for their gentleness and kindness. They all gave her their phone numbers. Some of them told her to call them if she needed to talk. One boy offered to let her come over to his house for the night; his mother did grief counseling at his church.

Sara looked around the group with her mouth slightly open. The tears stopped, "I don't know what to say. Thank you. Thank you all. I can't believe you are all being so kind. You don't know what a burden this has all been; it was really hard to come to school today. Thanks again. I may call you, but I think my mother will take me. I just needed to know that it was okay to go."

"Letting people know you care, even at a time of loss like this, is seldom wrong," Harmon interjected. The bell was getting ready to ring, and Harmon was striving for some sort of closure. "I can't imagine Philip's mother feeling anything but gratitude that you cared enough to come by."

She thanked them all again, and when the bell did ring, several students stayed to hug her and pat her on the back. She cried some more and continued to thank them through the restrained sobs.

Harmon thought about Sara often during that weekend. He had lived through the period of the many suicides, but none were students in his class, and no one from Homeroom had ever completed a suicide attempt. He was haunted by images of Sara. Her guilt must have been overwhelming, although she seemed to have a perspective on it. What haunted him most were her words, "If I wasn't part of the solution, I must have been part of the problem." He wondered how that applied to him and all the student suicides in the past. Was he, too, "part of the problem"?

Beyond the guilt, the empty space left by a suicide seems irreversible. There is no closure, no resolution, and no goodbye. Suicide is not some smooth cut in the fabric of life, but a ripping, savage tear with uneven edges. He was tempted to call Sara both on Saturday and Sunday, but he was always reluctant to initiate a connection with a student, especially a female. She had his phone number. Besides, with Sara's church affiliation and parental support, she seemed to have all the support she needed. Probably. He was successful at convincing himself that she wasn't alone.

School started again on Tuesday. Harmon looked for Sara in the hallways, but he wasn't really surprised that he didn't see her. During second period, he received a note form Allison asking him to stop by during his first free moment to talk about Sara. At the beginning of lunch, he went into Allison's office. "Sit down" she said, and he was immediately prepared for bad news. His stomach leapt into his throat, and if he had already eaten lunch, he would have lost it that instant. He felt as if his heart stopped. He feared the worse. He cursed himself for not calling Sara that weekend, but he sat. He sat because he wasn't sure his legs could support him. He was too frightened to speak except to reply to Allison's questions.

"Did Sara make it to Homeroom last Thursday?"

"Yeah, she was there. In fact, we spent the whole period listening to her. Why what's wrong?"

"Did she tell you about her friend Phillip at Main High School?"

"Yeah."

"She told you he killed himself?"

"Yeah."

"How did the other students respond?"

"They were great. They all gave her support and offered to help her any way they could. They gave her their phone numbers, they offered to drive her to the funeral, and at the end, they all hugged her."

"Yeah, well I called Main High School today to offer them my help with the crisis. They didn't know what I was talking about. There was no suicide. They have three students named Philip and each one was in class today."

"What? Maybe she got the wrong high school?"

"I'm afraid not. I called Sara's mother after I got off the phone with Main. Sara doesn't have any friend named Philip and, doesn't have any friend who killed himself. She spent the weekend at their lake house. She apparently has a history of this kind of thing. In junior high school she had her teachers convinced that her mother had attempted suicide."

Harmon sat in silence for several minutes before he could talk, "A lie? The whole thing was a lie?"

Allison nodded, and they sat in silence together.

Harmon spoke first, "I can't believe it. She cried. I mean, she more than cried. She sobbed almost hysterically at times. I mean, how do you fake tears like that? Why would you fake something like that?"

"I don't know, but if it's any comfort, she had me convinced too. She is very good."

"Have you talked to her today? What did she say?"

"I haven't seen her yet. I don't know what I will say to her," Allison stared at the picture of the parachute on her wall; she often looked at it during times of confusion. "I guess I'll ask her why she felt a need to lie to like that."

"She lied. I can't believe it was all a lie." He sat in silence, breathing very slowly. "I'll have to tell the kids in Homeroom; I think they deserve to know."

"I agree. I just hope they don't, you know, make things worse."

"You mean like attacking her or something?"

"Or something."

Harmon continued to sit, shaking his head back and forth, unable to respond or comprehend. Finally he looked up at Allison and said, "You tell her that…" He hesitated because he wasn't sure what he wanted Allison to tell Sara. "Tell her that it is okay to lie in Homeroom."

"Okay to lie?"

"I don't want her to feel that we won't welcome her back because she lied, or that we won't forgive her. Homeroom is not about confrontation."

"Do you really want to say it is all right to lie?"

"I want her to feel safe. If that means she has to lie, we will try to provide a place where she doesn't have to lie, but if that's what she needs to do…"

On Thursday, Homeroom began. Harmon started by asking them how they felt last week at the end of Homeroom. They went around the circle and each person expressed feelings of sympathy, pain, frustration and fear. One student shared that it reminded him of when he was suicidal and that the realization of the pain his death would have caused was one of the things that stopped him. After they had gone all around the group, Harmon asked them to remember that feeling; then he told them the truth. There was a silence for a very long time. Finally someone spoke out, providing what Harmon later came to view as one of his proudest moment in Homeroom, a moment that validated his faith in Homeroom. "She must have been really desperate to get attention that way." He could never remember who said it, but the whole group agreed and they expressed as much sympathy that Thursday as they had the proceeding Thursday. They were not angry or even hurt. They sensed that Sara was acting out of a sickness, and they felt sorry for her. He told them he was inviting Sara into Homeroom as a permanent member, and they unanimously approved. Sara did join Homeroom, but she attended only once. She may have felt uncomfortable in front of those people after what had happened, or she may have felt that she had lost all credibility. Or it may have simply been, as Harmon suspected, that she never felt that she could ever command their attention again. She never re-enrolled. When asked why, she said that one of the boys in the group scared her. He'd had a bad reputation in junior high school and she was afraid of him. Harmon didn't believe her.

BRUCE, THE REST OF THE STORY

Liars have always been attracted to Homeroom. Some of the liars seemed more desperate than malicious, lying more to themselves than to others. Hypocrite might have been a better term, but Harmon was never sure. For example, Bruce was lying when he said he was a published author and when he told of his self-admittance to an alcohol rehabilitation center. He had entered a treatment center, but his parents had admitted him for clinical depression. He had stopped taking his Prozac because he feared how it would mix with alcohol. Yet somehow, in Harmon's mind, Bruce's lies seemed almost innocent. When Bruce tried to impress everyone, when he tried to get sympathy, Harmon could forgive and accept because the attempts were more pathetic than manipulative.

However, during his second year in Homeroom, Bruce crossed over some line, and he became more and more unnerving. He had missed those few days after the prom not because he wanted Missy to gain a perspective on the prom, as he had led Harmon to believe, rather he had been absent because he had gone on a three-day drunk. Harmon was quick to adopt the story that Bruce was trying to drown his sorrows because of the bittersweet experience of his prom date with Missy, but the truth was much more disturbing. Despite his touching vows of sobriety, he had never stopped drinking. The prom was the exception rather than the rule.

The next year, his reckless behavior began to escalate and became more and more dangerous. At one of his parties, in a fit of spontaneous playfulness, he threw one of his friends through the second-floor window of a motel onto a parked car. Another friend complained that Bruce had burglarized his house when his family was on vacation. Bruce's driving became even more erratic. He drove onto sidewalks and over medians with glee. His friends were afraid to ride with him and he seemed bent on frightening them. He had several accidents. His lying became more pathological. All of his friends grew weary of the pointless and senseless lies.

When he didn't graduate that last senior year, he cried in Allison's office and begged to have another chance. All he lacked was a physical education credit, but that hadn't stopped him from skipping gym class 81 of the last 90 days, despite numerous warnings, detentions, and suspensions. On most of those days he had driven by his gym class and waved at the teacher. Still, his tears were real, and Allison intervened. She talked the gym teacher into giving Bruce another chance. He could graduate if he talked to the teacher, apologized, and took an exercise test, even if he didn't pass it. He never talked to the teacher, never took the test, and never graduated.

When school ended, Bruce's family moved, and he may or may not have moved with them. No one knew for sure. No one ever actually heard from him again. There was one rumor that he became a successful gambler in Las Vegas while another rumor cast him as a pimp in New Jersey. Somehow he was the source of both rumors.

Still, Harmon had few students more likeable than Bruce. Harmon saw in Bruce a tortured spirit who was more sensitive than harmful. Bruce was a desperate and lonely person who did not know how to let others touch him. He touched Missy, and she was not the only person. Later, whenever Harmon would see any of the members from those Homerooms, the first person they would ask about was Bruce. However, Bruce was incapable of letting any of them touch him in any meaningful way. Harmon questioned whether Homeroom had helped Bruce, or would enabling be a more accurate label for what had transpired?

And there were others in Homeroom who were less than honest in their self-disclosures. For example, Herbie came into Homeroom wearing gray dungarees, unfashionable loafer type tennis shoes and a Star Trek T-shirt. He wore thick, dark-rimmed glasses, and he looked as if he were in desperate need of a plastic pencil holder for his shirt pocket. His hair was wavy and sort of long, but combed up like the Everly Brothers in the fifties. He spent one entire period talking about his cocaine addiction and his recent return from a rehabilitation hospital. In actuality, the closest he ever got to cocaine was in his otolaryngologist's office, and the closest he got to rehabilitation was when his grandmother took him to the dermatologist. And there was Sandy, who said one week that she had received a Scholarship to West Point. The next week she reported her estranged father was dying from gunshots received from a drive-by shooting. The following week she told the group that her best friend, who lived in another state, died from cancer.

Harmon did not know how to deal with the lies. He never developed a successful policy. In fact, he was never quite sure how he felt about the lying. Especially when he thought about Tanya.

TANYA

Tanya was in the first Homeroom that was intense. Most of the students in that Homeroom were from of a study hall. They were a motley congregation, eight in number. Among the eight, were three who had attempted suicide, two problem drinkers, one drug user, a special education student, two honor students, three males, including one who thought he was the reincarnation of James Dean, a student recently returned from a psychiatric hospitalization for undetermined reasons, two students with histories of violent confrontations with teachers, and Tanya. After the first two or three meetings, nothing serious was discussed, and Harmon was questioning if Homeroom was accomplishing anything, if there was any value in Homeroom. He was thinking Homeroom might be an example of something that seemed better on paper than in reality when Tanya stepped in and changed the face of the program forever.

Tanya was an honor student. She was a little overweight, and she tended to wear too much make-up. Her hair was blonde but not naturally. Her style of clothing was not the most fashionable. Her mascara was darker than most people used, especially at school. She wore tennis shoes with nylons, and she always wore dresses or skirts and blouses.

One particular day, as everyone took a seat in the circle, they faced Tanya. She wasn't the geographic center of the circle, but she sat down first and held her head in her hands as everyone else filed in. She wept quietly, barely loud enough for anyone to hear but audible nonetheless. Everyone found it difficult to wait for the bell to ring indicating the start of Homeroom, but they managed to do so. Finally everyone was there, and Harmon asked her what was bothering her. He imagined all sorts of answers ranging from a suicide attempt to the death of a loved one. He was not prepared for her answer, "Oh, nothing. I'm okay."

Everyone in that room knew that she was not all right and that something was bothering her, but she denied it. Harmon tried to reconcile the contradiction between the two opposite images of her crying and her proclamation that nothing was wrong. He thought Homeroom was not about probing. Maybe this was a test to see if he would respect anyone's request for privacy. He started to accept her answer and go onto other business when one of the boys chimed out, "Come on, we know something is wrong. What is it? You can tell us. That's what we are here for."

At first she didn't answer. She did start crying a little louder.

One of the girls asked, "What is it? C'mon let us help."

Tanya looked up. She looked around the room. Then she took a deep breath, released one more sigh, and said, "I think I might be pregnant."

Someone released an audible gasp, and they all moved forward in their seats.

"I don't know what to do. I mean, the father is the youth minister at my church, and I can't ruin his career, not to mention his marriage. I mean he has two little kids."

"He should have thought about that before…" One of the guys started but then trailed off.

"How did it happen?" One of the girls asked, and then she seemed embarrassed at her question.

"Well," Tanya began. "We are in the choir together, and every Thursday he'd give me a ride home and we'd talk. Parked in front of my house, we'd talk, sometimes for an hour. I've always liked talking to him. He is so understanding. He helped me get over my boyfriend breaking up with me a couple of weeks ago. And then last Thursday, we were talking, and I was crying, and he put his arm around me, and he was comforting me and telling me that he didn't want me to cry, and…" She didn't finish her sentence; she didn't need to. She just lowered her head and wept more and more quietly.

All of the other members of Homeroom were on the edges of their seats and they sat like that throughout the period. They offered her advice on how to handle the expectant father and what to do next. One of the girls offered to take her to Planned Parenthood. One of the boys offered to cut his next period and shoplift a pregnancy test from the local drug store.

There was something in the way she rebuked all offers of help and diverted all advice that bothered Harmon. "First, if this had happened last Thursday, it would be a little premature to suspect she might be pregnant. Secondly, would a married man really have sex with a teenage girl in a car parked in front of her house?" Harmon asked himself. "What is more likely, a youth minister who would jeopardize his career and family, or that Tanya would make up the story for attention?" Although her story was within the realm of possibility, Harmon still felt that the latter was a more plausible explanation. So he sat back and watched with a skeptical eye.

Harmon kept his doubts to himself and ultimately was glad that he did. Tanya's story had a powerful, galvanizing effect on this Homeroom. The entire group gathered their resources together to help Tanya. It was obvious that they cared and wanted to help her. Tanya's story brought the group together closer than anything else that had happened. The closeness was not temporary. They stayed really tight all the rest of the year. Each meeting would end with a spontaneous hug among the members. They shared phone numbers; they met on school holidays and over Christmas break. The group went on to prevent one potential suicide, and made two of the members really evaluate their drinking and drug use. Harmon wished they would have committed to abstinence, but he saw their talk in Homeroom as a first step in that direction. Whenever Harmon thought about the course of that particular Homeroom, Tanya's revelation seemed to be the turning point.

At the time, Harmon certainly did not see Tanya's story as a positive development. Right after the meeting, Harmon felt extremely conflicted about how to handle her revelation. On one hand, he saw this as a challenge to the confidentiality rule. He felt he should inform her parents; he felt ethically bound to inform them. However, he also saw informing the parents as a risk for the whole program. No one would ever trust him or Homeroom again. If he could arbitrarily discard confidentiality the first time he was tested, how would he build trust? Still, he didn't feel comfortable withholding this kind of information from the parents. On the other hand, he wondered if he really had any information to give to the parents. He didn't know if she was pregnant. He decided to talk to Allison and get her advice before calling the parents. To go to the parents now, behind Tanya's back, would destroy the integrity of the program. Reinforcing his dilemma was the personal doubts he had about the truth.

Before talking to Allison, he decided to do a little investigation. He looked on Tanya's registration records and found the name of the church she attended.

He called to get the name of the youth minister, only to find out that there was no youth minister, and that there hadn't been one for several years. The choir director was a woman. Harmon was even more convinced that Tanya had been lying. Why? What had she hoped to accomplish? To Harmon, there was a more important issue. Should he confront her? Was Homeroom a place for such confrontations? He went to Allison for answers to these questions.

"Why? Why did Tanya lie? I mean, she could get attention in a lot of ways. She didn't seem that desperate. Why?"

Allison thought for a minute before she responded. "Look what she accomplished; Tanya's disclosure let the girls in the group know she was capable of attracting a man, a real, adult man, and she let the boys know she was sexually active. Both facts were powerful as a source of curiosity and attention. I mean what an appealing position to be in."

Harmon thought about what Allison said. "Should I confront her?"

"With what? She'll just deny that she lied. You'll come across like a bully, or at least a teacher."

"But the church doesn't have a youth minister."

"She'll just say she changed churches since she filled out the registration form, or something."

Harmon sat and contemplated what Allison said. He probably couldn't prove that Tanya was lying.

Allison didn't wait for a response from Harmon, "I'll bet you anything that at the next meeting of Homeroom she tells the group that it was all a false alarm and she isn't pregnant."

"So I don't confront her?"

"Well, it just seems to me that Homeroom is a support group not group therapy." Allison countered.

"Confrontation is more of a group therapy kind of thing?"

"Yeah, in my mind, support and confrontation are opposites."

"What do you mean? I mean, I understand what you are saying: I'm just there to support the kids in Homeroom, not to heal them or make them face their own demons, but do I let them lie without consequences?"

Allison furrowed her brow as she tried to clarify what she meant, "In a situation like the one you had with Tanya, any consequence should be natural and spring from the group, not the leader. In a way, what you believe doesn't matter as much as what the group believes. Besides, how would you prove that a person was lying? I mean, when she doesn't have a baby nine months from now, by then everyone would be aware that she wasn't pregnant."

"What about other lies?"

"Well, I'm just not sure that you want to spend that much time investigating all the possible lies. I mean, do you really want to play Sherlock Holmes?"

"So I should just look the other way?"

"What do you think you should do?"

"I don't know," Harmon's answer was as true years later as it was then.

"Confrontation is the only alternative?" Allison could understand Harmon's dilemma. "So how would you feel about not saying anything?"

"Phony."

"How would you feel about confronting?"

"Vulnerable."

"So, can you share vulnerability with your group?"

"I don't have a problem admitting incompetence. I do have some experience there."

Allison nodded. "I don't see anything wrong with being real and admitting your difficulty in believing someone."

"I would feel better if I knew what I was doing."

"Will you confront them with your doubts?"

"I don't know; I guess it depends."

And that was the closest Harmon got to forming a policy regarding lying in Homeroom, and he felt unsettled on the issue. However, one time his lack of a policy actually threatened the existence of Homeroom altogether. Harmon tried confrontation, and he was profoundly unsuccessful.

MICHELLE

Michelle was a junior. She was very social with friends on the drill team and friends who were cheerleaders, although she was neither. She had been a cheerleader in junior high but was not talented enough to survive the transition to high school. In some ways, junior high school was the highlight of her life. She seemed emotionally to be fixated in junior high school.

Michelle captivated her Homeroom with a story about the events of a Saturday night with Dana, a highly visible, popular, and personal friend of three of the members of one particular Homeroom. She started by asking for assurance that everything would remain confidential. Harmon assured her that he would not disclose anything unless it involved threat to self or others, and he reminded the rest of the group about the confidentiality rule. "But," he said, "if you don't feel comfortable sharing, you don't have to."

"I don't know what to do. I need help." She stopped and shed a few tears, capturing everyone's attention, before beginning. "Saturday night, Dana and I didn't have anything to do. Geoff, Dana's boyfriend had to go somewhere with his family; he had to take his sister to a rock concert. We knew these college guys, met them at fraternity party a month ago. They were real cute and nice, you know, polite, so we thought it would be fun to give them a call. We called them about ten o'clock. They said they were having a party and they invited us over. We didn't have a car. Actually, I did but I didn't want to drive to the campus on the other side of town, so they came to pick us up. Well, they took us to their apartment, and there wasn't anybody at the party except us and four guys, college guys. We started drinking—wine coolers and beer, nothing real heavy—laughing, having a good time."

"Wait, let me see if I've got this right." Harmon interrupted her. "You went over to a guy's apartment, four college guys, in the middle of the night, without a way home, and started drinking."

"Yeah, it sounds kinda of stupid when you put it like that."

"It sounds a whole lot stupid if you ask me." Someone else in the group spoke.

"But they had been so nice at the other party, and one of them is in a fraternity with Charlene's brother. Anyway, I think they must have put something into the drink, because I've drunk a lot of beer and wine before, but I've never been this drunk, ever. I felt like I couldn't walk or even talk. One of the guys started......touching me and trying to hug me. I kept pushing him away, but I could barely talk or move my arms. I sure couldn't stand up. I could see across the room that two guys were doing the same thing to Dana on the sofa. Then I passed out."

She stopped. All eyes were on her. She choked back some tears, composed herself and went on. "When I woke up, Dana was shaking me and trying to get me up so we could leave. She was holding her blouse together because the buttons were torn off. I got up and the guys took us home. They told us to give them a call next weekend. It was one o'clock."

"Was Dana raped?" asked Samantha with desperation in her voice. Samantha was a good friend of both Dana and Geoff.

"I think so, but I don't know for sure; we never talked about it."

"Were you?" Harmon asked.

"No, no. No. They left me alone."

"Why?" a male voice asked.

"Why?" She seemed stunned by the question.

"Yeah. Why would they rape her and not you?"

"Well, I got sick. I threw up all over the......couch I was on."

"I thought you passed out?" Samantha asked.

"I did. After. You know, I threw up first."

"Was this before or after the guy was grabbing you?"

"Huh? Oh, during. While he was touching me, I threw up. Some of it hit him. I passed out with my head in the waste basket. I mean, right after I saw them, Dana, fall off the couch. Actually she was pulled off."

"Were there two different couches?" Harmon wasn't sure who said this but it seemed like the same masculine voice that had spoken earlier.

"What? Well, there was this couch I was on, kind of a loveseat, and Dana was on this bigger sofa on the other side of the room."

The group continued to ask questions and Harmon could sense a tone of disbelief in the questions, but none of the questions were too abrasive and Michelle managed to avoid being defensive. The desire by the group to support her overcame their curiosity over details.

By the next afternoon, the story was all over the school, even in the teachers' lounge. Dana came to Allison. She was devastated about being the subject of the whole school's gossip. She told Allison that none of the story was true. She did finally admit to going on campus and drinking a beer at a party Saturday night. But she did not pass out, she had not been raped, and she didn't want Geoff to know about the party or anything. She didn't understand how everyone had found out, and why everyone thought she had been raped. Michelle came to Harmon in tears to tell him that someone in Homeroom—she was pretty sure it was Samantha—had broken confidentiality. Later, Samantha came to Harmon. According to Samantha, Michelle was responsible for spreading all the rumors. She was telling everyone the story and blaming Samantha.

By the time Homeroom was scheduled to meet the next week, Harmon had pieced together Michelle's conspiracy. First, she had destroyed the relationship between Dana and Geoff. Whether Dana had been raped or not, she had gone to the party without Geoff's knowledge, and Geoff didn't trust her anymore. Second, Michelle had destroyed Dana's credibility. If Dana denied the story, no one could blame her, and the more she denied it, the more everyone believed it. The more intense her denial, the more the story was believed. Third, Michelle had a perfect alibi. She hadn't done anything. Samantha was responsible by breaking Homeroom confidentiality, with Michelle being just an innocent victim. Four, Michelle had gone a long way toward destroying any trust in this Homeroom, if not all Homerooms. She had accomplished all of this while operating under the guise of being a concerned, helpful, misunderstood, friend. There was no way anyone could check out the truth of the story. It was Dana's word against Michelle's. Dana had a reason to lie. Besides Michelle had only hinted at a rape; she never said she actually saw what happened.

Harmon couldn't discredit Michelle's story, but he could verify the role Homeroom played in spreading the rumors. He checked with each member of Homeroom, and each one gave him the names of at least two other students who had told them about the incident. In each case, the story was traced back to Michelle as the original source of the information. Harmon was confident that he knew Michelle had been the source of the rumors, and he knew he had to confront her at the next Homeroom.

He wasn't sure what he was getting himself into, but he was sure that Michelle had stepped over some line and she needed to be held accountable. The day for Homeroom finally came, and the tone was very somber as everyone entered and sat down and moved their desks into a circle. Michelle was sitting slightly to Harmon's right and Samantha was directly across from him. He turned toward Michelle, fully focused on her, leaning forward in his chair and started gently to speak to her, "I think we have some unfinished business to attend to."

Michelle tried to look away and pretend that she didn't hear or know what he was talking about.

"Michelle, I'm talking to you."

"What? What do you mean?"

"I think we all want some sort of explanation about what you said."

"About what?"

"About Homeroom. You accused someone here of breaking confidentiality."

"I don't want to talk about it."

"I think we deserve an explanation. I think you owe us that."

"I don't want to talk about that. Let's just drop the subject."

He sat back and contemplated what to say next. Homeroom had always been based on the principle of not probing, but this seemed to be a time when that principle needed to be transcended. He cleared his throat and tried to maintain his composure and tried to make his voice as tender as possible, "Dropping the subject is not an option. You will have to face us. Explain yourself. I need to know, Michelle. I need to understand why you lied. Can you help me to understand?"

"Dana doesn't want me to talk about it anymore."

"That is not what I'm talking about, Michelle. I don't want to get side-tracked and all hung up on trying to prove what happened, or when, or if, or any of that. I don't want to go down that road. I want to know why you blamed Homeroom for breaking confidentiality, when it was you who did so."

"I said I don't want to talk about that."

"And I said I will not allow you to get away with this. You will not cop out. You will face us."

She started to cry. He expected her to. Her tears came slowly but when no one rushed to stop them, she began to cry harder. When she finally spoke, she sounded hysterical and was sobbing in great convulsive waves. "I never lied. I don't know why you are treating me so mean." She continued to cry, but no one was offering her sympathy.

Samantha broke the silence, "You did lie. You told Dana that I was the one who told everyone. But I didn't. You did."

"Dana didn't want Geoff to find out about…"

"I don't care about that. You lied about me!"

Harmon tried to intervene between the two before the conflict escalated. "I think what Samantha is saying is…" he stopped because Samantha's facial expression told him that she didn't want him speaking for her.

"Michelle," Samantha began in a very calm voice with a remarkable tenderness, considering the situation, "why would you lie like that about me? What have I done to you? I just want to know."

"We all want to understand," Harmon added.

Michelle sat weeping, tears flowing down her cheeks. She was obviously pondering the situation. He felt this could be some great opportunity for her finally to confront her need to lie. They, Homeroom, had done their job. They confronted her with as much empathy as possible. They stated everything in terms of wanting to understand and help her. They offered her an opportunity to be honest, to be real in a supportive environment. She rejected the opportunity.

"I don't know why everyone hates me. I just wanted to help Dana."

She jumped up and ran out of the room. Sharon ran after her. Harmon let both of them go. He knew Sharon would make sure nothing bad happened. But he still felt very discouraged. Michelle was not going to take an honest look at herself in front of the group. She had decided not to change, to maintain the same defensive posture, to try to divert attention off of herself, to cry for pity rather than confront for honesty. He felt sad and exhausted. He looked around the group. No one spoke. An ugly but necessary scene, had left them all drained. The balloon of anger had been burst, but there was no rush of cleansing, fresh air. And maybe they did feel guilty. The confrontation was hostile, and hostility is usually accompanied by some guilt. But, if Harmon felt any guilt, it was augmented by a profound sense of regret, regret for the lost chance, Michelle's last chance, certainly as it pertained to Homeroom. She never returned, and two weeks later she transferred to a private school, although in all fairness, this incident in Homeroom was not the only reason for her transfer.

The confrontation with Michelle left a bitter taste in Harmon's mouth. He never wanted to have another such confrontation in Homeroom.

TUESDAY AFTERNOON

CHAPTER 9

NEVER TRUST A CLICHE

The bell rang. "With deep philosophical implications," Harmon noted, "one period was over, and the next was about to begin." One of the things he liked most about teaching was incessant sense of fresh beginnings. Each semester was a new opportunity, each day a new lesson, each period a new class. It was time for a Homeroom, a new Homeroom, a chance for an angel to appear.

Clark was the first to enter the room. He helped Harmon arrange the desks in a circle. In this Homeroom, seven desks were needed. They took the first desk from the five rows, and the second desk from the outside rows, and circled them up, leaving room for Harmon's rolling chair. Clark nodded a perfunctory hello, but nothing was said. Harmon was not surprised at Clark's silence. Clark was a man of few words, as they say, but Harmon was not sure that Clark was shy. To Harmon, Clark seemed aloof, one of the more isolated members of Homeroom. He didn't have many friends, probably because he didn't display much in the way of social skills. However, he was very committed to Homeroom. He had been in a Homeroom in the fall semester, and now he was finishing his second semester. He seldom missed a meeting, having attended once with a fever that kept him home the rest of the week. Clark was tall, six-foot-one, and gangly; he couldn't have weighed more than 130 pounds. He had stringy hair, neither long enough to be stylish nor short enough to look well groomed. He wore wire-rimmed glasses and had a goatee, or, rather, he had a patch of hair on the bottom of his chin that resembled a goatee. He liked to twist and pull the hair, such that most of the time, the beard was unequal on either side of his chin.

Kaye came into the room shortly after Clark. In a previous Homeroom, she had revealed a painful past, full of sex and drugs. Her sexual activity had started early in life, initiated by an uncle, who provided her after-school care while her single mother worked. Later, her school bus driver had continued her sexual indoctrination. By the time she went to junior high, she had become well versed in seductive behavior, which had caused her shame, guilt, and anguish, but these skills were also an effective tool for manipulation that she had used to her advantage. By now, her senior year in high school, she was confused and had difficulty distinguishing any real sexual feelings from a desire to control her world. Alcohol had also entered her life in junior high, followed quickly by a variety of drugs, until she was completely confused about who she was and what it meant to be Kaye. In high school, she attended Al Anon regularly and was in the middle of a long journey toward self-respect. Harmon admired her strength and courage. In this particular Homeroom, Kaye never brought up her past and the group saw Kaye, in a limited way, as someone who had difficulty making passing grades. Apparently, she hadn't developed much trust for the group, but her respect for Harmon increased because he maintained confidentiality regarding her past. He completely left any disclosures up to her. Actually, the way she saw it, it was not a question of trust. Homeroom allowed her to have relationships based on who she was and what she did at that point in time, rather than what she had done and who she had been in the past. Her history never seemed to be an appropriate subject in this Homeroom, and she did not feel a need to force the topic into the conversation. She actually found this freedom to be very comforting.

They finished arranging the desks. Harmon always sat, as part of the circle, on a rolling chair. He liked not having a desk in front of him and he liked having the freedom to change his position to square off with whoever was speaking. Occasionally, a student would grab the rolling chair first and Harmon would sit in a desk, but usually Harmon's position in the chair worked best. There was no assigned seating, no prescribed order, and Harmon sometimes thought it was significant who would choose to sit in the chair opposite him. Sometimes it would indicate that the person wanted to speak, had something on the mind. He noticed that Abby took the desk immediately across from him. He was hoping that would be the case, because at last week's meeting Abby had been left with some unresolved issues.

During that last meeting, Abby had told the group that she wanted to break up with her boyfriend, Roger, but he wouldn't let her. He had pleaded with her. Finally, as a last resort, he had threatened suicide. Last year, before they had started dating, he had attempted suicide. She had to take his threat seriously. She hadn't known what to do but was certain she didn't want to call his bluff. The rest of the group, with Harmon's lead, had helped consider her options. She had decided to continue to date Roger but to try to talk to him about getting some help. Harmon wanted to follow up and see what had happened.

When the bell rang, everyone was settled into a seat. Harmon began. "Abby, we are all anxious to find out, how are things going for you?"

"Well, I tried talking to Roger, but..." Her voice trailed off. "He just wouldn't listen to me. He acted like what I was saying wasn't worth noticing."

"That must have been really frustrating," Brett said. Brett, a football player, a good one, was not the stereotypical jock. Football players and cheerleaders have a really bad reputation in many schools, which is often undeserved. They are seen as conceited, mean-spirited, shallow, and stupid, and there are perhaps many of them who fit this description. However, the majority of the jocks and cheerleaders have the same insecurities as all the other kids in high school. Many of their negative images come from the projections of the student body. A boy feels inferior to the quarterback and blames the quarterback; a girl feels less popular than the cheerleader and blames the cheerleader. That process is more common than the arrogant, mean bully in a letter jacket. One of the great delights for Harmon is exposing the fallacies of stereotypes and revealing them in Homeroom. Brett was as sensitive and intuitive as any student Harmon had ever seen. He was the leader of this Homeroom, a fact Harmon recognized even if no one else acknowledged it. It was usually Brett who made the empathetic comment, communicating a warmth that made the speaker feel safe. He was the angel in this Homeroom.

Harmon noticed that Abby had turned toward Brett after his response. Harmon leaned back in his chair, Brett leaned forward in his, and Abby's muscles began to tighten, as she spoke more to Brett than to Harmon. "I must have started four times trying to get Roger to hear me, you know, why I wanted to break up with him, and then why I needed to break up with him. He would just smile, change the subject, or say something like he loved me and expected everything to be okay. Finally I had to scream at him. When I finally broke down and started crying, he started to take me more seriously. But he still wouldn't acknowledge that I wanted to break up. He would say he loved me, like that was going to make everything all right."

She looked around the group and everyone was looking at her. She wanted them to approve of her actions. "I'm not a bad person; I'm not a heartless person; I'm not." She wanted them to understand.

The group did understand, but only Brett spoke. "No one thinks you did anything wrong. We feel sorry for you. I mean, I don't know what I would do." He said the words, but the group nodded their heads in agreement.

She seemed to feel better as she went on. "I finally told him that I couldn't stand the pressure anymore. I told him that he needed to see someone like a therapist or counselor. He didn't want to and I just started crying; it was the last straw, and I couldn't help myself. Finally, he promised to see someone if I wouldn't break up with him. What could I do? I promised." She looked down, obviously feeling defeated.

"So he acted like nothing was wrong, and I kept pestering him about scheduling an appointment. He thought the moment had passed and I was no longer PMSing, as he put it. Only nothing had changed and nothing was any better. I finally remembered something Mr. Harmon had said about Roger's parents needing to be involved in the solution, so I went and talked to Roger's mother. I told her everything. She was so cool. I mean, she took everything I said very seriously. She wasn't in denial at all. She was very worried and sad that I wanted to break up. She promised to get him in to see a psychologist, or counselor, or something. But she wanted me to wait to really break up until he was in therapy. In fact, I agreed to go with him to the first session. We have an appointment tonight."

"How do you feel about it now?" Mr. Harmon asked.

"I've been thinking about it a lot. I mean, it's hard not to. I can't seem to think about anything else. And like I'm beginning to get mad. I mean, I don't want to go with him anymore. I don't want to kiss him or anything. And yet I feel all this responsibility. It just doesn't seem fair. I don't want him to die, and I sure don't want to be the cause of his death. But, damn it, I'm seventeen years old. I shouldn't have to be in this position."

Brett responded. "Jesus, Abby, that must be…I can't imagine. That's gotta be….the weight has to be horrible."

As he spoke, Abby looked into his eyes and then shifted her eyes to her desktop. Her audible gasp was followed by a deluge of silent tears. She wept undisturbed for a few minutes. Clark went to Harmon's desk and brought the box of tissues Harmon kept available for just such moments. She smiled at Clark, mouthed a silent thank you, and tried to smile. She looked at Brett and back to Harmon. "No one knows what I have been going through. I mean, I feel sorry for Roger's mother. I really do, but she doesn't know what she is asking of me. I can't…." She just shook her head.

Harmon reflected. "You'd like nothing better right now than to just walk away."

She nodded, as she folded and refolded her tissue, wiping her eyes, "I just wish I could breathe again. You know, take one deep breath."

"Go ahead," Harmon directed her. "Take a deep breath right now. Inhale. Now exhale. Again. Do it again."

She did so several times and there was a visible change. Her shoulders lowered, her neck straightened, and her forehead became smoother. She relaxed, at least for a moment.

"Are you going to go tonight?" Brett asked.

"Yeah." She nodded. "I have to. I'm sort of looking forward to it. You know, the beginning of the end."

"Is there anything we can do to help?" Brett asked, and Harmon cracked the briefest smile.

"No. Nothing more than you've done already. Thanks."

There were a few minutes of silence, a calm between storms, as it were, before Alex spoke up. "Ah, endings, a subject I can relate to." Alex was short in stature but compensated by being relatively nondescript. He wanted, more than anything, to be a stand-up comedian, and Harmon felt that the main reason Alex came to Homeroom was to try out his material. He was generally quiet except when he expressed his wry sense of humor, usually once or twice during each meeting. He was obviously bitter and his humor was a coping mechanism against real or imagined pain. Harmon wondered if anyone else in the group was aware of the pain Alex's humor was covering.

"You might say I'm the expert on endings. Every girl I've ever gone with has broken up with me. You'd think at some point I'd have a chance to utter that magical phrase, 'I just want to be friends.' I've experienced all the classical lines: 'my parents say I'm too young to be serious'; 'I've just gotten over my last boyfriend and I'm not ready for a new relationship'; 'it's not you, it's me'; 'I can't handle commitment.'"

Brett responded, "You make it sound like you have gone with dozens of girls. Have you?"

Alex deflected Brett's attempt to clarify, "You don't even know the half. I mean, they're so good, or I'm so bad. They like make an art of breaking up with me. They break up before we start going together, preemptive strikes. Hell, I've had perfect strangers break up with me."

Everyone laughed. "That's the way Homeroom is," Harmon thought to himself, "pathos followed by a moment of surrealistic comedy."

Charlie was the next one to speak. She was a female athlete, in volleyball, basketball, and soccer. She was masculine appearing but had a boyfriend. She was a rare mixture of beauty with a complete lack of vulnerability. She was tough in many ways, physically and emotionally. Outside of Homeroom, she was usually in the company of other girls. If there was a gender confusion issue, the confusion might well have belonged to those around her more than to Charlie herself. "I hate breaking-up with guys; they always take it so personally."

"It's hard not to take a break-up personally." Alex's voice displayed some true pain and betrayed his flippant attitude. His hurt was accidentally revealed, and Harmon wondered if the group noticed or if they would respond.

Not surprisingly, Charlie displayed little sensitivity to Alex, "You know what I mean."

"No, I really don't know what you mean," Alex responded.

"They get all serious."

"As opposed to what?" Alex responded caustically, "Laughing? Cackling? Giggling? That's what I do. When someone breaks up with me, I follow with a long, protracted guffaw. Hardy, har har har!"

The silence was interrupted by Brett. "Sounds like you've been hurt more than you want to admit."

Once again, Harmon was impressed, not only by Brett's perceptiveness but also by the gentleness of his response.

Alex's eyes darted around the group, settling on the desk in front of him, "I just don't know what they want from me."

"Girls?" Brett asked. Alex nodded yes.

"I'd like to know that myself," Brett said. He looked around the group and asked,

"What do girls want from guys?"

"Well, I can tell you what they don't want," Charlie responded as if challenged to defend her entire sex. "We don't want someone who gives us flowers all the time, or calls every night or...or...or says they love you too soon."

"Actually some of that doesn't sound so bad," Kaye added.

"You know what I mean, Kaye. You hate it, too, when a guy won't let you have any space."

Kaye nodded, but Brett spoke, "I don't understand girls. I mean should we be nice or what? I mean, what if a guy just likes to do things for his girl? Is that such a bad thing?"

"Of course not," Charlie retorted. "As long as the gifts and everything come from the heart and aren't just some attempt to control. I want a guy who treats me as an equal. I don't want to be put on some pedestal. I don't want to be worshipped. I don't want the...."

"Responsibility?" Harmon asked, and Charlie stopped in mid sentence. She had not put it into words before, but that was exactly what she meant.

"Yeah," she said. "I have enough difficulty living my life; I don't want to live someone else's too. I can't be responsible for someone else's happiness. Am I wrong?"

Everyone acknowledged agreement but Alex wasn't quite satisfied, "How can you love somebody too much? I mean, what is that?"

Alex's question was just too random for the group to understand. The puzzled looks from everyone demanded an explanation from Alex. "The last girl who broke up with me said I loved her too much. How can you love somebody too much?"

"Maybe she just wasn't ready for that kind of commitment," Kaye suggested.

"Maybe she didn't feel as strongly about you and didn't want to lead you on," Charlie offered.

"Yeah, maybe." Alex settled for that. His questions might not have been resolved, but he was finished talking. There was a period of silence. Harmon, sensing that Alex wanted to change the subject and didn't want to reveal any more, turned his attention toward Mona, the only one who had avoided entering the discussion. She had sat quietly to the side, paying attention to the conversation yet not saying anything herself. She was usually talkative, and the change piqued Harmon's curiosity.

"Mona, you're really quiet today. Is there anything wrong?" Harmon asked.

"No," she said in a way that made everyone realize that something was very wrong. She looked down, knowing that she hadn't fooled anyone but not sure that she wanted to go any further. She hesitated but couldn't make a decision.

"You look really sad." She didn't reply so Harmon rephrased his observation. "I guess that was a question. Are you sad? Is something bothering you?"

"No. Yes. I don't know what I feel. I'm all confused. I mean, I feel so many things; I don't know what: I'm scared, I'm hurt, I'm worried, I'm angry, and I feel guilty, and...and" She started to tremble.

"You just seem overwhelmed by all these feelings. What's going on? One at a time, maybe."

She seemed to think it over before responding. "I had a big fight with Little Max." Everyone knew who Little Max was; she was Mona's best friend. Mother and daughter shared the first name, Maxine, necessitating the nicknames: Big Max and Little Max.

"What's wrong?"

"Big Max is in the hospital today for some laboratory tests, a biopsy. If it's malignant..." Her voice trailed off, and everyone was silent.

"I love Big Max like my own mother. I just can't..." Her tears said what her words couldn't. The group was appropriately reverent, with Clark again providing a tissue for her tears. No one interfered or tried to get her to stop crying. The topic of cancer is like that. Cancer and death command a universal respect.

Harmon remembered her confusion and sensed that something more was involved. "The surgery isn't what's bothering you."

She nodded but turned her face down toward the desk, and she seemed to withdraw.

"Can we help?" Brett asked.

"I don't think so."

"Do you want to talk about it?" Brett asked, with unmistakable gentleness in his voice. Harmon was impressed with Brett's ability to express so much with so few words and to provide an opening without probing. No one else was brave enough to risk saying the wrong thing; no one else was sensitive enough to know that more needed to be said.

"I don't know what good it would do." She looked at Harmon.

"I don't know if it will do any good," Harmon answered, "but will it hurt?"

"Maybe." She took a deep breath and started her story. "Last night I was over at Little Max's house. I knew she was scared; we were both really scared. We tried to comfort each other but mostly we cried together. We ended up talking about life and death and fear and dying, you know, the way you do with your best friend. If you know me at all, you know how religious I am. My church is the most important thing in the world to me. I go two times a week, and I pray every day. I read the Bible every day, too. Well we got to talking about death and what we'd do if Big Max really died. I know it sounds morbid, but it seemed like the right thing at the time. I mean, we even talked about the funeral. We were just talking. My views on death, you know, what I think happens when you die, what Heaven is like, just came out. Her views were..." Mona trembled, almost unwilling to complete her next thought. "Really different from mine. I've always known that she was Jewish, but until that moment I never thought about it. I mean, I never really thought about what it meant that she didn't believe in Jesus Christ; I never really thought about it and now...I can't think of anything else."

"And that's what you had the fight about?" Harmon asked.

She nodded.

"And that's why you feel guilty?" Another nod, and she continued nodding as he reflected all the feelings she had expressed earlier. "And hurt and angry and confused?"

"I don't understand," Charlie said.

"Yeah, what's exactly bothering you?" Kaye asked. Both Charlie and Kaye were genuinely confused.

Alex, an avowed atheist with Jewish ancestry, felt another emotion. "You know, in this country, people can believe differently than you."

"You don't understand." She spoke, her voice barely audible. "You just don't understand. I shouldn't have brought it up."

"You're right. I don't understand, but I'd like to." There was sincerity in Kaye's voice that attracted as much attention as if she had yelled.

Mona just sat silently, shaking her head, while Alex was sitting as close to being at attention as one could be in a sitting position. Harmon, sensing the tension, turned toward Alex and calmly said, "Mona and Little Max have been friends for 12 years, family friends. This is not someone who needs lesson on religious tolerance."

Alex was clearly agitated. "I can't stand this holier-than-thou attitude of Christians. Who gave you a monopoly on truth?"

Even Charlie seemed to agree. "So you go to different churches. So what?"

"You don't understand. I told you that you wouldn't understand. I shouldn't have said anything."

"This wasn't the first time you noticed a difference?" Harmon asked.

"Of course not. We've visited each other's church and synagogue. I've always accepted that. I'm not like Alex thinks. I accept people being different from me. I can tolerate difference. If she was in a different political party, if she was dope addict, if she was...any number of things."

"Tolerance is always easier at a distance," Harmon said.

"This isn't like she has a different fashion sense. I mean, if she was gay, or a Ku Klux Klan member, or mean, or just bad, there would always be hope that she could change. I don't want to force her to be like me, and I'm not trying to convert her. I am not like that. Damn it, I'm not narrow-minded! I've got friends that do drugs, friends that sleep around, that drink each weekend—all things that I think are wrong. I don't try to change them; I just let my lifestyle speak for itself."

As Mona continued to speak, her tone moved in the direction of anger but was still filled with anguish, "This is someone I love. How can I respect my own faith, how can I even say I have any faith, if I could so easily discard it when inconvenient? I can accept different religions; I am not a bigot; but how can I accept that my friend is going to hell? Everything else I can be accepting of, patient about. There would always be hope that the worst sinner will repent, and what is a sin, and what isn't, can be argued about. But there is only one salvation, only one way to get to heaven, and that is through Jesus Christ. I mean, I can't just shrug my shoulders; easy come, easy go. If I could, how real, how deep would my faith be? We're talking about their immortal souls!"

The desperation and intensity left everyone in the room speechless. The depth of her anguish was clear to everyone. Alex wanted to apologize and Kaye wanted to say she finally understood, but both were too awed to break the silence.

After he let the silence calm the atmosphere of the room, Harmon attempted to restate Mona's feelings in a serene tone. "On one hand, you respect your friend's culture, and heritage, and religion. You don't want her to change for you. But on the other hand, your beliefs are so strong that you can't just ignore them; the consequences are too dire. I'm not sure if we can help. You may want to talk to your minister."

"I have an appointment with him tonight."

"But I do know that we all respect the anguish you are experiencing."

"Exactly! And it is driving me crazy!" She burst into uncontrollable crying, part gasping for air and part screaming from pain. Her sobbing continued for several minutes. Harmon remembered descriptions he had read about primal screams, and he wondered if that was what he was witnessing. He began to feel quite frightened and wondered if he had gone too far, if he had opened a wound that was beyond repair.

The crying became weeping, and it eventually subsided to the point where Mona caught her breath when Brett finally spoke, "I wish I could help you Mona. I wish I could..."

She nodded, and the start of a smile crossed her lips.

"Flowers," Abby said. "Flowers always help."

"Roses" offered Kaye.

"A dozen roses," Mona said.

"Nothing is so damaged that a dozen roses can't fix it," Charlie offered.

"The universal fix," Kaye noted.

"Now you tell me," Alex added.

Everyone laughed much longer than Alex's quip deserved. When the laughter stopped, Mona thanked everyone, especially Brett. "I feel better. I know nothing is solved, but I feel better."

The lull between topics was interrupted by a knock on the door. Harmon went to the door and found a football player he did not recognize. The football player gave a ten-dollar bill to Brett. Harmon asked, "What was that all about?"

"Nothing. I'm just collecting some money from the football team," Brett said, with a kind of embarrassed shrug.

"Go ahead," Charlie goaded him. "Tell him what the money is for. Tell everyone."

"It's nothing."

But no one was going to accept Brett's attempts to avoid the subject, and after a little more prodding, he elaborated. "It's for Warren; the football team is paying for Warren's prom."

"Goofy Warren?" Alex chimed in.

"He's not goofy. He's just…Actually, he is kind of goofy."

"Who is Warren?" Harmon asked.

"He's the ball boy, the mascot for the football team."

"You mean like a trainer?"

"No, he couldn't…he's not a trainer. He just helps out."

"You've seen him, Mr. Harmon." Charlie wanted to clarify. "He's the guy that's always on the sidelines. He has real thick glasses, kind of a goofy grin, and walks funny, like his knees don't work."

"He's kind of handicapped." Brett sounded almost apologetic. "He's a special ed kid. And he just has always been nice to the football team."

"Yeah, I've heard the way you guys treat him," Abby said.

"Some of the guys tease him; what can I say? Some jocks are jerks. But everyone has chipped in to pay for his prom. I mean, maybe we tease him, but he likes it, and he has become a part of the team. When I sprained my ankle at the Lincoln game, after the trainer wrapped it and I was sitting on the sidelines hurting, he gave me a drink of water and said he was sorry. It meant a lot to me. Everyone on the team has a story like that."

"A regular Gunga Din," Alex joked. But Brett, who didn't like to joke about Warren, just nodded.

"I can tell you aren't going to tell the whole story, so I guess I will," Charlie said. "Warren is a senior. He has never had a date. He really is a sweet kid, but not very desirable, if you know what I mean. He knows. He's never asked anyone out; I don't think anyone would have said yes to him. But Warren really wants to go to the prom. Brett found out and talked Lorrie into going with him to the prom."

"Lorrie, the cheerleader?" Alex whistled between his teeth. "Lorrie, the Homecoming queen?"

Brett wanted to downplay the situation. "Lorrie's gone to the last three proms, and her boyfriend, Rob, is in college. He was on the football team last year; he knows Warren, and he couldn't take her this year because he's away at college. Rob and Lorrie are really tight, been going together for two years. They'll get married if romance is ever real. She didn't have any need to go to the prom, and she agreed to go with Warren. Rob has been really cool. He even called Warren long distance from college and pretended to be jealous. Warren knows it's kind of a pity date, but Rob made him feel better by warning him to be careful with Lorrie. I mean, you know, Rob was just joking. She is a real sweetheart, a genuine nice person. You just can't believe everything you hear about cheerleaders; she's living proof that all the clichés about cheerleaders aren't true."

Charlie nodded. "Lorrie is sweet, but Brett...Brett found out that Warren's father wouldn't let him go to the prom, wouldn't give him the money."

"His father is kind of mean." Brett tried to explain.

"There is a rumor that Warren's knees and stuff are due to abuse when he was young."

"No one knows that." Brett defended Warren's father with a swiftness that attempted to hide his fear that the rumors were true. "His father just didn't want people to laugh at Warren. He didn't want Warren's feelings to be hurt. In a way, he was just trying to protect Warren."

"Whatever." Charlie did not want to pursue the issue. "Brett got the rest of the football team to raise the money for Warren's tuxedo, his part on the limousine, the corsage for Lorrie, dinner—everything he needs."

"I guess the clichés about football players aren't always true either" Harmon said.

Brett blushed but turned toward Harmon, "Well, I was just following your lead."

"Me? What did I do?"

"Remember last year when Claude said he didn't have his homework?"

"No, sorry. Can't say that I remember it."

"Well, he said he didn't have his homework, and he had some lame excuse. No one in their right mind would have believed him, certainly no teacher I ever had. But you did; you accepted his paper late. When I asked you why, do you remember what you said?"

"No, sorry."

"You said everyone chooses what kind of a person to be, and you'd rather be the kind of person who believed Claude than the kind of person who didn't."

Harmon looked puzzled and opened his arms out from his body as if to ask what Brett meant by that.

Brett answered, "That's how I got Lorrie to agree to go with Warren; I just asked her if she'd rather be the kind of person who goes with Warren or the kind of person who wouldn't. She didn't think about it for long. She called Rob, and he said he was proud of her decision. She's the one that's really great."

"But you collected the money, and you came up with the idea." Charlie wanted to make sure the credit went where it was due.

"Yeah, but it's all Mr. Harmon's fault. I'd rather be the kind of person that helps Warren than be the kind of person that doesn't."

Now it was Harmon's turn to be embarrassed. First he tried to joke his way out of recognition. "I'll try to take as much credit as I can." Suddenly the bell rang, and everyone got up to leave.

As everyone shuffled out the door, Harmon tried to summarize, in his own mind, what had just transpired in the last hour. Had Homeroom helped Abby? Harmon couldn't quite see that yes was the appropriate answer. Perhaps Homeroom gave her some support to go to the therapist with Roger. Perhaps. On the other hand, Homeroom gave Alex attention for being flippant about his feelings. If Homeroom had done anything that could be defined as helpful for Abby, then hurting Alex, enabling him to joke his way through his feelings, might be an appropriate label. Mona's problem was too great, too fundamental to have any resolution in one hour. Harmon felt sorry for her, and he was sure that the rest of the group had newer and deeper respect for her dilemma, but that didn't mean they had helped her. Charlie talked but never introduced a subject, never owned a topic. Kaye never talked about her drugs use or sexual experiences. And Clark? What did Clark get, except maybe training for a job as a tissue dispenser? Perhaps Charlie, Alex, and Kaye all needed to be confronted more assertively. Perhaps. Harmon had enough of a background in psychology to recognize their defense mechanisms, and he had a sense for which ones needed to be confronted. However, he was a high school teacher, and this was a class period. He recognized the limits of time and place. He had faith that avoiding confrontation was beneficial, although sometimes his faith was tested, daily. In many ways this had been a typical Homeroom. There was sameness even in the uniqueness. Every Homeroom was different, yet every Homeroom was the same. Perhaps that is exactly what he found so confounding about Homeroom. The tears and laughter were from different sources but there was universality to the suffering and even the joy. The difference was just a matter of degrees. The students for the next class were already shuffling into class.

Harmon showed the same movie as he had shown the other periods, and he sat in the back of the room and continued to ponder Homeroom. Each Homeroom was an hour long; they would laugh together and sometimes cry, but had any good come from those meetings, anything measurable? Harmon feared that the answer was no. Dread of facing the Board with nothing tangible tempted him to consider canceling his presentation. Then he remembered what Brett had said, and he had to ask himself, "Do you want to be the kind of person who believes in Homeroom, or do you want to be the kind of person who doesn't?"

When the last period was finally over, he dragged himself down to Allison office to see if she had any last-minute ideas for his presentation. Secretly he hoped she could allay his new-found doubts. Sharing his doubts with Allison was certainly not a unique event, more like a recurring pattern. He often shared his insecurities, and this time, like so many other times in the past, she listened intently to all of his self-questioning. He told Allison that their earlier discussion about Cindy had made him question the validity of Homeroom. He felt the lack of a consistent, effective policy regarding lying to be the greatest failure of Homeroom. He understood that Homeroom was more geared toward support than confrontation. He understood that confrontation was difficult to do constructively without being abrasive, but he also knew that confrontation was just not his style. He was not comfortable doing it, and when he had tried to do it, he hadn't done it very well. He was haunted by the idea that his lack of skill at confrontation was due to his own rationalizations. Every time he avoided a confrontation, he felt that he was copping out, giving in to his own frailties. Even worse, when he refused to confront, he knew that he was betraying everything he believed, and he was compromising the principles on which Homeroom was based.

"If I want to establish a program based on a Rogerian model," he told Allison, "then I must be congruent and genuine. Every time I ignore a deception and back off from a confrontation, I am not being genuine; I am being a phony. Ultimately that seems to be the biggest threat and challenge to Homeroom. Am I brave enough to be real? Apparently not."

"The students don't see it that way."

"What do you mean?'

"Well, your standards. I hesitate to call you a perfectionist, but you do have some pretty high standards for yourself. You are not perfect and that seems to bother you more than it bothers your students."

"I've never seen myself as a perfectionist, but I see what you mean." He thought a minute. "Actually I have no idea what you mean. What do you mean?"

"It's harder to see accurately where you are, if all you look at is where you aren't. You can't judge a donut by looking at the hole."

"I've had a long day. You are going to have to back off the metaphors and speak a little more clearly."

"Okay, look at it this way. You concentrate on where you've fallen short with Homeroom, where you have failed. You miss where you have succeeded, what you've accomplished."

His silence gave her a hint that he still wasn't sure what she meant, so she tried rewording her answer one more time. "As one of my professors would say, 'You're shoulding all over yourself'. You tell yourself you should help every kid; you should always be genuine; and then you see that you have failed to do all those things. And that brings me to my second point." She hesitated for a second to let the first point sink in. "You do not have exactly the best vantage point for judging the success of Homeroom. You are too much of a 'participant observer' to maintain objectivity."

"If you are telling me that I can't accurately assess Homeroom, what alternative do I have?"

"That's not exactly what I'm saying. I think you have to evaluate the program, especially with the goals you have stated. There is no other objective data out there. But you have to keep in mind that your viewpoint is skewed."

"My viewpoint is screwed? Then the whole program is screwed."

"Skewed, not screwed. Skewed. Skewed. Not accurate, off center, out of balance."

"What do you mean? I know skewed. Are you saying that I can never assess Homeroom accurately?"

"Not exactly. What I'm saying is that your viewpoint is different from that of the student's and you need to take that into consideration."

"Okay," Harmon said fully aware that he didn't understand her at all.

"When you, when anyone judges anything, you have to compare it to something else, and you have created a difficult yardstick for Homeroom. You look through an adult's eyes. That's your viewpoint. It's not wrong; it's just different."

"Oh, God! I've become an adult! I never thought anyone would accuse me of that!"

"It happens. Even to the best of us."

"OK, so I look at Homeroom through aged eyes instead of adolescent ones. You are saying that I put adult-like standards on the experience?"

"Yeah, sort of. You compare Homeroom with how it <u>could</u> be, based on past Homerooms. Every Homeroom is judged up against those past successes, which is a pretty high standard."

"I see Homeroom as it could be...instead of how it is?"

"Not exactly. You see Homeroom as it <u>could be</u>, but they compare it to all the other things <u>that are</u> in their life."

He sat in silence, trying to digest Allison's words. She was saying that his negative judgment of Homeroom was due to his comparing it with the wrong standards.

Allison went on. "Don't you see? You have a vision. Whether you articulate it or not, whether you are aware of it or not, whether you like it or not, you have a vision of what Homeroom should be. And you judge it by that vision."

"You're saying that the students don't have that preconceived notion, so they judge based only on their experiences?"

"Yeah."

"I don't know if I agree. I try not to put any expectations on each Homeroom."

"Maybe it's not expectations. Let me put it this way. You judge yourself harshly for being incongruent because you see what you withhold and how you fall short. But they judge you as being completely genuine because they see an adult being vulnerable and sharing his feelings. How often do you think they see that?"

He nodded.

She hesitated several minutes to let everything sink in before she expanded on her idea. "Don't tell me that they're wrong; they're not. You may be right that you cop out and don't share yourself fully. You're not completely genuine; you're not congruent, all the time. And you are right. Who the hell is? <u>But you try!</u> Don't underestimate the power of your struggle! Especially if you compare yourself to the other teachers, and other adults they come in contact with. Trust the kids' wisdom as much as yours because both of you are right."

He thanked her once again. She had shown him a new way of viewing Homeroom, and, more importantly for his own sanity, a new way of viewing himself. Perhaps he was too hard on himself. Perhaps his doubts said more about his own self-esteem than an accurate assessment of Homeroom. Allison had given him an alternative perspective on viewing Homeroom. "Thanks" was the only appropriate response he could muster, but he meant a more profound thanks than the word alone could express. He'd known for a long time that self-confidence for him was like a coat he could put on and take off with remarkable speed, but this latest crisis of self-doubt had been resolved in record velocity, even for him.

He left her office and walked down the hallway to go home, when he saw Mona.

She had a big smile on her face as she greeted him. "Thanks. Thanks so much. It really made my day. They were perfect."

Harmon turned to look at her more closely. Her smile was more radiant than he had first realized. Although there was a hint of tears in her eyes, she glowed with deep, resonant warmth. He was eager to find what had caused this radical transformation in her mood from earlier in the day. "You're welcome. But what did I do."

"The roses."

"What roses? What are you talking about?"

"When I went to my locker after last period, there were a dozen roses in my locker. Didn't you put them there?"

"No, it wasn't me."

"Then who?"

"Brett?"

"No. My first thought was Brett, but when I thanked him, he said the same thing as you. Are you sure it wasn't you? And him?"

"No, really. It must have been someone else in Homeroom."

"Who?"

"Alex? Maybe one of the girls. Or Clark."

"That doesn't sound right. It's really weird. Who could have sent them?"

"Does it really matter?"

"No, I guess it doesn't matter. No. In fact it doesn't matter at all. It makes it kind of even more…special. I mean, I sure appreciated those roses. I don't think I've ever received anything that has meant as much to me. I don't know why. It was like they were…." She started to cry.

"Validation."

"Yeah, exactly. Like it was okay to be me. Whoever sent the roses was saying it was okay to be upset and everything. I mean, I don't know if this sounds weird or what, but I never felt so…accepted. Is that crazy?"

Harmon just nodded. "No, it's not crazy." He patted her on the shoulder as she wiped the tears away and regained her composure. She smiled at him as she started to leave, but he stopped her and said, "I guess roses really are the universal fix."

"Yes! They really are!"

He was ready to defend Homeroom to the Board.

TUESDAY EVENING

The 70 paces down A Hall from the stairwell to the Hub were actually the last steps in a very long journey he had been traveling for three years. He had carefully mapped his journey and planned every detail. He had studied the hallways before school and during school. During his junior year, he gathered data for his major statistics project; he analyzed the traffic patterns. He knew exactly how many kids would be in any given hallway at any given moment of any given day. The largest congestion of students was, of course, an assembly or Pep Rally, but during a normal schedule, the Hub right before school could be counted on to have the largest, single collection of students on any normal day, and of added benefit to him, they would be all upperclassmen. He could count on between 100 to 200 students casually milling around in random groups suspecting nothing.

Another time and another hall might have more students, but the students would be closer to classroom doors and moving in specific directions. Before school, in the Hub, there would be upperclassmen with little going on in their vacuous heads resembling alertness. No one would be prepared to respond quickly in this environment this early in the morning.

He had painstakingly thought out other tactics. At one point he had considered approaching the Hub from D Hall, but he thought that would give too many people an opportunity to escape down the great stairway, as well as down A Hall. To block the escape route, he considered coming up the stairway. Then he would be between B and C Halls. But there would be too much distance between him and the groups at the opening of A Hall, and he feared that the juniors around the stairs would be too close; they might be able to jump him before he could get off enough shots to eliminate all of them. He was confident that from A Hall, especially the corner where A Hall opened into the Hub, he could eradicate the seniors across from him and eliminate all of the juniors before they could provide a threat to him. With the rest of the groups, it would be like shooting ducks in a shooting gallery except with a rapid-fire weapon.

At one point he had thought of using bombs. He knew he could actually get more kills with bombs. He had even worked out an elegant plan. He would plant two bombs, one each in the library and in the cafeteria the morning of a Pep Rally. He got the plans for a bomb from the Internet and was confident he could make a powerful yet inconspicuous one. He would disguise it in a lunch box, and hide it underneath books in the library and in the trash cans in the cafeteria. Then in the middle of the Pep Rally he would hurl his backpack full of much more powerful explosives onto the middle of the gymnasium floor right in the middle of a cheer. He could just picture the look on the cheerleaders' faces. At the same time, the other bombs would go off. Every student would be in the cafeteria, the library or the Pep Rally. He calculated that he would have a 90 percent fatality rate, much higher than the 200 or so he was planning in the Hub massacre. He gave up on the bombs because he thought it was too risky and too complicated to coordinate, but mainly, the bombs seemed too impersonal. He wanted to see his victims. He wanted to see them bleed. The bombs would have robbed him of the greatest reward of his endeavor.

He settled on his original plan and his 70 paces to doom, down A Hall with one hand on the handle of his Uzi, gripping the trigger, and the other hand fondling the barrel, all underneath his jacket, where no one could see what he was doing or what terror he was holding. This, this was so much better! He ignored the couples in A Hall, as they ignored him, too engrossed in each other to notice. He didn't notice what the others were doing or studying as he diligently walked down the hallway to deal out his brand of destiny.

He took his place at the corner of A Hall and scanned the scene of the Hub. The usual groups were there, with a slight variation. Two small groups close to the stairs by B Hall might be a challenge, but he wasn't really worried about them. "If one or two escape down the stairs, more power to them," he thought to himself. He wished them well. There will still be enough gore to satisfy him. They were certainly too far away to provide a threat to him. He was sure he could mow most of them down before they could travel the 25 feet to him. The rest of the Hub provided nothing for him to worry about, and certainly A Hall was inconsequential. His attention turned to the senior group across from him, the self-appointed leaders of tomorrow, the anointed ones. The focal point was a football star, the quarterback, with his letter jacket and symbolic leather footballs sewed up and down the sleeve marking his accomplishments. Girls were on either side of him hanging on his every word.

"Hey Mr. Football Man, catch this, you simian imbecile!" he shrieked. Completely caught off guard, the quarterback slowly turned. An explosion of blood spread across his chest followed closely by a large bang and a prodigious gush of blood from his back. His knees buckled and crumbled, but by then the bullets were careening everywhere and everyone was collapsing in a macabre ballet.

He changed clips and swung to his left and to his right emptying more rounds. Some were screaming, begging for mercy. Some were falling as they tried to run away, and two actually tried rushing him, but he was too quick for them. He cut them down decisively; he pumped a half-dozen bullets into each one, mostly to their heads. He changed clips again, cleared A Hall definitively, and started slowly walking down the Hub toward D Hall, shooting anything still moving and most bodies not moving. He stepped over one body, slipped in the puddle of blood, and almost fell down. He steadied himself and continued to walk. He took his barrel and pushed one body over and shot it again. Then he nudged another body and it flopped over. Suddenly, he stopped. This body had a face. He recognized the face on this last body! He stared at the face, fell to his knees, and he knew, nothing would ever be the same.

CHAPTER 10

IN THE RING WITH THE CULT

That night was a beautiful, warm, spring night, the kind that makes you want to go for a walk and look at the stars. Harmon pulled into the parking lot in front of the Administration Building feeling optimistic. He had resolved his own doubts, and to him that was the most important first step in his confrontation with the Board. He was ready.

The Administration Building, located on Main Street, right off of the old town square, had been the only school during the Depression—one building, all grades, two floors. By the time the first high school was built, and then the other schools, the Old School House had gained too much loyalty in the community to be torn down. That, and the prestigious address of One Main Street, caused everyone to vote and re-vote for costly renovations and enhancements to the Administration Building, resulting in an exterior that was old fashioned and stately, while the inside was very sleek and modern.

Harmon was filled with a sense of awe whenever he entered the building. The stone archway and large wooden doors, which must have been twelve feet tall, made a regal impression. The stoic stone guardians had borne witness to some sixty years of students. As he walked into the entryway, he looked at all those pictures of past graduating classes, and he saw the same eyes that looked back at him each day in class. He saw the pain of today's youth in their eyes. Details change, but the struggles of youth are universal. There is sameness to the fears, battles, and struggles of youth. In the end, adolescence is when one learns to deal with pain and rejection. That was true, that is true, and that will always be true. And Harmon was not sure what role, if any, he should play in this process.

Off to the left of the entry hall was the large carpeted Board room. The door opened onto three rows of wooden chairs which are reserved for any visitors or general audience. In front of the chairs was a large mahogany table with three plush chairs for presenters where he would sit during his presentation. Facing the presenter's table, about twenty feet away, was a very large, redwood table for all five of the Board members and the superintendent. Their chairs were throne-like, rocking chairs on rollers. In front of each chair was a small stack of papers, a copy of the agenda, and any reports to be considered. As Harmon entered the room and took his seat in the back, the principals were finishing their budget reports and making their recommendations. Not surprisingly, no one challenged the reports. After a series of quick, obligatory rubber stamps, Harmon was next on the agenda. He was grateful no audience was there to witness his presentation. He thought that the size of the meeting would work to his benefit.

Randich, having finished his budget requests, introduced Harmon. "One of my faculty members, Mr. Harmon, wants to make a presentation to the Board. I have recommended that Mr. Harmon teach one extra section next year, which would require his sacrificing a program that he has developed over the past five years. My recommendations are based solely on monetary considerations. Mr. Harmon would have the Board consider other criteria. I have invited him to make his plea, and describe the merits of the program, directly to the Board."

Harmon took his seat directly in front of the Board. There was stillness in the room as he spoke, although each Board member seemed to listen intently. He began by thanking them for their attention. Then he described Homeroom. After the presentation that he had practiced all day, he talked spontaneously. "I believe in Homeroom, but I do not believe it is a program that can be judged by numbers." The faster he talked, the harder it was for him to find the right words. "I know it is….an antidote to the alienation and loneliness experienced by many students. I believe Homeroom is a…successful…useful…drug and suicide prevention program. I hope you can look beyond the numbers. Can I answer any questions that will help you reconsider the continuation of Homeroom?"

He was sure that they had been listening, but he was not sure if they had heard him, or understood him. His words were just the prelude, the preliminary bout, so to speak. The tension in the room became visible once Harmon stopped talking. Everyone turned expectantly toward Hitchcock. He cleared his throat, pushed back in his chair, and said, "I have a few questions."

Hitchcock was wearing a powder blue suit with a heavily starched white shirt, with a pointed collar. His tie was a navy blue. Harmon's dark blazer, light blue, button-down collar, and bright red, silk-patterned tie seemed to provide the perfect contrast to Hitchcock. They looked like opposite ends of a continuum, as if one were the photograph and the other the negative. Sometimes appearances are not deceiving.

Hitchcock snorted. "I completely reject the philosophy behind your program; I couldn't disagree more…"

He was interrupted by Dr. Henderson. "I am curious, Mr. Harmon. Do you have any research to support your approach? For example, most of the research I am familiar with supports the idea that a clear zero-tolerance policy is the only effective drug policy, and you seem to be advocating something else."

"Homeroom is not a district policy issue. I mean, I'm not here to try to convert anyone to my philosophy, and I would be very reluctant to force my approach into a total curriculum. I know I would have serious reservations about implementing the Homeroom philosophy on a district level. But I do think my approach has a place within the total high school program. Homeroom is not the answer for everyone. But Homeroom is my approach and it has worked to some extent with the students I have come in contact with. It may not work in a different situation, a different environment. I don't know. I think it probably would, but I can address only my experiences."

Henderson sighed.

"Nothing works all the time," Harmon said.

"And everything works sometimes." Henderson finished his thought. He could tell her curiosity was piqued. She liked to approach things on a grand, philosophical level. She wanted the rationale, the pedagogy underlying Homeroom. She asked, "Do you have any authentic, validated research or theory to base your ideas on? I mean, is your Homeroom just a product of your opinion?"

"I understand," he said, and he did. She wanted a label, something to help classify Homeroom and give it a context. "Homeroom is based on the theories of Carl Rogers." Then Harmon launched into a five minute-lecture on Rogers' theories, and how they were implemented in Homeroom. "My goal is to create an environment marked by the three characteristics that Rogers hypothesized as being necessary for healthy emotional growth: empathy, positive regard, and genuineness or honesty. I try to create a psychologically safe environment where these traits can be nurtured. Then the students can find their own directions and answers to their problems."

"I am familiar with Rogers' work," Henderson said disdainfully. "I don't disagree with Rogers as much as I have never had the patience for him. His theories always seemed like such a waste of time."

"Rogers is not hard to understand, just hard to believe in," Harmon said, nodding his head. "However, even if you don't buy the validity of his theories, they still seem to be the safest approach. I mean, if we are in the business of changing people, and that is what education is about, especially drug or suicide prevention, then the Rogerian approach avoids the dilemma of selecting the direction for change. I mean, who is wise enough to know exactly what student should do and be? I know I don't feel comfortable making all these value choices for every student I come in contact with, and I sure wouldn't feel comfortable imposing a direction that was contrary to what their parents had given them. With a nondirective approach, values are not an issue. The school, me, we don't select direction or values for the students."

Hitchcock could contain himself no more. Harmon had obviously hit the button Hitchcock had been waiting for someone to push. Everyone was shocked by the intensity of his next words. His passion would have been scary in a different context. Here he just stunned everyone. "This is the type of secular humanist crap I have always been fighting! Where are these kids supposed to get their values if the adults in their lives don't provide some guidance, don't tell them what is right and wrong? If we don't make it clear, if we shirk our responsibility in this area, if we say that all values are equal, then we are making a value judgment. A dangerous value judgment. To say that no value is superior to any other value is the same thing as saying that there is nothing of value. **Morality is not relative!"**

Hitchcock was almost raging. Harmon felt that he could say the wrong thing, or perhaps the right thing, and push Hitchcock over some edge. Harmon found himself feeling sorry for Hitchcock. Harmon thought, "How painful it must be knowing you're right when everyone else thinks you are wrong. Being wrong when everybody else is right doesn't exactly help." Harmon heard his own voice coming out surprisingly soft and gentle. Instead of rising in intensity, it became subdued as he spoke, until he was almost whispering. "I understand what you mean, Mr. Hitchcock. I hurt when my students get involved with drugs, and I ache even more when they answer 'it all depends' to every moral question posed to them. And I agree, sometimes, they don't seem to have much of a moral standard. But I don't think the problem is a simple lack of clarity on right and wrong. They know the difference. What they lack is not knowledge of values. What they seem to lack is a commitment to their own values. Sometimes they seem to reject their parents' values, but it's more a questioning and searching. However, in my experience, they find their way back to their original moral values a lot quicker if they are allowed to explore rather than having to defend their attempts."

"Besides," Harmon continued. "I don't operate in a moral vacuum. I let my students know how I feel. I make it very clear that I am opposed to drug use. But I do spend more energy trying to understand rather than judging their behavior. The message of caring about them and trying to understand them speaks louder and is more powerful and more effective than lecturing to them. Furthermore, there is nothing I could tell them that they don't already know."

The effect of his tone on the Board was dramatic. The meeting seemed to turn even more calm. The hysterical tone Hitchcock had introduced had subsided. There was a brief silence that was finally broken when Hitchcock spoke. "The inherent danger of certain issues makes a direct, forceful intervention imperative. I mean, drugs can kill people."

"I hope you don't think that I wouldn't intervene if I thought a student's involvement with drugs was dangerous or out of control. That is one of the exceptions to confidentiality that I explain to the students. I also would not sit silently if a student was talking about suicide or hurting someone else. I have gone to parents with each of these issues. In the case of drugs, usually the parents know already but don't know what to do."

"Denial?" Hitchcock asked.

"No, not really. Parents of high-school-age kids often experience a dynamic that seems beyond a technical term like denial. Resignation, maybe. In the case of suicide ideation, normally the student wants me to tell someone. I usually get their permission to talk to a parent. Only once has a kid refused to let me tell his mother about his suicide plans."

"What did you do?"

"I told the mother anyway."

"Why? I thought confidentiality was the cornerstone of your program."

"I did so because I felt that I had an ethical obligation to do so, because I felt that I could not handle the situation without outside professional help, and because I could not live with the consequences if the student acted on his feelings and I hadn't told someone. That is too heavy a burden for me to handle. Besides, one student's life is more important than my principles."

Suddenly Harmon realized the essence of the differences between Hitchcock and him. Hitchcock wanted to teach kids the right dogma, and Harmon viewed all dogma as the enemy. He wanted his students to think for themselves because he trusted the conclusions they would eventually reach. His approach was the antithesis of Hitchcock's approach.

Hitchcock was not ready to let Harmon off the hot seat. "Don't you think Homeroom is providing psychological services beyond what a school can provide? What gives you the right to probe into their psyches? I mean, if you provide therapy don't you need some sort of license or certification or something?"

Harmon exhaled, expressing some weariness. He was losing his patience with Hitchcock and was just plain tired. He wanted to go home. "Mr. Hitchcock, I do not provide therapy. I make that very clear to my students on the permission slip that the parents have to sign."

"Well, then what do you do?"

"I listen. I talk, and listen, mainly. That's all I do. I talk and listen, hopefully more of the later than the former," he said with a sigh. "The whole essence of Homeroom can be summed up in one simple sentence: I believe there is value in communication. That's it. That's all there is to it."

"I still think you have to make clear to students the right values; you have to give them some sort of direction."

"You know, Mr. Hitchcock, I think we agree on where we would like students to be. I think we would make the same choices for students if we could. Neither of us wants students to use drugs, nor do we want them to be sexually active, but the question I would ask you is: how do we achieve those ends? I wish that I could say 'Don't do drugs! Don't have sex' and they would all stop. But the truth is I don't have that kind of power. And if I did have that kind of power, I would be afraid of abusing it. So, the question becomes how do you get them to come to these decisions? How do you get them to make the right choices? Mr. Hitchcock, this is the Terrible Paradox of Education. It doesn't seem to me that we have accomplished much if we teach kids how to balance chemistry equations if they commit suicide. What good is it if a student can balance the quadratic equation but can't stay sober? And is mankind improved if we graduate students who can program computers, but can't tell right from wrong and have no sense of direction or connectedness to other humans? You see, we can teach all these beautiful, intricate, wonderful, and academic operations better than we can teach the human conditions necessary to ground these operations. Without strength of character, and moral integrity these academic behaviors are intellectual parlor games. However, to teach the necessary values requires a different paradigm. These lessons can not be taught through direct instruction with worksheets and homework and lectures. These lessons require…what?…something else…teachers as role models, perhaps…discovery learning, and student-centered instruction rather than teacher-directed. And that is the terrible paradox: the most important lessons for students can't be taught; they can only be learned."

"You advocate the use of the nondirective approach to trick them into it?" Hitchcock asked sarcastically.

"No, trickery is not the right word. I want to let them find their own answers, not my answers because I trust them to do a better job than I could." He heard the sound of his voice, and he couldn't help but feel that he was pleading more than speaking. "Don't you understand? My students, at worst, are bored and lonely. Alienated. Lost. Confused. Works in progress. Sure they need direction, but even more, they need to find their own direction; it can't be imposed. It has to be discovered. You want me to give them direction, and I think it is more important that I have faith in them. Ultimately, faith is more powerful than directions."

With that, Harmon felt a sense of completion. If they did not agree with the program, there was little he could add. He had explained it; he had defended it. There was nothing left to say. Dr. Spaulding called for closure on this issue, thanked him, informed him that they would be voting later this evening, and told him he was welcome to stay to hear the results. He didn't really want to stay around, but he felt he should demonstrate his commitment to Home-room. He waited around in the hallway for a few minutes. When nothing was forthcoming, he went outside to savor the night air and contemplate the past half-hour. He thought about his confrontation with Hitchcock. As uncomfortable as he had been, he had managed to avoid an ugly, acrimonious scene. It could have been worse. Strangely, he couldn't help but feel some respect for Hitchcock. Although he disagreed with everything Hitchcock had ever said, they both wanted the same thingl. Their greatest disagreements were procedural; Hitchcock couldn't agree to Harmon's methods, and Hitchcock didn't really offer any methods. In the end, Hitchcock cared. He cared with more emotion than logic. To his credit, he operated from an agenda that was anything but selfish, imprudent perhaps, but not selfish.

Harmon looked around the parking lot. In the sky, the night was clear and stars were shining bright. On the street the traffic was sporadic. He heard the sound of a match scratching across a match book, and he noticed someone else standing off to the side. He wasn't sure when the second man had appeared, but he knew he was alone when he first came outside. The stranger was in his late fifties, somewhat unkempt, although he was wearing both a tie, loosened, and a sports coat, wrinkled. His hair was white and long, not fashionably long but looking as if it hadn't been cut in awhile. His tan coat was baggy. He was puffing on a cigarette, and smiling at Harmon with a familiarity that seemed unwarranted. "You kinda had a rough time in there, eh?" he asked.

Harmon looked at him suspiciously, "Not too bad. In fact, I thought it went pretty well, considering."

"Oh yeah. Considering what?"

"I don't know."

The man took a long drag on his cigarette and slowly blew the smoke out, "They won't let me smoke in there anymore. I have to come out here." He took another drag, "It's been awhile, longer than I like." He looked at Harmon from head to toe while still sucking on his cigarette. "You know, Hitchcock never served in Viet Nam. I think he regrets that. When he looks at you, he sees tiedyed shirts and peace signs."

"I was barely alive in the sixties."

"Yeah, but you wish you could have marched for peace and civil rights."

"No, I don't," he said, wondering how the stranger knew.

"Yeah, okay, if you say so." He took another long drag. "Anyway, it was a pretty good show. Added a little pizzazz, you know what I mean? Usually these meetings are more boring than…." He stopped to inhale and think of the best metaphor. "Salt."

"Salt?"

"Well, you know what I mean."

Harmon nodded, hesitated, and said, "No, I don't."

"Well, these budget meetings are usually just a bunch of rubber stamps. Administrators' recommendations. I figure they brought you in to entertain Hitchcock. Divert his attention away from anything important."

Harmon looked quizzically at the old man, but he didn't say anything.

"Well, maybe I'm just being cynical, but your program never had a chance to pass. I figure, Spaulding used you to make Hitchcock feel like he had some power. You know, placate him. He sacrificed you to Hitchcock; my guess is he will exchange the veto on your program for support on some other issue that he really does care about."

Harmon turned toward the white-haired man, and his face must have showed his dismay.

"Well, you know, a lot of people think I'm cynical. Too cynical," the old man said.

Harmon continued to stare at him, and finally asked, "Have they taken the vote yet?"

"You didn't know? They took it a few minutes after you left. You lost."

"They already voted?"

"Yup."

"No debate?"

"None."

"Unanimous?"

"Sure."

He felt numb. "Well, that's that." He sighed, took a deep breath, exhaled, and looked back at him, "Who are you?"

"Lassiter, Ken Lassiter."

Harmon recognized the name. Lassiter was a reporter for the local paper. Education was his specialty. His articles created controversy whenever possible. Not that he was dishonest, but he wanted to entertain readers. Harmon did not automatically accept Lassiter's interpretation. Lassiter was cynical, and his viewpoint wasn't exactly unbiased. To Harmon the truth was different from what Lassiter had said, but even more disturbing for him.

"I don't think you are right, Mr. Lassiter. I think you got this one wrong."

"Oh? How do you see it?"

"The decision was made before I got here tonight. I'll grant you that. That's obvious, but I don't think they listened to my presentation and asked me questions to placate Hitchcock."

"You don't suffer under the delusion that they were trying to placate you, a mere teacher?" He said the last phrase with obvious disdain.

"No, it certainly wasn't to placate me. It had nothing to do with me. I think the Board and Spaulding needed me for themselves, to give themselves the illusion of....."

"Of what?" Lassiter was staring at Harmon and, for the first time, he was oblivious to his cigarette. Harmon was too busy looking for the right word to care whether Lassiter was looking for a quote or an issue for his next article.

"The illusion of something, of...compassion. I guess. The Board, the superintendent...they need to feel that they are concerned about the lives of children, but, here is the really depressing part, they don't care. No. That's not accurate. No. That's not really fair. They care. They care deeply. They just don't have any contact with the real lives of children. They are just...accountants."

Soldiers for the great Cult of Uniformity, he thought but did not express out loud to Lassiter.

He looked around at the sky, gazed at the beautiful stars and kept searching for the right words, the idea he was trying to express. "I've learned something tonight. I think I've seen the future of education. The Board, all of them, see education from the context of a ledger sheet. Spread sheets. Databases. Demographics. Test scores."

Harmon took a deep breath, and exhaled slowly, before he continued, speaking deliberately. "I don't disagree with the decisions they make, most of them anyway. But everything is decided with numbers and structure and order and logic. I guess that is the safest way, perhaps the best. I don't know. Mostly, I think it is. But I do know that we are dealing with a product that is not structured or logical."

"Students?"

He nodded. "There is something mechanical and dehumanizing about the system that is evolving. The more efficient we become, the more removed we become from the lives of children. Something is lost."

He looked at Lassiter and saw his scraggly face and found no comfort there. Nor was there any comfort forthcoming from the deep sky. "I know their world. I can function in it, flourish even. I don't mean to put it down. Really. I mean, organization is a good thing, the best way, certainly the safest way. Least likely to make catastrophic errors, you know."

"But?"

"I understand their world; I live in their world. But they don't live in mine."

"Yeah, well." Lassiter flicked an ash off of his cigarette. "Cassandra is an easy role to play."

"No, I'm not making any dire predictions. I just feel.....sad. Like something has been lost."

"What, what has been lost?"

Harmon looked at the sky. He looked at the nearly empty parking lot. He turned slowy toward Lasiter.

"Passion," he said. And passion, he thougth to himself, is intolerable to the Cult of Uniformity.

WEDNESDAY MORNING

It would be today. All his planning, all his dreaming, came down to this day; he was ready. He stepped out into the middle of A Hall from the stairwell. Under his jacket he clenched and unclenched the handle and trigger of his Uzi; his left hand ran slowly up and down the barrel as if to comfort the beast but more to calm his own nerves, although in truth, he found that he didn't need to. He was strangely serene as he started his journey down the hallway. He didn't want to be too conspicuous with his slowness so he picked up the pace just a little. The kissing couple on his left didn't notice him at all, nor did the rest of the people in the right half of the hallway. There were the customary two couples flirting, and the others were studying and doing homework. No one noticed him. "Invisible, as usual" he thought.

When he got to the end of the hall and took his spot in the corner, he surveyed the scene. To the left, a small group of juniors were playing hackey-sack, too far from the stairs and too far from him to pose a threat. Dispersed through the Hub were several more groups, nothing out of the usual. He took a few minutes to look around, once more to savor the last few seconds of calm before the storm he was about to unleash. Then with determination he tightened his grip on his gun and turned his attention to the seniors across from him. The circle was its usual size and the boy in the center had his back to him. As he raised his weapon, he called, "Hey, Leader of Tomorrow, meet TODAY!"

Slowly, Brett turned to face him. Brett! He looked at Brett, and then he felt something funny in his right hand. His gun felt soft and rubbery. Standing next to Brett was Mona. She turned to face him, too. He felt his Uzi melting. He looked down and could see his gun losing shape, morphing into an unrecognizable blob, melting into a puddle, and he stood there facing them in a puddle of water.

CHAPTER 11

SHELTER FROM THE STORM

Few cars were in the parking lot when Harmon showed up at school the next day. Nothing new. He was usually one of the first to arrive, but there was always someone ahead of him. As he walked across the parking lot, the warmth from the evening before seemed to have had an inertia that washed over him. Everything was bright, sunny, clean, and crisp, as if to mock the mood he was in. He signed in at the office and headed for his room. On the second floor, his room was at the end of A Hall closest to the stairwell and furthest from the Hub.

As usual, A Hall wasn't completely empty, even at that time of the day. Today a boy and a girl were sitting by an open locker pretending to do homework while flirting with each other. Soon there would be others, usually about a dozen kids by the time first period started. Some things never changed. He was struck by the fact that nothing was any different from any other morning. Normally the predictability brought him a certain comfort. Today, however, it only highlighted his sense of loss. Homeroom was no more. It should have been raining. The hallways should have been completely empty to reflect the emptiness he felt. Instead, it was a bright, warm, inviting day. The type of day that says everything is right in this best of all possible worlds.

He thought about going to see Allison but decided against it. Somehow, he felt that she already knew last night's outcome, and he just didn't feel like talking. He shuffled down the hallway to his room, unlocked the door, turned on the light, sat in his chair, and slumped onto his desk. His desk faced the wall on the left side of the room away from the doorway, in the back corner. The student desks were directly behind him, and they faced the door at the front of the room. The effect was that his desk was never between him and the students. When he was teaching, the students were facing him. He never sat with his back to the students because he never sat while students were in the room. Now he sat with his elbows on the desk, cradling his head in his hands, his back to an empty classroom. He probably looked terribly depressed or, at least, deep in thought. Actually, he was mostly tired. He hadn't slept well last night. He kept thinking of things he should have said to the Board. He had finally fallen asleep when he had accepted emotionally what he knew intellectually, that nothing he could have said would have made the slightest difference. Homeroom had made a good run, but it was over, and that was that. In the broad range of human events, this was not a major tragedy, and if this was the worst thing that life would hold for him, he would die a very fortunate man.

He poured some coffee from his thermos and took a sip. He was sad that Homeroom would be no more. He revolved in his chair and slowly looked around his room, which basically hadn't changed in twelve years. There was the same desk, now facing in a different direction, in which he had found Nancy Swenson years ago. There was the graffiti board at the back of the room, filled mostly with the same kinds of quotes from year to year, most of them remarkably uncreative. He turned to face the cork bulletin board above his desk. He looked at it without reading the schedules, memos, school calendars tacked to it. To the right was a large, framed poster. It was the first thing Harmon had ever bought for his classroom, the first thing he put on his wall. An essential addition to the classroom, the poster said something important to Harmon. He liked it the first time he saw it, but over the years, he realized it came closer to summarizing his philosophy of education than anything else he had ever found. It was a quote credited to Lord Buckley, and although he had only a vague idea of who Buckley was, he endorsed the sentiment: **"The flowers, the gorgeous, mystic, multicolored flowers, are not the true flowers of life. But people, yes people, are the true flowers of life. And it has been a most precious pleasure to have temporarily strolled in your garden."**

He sat quietly drinking his coffee, reading and rereading the quote. It was a permanent part of his classroom, and more than a few students and parents had commented on it. He slowly became aware that someone was saying his name. He turned to see a young woman standing inside his doorway across the room from him. She looked familiar but he couldn't place her.

"Do you remember me?" she asked.

"Of course." He lied. He had no idea who was standing in front of him. This sort of thing had happened before and with a frequency Harmon found unnerving. He had averaged nearly three hundred students per year for several years, and nearly two hundred for the past half dozen years. Although he didn't immediately recall this student, he had faith that he would remember her by the end of the conversation. "How have you been? What are you doing these days?"

She smiled. "Well, I went to college, for awhile. I didn't like school very much. I was going to major in psychology, thanks to you. But, you know how it goes, not much fun. Too much math, too much reading. I was never big on academics."

There was something familiar in her voice and the way she moved toward him, holding something behind her back. She was touching one desk and then another, tentatively moving towards him. He couldn't quite recall who she was although everything she did seemed so familiar. He had a memory, a vague image of her standing in the same place, moving the same way, only much younger. But there was something fundamentally different about her that kept him from recognizing her. Her eyes. He could see her eyes. That was what was different. When he pictured her some years ago, her head was down, her eyes darting back and forth, avoiding any real eye contact. He could not remember her accurately.

She made her way until she was standing right in front of him, above him as he was still sitting at his desk. She was confident in her bearing and proper in her posture as she spoke. "I'm a mother now. I've got a wonderful, beautiful, bright daughter, two years old, Paula. Looks like me but has her father's smarts. My husband is a laboratory technician for the Environmental Protection Agency. We met at college, in biology class, only he passed. We've been married five years."

She was smiling and he realized that was the obstacle that kept him from recognizing her. "I'm not used to seeing you smile," he said.

"I didn't have many reasons to smile back in high school." She lowered her eyes and frowned, and he immediately knew who she was.

"Vanessa," he whispered loud enough for her to hear. "How are you?" They both knew what he was asking.

She looked at him and smiled, the brightness returning to her eyes. "Oh, Mr. Harmon, things couldn't be better. I never thought I could be this happy or make my life work out so well. I've been sober for six years. In fact, my wedding was my husband's gift to me to celebrate my first year of sobriety. I don't go to AA any more. I don't need to, and my schedule is too busy. Paula keeps me busy. I know that AA is still there, but I don't think I'll need it. My mom and I have become best friends; we are going to have breakfast today."

He stood up to face her directly. Vanessa was an alcoholic in high school, although in some ways, drinking was the least of her problems, really more a symptom than anything else. She had attention deficient disorder and never had much success in a classroom environment. She was intelligent enough, but she could never maintain any motivation. She developed a hostile relationship with her mother. She had a boyfriend who abused her, but she felt that she deserved to be mistreated. Harmon could remember her saying she would get him mad because she wanted to. She had low self-esteem and she drank to cope.

"I don't spend a lot of time thinking about high school these days, not that I could. I mean, most of it was a blur," she said. "You know, the rest of life isn't like high school. I didn't know that. I wish I had. Things would have been better. Somebody should have told me."

"Would you have believed 'em?"

"No. Of course not." She laughed. "But that's not what I came to talk about. I don't spend much time thinking about high school, but I thought of you last night, and I had to come see you today." Her voiced cracked. "I'm pregnant again."

"Congratulations, that's great! But I'm confused, why did that make you think of me?"

"The pregnancy? That's not why I came to talk to you…This is so hard."

He nodded. "Take a deep breath. It's okay. Talk to me. Tell me what's wrong."

She took her deep breath, and sat on a desk top, while still clutching something in her arms. "Nothing is wrong. That's kind of what I wanted to tell you."

He was confused but totally focused on her.

"I recognize that look. You used to look at me like that in high school when I needed to talk." She laughed. "Last night I was sitting on the floor playing with Paula, listening to some music, changing her diaper. Changing her diaper. Can you imagine that? I mean, did you ever picture me changing a diaper?"

He just shook his head while they both chuckled.

"There I was gleefully changing my daughter's poopy diaper, thinking about the new baby, and asking myself how could I be so lucky? And I thought of you"

He sat there numbly. He could feel his throat tightening and he swallowed hard.

"So I made this for you. It seemed like the appropriate thing to put in that little window on your classroom door."

She handed him the poster board she had been clutching. It was a picture of an open, red umbrella with rain falling all around. In big, red, scripted letters outlined in yellow were the words "Shelter from the Storm"; it was repeated on other side. He took it, looking at her and back at the poster. He opened the drawer on his desk, got out his scissors and tape, and walked to the door. He trimmed the picture and taped it to the little window on the door so that it could be seen by anyone on either side of the door. They both stepped back and admired how it looked. "You were always artistic," he finally said. "This means so much to me. Thank you."

"No, thank you. That's why I came here today, to thank you."

"I didn't do anything. I just…"

"No, I owe you. More than you know. More than anyone knows. I've never told anyone this, but…this is why I came here today, to tell you." She stepped closer and lowered her voice, "That last year in high school, one day, Sunday, my mother was at church. I was hung over. I had spent the first part of the morning throwing up, and then the headache set in, the hangover. The night before, my boyfriend had broken up with me. I was failing English, and I thought I might not graduate. I went into the medicine cabinet and got out my mother's bottle of sleeping pills."

She stopped and looked around the hall to see if anyone was listening. Her voice was shaking as she conjured up images that were too painful to recall. "I took the bottle into my room. I sat with it in front of me at my desk. I poured out the pills. I stared at those pills. I thought of all the people who would be better off with me dead. I couldn't think of one reason to go on living. I sorted the pills. I made one pile for my mother, another pile for my father, who I hadn't seen in twelve years, a pile for my ex, another pile for my teachers. And that's when I thought of you."

Her eyes were filled with tears and they were beginning to flow down her cheeks. "I knew, I <u>knew</u> you would cry, you would hurt if I took those pills. And I swear, I swear to God, I heard your voice say 'Don't'. It shook me. I sat there trembling. I mean I was on the verge of…." She shook her head back and forth, and then she looked directly at Harmon. "You know what I did next? I reached for some paper and my psychology textbook, and I did my homework, a worksheet, just a simple vocabulary list. I think it was the first assignment I'd done all semester. I made a 65 on it, didn't even pass. I still have it. It's the only thing I have from high school; the only assignment. You see, Mr. Harmon, I owe you…my life, and the life of my child, eh, children."

He looked at her. They hugged. "Thanks." His voiced cracked as he spoke. "Your timing could not have been more perfect. I needed something today."

She wiped away a residual tear from her eye, regained her composure, and looked puzzled. He realized that no one knew about last night's decision. "The Board voted last night to do away with Homeroom. It will be no more."

"What's Homeroom?" she asked, and he realized that she had never been in Homeroom.

"A support group I've been doing for the past six years."

"Oh," she said, "that's too bad they cancelled it. I'm sure it was a positive program." She was beginning to feel self-conscious, "I need to be going. I'm going to meet my mother for breakfast and tell her the good news."

She turned to leave, and he watched her walk down the hall toward the Hub. They waved to each other when she reached the stairs at the end of the hall, and he turned to walk back into his room. As he approached his desk, he felt as if he had been hit by a blast of hot air, like when one leaves an air-conditioned building and goes into the summer heat. He blinked and sat down. He took a deep breath. "She hadn't been in Homeroom," he whispered out loud. "Neither had Nancy Swenson. Neither of them had been in Homeroom."

"Who? Who hadn't been in Homeroom?" Allison was standing at the door.

"A former student. She gave me the sign for my door."

"I saw it on my way in. It's really nice. I like it. It says a lot that she would go to all that trouble, not to mention the content."

"Thanks." He was feeling almost dizzy. His thoughts were spinning from Vanessa's visit when suddenly he felt clearheaded, crystalline clear. If his first realization was like a blast of heat, this was more like a cool breeze. He was experiencing an epiphany, a very slow-developing epiphany, as contradictory as that was. "The Board cancelled Homeroom last night, and I just realized that it doesn't matter. It really doesn't matter. All the Board can do is cancel a program. The only power the Cult of Uniformity has is over ink on a piece of paper. That's all they can do. Change paper. But Homeroom isn't really a program; it is an attitude, a relationship, a state of mind. The Board can cancel Homeroom, but it can't kill it. The greatest legacy of Homeroom was the caring that it expressed. The Board can't touch that. The Cult is powerless against caring. Caring is the essence of Homeroom under any guise or title or program. Homeroom is not a noun; Homeroom is a verb."

"A verb?" she asked.

"Yeah, Homeroom is not something you do to someone but with someone. It is a 'Shelter from the Storm', and the shelter is as much a state of mind as the storm. Don't you see? Homeroom is…a process not an event."

Allison smiled, "I'm glad to see you're taking the cancellation so well, but we don't have time to talk about this now. Something has come up."

"What?"

"You are needed in the office."

"But.."

"This takes precedence over everything!"

She turned on her heels and swiftly moved down the hallway. Her swiftness told Harmon that something was very wrong. They didn't speak as they rushed, nearly running, down the stairs into Randich's office. He didn't know what to expect so he didn't feel any shock as he entered the room and viewed the frozen tableau in front of him. Randich was behind his desk, a middle-aged woman whom he didn't recognize sat in front of his desk to the right, crying into a handkerchief, Allison took a seat in a chair reserved for her behind and to the right of the woman, and Police Officer Chandler was standing next to someone Harmon couldn't recognize. This unknown person, bent over with his head in his hands, was in the center of the room and the focus of everyone's attention. When Harmon entered, he lifted his head out of his hands.

"Clark?" Harmon gasped.

Clark's eyes looked desperate. His nostrils were flared. He looked like a cornered animal, but as soon as he made eye contact with Harmon, his face changed, almost sagging. Harmon expected to hear a shriek but was surprised to hear, instead, a well-modulated voice.

"Mr. Harmon, you have to tell them. You have to make them understand."

But Harmon had no idea what was happening and could think of no appropriate response. He looked around at everyone for some sort of answer.

"Mr. Harmon." Dr. Randich broke the silence, demonstrating that he was the one in charge. "Clark insisted that you be here. He felt that you could…serve some purpose although I don't know what purpose he has in mind."

Harmon looked around the room, trying to find clues as to what was going on. He guessed that the woman was Clark's mother, that Clark had done something to warrant Officer Chandler's presence. He guessed that whatever Clark had done, it had something to do with the notebooks lying on Randich's desk. Randich waved one of the books in the air as he began to explain the situation. "Clark's mother found this journal early this morning, and it contains some profoundly disturbing…plans." Clark looked up as if to interrupt Randich, who raised his hand in a gesture of acknowledgement. "Fantasies. At least, Clark maintains that they are fantasies, not plans. That's why we are here: to try to ascertain how serious these writings are."

Harmon started to say "what" but it never came out.

Randich continued. "When she brought the journal to me, I read the first few pages and immediately called Officer Chandler. He found Clark in the parking lot and brought him in here. This journal contains a detailed plan to shoot, to kill most of the upperclassmen in the school."

Harmon froze. He sensed that he was not the only one holding his breath, but he wasn't sure if the others felt that their breath had just been sucked out of them with such intensity. Randich turned toward Clark as he turned the pages of the journal, "There are detailed studies of student traffic patterns between classes, charts to determine the most crowded hallways correlated to times day and days of the week. He has estimates of people in hallway junctions between classes, the number of paces to nearest doorways. He has estimated the number of fatalities from various locations and directions. He has maps of the school with numbers of potential student fatalities marked in front of classrooms. He has projected body counts from the bottom floor moving up, and from the top floor moving down. He has systematically determined the best route to maximize the kill rate. He has been meticulous in his approach, rather impressive. When confronted a few minutes ago, he said that this was all just daydreaming. That he didn't mean any of it. That's why you are here, Mr. Harmon. He says you are the only one who will understand and believe him."

Harmon felt like his knees were about to buckle. He touched Randich's desk to steady himself and turned to Clark, but all that came out of his mouth was a feeble, "Clark?"

"Mr. Harmon, you have to believe me. That's not me. I wouldn't do that."

"Do you deny you wrote this?" Officer Chandler asked.

"No. No. I wrote it."

"But it was just a joke. Rather elaborate for a joke don't you think?"

"No. It was no joke."

"But you didn't mean it?"

"No. I meant it. I meant it; you don't even know half. Let me tell you; I'll tell it all, now that Mr. Harmon is here." And he told them everything. He told them about the years of planning, the statistics class project on hallway traffic patterns, working at McDonalds to save money to buy the Uzi, and the countless hours of practice in changing magazine clips. And he told them that he figured he would kill close to 200 kids.

When he finished, everyone remained silent trying to imagine the carnage. No one knew what to say, and Clark didn't seem finished. He turned his head down and slowly shook it back and forth. "But that was then, not now." He jerked his head up, "That's what I want you to know, Mr. Harmon; that was then, not now."

He had obviously said something very important to him and he wanted to be understood, but no one, Harmon included, knew how to interpret his remarks.

"I know what I just told you sounds horrible. I know it's not normal. I don't care what they do to me, or what they think. But Mr. Harmon, I do care what you think. I want you to understand, to know that I would never do those things. Not now. I was ready to; in October and November. I'd even picked a date, a Wednesday, early in May, today, as a matter of fact. I was just biding my time. And then I…"

"Let me guess." Officer Chandler was going to lead any inquiry. "You had a change of heart."

"Yes! Damn you!" Clark spit at Officer Chandler.

"What changed your mind?" Chandler said in a voice dripping with sarcasm, "What happened?"

Clark looked up, glanced toward Harmon, and spoke very quietly, almost reverently. "Homeroom. Homeroom happened."

Harmon rocked back on his heels, and his jaw fell ajar slightly as Clark continued to tell his story.

"Mr. Harmon invited me into Homeroom, and I figured I might get some new ideas about my plans. If nothing else, I figured I'd get some additional reasons to hate everyone. I was elated when I saw Brett and Mona were in my Homeroom. They were like the epitome of everything I hated. I couldn't wait to hear them. Instead, something else happened."

"Yeah, what happened?" Chandler asked.

"I got to know them." Clark stood up and walked around behind his chair. He turned toward Chandler. "I don't expect you to understand me, or even believe me." Then he looked around the room, making eye contact with everyone else before he settled on Harmon.

Only Harmon nodded.

"At first everything was like I expected. I remember Brett talking about scoring a touchdown. He was obviously proud of himself. But he didn't put anyone else down; he just wanted to share his happiness. Later when Kaye was talking about something happening in the cafeteria during the pep rally, Brett didn't seem pissed that she wasn't in the pep rally. Do you understand what I'm saying; am I making any sense?"

No one moved, but Chandler was shaking his head back and forth.

"One time,—I'll never forget it—Alex was talking about something—I don't know what, not school-related, and then Charlie began, and Abby. What I remember was that Brett paid attention to each one. I mean, he really paid attention. I was impressed and I remember thinking that he was different, and there was like this voice inside my head that said he didn't deserve to die. I should have known then that it was all over."

"One day in February the countdown on my calendar was like 68 days. I was at home practicing loading new clips, dropping the old ones, as quickly as possible, and picturing all my victims at the same time, when suddenly, one of the victims had Brett's face. I saw Brett." Clark's voice cracked and he had to stop and take a deep breath before continuing. "I tried to get him out of my mind, but I couldn't. If I really concentrated on other people, I could force myself not to see Brett. But the next day, Abby was one of my victims and Brett was there again, and I saw them both dead with blood flowing out of their heads, and I cried."

He stopped. Harmon could see the tears in Clark's eyes. There was a brief moment before Clark could continue. "From then on, whenever I'd picture my rampage, Brett would be there. Against my will. Mona, Kaye, Alex and Charlie, all the members of Homeroom, started showing up. One time I even pictured you, Mr. Harmon, and you were crying. I just couldn't take it any more. It was all over. I knew I wasn't going to shoot anyone. Mr. Harmon, you have to believe me."

Harmon looked at the desperation in Clark's eyes and tried to reconcile his vulnerability with the horror he had just described. Through most of the last year, Clark had actually been planning this terrible slaughter. Harmon was stunned and had no other appropriate response. He wanted to believe Clark. He thought of Brett's words. He wanted to be the kind of teacher who believed in his students, but he couldn't shake the images of death and destruction that Clark had painted. It was especially troubling knowing that these plans had existed during most of Clark's time in Homeroom.

Officer Chandler broke the silence. "This is all very nice. You want us to believe that you've changed your mind, shrug our shoulders, and go on like nothing has happened, but there is just one problem, one tiny stone left unturned." Everyone looked at Chandler, including Clark. "The Uzi. Where is the Uzi? The police have a search warrant and have just come from you house. There is no gun in your room. Where is it? It's not in your locker; we've looked. How do we know you don't have it hidden somewhere here at school, waiting."

"I got rid of it." Clark was answering Chandler but his focus was on Harmon; his eyes never left Harmon.

"Yeah, right." Chandler continued to badger Clark. "You have this gun of unbelievable, destructive power. You nursed it and pampered it and obsessed with it for over a year. You plan in gory detail to use it, you practiced daily with it, and now, because of a few visions, you get rid of it? You want us to believe this? What did you do with it?"

Lowering his eyes, Clark answered slowly and quietly. He was defeated. He sensed no one was going to believe him, and the pain of losing Mr. Harmon's respect was unbearable. "It doesn't matter now. I sold it, pawned it. Yesterday, actually."

"Where?"

"You won't believe me."

"Probably not." Chandler was not going to let Clark get off the spot easily, "Try me anyway."

"Some pawn shop on Madison."

"Got a receipt?"

Clark shook his head, resigned to any fate.

"What did you do with the money?"

There was a long hesitation before he whispered, "Some of it is in my drawer at home, and with some of it, I bought some flowers."

Harmon's looked up off the floor. "What did you say?"

"He said he bought some flowers," Chandler replied mockingly for a silent Clark.

"Roses." Harmon spoke-up and gave Clark the confirmation he so desperately wanted and frantically needed. "I saw the roses."

"The universal fix." Clark said as he looked up and locked eyes with Harmon.

"I saw the roses, or at least I saw the person who got the roses, and it was a wonderful, insightful gesture. I believe Clark's story about the gun, and more importantly, I believe in Clark. He is not capable of shooting anyone. He may have been at some point, but he is not anymore. He is not the person he was. The person he is now is a sensitive, caring human being. I will vouch for him, and I'm sure everyone in his Homeroom will also stand by him."

"This is all too touching for words, but I can not take the chance." Chandler spoke as he reached behind his back for his handcuffs and moved towards Clark. Harmon stepped between them, and Chandler warned him, "Mr. Harmon, you do not want to do this."

"If Mr. Harmon vouches for Clark, that is good enough for me," Allison said as she stood up. "Mr. Harmon would not make this kind of judgment without merit; I know him and I know he would not do this lightly. I trust him completely."

Chandler continued to move menacingly toward Clark.

"Officer Chandler." Dr. Randich's voice was not so much loud but unmistakably definitive. "This is still my office, and I will decide the course of action here. Mr. Harmon, you are taking quite a risk here. Are you sure that you can trust your instincts about Clark? If you are wrong, lives could be at stake."

Harmon nodded.

"That's good enough for me. I trust your judgment." Randich said. "But unfortunately that does not entirely resolve this situation." Randich turned his attention to Clark. "I am charged with the safety of the student body. I mean, you tell us of your detailed plans for a massacre and you tell us you've changed your mind. I believe your sincerity, especially because Mr. Harmon vouches for you, but can I take that chance? Legally, I'm not sure I have many choices. You did buy an illegal weapon. You did plan on using it. What if you change your mind again? What if..."

Clark interrupted Randich. "I understand. I mean, I know. Even if I never killed anyone, going home practicing and dreaming about it is not exactly a model of mental health. I understand that you can't ignore this. I accept whatever you do. I really do. I just wanted Mr. Harmon to believe me. I couldn't stand it if he didn't understand and if he didn't explain to the rest of Homeroom." Clark turned from Randich to Harmon. "Mr. Harmon, you tell the kids in Homeroom about what happened here today. You make sure they understand, and you thank them for me. Especially Brett. You make sure they understand, that everyone in Homeroom understands. You do that and I'll accept any punishment they have for me"

"I will." Mr. Harmon moved toward Clark and put his arm around him. "I will. I promise."

Clark had tears in his eyes as he looked around the room and spoke. "What, what's going to happen to me?"

Allison answered, "I think I might have a solution. Instead of going to prison or court, you will need to go to a psychiatric hospital. There you will undergo a thorough diagnostic examination. You will not be allowed to reenroll at school until you are cleared by the hospital. This type of thing usually takes a 30 day confinement. By then the school year will have ended. You will take your final exams in the hospital, and graduate during the summer."

"No graduation." Clark said in a way that was not a question but a dull statement of fact. "I was really looking forward to graduation. I wanted to see everyone walk across the stage."

"I don't want you anywhere near graduation under any circumstances," Chandler warned.

"Do we have to take that away from him? He doesn't deserve this." Harmon was pleading to Randich rather than Chandler. "I mean, he didn't actually do anything. He only thought about doing something. Graduation is all he has. What else does he have? Don't do this to him."

Randich nodded, and then shook his head before he spoke slowly and deliberately. "I have to agree with Chandler that there is too great a risk to allow Clark to walk the stage at graduation. I don't think I can legally allow that. But Mr. Harmon is right, also. If we don't care about an individual student, what kind of educators are we?"

Randich rubbed his forehead. "We'll have to compromise if Mr. Harmon is willing. Clark may attend the graduation ceremony under two conditions: first, the hospital has to clear him, and second, Mr. Harmon has to pick him from the hospital and return him after the graduation. Is that acceptable to everyone?"

Everyone nodded yes. Everyone stood, and Officer Chandler started toward Clark with the handcuffs, but Randich shook his head no. Chandler escorted Clark and his mother out of the office and out of the school. Harmon and Allison were left with Randich. The three were in dumb silence until Randich spoke. "I don't' think I've ever experienced anything quite like this last half hour. All the blood has left my body; my knees are weak. I would stand, but I think I've urinated all over myself."

No one moved or said anything. "That's a joke," Randich explained.

No one laughed; no one felt like laughing. Randich understood. "I don't know whether to cry or curse or what. I hope you understand, Mr. Harmon, that I had to do what I had to do. Clark left me no choice. I couldn't just let him back into school without some legal clearance; I think the psychological evaluation will work out. In fact, to call it appropriate would be an understatement. I hope you don't feel too bad. If you do, think of all the lives you and Homeroom just saved. It may be of little consolation right now, but I think,

Mr. Harmon, you should plan on doing Homeroom next year. I think today demonstrated how much we need this program. I'm sure the Board will share my newfound faith in Homeroom. I hate to think what would have happened today if there had been no Homeroom..."

Harmon nodded. At last he knew how Randich would have handled the Swenson affair. He walked in silence down the hallway into Allison's office.

CHAPTER 12

PLANTING SEEDS

Harmon accompanied Allison to her office. There was still some time before first period, and he needed some time to process the events of the morning and come to some sort of emotional terms with them; they both did. He flopped into his usual chair opposite Allison's desk. Then he leaned forward on his elbows, resting his head in his hands, and he wept. He actually wept. It was quiet weeping, with few tears, but it was an emotional outpouring after everything he had experienced in the last hour. Allison sat back and let it happen.

He finally leaned forward and spoke. "The sign Vanessa gave me, Homeroom's restoration, I should be on some kind of euphoric high...Instead all I can think of is how close we came...how much rage and pain in Clark...who knew? The loneliness...all year and no one knew..."

"You knew," she replied gently.

"I knew nothing," he said almost angrily.

"If you didn't know, why did you invite him into Homeroom?"

"He seemed different, he seemed...alienated, you know, but I didn't know what was going on, I didn't have any idea, I didn't...."

"Yeah, you didn't know any of the details. No one knew any of the details. But you sensed something. You sensed that Clark needed someone to reach out to him, and you did. And I would like to point out, it is pretty damn good thing you did. You and Homeroom did one heck of a job; you saved the lives of a lot of students in this school."

"He never let us know his pain, his rage. I never helped him. He hurt, and we were…" He shook his head vigorously. "Make that me. I was impervious. I feel so useless."

Allison sat back and sighed. She sensed that Harmon was inconsolable right now. He needed time to think and feel.

He just shook his head and continued to vent. "I feel so overwhelmed, so frustrated, so disjointed. I feel like I'm a gong being hit and banged randomly."

"You feel at odds, discordant with what's going on around you."

"Yes, I feel like I'm in this rich pageant, school, this rich symphony and I'm some…isolated, incongruent, unharmonious note. Really, I'll be okay," he said. "I just feel so…disassociated." He looked around the room, staring at nothing, awkward, uncomfortable, and inarticulate. "You know what the hardest thing is about this job? The hardest thing is that everyone I meet, every connection I make, is so temporary. You know what I mean? I have been thinking about this a lot the last day, and almost every kid I've known…It is all so transient. I know so little about them. I don't know their past and I don't know their future. Take Clark, for instance. I have no idea what went on inside of him, what brought him to this point, and chances are I won't know what happens to him, how he ends up. All these people, through the years, these wonderful, amazing people that I have known I don't know where they are or what they are doing. With a few exceptions, I seldom know what happens to them; I care about them, I…"

"Love them?"

He nodded but avoided the L word. It seemed too trite, too maudlin. "What I feel, what I experience is so temporary, so disconnected from the past or future. I cross intersections with them. Here and now. That's all. Random acts."

"You're not getting burned out on me, are you?"

"No. I just feel drained, deep-down emotionally drained." He knew that teaching was what he needed, that teaching would energize him. He stood up. "I'll talk to you later. Right now I want to go back to my classroom; I need to get back to my classroom."

"Wait, I have something for you. You look like you need this now so I'm going to give you an early end-of-school-year gift. I found this at a bookstore a week ago; it got some good reviews. I thought you'd like it. It sounded like something you would say."

She handed him a book entitled <u>The Gorgeous, Mystic Flowers: Lord Buckley's Influence on Pop Culture</u>, by Nancy Lamont. He took it and looked up at Allison. "You didn't need to do that; this looks great. I've always wanted to know more about…." Abruptly, he stopped. He looked at the picture of the author on the back page; she looked familiar. He was stunned and had to sit down. He read the biographical sketch of the author: married, two children, freelance writer, former journalist for some fairly prestigious magazines. Harmon recognized her! Her hair was longer. She wore glasses and had an uncharacteristically large smile but it was still unmistakably Nancy Swenson.

"Do you know who this is?"

Allison only nodded. "Look on page 8 of the acknowledgments."

Harmon read out loud, "Last, I want to acknowledge my high school teacher, Mr. Harmon, who introduced me to Lord Buckley in his room A 216. Although I'm not at all sure he had this in mind, he planted a seed, and this book is the fruit it bore. He was right all along. The best places are not the places you go to, but the places you take with you."

Harmon looked up and had to blink twice. Allison broke the silence. "Mr. Harmon, you plant seeds."

He nodded. He turned to leave, but not before silently giving her a very long hug.

He walked up the stairs to the Hub and toward his room. The halls were filling with students hurrying to their classes. He walked down the hallway, staring at the students. He was haunted by the images of terror Clark had described. "If they only knew," he thought. Standing at the corner of the Hub and A Hall was a girl draped in a long black cape. As he approached her, she pivoted away from him and twirled her cape in a flamboyant, dramatic gesture. Harmon passed her, but stopped and turned back toward her. "Nice cape," he said.

She was stunned. Her cape often drew reactions from teachers but seldom a positive one. She looked to see if there was any sarcasm in his eyes. Sensing none, she mumbled thanks.

"Where did you get a cape like that?"

"I made it myself."

"That's really cool. By the way, I'm Mr. Harmon. I am a teacher."

"Yeah, I know who you are. You run Homeroom."

"Yes. Yes I do. You ought to check it out. You might like Homeroom. I mean anyone who can make a cape like that…"

"Thanks, I was going to ask you about getting into Homeroom next year."

"Good. I've got class now, but see me later, okay? What's you name?"

"Chloe."

"Well, I'll see you later, Chloe. Nice meeting you."

They parted and went their separate ways, both feeling better than they had felt before they met. He watched her walk away, down the same hall that Vanessa had walked earlier. It was through this same hall that he had carried Nancy to the nurse, and in this same hall Clark was going to slaughter the student body. It was the same hall, and yet nothing was the same; nothing would ever be the same. And he thought to himself, "I wonder if there are angel's wings hiding under that cape?"

978-0-595-40830-6
0-595-40830-3

Printed in the United States
60797LVS00004B/72